By the same author:

FICTION
Light in the Sky
Blaze of Glory
Clown of the Gods

NONFICTION
Stage Costuming
Recurring Cycles in Fashion
Scalpel
The Women and the Crisis: Women of the North in the Civil War
Men Who Made Surgery

The Town
and
Dr. Moore

by Agatha Young

Simon and Schuster, New York

This book is for Bill and Madeline Krause
and for
Hugh and Gerry Hermann

Author's Note

In the course of writing this book it has been necessary for me to lean heavily on the good will and knowledge of a number of doctors, hospital administrators and head nurses. Chief among them have been two constant mentors and staunch friends, Dr. William H. Krause of Windsor, Vermont, and Dr. Hugh P. Hermann of Woodstock in the same state. With unprecedented generosity they have made available their technical knowledge, given freely of their time, and of their understanding of the special demands of rural medicine. It is my pleasure to acknowledge the greatness of my debt of gratitude to these two.

Outstanding among others whose extraordinary kindness to a layman has lightened and made memorable for me this task of writing are the late Dr. Robert W. Ballantyne of Windsor, Vermont, Dr. Richard H. Cardozo of the Mary Hitchcock Clinic, Hanover, New Hampshire, Dr. George E. Wantz of The New York Hospital, and Dr. George F. Egan, also of The New York Hospital. These doctors, however, are not responsible for anything I have written.

Head nurses in small, rural hospitals contribute more than is generally realized to both their hospitals and the community. They are fine and often heroic women. It is a pleasure to acknowledge the gratitude and admiration I feel for the one I knew best, Mrs. Lena E. Sisco, head nurse of Windsor Hospital, recently retired. The head nurse in this story, Edna Judson, was created before I met Mrs. Sisco, or I might have been able to write with more understanding of the task these women so willingly perform, for she taught me much about the workings of a country hospital and its relation to the community.

The principal source of a fiction writer's material is reality, and the reader, knowing or sensing this, frequently assumes that the characters in a novel are real people. Actually, portraiture in fiction is neither wise nor particularly feasible. The fiction writer, bound by the requirements of the medium, strives for reality, not for actuality. For this reason and for other reasons as well, the charac-

7

ters in this book are not real people. The doctors and nurses and other people in the story may seem to be familiar types, and it is hoped that this will be the case, but as individuals they are all of them wholly and in every respect products of the imagination. Any resemblance to living persons is accidental and the product of chance.

The names used in this book are common in Vermont, and were selected to add verisimilitude. A serious effort was made to avoid using first and last names together that might belong to any real person. However, it is impossible to be sure, and if such a person exists, it is without my knowledge.

This is not a routine disclaimer, for it means exactly what it says. There is one exception. One of the characters is intended to be an exact portrait. This is Fluffy, the cat, who enriches life in his home town of Woodstock, Vermont.

Though Fluffy graces the streets of Woodstock, the town of Haddon in this story is not Woodstock, which in many respects is not typical of Vermont, as Haddon is intended to be. There are many towns like Haddon in Vermont, but "Haddon" is not intended to be a pseudonym for any one of them. And incidentally, I have never known a Vermont town to be without a doctor, though it could happen as it does in the story, and has happened elsewhere.

In the course of writing this book I have made many visits to hospitals, especially to the hospital at Windsor, Vermont. The privately owned hospital in my story is not patterned after any of them. Its problems and circumstances are all imaginary, for I have never visited a private hospital.

If this "Note" seems wearisomely long it is because some readers have a desire to believe people and places in a novel are real, and want to persist in this belief in spite of anything the author may say.

—AGATHA YOUNG

8

The Town and Dr. Moore

I

THE CLOCK IN THE CHURCH STEEPLE at the far end of the village street slowly struck ten. The sound came softly through the open window of the hospital room, muted by distance and by the golden haze of the September morning. Dr. Moore bunched up his stethoscope, pushed it into the pocket of his old tweed jacket and gently pulled the bedclothes over the lifeless form of the old woman.

While he did these things, a part of his mind was aware of sounds beyond the closed door of the room, familiar, well-loved sounds that meant the smooth running of his hospital. Someone passed in the corridor with light, hurrying steps. Someone else passed, wheeling a cart on which utensils rattled. That would be Helen coming away from the operating room—a better instrument nurse than she knew or than a hospital the size of this one had any right to expect. Farther off, he heard the loud voice of Dr. Perkins, the only other staff member of Haddon Hospital. Howard Perkins was one of those surgeons who come out of an operating room a trifle above themselves, not boisterous exactly (though Moore had seen that too) but added to, so to speak, every dimension of personality enlarged. The hospital awoke to an intenser life whenever Perkins was within its walls.

The brief stocktaking ended, he returned his attention to his more immediate duties. On the opposite side of the bed there sat a small, incredibly wizened old woman staring at him with the bright, fearful eyes of a mouse. He met this intent gaze pityingly. "Alice," he said, "your sister's troubles are over now."

She made no reply, and thinking she had not understood, he came around the bed to her. She shrank from him as though he threatened her, and made a darting movement like a trapped animal. Again he thought of a mouse. Then, startlingly, she shrieked at him.

"No!"

She bowed her head, gnarled fingers came up over her face and she wept such a flood of tears that it was a marvel to him that such a dried-up body could produce them.

Dr. Moore put his hand on her shoulder, giving it a slight pressure. Tears ceased as though after all there were not so much juice of feeling in her, and her trembling hands came away from her face. He could see self-pity beginning to crowd out the brief burst of sorrow and knew she had found a means—unlovely but serviceable—of coping with her trouble. She would be all right now—if you could apply those words to so pitiful and inadequate an object. He looked at his watch, remembering that he had a crowded day before him, and that he must cut his comforting of old Alice as short as he decently could.

Like the rickety mechanism of an old clock getting ready to strike, she gathered herself for speech.

"I ain't agoin' to live long now, Doctor." She spoke as though that would serve the world right. "I tell you I ain't goin' to. I ain't agoin' to live very long." Then in a kind of screech that made him shudder, "What am I goin' to do? You tell me that. What am I goin' to do?"

"We'll talk about it after you've had time to rest a little, Alice. I have to go now but I'll send someone to look after you."

Looking back from the door, he saw that he had already dropped from her mind. She was leaning forward, gazing at the dead woman with an expression of disbelief and, unmistakably, of resentment. Chilled by this look, he shut the door behind him.

Faintly, through the open windows, he heard the rattle of dishes that indicated the preparation of lunch, and a burst of radio music coming from the maternity ward. There was here in the hospital a life, a character, and after thirty years of existence even a kind of maturity independent of him, its creator. Like a child grown up, he thought, but still financially dependent. Every year the hospital failed, by a slightly greater amount, to earn its way. Dredging in his own pocket and increasing bank loans were no longer sufficient, and some new approach to the question of money had become essential.

The burden of these gloomy thoughts had slowed his pace so that only now he arrived at the top of the broad, massive staircase that had been the chief grandeur of this mansion before it had been converted into his private hospital. At this point Dr. Moore stood still, his attention caught by a worn place in the linoleum just at the top of the stairs. The floorboards, he saw, were actually showing through. Dr. Moore scuffed with his toe at the edges of the worn place. They were tight enough. No danger that anyone would trip and fall downstairs. Still, this was the sort of thing the inspectors for the Hospital Accreditation Board fastened on. Frowning, Dr. Moore looked around and saw that the rest of the linoleum was in good enough condition. A patch would do. He went on down the stairs.

The hospital had an elevator in a brick wing that had been built at the back of the old house when Dr. Howard Perkins had come here fifteen years earlier. The wing had cost fifty thousand dollars, supplied by Perkins, though the money was actually his wife's. Because he had, so to speak, built it and because it contained the operating room, Perkins regarded the wing as his special province and in his goings and comings he always used the elevator.

Moore used the staircase and not alone because the elevator cost money to run. The solidity of the stairs pleased him, for he was a big man, solidly built himself, his body not betraying his sixty-five years except in the stoop of his heavy shoulders.

From halfway down the stairs, Dr. Moore looked into the square hall below where his elderly head nurse, Edna Judson, sat at a desk writing. At the sound of his familiar step, her impassive face, as grim as a portrait on a parlor wall, softened into an expression he recognized as reserved only for himself. She seemed, he thought, to stand behind a line she had drawn for herself that she never overstepped, but at the same time she appeared to recognize subtly the existence of a special relationship between them based on years of regard and trust. She laid down her pen and arose to stand waiting. Tall and thin and angular, she had to his mind an attenuated look of being compressed sidewise, an improbable, a Gothic look. The effect was increased by what he regarded as a monstrosity she wore on her head, a white cap rising high from a black band and ending in a forward peak like a Punch's cap. What school of nursing it symbolized he did not know, but it had the appearance of being integral with her. Though in the operating room he saw her without the ludicrous thing perched on her gray hair, he had never grown used to its absence there, and through the years it had added not a little to his natural enjoyment of life.

"Well, Edna," he said from the bottom of the stairs. The cap bent forward with a beaklike motion. "Ila Henderson is gone. Alice is up there. She's taking it all right. Will you go up and see to her?"

"How is she going to carry on in that tumbledown old Henderson place all alone, Dr. Moore?"

"She's no worse off than lots of others in the back country. The neighbors can look after her for a while, poor old soul. I don't suppose there's any coffee in the kitchen, is there?"

"I've been keeping it hot for you."

"Fine."

He turned away, his expression growing preoccupied as he crossed the hall to the door of the partitioned space he had allotted to himself for an office. In the doorway he paused, looking around the cramped little room, at the old desk littered with papers, at the black-framed license to practice medicine in Vermont hanging crooked on the wall, at the battered swivel chair and the faded photograph of a much younger Dr. Moore standing on the walk in front of the hospital on the day it was opened. This looking around, this renewing of his contact with his own special environment, was, in a sense, a reaffirmation of himself, and he would have been surprised to know that it was a habit with him whenever, as today, death had dealt him a defeat.

Dr. Moore let himself down heavily into his swivel chair, pulled the telephone toward him and said, "Get me Nortons', will you please?" He was speaking to the central operator, exerting his self-assumed prerogative not to be bothered with numbers. By such simple means as this he managed to avoid, pleasantly and without making an issue, much of the regimentation of modern life.

A cheerful, metallic voice said, "I'm ringing, Dr. Moore."

Listening to the distant sound of the bell, he allowed himself a pleasing, mind's-eye view of Ianthe Norton's ample figure and intelligent brown eyes. At the sound of her voice, Moore straightened in his chair, putting off weariness. "Ianthe? Ed Moore. How is Nat today?"

He listened to her reply, his expression composed into lines of thoughtfulness; then he raised his head as Edna, rustling austerely, came in carrying a cup of coffee. He nodded his thanks and, making room in the litter on his desk for her to set the cup down, still listened attentively. His expression was grave, as he said into the telephone, "Perkins thought it looked like a fatty tumor, not a recurrence. But we'll get a report from the pathology laboratory in a couple of days. I'm going to try to get to New York tomorrow to look for a young surgeon to assist here and I'll get in touch with you when I get back. Nat will be all right, but don't let him worry if you can help it. . . ."

Moore was drinking coffee with one hand and with the other searching through the litter on his desk for a death certificate blank when the door was thrown open with some force. He looked up to see Dr. Perkins standing there.

Dr. Perkins filled the doorway, for, like Moore, he was a big man. People thought of him as even bigger for he held himself with a chest-out erectness, and the impact of his personality was of the kind associated with largeness. He looked angry, which was not unusual, and Moore's manner became placatingly mild.

"Hullo, Howard. Come in. I was just talking to Ianthe about the growth below Nat's clavicle that you took out. I said it was a fatty tumor."

"You know damn well it wasn't, and it's my guess Nat knows it too." Perkins dropped into a chair, crossed his knees and hit the wooden arms a smack with the palms of his hands.

"Well, don't contradict me, if you see either of the Nortons. Give them what peace they can get."

"I came in to tell you the goddam Bovie broke down in the middle of things this morning. I've been operating alone for more than a month while you've been trying to find a replacement for that worthless bastard that got sick, and on top of that the electric cautery quits, so instead of burning the blood vessels shut I have to tie off every stinking tiny one by hand."

"We'll get the Bovie repaired, Howard, and in the meantime we can borrow one from Warwick Clinic. We've done it before."

"Borrow, hell! We've got to have a new one, Ed."

"You couldn't see your way clear—"

"No, I couldn't. Remember our agreement? Fifty thousand—all

the money Adele inherited, all the capital we had—and that was to be all."

Moore sighed. "Anything else?" he asked with a heavy sarcasm wasted on Howard Perkins.

"Sure. The operating table was war salvage—World War I salvage, by the looks. The autoclave leaks steam and Helen got a burn. No assistant, a borrowed anesthetist because that old woman had to pick an operating morning to die, and you wouldn't let her do it alone. No Bovie, and an instrument nurse with a burned hand. Christ! You've got to take drastic steps, Ed, or we're all going down the drain."

"You know I'm planning to."

"Plans. You're a dreamer. You—"

There were quick footsteps outside, the door opened and Edna Judson looked in.

"Dr. Perkins. Excuse me. The little Jones girl with the tonsillectomy is hemorrhaging."

Perkins stood up. "All right, Edna. Get her into the operating room. Ether drip."

He turned to Moore and spoke pleasantly, as though there had been no loud words. "Remember the good old days when we didn't have these secondary tonsillectomy hemorrhages? The bugs have been mutating, I suppose. I'll handle the ether myself—no need to bother you. I imagine you've got plenty to do before you go to New York tomorrow."

Left alone, Moore sat for some time without moving, head bent, deep in thought. Then he swung his chair to face his desk and found, after a little looking, some typewritten sheets clipped together, with columns of figures on the right-hand side. The typing was not expert, for most of the clerical work of the hospital was done by Helen Pierce, the instrument nurse, in her afternoons, but this did not bother Moore except for Helen's sake. He studied these pages, turning them back and forth. While he read he frowned, and sometimes his lips moved, for accounts were not his strong point. After a little of this he reluctantly accepted the conclusion that when he had asked for the last bank loan his reckonings had been a good deal too optimistic.

● ● ●

Though Moore came to the bank fairly often, it always seemed to him an alien place. The thin-faced, precise-featured tellers, each enclosed in a glass cage, did not strike him as quite ordinary people, though he called all four of them by their first names. He raised a hand in greeting as he passed them, conscious of the contrast between their neatly pressed dark suits and his own light tweed. These young men added to the inadequacy he felt whenever he had any contact with financial matters.

The door to Timothy Stoner's conservatively well-furnished office stood open, and on hearing Moore's step Stoner whirled his desk chair around and stood up.

"Come in, Ed."

Stoner, tall, thin and bloodless-looking, came a few calculated steps forward and held out his hand. In this small town, where the important men met frequently, Tim Stoner was the only one who went through the formality of shaking hands, and always Moore, forgetting this, was unprepared. The hand Stoner gave him was thin, large-knuckled and a little damp.

Stoner waved at a green leather chair. "Sit down, Ed. What's on your mind?"

Moore lowered himself into the chair and crossed his hands on his lap in the self-conscious attitude of a man sitting for a portrait.

"One thing only," Moore said, and Stoner laughed. The quality of the laugh made Moore angry, though he was fully aware that he must, in the interests of the hospital, preserve an atmosphere of cordiality.

"Money, Ed?"

"I was too optimistic in my estimate when I asked for the last loan. There are some repairs that have to be made before the Accreditation Board examiners show up again."

Stoner, his eyes on Moore, swung gently back and forth in his cushioned desk chair without making any reply. Because of the curious lenses of the dark-rimmed glasses he wore, the look he kept steadily on Moore was one of magnified intensity, of supernatural penetration. These glasses, by convincing those he turned them on of the unusual force and keenness of his intelligence (an impression not very far from the actual truth), helped to emphasize his prestige. He was fully aware of this and used their effect with deliberate calculation. Without the glasses he was virtually blind and his gray eyes took on the misty, diffused look of light on a foggy day. His dimness of vision he also used with calculation. When he wanted to make some decision, or merely to think something through free from the pressure of an opposing personality, he took his glasses off and was at once alone in the mists of his private world. He seldom took them off in Moore's presence, for he suspected they had the effect of cowing Moore slightly, and this Stoner enjoyed.

After giving the glasses time to take effect, he said crisply, "How much do you want?"

"I was thinking of five thousand—eight, maybe."

"Look here, Ed, I've been meaning to have a talk with you for some time. Your loan here has slowly been getting larger and larger. You realize that, don't you? And you have no better prospects of paying off than when you first started borrowing. Meanwhile your building and equipment have been going steadily downhill and you and Howard aren't getting any younger."

"Howard's only forty-eight."

Stoner smiled and waved his hand deprecatingly. "I want to ask you another question, Ed. In view of these discouraging facts, why do you think this bank has been willing to keep on lending you money?"

"Because the hospital is an essential community service, damn it! It's the town hospital, and—"

"It's your own hospital. You own it. However you administer it for the public good—and I'll have to say you've done a good job of that—the fact remains it's a *private* hospital. Run—theoretically —for your own private profit." Stoner laughed at his grim joke and Moore smiled wryly.

"What are you getting at, Tim? You know damn well the town wants the hospital and needs the hospital."

"I don't like to say this, Ed, because we've been friends ever since you came to town and you've done a fine job here, but that's precisely where, in my view, you're wrong. Thirty years ago, maybe —or even twenty—I grant you Haddon did need a hospital. Now the Warwick Clinic has grown to a modern two-hundred-bed hospital and it's only thirty miles away on perfect roads. Haddon doesn't need a hospital any more."

"Timothy, damn it, you're absolutely wrong. This town—"

18

"Ed, wait till I finish, will you? I happen to think this town would be better off with no hospital at all than one that's rapidly getting to be second-rate. But I don't want to argue about that now. I only want to disabuse you of the idea that the bank is carrying you because the hospital is an 'essential community service,' as you call it. It isn't. Are you interested in the real reason why we've been lending you money?"

Moore jumped up and, with his hands jammed in his trouser pockets, began pacing up and down in the narrow space opposite Stoner's desk. Stoner watched him silently. After a moment Moore stopped, shrugged slightly, said, "I suppose so," and went back to the green chair.

"A pretty good proportion of your cases at the hospital are sent to you by one or another of the manufacturing plants at Silver Springs, aren't they?"

"Yes—mostly surgical."

"Now, Silver Springs is thirty-*eight* miles from Warwick, which is too far to transport most industrial accidents, even with the kind of first aid they're doing at the plants now. And a little too far for families to go visiting. Thirty-eight miles to Warwick, but only eight to your hospital here. See what I'm getting at, Ed?"

"You're saying the Silver Springs plants need the hospital. And I'm telling you, my God, they use us all the time."

"And the Silver Springs plants bank with us and we want to keep them from moving to places where they can get better facilities, so . . ."

"So you lend me money to keep my hospital going because they need it and it's good business for you to keep them happy. Well, in that case . . ." Moore pushed himself up straighter into the chair. "This bears out my conviction that the way to lick my financial problems would be to expand. We're full most of the time, but it's running costs that are killing us. Add more beds, a couple of really well-trained young men and your prestige and earnings go up but your running costs don't rise proportionately. I tell you—"

"Hold your horses, will you? What you're saying is pure poppycock."

"I've given it a lot of thought."

"You never had a business head. Leave it alone, will you? Let me finish. I've been telling you why this bank has been willing to carry you in the past. The future is another matter. Let's get back to the Silver Springs plants. The medical benefits the employees get have been increasing fast. Most of them now get all their medical expenses and those of their families paid both while employed and after retirement. That costs a company around twenty-seven-fifty per man per month."

"I didn't realize it amounted to so much."

"Listen to me, Ed. I said, costs the company—not the union, the *company*. That means that the company has a very direct interest in how that money is spent. Roughly speaking, a company has two choices. It can hire a company doctor, put in a surgery with X-ray equipment, and so on, and take care of everything short of really necessary hospitalization itself. Or it can use the nearest available hospital, which tends to be cheaper and more practical in the long run. Do you see where I'm getting now?"

"No." Moore said it shortly, for the thought had occurred to him that Stoner was enjoying the giving of this lecture.

"Well, then. If the plants are going to rely on a hospital, they want it to be a good one, and not a privately owned one. Now, all five plants in Silver Springs have old, inadequate buildings, and it wouldn't take much to make them move elsewhere. I don't say hospital facilities would be the deciding factor, but they would be *a* factor. And another thing. This is confidential—if anything ever is in this town. There's a company—I won't name it—looking for a location to build a plant for four thousand workers. Four thousand. They *might* come to Silver Springs, if . . . See what I mean now?"

Moore grunted and shifted uneasily in his chair. Abruptly, Stoner leaned forward and pointed a long finger at him.

"Now, look here, Ed. I'm being very frank with you because we've known each other a very long time. I like you personally, though I think you've never believed that because our business relations have not always been conducive to friendliness. But I've always liked you. You've done a fine job with your hospital all these years. You've served the town without self-interest and at considerable sacrifice to yourself. What I wish I could make you see is that I try to serve the town too. I try to do it intelligently, in

20

the best interests of the town, and our seeing those interests in a different light is just unfortunate. But, Ed, I wish you'd at least give me credit for being something beyond a hard, calculating and heartless banker. I love this town. I want to use the position I have here, to the greatest extent I can, for what I sincerely believe to be its good."

Moore made another inarticulate sound that Stoner ignored.

"It's because of the town's pride in you that I don't hesitate to ask you to do a difficult thing. I want you to give up your hospital."

"That I absolutely refuse even to consider."

"Make way for a new one at Silver Springs, not here, Silver Springs."

"I've heard of no such project."

"Of course not. So far, it's only in my mind." Stoner tapped his forehead with the blunt tip of a long finger. "As a banker I have to think ahead and make plans, and even you will have to admit that Silver Springs is the logical place for a hospital, and also that there can't be two hospitals only eight miles apart. Not to mention that my bank would be expected to participate in the financing of a new hospital and couldn't very well do that and keep up our loans to you."

Stoner had pulled back his pointing finger and wrapped his hand around it as though it hurt him. Moore was sitting in stunned silence. After a moment Stoner cleared his throat and went on.

"I am going to work for this scheme of mine, for this is where the best interests of the bank lie. As I say, I want you to give up your hospital—voluntarily. Retire. Stick to your private practice. Do anything you like, but make way for a new hospital."

"And I'll be God-damned if I'll do anything of the sort!"

Moore jumped up and going behind his chair, seized the back and leaned over it toward Stoner, speaking in a voice that made Stoner glance nervously at the door that led to the main part of the bank.

"After more than thirty years of giving this town the best medical service it ever had, you've got the God-damned gall to tell me to shut my hospital and get out. Well, I'm not going to do it. This town wants my hospital and trusts me. They'll trust whoever I pick out to follow me when the time comes. *They don't want* to be forced to go to a strange hospital, with strange doctors, at Warwick or Silver Springs or anywhere else. If the bank won't back me, I'll go to the people at Town Meeting next February—"

"The town people didn't help you when you went to them for money thirty years ago. You had to use the money your wife left you, didn't you?"

"The town feels differently now. They've found out what the hospital means to them."

"And I'll stand up and say that a half-dead hospital is worse than none, and the town trusts my judgment. And, Ed, don't forget there are other ways of closing your hospital than by cutting off your loans. Remember, part of your building isn't fireproof, and with a new, safe hospital building only eight miles away, do you think the government inspectors wouldn't shut you up? You must think of that. They'd really do it, you know. About the loan you want now. I'll let you have your five thousand, and you can even count on help to keep you going until the plans for a hospital at Silver Springs are a certainty. After that I am, frankly, your enemy, or rather the enemy of your hospital."

There was a pause, dead and heavy. Stoner went on speaking but in a lower voice.

"Ed, I'm sorry, because I know you love your hospital and I like you personally, but . . ."

Stoner stopped because he was talking to Dr. Moore's back. Dr. Moore was making for the door, and when he went through it he slammed it behind him, hard. But because he was a peaceable man, whom anger physically upset, he stopped by the closed door and put his hand on the wall, leaning on it until the heavy thudding of his heart had lessened a little. Then he drew a long sigh and went resolutely on his way.

II

Jᴇʙ ᴛʀᴜᴇʟᴏᴠᴇ sᴀᴛ ʙᴇsɪᴅᴇ ᴛʜᴇ ᴅᴇsᴋ of the personnel manager of the Silver Springs Machine Tool Company, and blinked at that young man with stolid resentment. Jeb was the company's janitor, though he preferred to be called its custodian, and he thought it a hell of a thing that the only time all day he would get to sit in a comfortable chair he had to listen to this young whipper chew him out.

The personnel manager thumped his open hand on the file folder on his desk. "The record is here, Jeb. You've had the greatest amount of sick leave of any employee we have."

"I'm entitled to me sick leave and me sick benefits, ain't I?"

"If you're honestly sick and not malingering."

"Like I say to Doc Moore, 'Me back hurts,' and like Doc says to me, 'I think you're a liar, Jeb Truelove, but I can't prove you are.'"

The personnel manager regarded Jeb with a steady look of profound dislike. Headaches and backaches. The incidence of these two maladies was high among the employees for exactly the reason Jeb had pointed out—nobody could prove they weren't real.

"Jeb, I wouldn't be surprised if you were the laziest man the company ever employed. I'm warning you, that's all."

"You'll hear from me union if you go any further than that."

"Get out of here. Go back and at least pretend to do your work."

Reluctantly Jeb pried himself out of the comfortable chair. He closed the door behind him and said to the lettering on it, "Young bastid. Goddam young bastid."

He plodded on, muttering, through a forest of noisy machines and made his way to a private lair he had built for himself out of stacked packing boxes and which he called his "office." He should at this moment be attending to the first duty of each morning, which was to run the flag out on the pole that projected from below a window on the top floor. He felt, however, that after what he had been through he had earned the right to pamper himself a little. He pawed around behind some mops and brooms in his "office" and pulled out a paper bag containing three cans of beer that he had brought in, against regulations, to refresh himself with at slack times of day.

He opened one of the cans and drank it rather fast because he was stimulated by anger. When he had finished, he examined the state of his wounded feelings, found himself to be still unappeased, and opened the second can. The third he put in his pocket and slowly set out to attend to the flag.

The building that housed the screw machine company had originally been constructed for the manufacture of uniforms during the Civil War. It was five stories high, solidly made of brick, and had tall, slim windows like an old prison. A great boxlike elevator went only to the third floor, the top two stories not being in use, and from there on Jeb had to force his paunchy body up the stairs. He did this slowly, with many grunts.

The top floor under the slate roof was stifling, and Jeb felt compelled to rest a bit before tackling the business of the flag. He sat down on a broken chair he kept here for this purpose and put his feet on a stray carton. Finding himself still at outs with the world, he decided to open the last can of beer.

At the moment when Jeb was receiving pleasurable sensations from being about to punch a hole in the beer can, Dr. Moore was going into his office at the hospital eight miles away. Jeb punched; Dr. Moore pulled his stethoscope out of his pocket and laid it on top of a sectional bookcase between a pile of medical journals and an ancient, never used microscope. On the other end of the bookcase there stood a framed photograph of a woman with direct, inquiring eyes, dressed in the fashion of twenty years ago. Alive, she had been Matilda Moore, Mrs. Edward Moore, and a short time after this photograph was taken, wearing this same dress, she had been carried to her grave. Edward Moore did not look at the picture, but, aware always of its standing there, he felt its presence as a kind of warmth.

24

Hurrying a little now, he began divesting himself of the baggy tweed jacket he kept here to wear on his hospital rounds. He hung it on a pair of antlers, present from Howard Perkins, who had the (to Edward Moore, inexplicable) urge to hunt and to destroy. For his jacket he substituted a gray suit coat, picked up an old and shabby Gladstone bag, and left the office.

Dr. Moore found Edna Judson waiting for him by the front door, the half-moon of stained glass above the doorway spattering her white uniform with gules and lozenges of colored light. She said, "What about Ila Henderson's death certificate, Doctor?"

"It's on my desk signed, but not all filled in. I'll have to get answers to some of the questions out of Alice when I get back. She won't know them, but I'll try. I've just about got time to make a call at Harris's on the Cabot Pitch before going to the airport, so I guess I might as well."

She nodded acknowledgment with the ludicrous motion of the forward-jutting cap. "No hat or coat, Doctor?"

"It's still summer—warmer in New York than here, I expect."

She opened the door and he stepped from the coolness of the solid old building into the warmth of the outside air.

"Good luck, Dr. Moore, and good-bye."

"Good-bye, Edna."

He knew as he went down the steps that she was still standing in the doorway, ugly, upright, reliable. It had been years since he had thought about her in any other way than as his head nurse, but a quality in these good-byes, a depth, coming, perhaps, from shared responsibilities, from mutual love of the hospital, made him do so now. Edna was getting old—and in this also she was like himself. What would she do in the years ahead? (And for that matter, what would he do with the unimaginable leisure of old age?) He knew almost nothing about her outside of their hospital relationship. To such an extent was this true that on those rare occasions when he had met her, out of uniform, on the village street, she had seemed like a stranger to him. She was not a "native." Probably she had no relatives, at least not in this part of the world. And that was the sum of what he knew. Friends? He had no idea. Interests outside the hospital? Unlikely, unless perhaps something like African violets on a windowsill.

It occurred to him now that he had a responsibility toward her, to make sure that she was what one called "well fixed" for her old age. It might be wise, he thought, to talk to her about it sometime, and at the thought of anything so intimate, so out of keeping with the carefully preserved impersonality of their relationship, a feeling of embarrassment afflicted him. Such a letting down of bars would only result in making her too acutely uncomfortable, and yet he thought he must someday attempt it all the same.

As he crossed the parking lot at an angle from the front walk, he saw that midway he would meet Dr. Perkins, who was crossing the lot at a similar angle from the emergency entrance in the wing. Any meeting with Perkins, however casual, was likely to have an air of portentousness about it, and Edward Moore, recognizing this anew, stopped to see if he were wanted. Waiting for Perkins to come up to him, Moore thought that it would be easy for a stranger to tell which was the surgeon, which the medical man. Perkins carried his conspicuous good looks with an easy confidence. Man of action, man of attack. Surgery fitted something deep in his nature. Moore thought a moment and decided the word he wanted was "fulfilled." The handling of a knife "fulfilled" a need in Howard different, he believed, from any fulfillment he himself found in medicine.

When he was still some paces away, Perkins said in his big voice, "Well, Ed, you're off on your wild goose chase, are you?"

"I'm hoping it won't prove that."

They had, of course, been all over this before, but, Moore knew well enough, it was not the other's way to relinquish a point of view. He was saying now just what Moore expected him to say. "I still think you're more likely to find a man through the usual channels. Write around. Give a glowing picture of our thirty-bed hospital here. Touch on the current revolution in rural medicine . . ."

"I suppose there is a revolution, as you call it, but I've been too close to things to know much about it, Howard." Dr. Moore, hoping to sidetrack his colleague, did not succeed.

"That old friend of yours that you interned with—I thought his reply to your letter sounded pretty vague."

"Still, he thought he might know someone. And I really believe that if we can find someone this way, he'd be likely to be a better man than we'd get through advertising."

26

"But did you have to go chasing off yourself?"

"He may need some persuading even to come and look us over. I thought I could do that better in person."

They had been walking toward the line of parked cars and they came to a halt behind Moore's dusty red jeep. Perkins said with sudden violence, "And what makes you think a good man would come to practice here?"

"You came, didn't you?"

There was a silence. Then Perkins said abruptly, "Well, good luck, Ed," and Moore said, "I'll be back as soon as I can, Howard."

He threw his bag in the back of the jeep, and because he was in the habit of keeping a knowledgeable eye on the weather, he glanced upward. The sky, seen through a tracery of leaves, was a faultless blue, and as he looked, a breeze, coming from nowhere, stirred the treetops and died with a sigh. A fall wind, brief but premonitory, and cooler, fresher air stirred around him. Then, also sighing, he cramped his big body with practiced ease into the limitations of the jeep. He watched while Perkins drove past in his secondhand, but impressive, Cadillac. Then he started the jeep and sent it expertly backward in a long curve.

On the sixth floor of the Silver Springs plant, Jeb drained the last of the beer into his mouth, threw the can into a carton where it clinked against other empty cans, sighed and reluctantly rose. Instead of making him cooler, the beer had done just the reverse, and his face and neck and hands were wet with sweat. He slouched across to the window above the flagpole, opened it and poked his head out. From here he looked down on the main, the "executive," entrance to the building, where shrubs and a few ornamental trees had been planted to camouflage the grimness of the old structure. He performed his daily ritual of spitting to see which way the wind blew and pulled his head back in. The flag lay in a heap beside him. He picked it up and slowly fastened it to the lanyards that would carry it outward to the end of the pole.

The ropes were old—he had been meaning to replace them for some time—and while he was hoisting the heavy flag to the windowsill, he saw a place so frayed it would have to have immediate attention, and beyond it another place where the rope was in the same bad condition.

He should have gone downstairs to the Storage and Issue Department for a new rope, but the thought of the weary climb back up those stairs was too much for him. He leaned on the wall and thought about it, feeling just a trifle giddy from the heat and the three cans of beer. Finally he said, "To hell with it," and after a good deal of fumbling got two knots tied in the weakened places.

He gathered up the flag, let it fall outside the window, and pulled the lanyards. The flag went outward by jerks for about four feet and then a knot caught and it would go no farther. Jeb yanked several times and swore, realizing that he now had no choice but to go down for a new rope. He began to haul the flag back in and the other knot caught, making it impossible to move the flag more than a few inches in either direction. He tried leaning out the window to pull on the flag itself, and found it annoyingly a foot beyond his hand.

He thought it over glumly, and decided he would have to unship the heavy pole, for which he would have to call help and so expose the result of his laziness. The alternative was—and the thought made him a little sick—to sit on the windowsill, lean forward, grab the flag and cut the nearest knot with his pocketknife. If he kept hold of the pole with one hand there would be no real danger, he would not be exposed to ridicule and the job would be done in minutes instead of an hour or more.

He put one foot over the sill and then, careful not to look down, the other. Feeling his sweaty hands on the polished wood of the pole, he thought he should have dried them, but it was too late now. He got the flag in his fist, jerked it hard to get the knot closer, lost his balance and fell.

The flag, before it tore loose, broke his fall a little. The tree he fell into broke it still further. The manager's secretary, who was taking dictation and gazing out of the window while her boss composed a sentence in his mind, saw Jed hurtle down out of the tree, and screamed. Jed was alive but unconscious and obviously so badly injured that the manager, himself white and shaken, decided he must be left lying in the shrubbery until a doctor could be brought to him. There had been no doctor in Silver Springs for three years and the manager left Jed to go in to telephone the hospital at Haddon. Edna, sitting at her desk, answered his call.

"Dr. Moore has gone to New York. . . . No, I'm sorry, he left just a little while ago. I'll call Dr. Perkins and ask him to go right out there. Cover him with something but don't move him at all until Dr. Perkins gets there."

Adele Perkins answered Edna's call in high, clear tones. She had a manner of speaking that Edna, who was not familiar with speech as it is taught in boarding schools of the expensive sort, thought affected and strange. Adele seemed to Edna aloof and cold to the town and its people, which she considered not a proper attitude for a doctor's wife. Adele told her that just a moment ago Dr. Perkins had come home, but he had a call and had gone right out again. She didn't know where the call had come from. But did it really matter? There was, of course, Dr. Ladd. . . .

Irritated, and telling herself there was no cause for it, Edna said to the operator, "Get me Dr. Ladd, will you please, Della?"

With the phone distantly ringing, Della said, "What is it, Miss Judson? Somebody took sick?"

"Accident out at Silver Springs. Man had a bad fall."

"Gee, and it looks like Ladd's ain't going to answer."

"Keep ringing."

When, a few minutes later, Edna put the telephone down, she looked grave and frightened for she was facing a situation no one thought could happen—an emergency with no doctor in the town. She snatched the telephone up again and said, "Della? Listen—go look out the window and see if Dr. Moore's car is parked anywhere. He may have decided to stop for something. If it isn't there, he's already gone to the Cabot Pitch and there's no phone there. Call the state police and get them to head him off. Then call me back."

Della took off her headphone, slid off her stool and leaned out of the window as far as she dared. The jeep was nowhere to be seen. With the two other operators watching her, and trying to sound calm, she called the State Police.

Moore actually had stopped in the town, but the reason Della failed to see his jeep was that he had parked it in a driveway between the drugstore and the building that housed the telephone exchange on the second floor. He was at that moment meeting Dr. Harlan Greer, retired and wealthy surgeon from New York.

29

Greer said, "Ah, Moore, just the man I want to see," at the same time Moore said, "Dr. Greer, how are you? Your place didn't run out of water in the drought, did it?"

"No, thank goodness. Come over here a minute. I want to talk to you."

He drew Moore to a spot close to the drugstore window, away from the shoppers on the sidewalk. Greer was a thin, scholarly-looking man with long, very thin hands—as different from Perkins as he could well be, and both types, in Moore's opinion, could be equally neurotic in relation to a knife.

Greer was saying, "I hear you've a new man coming to join your staff at the hospital. That right?"

"I wish it were. It's still a matter of hope."

"What happened to the man you had? I heard he got sick."

"T.b. Gave us all quite a scare at the hospital when he came down with it."

"I dare say. . . . I'm just on my way to Warwick. Perhaps you've heard that they have let me do a little lecturing to the medical students? I enjoy it. But I wanted to hear about this new man. There's a lot more to draw a good young doctor to a country practice than there used to be. In my day, as a young man, I wouldn't have considered it. Rural medicine . . . but I prefer the term 'exurban,' don't you? For a town like Haddon that isn't really country any more . . ."

Moore made an indeterminate sound, not caring to admit he had never heard the term before, and didn't like it.

"Exurban medicine is changing so fast. There's no longer any reason for a patient to get inadequate care because he lives in the country—"

"There's the shortage of doctors."

"There's that, true. But you doctors here in Haddon should get a move on. You're way behind the times."

"I'd like to talk to you about it sometime. And about an extraordinary talk I had yesterday with Stoner at the bank."

"Glad to. It interests me, because—*Oh! Good heavens!*"

Dr. Greer leaped backward with agility and gazed down with an expression of startled disgust at a large and shabby Angora cat that had just rubbed against his leg and was attempting to do so again. Moore stooped, picked him up, and held him under one arm. The cat made a plaintive, wearied sound. Moore said, "You don't mean to say you don't know Fluffy? He's a village character, the town cat."

"I can't stand the creatures."

Moore looked down with tolerance at his burden. The cat's ears had suffered much in past battles and one of them was newly torn, and bleeding.

"Fluffy, you've been fighting again."

The cat struggled to be free, seemed to realize the hopelessness of his situation, and turned up at Moore a stare of stolid malevolence and boredom. Greer seemed anxious to get away from the cat's proximity and Moore said, "I haven't had time to think about these things very much—not enough to get a clear picture in my mind of what's going on in country medicine. It might really help to talk to you. Thanks. So long."

Almost over the heads of the two doctors, Della was listening to Edna saying in a voice high with strain, "Try Dr. Harlan Greer. I know he doesn't have a Vermont license, but this is an emergency. If you can't get him, try old Dr. Hull at Finlay Three Corners. Oh, and call the general store at the turnoff to the Cabot Pitch and get someone to stand in the road to flag Dr. Moore in case he gets there before the police."

Still carrying Fluffy, Moore went into the drugstore. He put the cat down on the prescription counter and held him against an evident passionate desire to leap for freedom. With the struggling cat pressed against him, Moore called out to the top of a bald head just visible over the partition, "Jim, have you got an open bottle of Merthiolate around somewhere?"

"Sure, Doc."

In a moment made active by Fluffy's struggles, Jim came around the partition with a bottle in his hand and saw the cat. "Turned veterinarian, have you?"

Jim held the bottle carefully away from his white coat while Moore, with his free hand, took out the stopper and looked down. The cat, who had ceased to struggle, turned up at him an unblinking stare from eyes deep and luminous with apprehension. Moore paused, for he had seen that same look in the eyes of a naked savage child in a movie of some New Guinea tribe, and he wondered if this primitive expectation of harm might not lie at the beginning of the road to thought. To soothe himself as much as the cat, he made a murmur of distressful pity, redipped the glass rod of the stopper in the Merthiolate, covered the raw area on the cat's ear with one quick swipe, and stepped back to avoid Fluffy's frantic leap to freedom.

"Fluffy's getting old," Jim said, wiping the glass rod and putting it back in the bottle.

"We all are. Here's a prescription for you."

Jim took it and read it with interest. "Old woman on the Cabot Pitch takes a lot of this stuff, don't she, Doc?"

"Keeps her amused and doesn't cost me much."

"I got some drug house circulars I've been saving for you, Doc." He pulled open a drawer, took out a pile of folders and laid them on the counter. "Look through 'em and see if there's any you haven't seen and I'll throw the rest out."

"Thanks, Jim. I've about been practicing medicine out of these things, last few years." Moore sorted rapidly through the pile, laid two aside, and shoved the rest toward the druggist, who was making a neat blue package of a bottle of brownish capsules.

"You don't use so many of the new drugs at that. Dr. Ladd don't use any."

"When I do use them, the bill for them usually runs more than my fee. A lot of my patients can't afford them." He folded the circulars and put them into an inside coat pocket. "Thanks, Jim. So long."

The operator was almost crying with nerves and anxiety. "Dr. Greer's gone to Warwick, Edna. Dr. Hull has flu. What you want I should do?"

"Call Boardman's, tell Orie to get the ambulance out and go get that accident and take him to Warwick. Tell him to hurry."

"Orie's out laying linoleum at Mrs. Henry's. Doris is alone in the store. I happen to know—"

"Call Orie at Mrs. Henry's. Tell him *quick*."

Moore backed out into Main Street and set off in the direction of the Cabot Pitch. The operator, her finger on the lever, listening to the telephone ringing unanswered in Mrs. Henry's front hall, was looking out the window and saw the familiar MD license plate on the back of Moore's muddy red jeep. She took her finger off the lever and said to the girl next to her, "Well, thank God. He's headed right. The state police'll get him quick now. If he wants the ambulance, he can call it himself when he gets to Silver Springs. I'm a wreck. Watch my board a minute, will you? I'll call Edna when I get back."

Moore crossed the upper bridge over the Little Torrent, deriving a moment's enjoyment from the rattle of loose planking and from the miniature dust storm raised by his passing. On the other side he looked at his watch and decided that he was cutting time a little short for the regular road to the Cabot Pitch. There was a back road up the near side of the mountain, much shorter, and no more than a logging track, but with the dry weather it ought to be passable. He decided to try. He therefore turned left instead of right, and the stubby rump of the jeep had just gone over the crest of a rise when he heard the loose boards on the bridge rattle under a passing car. He had no way of knowing that this was one of the two state police cars that were hunting for him. The other car was already parked on the regular road to the Pitch, confident of catching him going or coming.

Scrabbling up through the hollows and over the exposed ledge of the logging road was an experience he thoroughly enjoyed, for it gave him a good shaking up and something to fight against that would relieve feelings of the combativeness aroused by Timothy Stoner. When he came out on the grassy plateau where the house stood, he guessed at once by the absence of shouting children and barking dogs that the house was empty. They would all be off somewhere in their ramshackle truck, and he would not be sorry to leave the medicine and depart without seeing any of them. The back door was unlocked and he went into a room that was kitchen, parlor and dining room all in one. The place was filthy and filled with the indescribable smell that accompanies family living below a certain economic level. He looked around with distaste at the black frying pan containing scraps of what was certainly illegal trout, at the broken-down rocker and the cot where someone had been sleeping—and at a large, expensive television set standing in the corner. He stared at it angrily, thinking of the bills these people

33

never paid, and it stared back at him with blank indifference. He put the medicine down on the table and stamped out.

The sight of the television set had raised his blood pressure with anger, making him feel like being up against something physically tough, and so he elected to make the far more perilous descent of the logging track instead of going by the regular dirt road down from the Pitch. The two state policemen waiting for him comfortably in the shade by the roadside did not realize they had missed him until he was guiding the jeep into a parking place at the airport.

At just this time Edna was walking down the wing corridor to get some lunch in the nurses' dining room. Edna was tired out, but her mind was at rest for by this time the state troopers would have located Dr. Moore. She figured that he must be most of the way to Silver Springs already.

She went into the dining room with a tray of food and found Helen, the instrument nurse, sitting at the end of the table with a cup of coffee. Helen was a big-boned, calm-faced young woman with brooding dark eyes, who did her work with steady intensity at a fixed, efficient pace. She was still wearing a green operating-room gown and a white snoodlike cap that she had pushed back, showing her dark hair. There was a bandage across the back of her left hand where the steam from the autoclave had burned it.

Helen was, if not a close friend of Edna's, at least high in her esteem, for they had worked together in the operating room long enough for each to know and appreciate the quality of the other. The two women smiled tired smiles at each other, and Edna, setting down her tray, began to unload her dishes.

"Is the crisis over?" Helen asked.

"Yes, thank goodness. Della saw Dr. Moore's car just leaving Haddon and she got the state police to head him off. They probably got him on the Pitch road, if not before. He must be nearly at Silver Springs by now. It's too bad his trip's spoiled, but I hate to think of what might have happened if we hadn't got him."

"The town shouldn't be without a doctor."

"I don't suppose it ever was before." Edna arranged her silverware with precision. "Who would think, with three of them—

four, if you want to count Greer—that not one of them could be reached."

As Edna was about to sit down, she turned to look out the window, for she had the country woman's hour-by-hour interest in the weather. The window looked onto the parking lot, and she saw with mild interest that a light truck had pulled in and that three men were taking something heavy out of the back. They were doing this with so much concentration and care that she continued to watch, curious to see what it might be. With a shock she saw that the thing they were sliding out of the truck was a man on a stretcher.

"*Helen, they've got that accident case out there.*" The shrillness of her voice made Helen jump.

"What are you talking about, Edna?"

"My Lord, Helen, they've brought him here."

Helen went to stand beside her at the window. "Isn't Dr. Moore with them?"

"No, he isn't. And the jeep isn't here. They must have thought they'd meet him on the Silver Springs road, and missed him—I don't see how. Helen—you don't suppose the police never found Dr. Moore, do you?"

The two women faced each other in consternation and Helen said, "That has to be it. That has to be what happened. Edna, what are we going to do?"

For a moment Edna thought in silence, her thin mouth drawn tight, striking her closed hands together. Then she looked swiftly at her watch.

"There's time to get Dr. Moore at the airport. Thank God. We'll have to do the best we can until he gets here. Get the emergency room ready . . ."

There is no sound in a hospital more ominous, more productive of alarm, than the sound of someone running, which is why nurses, though they move swiftly, never run. Edna ran, and Helen, pulling down her operating-room cap, followed her.

The mountain airport was small and windblown and the plane, an ancient DC-3, had a weight fastened to its tail. One of the two airport attendants stood by this weight, ready to unfasten it, while the other stood by the steps helping the last of the passengers to board. Moore parked the jeep where it would await his return, snatched his bag and ran. As he passed the offices, which were little better than a shack, he heard a telephone ringing and experienced the sudden alertness, the reflex urge to action, that is everyone's instantaneous response to a telephone bell. Realizing in the same instant that this was no concern of his, he hurried on.

The muscular young man by the steps said, "Hi, Doc. Just made it."

"Hullo, Henry. Your phone's ringing in there."

"They'll have to wait. Have a good trip, now."

As Moore sank into his seat and fastened the safety belt, the plane began to roll away.

"Phone's ringing, Henry," the other young man said.

"Yes, I know. Time I get there it'll stop."

They stood side by side to watch the takeoff, and then Henry, realizing the phone was still ringing, dogtrotted back to the shed.

A few minutes later he came out and sat down on a luggage cart out of the wind. "Wanted Dr. Moore," he said. "Emergency. I said he'd gone. I wonder should I have called the plane back?"

His pal pulled a pack of cigarettes out of his shirt pocket, expertly shook one loose and sat down to enjoy it. "Naw. Quicker to git another doctor."

In the front hall of Haddon Hospital Edna's peaked cap sat on her desk as though monitoring the hospital in her absence. Edna, in the emergency room, was wearing no cap at all, for after her first look at Jeb she knew that there was no time for anything else. She was standing at the side of the emergency table and Helen at the head, both women bending over Jeb Truelove's smashed, unconscious form. Helen was holding an oxygen mask over his lacerated face, and Edna, straightening up, took the prongs of a stethoscope out of her ears.

"I still get a faint heartbeat. I don't think there's anything more we can do until the doctor from Warwick gets here."

"How much longer do you figure?"

Edna glanced up at the big clock on the wall. "I called soon as I was sure the airport wasn't going to answer. Twenty, twenty-five minutes ago, I guess. I should have looked at the time then. He should be here in ten or fifteen minutes, shouldn't he?"

Helen looked down at Jeb's battered head. "I wish they'd taken him straight to Warwick when they had him in the truck. If he starts to go while there's no one but us here, what are we going to do, Edna?"

"I don't know. I've been trying to think. We can't use heart massage with his chest smashed like that. I'm sure he's been bleeding a lot internally."

"Epinephrine into the heart?"

"I just don't know, Helen."

"Would you dare?"

"Yes I would, if I thought it would help, but I just don't know . . ."

Edna slipped the stethoscope back in her ears and applied the diaphragm to Jeb's shattered chest. She moved it two or three times, listening, and Helen, frowning, watched. Then Helen saw that Edna's lips were silently, slowly moving as she counted the heartbeat, and she watched the lips. They moved and stopped, and moved again. They stopped, and seconds passed and they did not move. Very slowly, Edna took the stethoscope prongs out of her ears.

"He's gone."

They stood looking at each other. After a moment Helen remembered that the oxygen was still flowing and she turned it off.

Dr. Moore, who was not accustomed to flying, watched from a window the takeoff of his plane. As soon as it was in the air, however, he was deep in thought about his problem of the hospital. He proceeded much as he would if he were making a difficult diagnosis; that is to say, he made sure he had all his facts and understood them before he attempted to draw any conclusions about the nature of the trouble or make any plans for its remedy. He made a conscientious effort to do this without letting prejudice or emotion distort his view. The result was that when he arrived at La Guardia, after what seemed to him a surprisingly short trip, he understood a good deal more than he had about the character and extent of the threatened attack on his hospital. He still had

37

no idea what to do about it but he felt that at least he had achieved a degree of clearheadedness.

He stumbled out of the plane into the hot, humid New York afternoon, and came out of his preoccupation sufficiently to experience the traveler's feeling of unreality and disorientation. He found a taxi and because so long a time had passed since he had been in New York, he decided to forget everything else and enjoy the ride. The taxi had not gone half a mile before he was once more lost in thought.

He remembered the hotel to which he was going as quiet, inexpensive, and comfortably shabby. He found to his surprise that it was no longer any of these things. The lobby, once a restful place of dark paneling and deep leather chairs, was now garish with color, mercilessly lit, and furnished with grotesque chairs in which it seemed to him impossible to sit normally.

As he waited in line in front of the desk, it came to him that the feelings of mental discomfort he was experiencing were not so much a product of these distressing surroundings as of his having in a deeper sense no relation whatsoever to this environment. His presence here had less effect than a tossed pebble on the surface of a lake. It added or took away nothing. This to him, if not a new experience, was one he had not encountered for so long a time as to find it strangely disconcerting. And for just a moment he had a strong longing to be back where he came from, where he was thoroughly and comprehensively known.

An irritable clerk assigned him a room without once looking fully at him, slapped down a key and turned him over to a bellboy with an air of having well disposed of him. As he followed docilely behind the bellboy, who was carrying the bag he would have preferred to carry himself, Dr. Moore wondered how it would seem to practice medicine in a place where most of the people you met, including many of your patients, were strangers. He thought this over while they joined the throng waiting for elevators, and it came to him that the practice of medicine in a community like Haddon, where his patients were known to him in ways other than medical, might have values he had not always fully appreciated. He would certainly feel himself seriously handicapped in both diagnosis and treatment without a knowledge of the home life, the economic and emotional problems of those who brought their physical ills to him, a knowledge that the city man, in the nature of things, must in most cases do without.

In the elevator, where he was pressed into closer proximity with strangers than he had ever experienced with friends, he endeavored to surmount distaste for this physical contact by sticking to his train of thought. Stack up on the other side of the scales from this undoubted disadvantage of the city man all his many advantages. Scientific and hospital facilities of the best. Association with men who were leaders in their fields. Research facilities. Even ease of transportation—not a minor factor when one considered that a country doctor must cover a radius of about thirty miles, night and day, in every sort of weather. Then where was the balance of the scales? Thinking about it as he stepped off the elevator and walked down a corridor in the bellboy's important wake, Dr. Moore decided it depended somewhat on the point of view—doctor's or patient's—and, in any case, he did not feel qualified to make an evaluation. Sum it up by saying that the city man probably tended to treat the disease, not the patient, while the country doctor treated the patient and did the best he could under the circumstances about the disease. An oversimplification, of course. But as Howard Perkins had remarked, the whole character of country medicine was changing. Perhaps in time, though perhaps not in his time but in that of a new medical generation, a better balance might be struck.

When he entered his room, he saw with regret that it had been "modernized" with as much ruthlessness as the lobby. The bellboy deposited his bag, flipped a switch on the air conditioner, another on the television set, accepted his quarter and departed in an aura of artificial briskness. Dr. Moore glanced with suspicion at the studio couch on which he feared he was to sleep, then also moving briskly, he turned off the television just as it started to blare at him, went to the air conditioner and turned that off, and attempted to open the window. It was fastened shut. He sighed and turned the air conditioner on again.

There remained the need to take prompt steps toward what he had come here to accomplish. He located the telephone and the massive directory in a recess behind the built-in studio couch. He laid the heavy Manhattan book across his knees and hunted out the office telephone number of his former medical school classmate, Dr. Adam Fairchild. Then he lifted out the telephone, found the wire too short to reach beyond the couch (apparently guests were expected to do their telephoning supine) and dialed in discomfort with the instrument on his knee.

Waiting, he discovered a small metal sign affixed to the arm of the couch, directly beneath an object that resembled the handle of a carving knife. He leaned forward and read: TO CONVERT THIS COUCH INTO A BED, PULL HANDLE FORWARD IN SLOT. TO LOCK INTO POSITION, MOVE HANDLE TO RIGHT UNTIL CLICK IS HEARD AND HANDLE HAS BECOME IMMOVABLE. TO REVERSE . . .

So diverted had he become by this that when a voice said, "Doctor's office," he had to reassemble his wits.

Dr. Fairchild, it seemed, was occupied with a patient and could not be disturbed. Dr. Moore said he would call later, returned the telephone to its niche, stood up, grasped the handle firmly, and pulled. The front edge of the couch lifted itself in the air, slid backward, and returned toward him, other side up, presenting a bed as tightly made as a Pullman berth. He contemplated this surprising phenomenon, the corners of his eyes crinkled with amusement, and said, aloud, "I'll be damned."

Moore left the contraption bed side up and busied himself taking his possessions out of his bag and distributing them in the room and in a closet-size bath of almost surgical cleanliness. He took from the bottom of his bag a small bottle of Scotch and went in search of a tumbler, which he found on the bathroom shelf, sealed in cellophane. He poured himself a modest drink, ignored a button labeled ICE WATER, added some water from the faucet and wandered with it back into his room.

He stood at the window with the glass in his hand, looking out over the air conditioner toward a city that had never been familiar to him and was now no longer even recognizable. Like body tissue, he thought, that is said to renew itself every seven years, the skeletal structure of the streets alone remaining without change. Haze hung over the city into which the sun had begun its decline, tingeing the East River, like a great artery, with a reddish glow.

He finished his drink, set the glass on the projection of the air conditioner, and turned back to face the room. He stood there, an expression of surprise gradually forming. The astonishing realization had just dawned on Dr. Moore that, for the first time in as long as he could remember, he had nothing whatsoever to do.

And then immediately, as though the having nothing to do had paved the way for it, he made the second discovery: that he was very tired—tired beyond the accepted, everyday condition of tiredness. He felt weak with it. He felt that in a moment more his body might begin to tremble.

He walked heavily across the room and sat on the edge of the bed, bowed forward, hands hanging limply between his knees, and thought about the probable cause of the weariness that had overtaken him. Years of driving himself too far. A little bit of himself that each day had not rested, and this residue of each day's tiredness adding itself to all the leftover fatigues of all his former days, suddenly overwhelming him.

Wearied even by this clinical analysis of his own weariness, Dr. Moore stooped down, slowly unlaced his shoes and took them off. Then he stretched himself out on the couch and presently he slept.

III

Dr. MOORE AWOKE WITH A START to the familiar, oppressive sense of duties to be done, his mind groping to assemble and order them before he realized where he was. When this dawned on him, he relaxed again, resenting the strange bed's resistance to the demands of his body, discovering that he ached a little here and there because of it. Then, with a start, he remembered that he must try again to reach Adam Fairchild. He looked at his watch, not focusing very distinctly. Ten minutes to five. Time enough. He pushed himself up reluctantly, balanced the telephone on his lap, and dialed.

Dr. Fairchild had gone for the day. Moore looked at his watch again in disbelief. At this hour he himself would still be in his Main Street office, the big office in an old building, with windows looking on the river, where he saw most of his patients. He would be hoping to be finished in time to look in at the hospital and to snatch an hour in which to cook himself a meal before his evening office hours began at seven o'clock. Trying to keep his feelings out of his tone, he told the crisp voice at the other end of the wire that he would like to have Dr. Fairchild's home telephone number. The voice replied that she was sorry she could not give it out, but if it was an emergency, she would be glad to contact Dr. Fairchild. Was it an emergency?

Dr. Moore conceded that it was not, thought a moment, and asked what time Dr. Fairchild would be in his office in the morning.

Dr. Fairchild would be operating in the morning from eight-thirty on. He would not return to his office until two-thirty, but all his appointment time was filled. There might be something later in the week—almost surely in the early part of the week following. . . . Dr. Moore could hear the pages of an appointment book being turned over.

Putting the telephone back in its niche, Moore swore with feeling. Then he lay back comfortably and marveled, and after a while he went to sleep again.

He reached the hospital at seven-thirty next morning. The ground floor of the great institution was not yet aroused to the day's activity. The huge lobby was still in semidarkness, and in the cathedral silence Moore's footsteps on the marble floor rang hollowly. At the far side of the lobby, on a counter, a desk lamp burned starlike in the shadows and behind the counter an elderly woman in a print dress sat reading. Moore walked toward her thinking that she looked like a nice old cup of tea, and that in one guise or another he had known her since student days. A privileged character who mothered interns and with whom the important doctors joked familiarly. Old biddies of this stamp seemed to relish being part of the life of a big hospital. Lucky old girls with jobs that kept them from loneliness.

This edition of the familiar genus laid her book down, smiling, making herself the hospital's official welcome, adding to it something of her own.

"Good morning, Doctor. What can we do for you?"

So she knew by the look of him he was a doctor, did she? And also, no doubt, that he was a country doctor on a visit. Amused, he said, "I want to talk to Dr. Adam Fairchild, or get a message to him. My name is Edward Moore."

"He's here, I know." She pulled the telephone to her, dialed, gave her message and was, apparently, told to hold the line. With half of her attention given to the telephone, she kept her eyes on Moore as though holding him there, keeping up friendly communication with him.

"Have you been with the hospital long?" he asked because he knew she would like answering.

"Twenty-one years, ever since this building was built. They almost put it up around me. *Hullo* . . ."

After a moment's talk she replaced the telephone. "He's up on the operating-room floor and he can't come to the phone. But he sent a message that he's awfully glad you're here and if you won't

43

mind waiting he'll send someone down." She looked at Moore with new interest, and he checked an impulse to tell her that he and Adam Fairchild had been students and interns together. "There's a place to wait just through that arch to the left." She leaned forward and pointed with a pencil.

He thanked her, and about to move away, he had an impulse to make some small, further acknowledgment of her friendliness in these impersonal surroundings. He said, "I'd like to know your name."

Surprised, she looked at him and quickly down again.

"Dora Mathewson."

She began nervously picking up various things on the counter and putting them down, giving the impression of tidying up without accomplishing anything. By asking her name he had intended only to give her a slight recognition of herself apart from the institution she served. He saw that he had made a mistake, that she passionately identified herself with the hospital where she was sheltered, secure, part of its greatness. Separated from it she might well be insecure, alone, perhaps even afraid. She said with a resentment he felt he merited, "Nobody around here calls me anything but Dolly."

He looked off into the shadows of the lobby. Then, with gravity, he again said "Thank you" and moved away.

Through the arch and around the corner he found empty benches in rows, facing two banks of elevators, a grim arrangement, it seemed to him. He sat down and became aware of a silence around him so profound that it was hard to believe that in most of the hospital morning activity had begun. From time to time a mirrored door of an elevator clashed open to let out tired-looking young doctors in rumpled white, their tour of night duty ended. Other doctors, their white coats stiff with starch, came and stood in silent groups of three or four, waiting to be carried upward. Some student nurses appeared, wearing striped dresses and caps with lovely, flightlike lines that pleased him. Then one elderly nurse came by herself, carrying her cap in her hand and a bulky chintz knitting bag on her arm. "Special," he thought, recognizing the knitting bag as the distinguishing sign, and watching her with mild enjoyment as she pinned on her cap in front of the mirror on the elevator door.

44

Then the door clashed open, and a doctor, so young he had to be an intern, came briskly out, saw Moore, and made directly for him. Dr. Fairchild's emissary, Moore thought, and arose, encountering eager, dark eyes, a sensitive, intelligent, only partly Americanized face. He thought, second-generation something. They're often the best medical material we have. . . .

"Dr. Moore? I'm Dr. Kopf. Dr. Fairchild sent me down."

Even the lad's voice sounded eager, as though his internship were still a great adventure.

"That's most kind." Inconceivable that he and Adam Fairchild had ever looked so young, so filled with high resolve, so empty of experience.

"Dr. Fairchild is operating this morning, as you know, sir. He said to tell you he's awfully glad you're in town. The op is on closed-circuit television—open heart—pulmonary valvulotomy." A pause and a flush mounting under the dark skin. "I'm scrubbing with him, sir."

"Congratulations, Doctor. First time?"

"First with him, sir. I'm mighty lucky. The thing is, Dr. Fairchild wondered if you would like to watch on television and then have dinner with him at the Union Club tonight. And if you can, would seven-thirty be convenient?"

"Glad to. Seven-thirty would be fine."

"The projection room's on the OR floor. Shall we go up?"

"All right. Thank you." He almost said "son," and amended the sentence. "Thank you, Dr. Kopf."

Waiting for the elevator, Dr. Kopf said, "You and the Chief were in medical school and interned together? He must have been a brilliant student."

"Run of the mine." Brooding, Moore saw young Adam, thin, pale eyes, quick to anger, industrious with the scalpel and in nothing else. "He always liked to operate. None of us thought he was slated for glory."

"*Really*, Dr. Moore? I should have thought . . ."

Disbelieving, and hurt by this denigration of his ideal. Feeling compunction, Dr. Moore said, "A lot of other things go into making a good surgeon."

The mirrored doors clashed open again and the elevator engulfed them. Leaning his slim, white form against the guardrail, hands behind his back, dark eyes deep with desire to understand, Dr. Kopf said, "What sorts of things, sir? I wish you'd tell me."

But they were stopping with a controlled rush at the fourth floor, and Dr. Moore shook his head and smiled faintly. He was not, come to think of it, at all sure he knew, except that he had a strong impression that those surgeons who, like Adam, became successful had one thing in common. Each one was sure, absolutely positive, that he could operate better than anyone else. That faith seemed to be an essential ingredient. Adam had it. Even as an intern, and with nothing to back it up, he was sure of himself, burning with his desire to be on his own.

At the fourth floor a lively covey of student nurses crowded into the elevator and burst into giggles the moment the door was shut, casting veiled and challenging glances at the young doctor who, Dr. Moore was amused to note, had become stern and slightly red in the face. At the sixth floor an orderly with a wheeled stretcher was waiting and everyone moved to the sides to make room. The woman on the stretcher was so motionless that each blink of her eyelids was startling, but her eyes, staring straight ahead, were alive with terror. At the eighth floor the student nurses all departed, each one as she left the elevator cloaking herself wonderfully in demure efficiency. At the twelfth floor, Dr. Kopf straightened himself, said, "This is ours," and gave the orderly a hand with the wheeled stretcher.

The corridor of the operating-room floor was full of activity and seemed to Moore as long as a city block. The pale green tiles of the walls gave the light an odd, underwater quality. Soundproofing created an uneasy hush in which each sound became noteworthy, meaningful. The deadening, the strange, unfocused light, made the intense, hurried life in the corridor seem remote, dreamlike.

Young Dr. Kopf's voice, transmuted by the soundproofing, came as through a cloud bank, making the triviality of his remark sound ridiculous.

"I'm afraid that the projection room is way at the other end of the floor, sir."

Walking along, Dr. Moore felt himself becoming again that troubled young intern of long ago, coming on duty in his ill-fitting whites, felt again the wave of physical weakness that made the simple business of stepping off the elevator on the OR floor an act

46

requiring resolution. Unconsciously, he slowed his walk to that former self's reluctance. His dislike of surgery, which had been the strongest emotion of his young life, was calloused over now by long necessity, but thinly, so that from time to time this protection broke, leaving him as rawly sensitive to the sights and sounds and smells of an operating room as he had ever been.

They were halfway down the corridor, coming abreast of a long counter that enclosed a nursing station. Two doctors and a nurse were using the counter as a desk. All wore round caps, and their masks hung loosely under their chins. Inconsequentially, Moore noticed that the nurse had pulled her smock tightly around her slim body with a broad band of surgical tape. To Moore, these OR nurses seemed a race apart, different from nurses on other floors in aptitudes and in appearance. As they passed, this one raised her eyes and looked at him with a deep, thoughtful, but unseeing gaze of pure intelligence, then went back to her writing.

Walking on, Moore felt around him great, softly moving air currents sweeping the corridor clean. In his day, the odor of ether hung over everything. It had seemed to cling to his hands, scrub them as he might, so that at meals in the cafeteria he inhaled it with each forkful of food he raised, and waking at night he found it still clinging inside his nostrils, sweetish and sickening. Now the ventilation left such smells no chance to linger.

A colored orderly passed them, trundling in front of him a cyclopropane apparatus on casters. Its pendulous black bag swung back and forth. The rumble of the casters rose crescendo and died behind them. Nurses in wrinkled scrub smocks came and went, moving swiftly, lithe, incredibly slim, pre-Raphaelite figures striding silently in their clumsy, prehensile white shoes. They seemed one with the currents of air stirred by their passing. Remarkable creatures, Moore thought, a type new since his day, a superrace, with bodies that seemed formed by the special exigencies of their work, and, irrelevantly, he saw in his mind the rigid figure of Gothic Edna.

They came to a bend in the corridor and rounded it. Here all resemblance to a hospital vanished. The floor was tile in squares of black and white, the walls were rose-colored, and sets of double doors with carved entablatures opened from the corridor on both sides. The place looked, Moore thought, like a theater lobby. It looked endowed. "What's all this?" he said, and was relieved to find that the blanket of soundproofing had been lifted.

"Lecture halls and the projection room, the room where they hold Grand Rounds. I suppose in your day, sir, it really was Rounds —I mean, everybody trailed after the Chief from bed to bed to listen to him lecture about the cases."

"They did." And it was, in his opinion, one of the very few things done more humanely today. No victimizing of each charity patient, discussing him and his ailment as though he were not entitled to any privacy, as though he had no feelings.

The projection room, to Moore's surprise, was like a small theater with steep tiers of seats and a huge screen that was, at the moment, blank. The only light came from the luminescence of this screen, and by it Moore saw that there were others present. Doctors, some in whites, some in ordinary clothes. Groups of student nurses, their winged caps, like flocks of birds, seeming in the half-light of more moment than the wearers.

"Where would you like to sit, sir?"

"Right here would be fine." Moore stepped into an empty row of seats toward the back.

"Would you like me to come back and get you when we're through in the OR?"

"Thanks, I guess I'll be able to find the way." What did the youngster take him for—a geriatrics case? Aware of having been brusque, he said "Thanks" again.

"I'll leave you, then. I have to scrub." Suddenly Dr. Kopf smiled. It was a boyish smile that did disturbing things to Dr. Moore. Young lad, not fully licensed yet. He searched his memory for a phrase, and found it—"practicing provisionally," until the end of his internship. The best of life and medicine still ahead of him.

Dr. Moore said, "So you're scrubbing with the Chief himself, for the first time. Good luck, Doc." And because it occurred to him that probably the title still had a glow of newness, he changed the formula. "Good luck, Doctor." Moore held out his hand.

The wait for the screen to come alive was a long one. Moore closed his eyes and let his thoughts drift into nothingness, but he could not quite escape, though he would have liked to, the shadowy companions to his thoughts, himself and the Adam Fairchild of long ago.

48

Once he heard his name spoken softly, and thinking he must have been dreaming, he opened his eyes. One of the Pre-Raphaelite unrealities was standing in the aisle, holding out a folded piece of paper. He took it, thinking that no one in this place appeared to have the slightest difficulty identifying the doctor from the country. He opened the paper and found it to be a note in tall, thin, somewhat ornamental writing that said, "Keep an eye on my first assistant, whose name is David Armstrong. He may be the man you're looking for. Adam."

He was thinking about the utter improbability that a first assistant to Adam Fairchild would be willing to consider a country practice when a voice, loud and disembodied, like a god's, startled him. He sat up to find the amphitheater filling with students, and the screen imageless still but alive with quivering light.

The great, hollow voice was saying in a pedant's tone, "You are about to see a pulmonary valvulotomy to open the stenosed pulmonic valve. The patient is a twenty-six-year-old white male. For the past year and a half he has had progressive dyspnea on exertion ..."

Moore moved restlessly in his seat, irritated by the technical language he himself never felt called on to use. And some of it was new since his day, though he could follow it all right—a young man suffering from shortness of breath because a heart valve was partly blocked and not letting enough blood go through to the lungs.

". . . radiograph revealed enlargement of the right side of the heart and of the pulmonary artery. The stenotic valve will be opened, the arterial defect corrected, and the inside of the heart explored for possible defects not disclosed by radiography or cardiac catheterization."

All right—they were going to clean out the valve and take a feel around the inside of the heart.

The booming voice dropped suddenly and the tones became human, but Moore ceased to listen, for forms, shadowy and vague, were appearing on the screen. They wavered, steadied, became clear, and he found he was looking down from above, as though now he were the god, at the figure of a young man sheeted to the waist. The body was fine, even beautiful, and seeing it, Moore was moved to admiration (not altogether aesthetic or wholly professional) that the marvels of human anatomy had never yet failed to arouse. The head was tipped back, the black-lashed eyes were closed. A complex of hoses and dials was strapped to the forehead, the arms were supported almost in the form of a crucifixion, the hands palms up, relaxed, half open. The anesthetized mind was in abeyance, body yielded up. The submissive acquiescence seemed to him deeply touching. He fought off this emotional weakness by trying to orient himself in an operating room seen so illogically from above, and said irritably, without knowing he was speaking aloud, "Where the devil is the camera?"

Someone behind moved and leaned forward. "It's fastened to the outer rim of the dome light toward the foot of the table. There's another at the head, as you'll see presently."

Moore said "Thanks" without turning around.

A gloved hand appeared and rested on the young man's chest. A gowned figure materialized and turned a capped and masked head upward to the camera. Not Adam, Moore thought. The mask moved and the same voice, no longer disembodied, spoke: "The vein cutdown has been done. The patient will be kept on very light anesthesia, especially when the pump takes over the function of the circulation. The anesthesia is nitrous oxide and oxygen, Pentothal induction. As you can see, the patient's breathing is being controlled by a respiratory cycler."

Moore sat forward with interest, for this was a mechanism he had never seen. There it was, beyond the patient's head, a glass cylinder containing a bellows that was rising and collapsing rhythmically, pacing the lungs, monitoring the quantity of the air it gave them. Moore, thoroughly unmechanical, gazed at the cycler with awe. The thing seemed so self-sufficient there by itself, quietly preoccupied, making a gentle, introspective hissing sound like a steam radiator on a chilly morning.

He had lost some of what the lecturer was saying, and now he listened guiltily to the long list of the operation's personnel, surgeons, anesthesiologist, anesthetist, technicians, nurses—twelve or fourteen all told, he thought. The voice behind him said chattily, "This your first open-heart, Doctor?"

"I've never seen a living heart."

Moore felt that he had stated a thing of far greater importance to himself, though he guessed that the individual behind him did not perceive any difference. He tried by a movement of his shoulders to make it plain that he considered conversation undesirable. The gloved hand resting on the patient's chest, rising and falling to the cycler's rhythm, had a hypnotic effect. The sound track was saying, "Dr. Fairchild will use the approach to the heart through the sternum, instead of removing rib sections."

It occurred to Moore with a start that the speaker might well be the first assistant. He grunted and leaned forward, and found that the second camera had taken over, for he was now looking down from somewhere above and behind the patient's head. A moment later four surgeons had moved close to the table. Moore could not see their faces, and he was disturbed to find he did not recognize Adam Fairchild, though he knew he must be the thin figure standing near the head of the table on the patient's right. Young Kopf would be the one standing with an air of diffidence in a bad location, holding up his gloved hands against contamination in the attitude of a begging puppy dog. If the lad were permitted to snip a couple of sutures in the closing, he would count himself lucky.

The tallest of the four raised his head toward the camera, and Moore, startled, found himself looking directly into the pale eyes of Adam Fairchild. He was unquestionably Adam, but at the same time, he was also a stranger. With a feeling of disturbed equilibrium, Moore stared at him. The illusion that Fairchild's cold, impersonal gaze was directed solely at himself was so strong that Moore sat back with tingling nerves.

Then he remembered to look at the first assistant, who would be the surgeon directly opposite Adam, but like the others, his face was hidden. The next few moments were pure frustration, for the surgeons bent over the table and all Moore could see were the backs of four heads with mask tapes tied over their caps and four pairs of gowned shoulders blocking his view of the patient. He suppressed an impulse to rise from his seat, as though by standing he could see better. The man behind him breathed in his ear and said, "They haven't got the televising of operations licked by a long way."

Moore drew his head away. The camera jerked, moved giddily by some remote control, and came to rest on a screen on which a dot of light leaped up and down, up and down, as it made its way from one side of the screen to the other. It vanished, instantly re-appeared, and began to cross the screen again, up and down, up and down. . . . A new voice, speaking with a faintly British accent, said, "You see here the oscillograph, measuring the patient's heart-beat. You will note that the beat is erratic. This screen and an-other, registering arterial pressure, will monitor the heart pump.

"I will now show you the pump that will take over the function of the circulation during repair of the valve. The pump will re-ceive the venous blood flow, as normally the lungs do, putting oxygen into it, which is the normal function of the lungs, and returning it to the patient's body, reconstructed as arterial blood. Camera, please."

The camera, inexpertly handled, produced a quivering image of another outlandish piece of mechanism with dials and hoses. A hand appeared and rested on a horizontal glass cylinder. "This is the chamber in which the blood is oxygenated. Inside, moving discs pick up cell-thin layers of venous blood, presenting them for oxygenation. Readings of the oxygen content of the blood will be made by a technician stationed outside the operating room." He talked for some time and Moore ceased to listen closely.

The camera made an erratic sweep to its former angle aimed at the head of the table. The voice said, "While we have been look-ing at the pump, the incision has been made. In a moment the electric bone-cutter will be used to divide the sternum. The ster-num will be spread apart; the pericardium, the sac that encloses the heart, will be opened and sutured to the edges of the incision, exposing the heart."

Exposing the heart. Moore's pulse began to beat faster. His hold on the back of the seat in front of him tightened. He looked down on the surgeon's heads with an occasional glimpse of the long opening in the patient's chest. Silence, except for the rhythmic hiss of the cycler, and now and then the metallic click of an instru-ment. That sound, at least, was familiar in his own operating room.

He saw Fairchild hold out his hand and the flash of chrome as he received an instrument with an electric cord attached. He heard a snarling buzz and knew that the sternum was being slit for its entire length. Again he had the impulse to stand up, and heard his own long-drawn sigh. The voice behind him said, "Maddening not to see, isn't it?" and he made no reply.

Another interval, during which Moore watched the first assistant. He could see little more than swift, very sure motions of his gloved hands, not even what the hands were doing. That told Moore little, but it seemed to him that there was, probably by intention, nothing spectacular, nothing virtuoso, about these motions. He thought they might be, probably were, the product of study and discipline, that they might imply a desire for efficiency and a dislike of showiness in technique—desirable traits, if these conclusions were right.

After a while Fairchild again raised his head, seeming, in that startling way, to be looking intently at Moore. Then he and the others moved slowly backward, and Moore was looking directly down into the young man's open chest.

The heart lay exposed. Moore, mind fogged by the intensity of his desire to receive impressions, saw first its motion. And he thought, "It's not a beat. It's not at all a beat. It's like the heave and roll of the sea." He watched hungrily the tremendous movements confined inside, beginning from below, rolling upward, bulging the outer surface of the heart, dying away, beginning its great roll once more.

There was sweat on his forehead and in the palms of his hands. He remembered he must be quick, see it all, let nothing escape him. The structure of the heart he knew from those lifeless, acquiescent bodies on the medical school dissecting slabs. Here again was the same, always unexpected cant of the heart, the same impression of the muscles' hardness and power. Here was the vinelike network of veins clinging tightly to the heart's surface, not inert, as he knew them in the cadavers, but moving with the heart's rolling waves. He saw the two great arteries curving upward, pulmonary and aorta, their rhythmic swell in slight syncopation to the heart's rhythm. And then he saw the damage to the pulmonary, the ballooning above the obstructed heart valve, and guessed the weakening of the artery walls.

Then Fairchild's gloved hand appeared as he laid a finger on the pulsating pulmonary. Moore felt in his own fingertips the weird, disturbing sensation. Then he heard Fairchild's voice and sat back feeling giddy, for the voice of this masked stranger was entirely familiar.

Fairchild spoke with a calm authority that in the intern's well-remembered voice had seemed ludicrous, as though this were a joke. "Note the enlargement of the pulmonary artery at this point. The blood is coming through the partially blocked valve in a jet that makes a palpable buzzing under my finger. Note the enlargement of the right side of the heart."

Feeling weakened, Moore sat back, and the voice behind him whispered, "Adam Fairchild in an operating room thinks he's God Almighty." Moore groped for his handkerchief and wiped the palms of his hands. He felt that what remained, however skillful, however technically perfect, must be secondary to his first sight of the living heart.

Fairchild was working now with swiftness and concentration, the illumination from the dome light brilliant on the back of his neck and the curves of his ears. Temporarily, there seemed little for the first assistant to do, and once the camera inadvertently caught him gazing into space with the almost dreamy look that Moore had seen in operating rooms before during a moment of idleness. It was like a pause between two worlds. It added nothing to his impressions of this young surgeon, but it brought back a thought out of the past about surgeons and surgery in general, that there exists a sharper division between the operating room and the "outside" than there is between the work and daily lives of any other occupation except, perhaps, in the actor's relation to the stage.

A dreary, almost boresome hour passed in minute preparation for detaching the pulmonary artery from the heart, broken into once by Fairchild's saying to the anesthesiologist, "I want the patient kept very light when we go on the pump." The voice replied, "He is light. He's been moving his head a little." Then, as though he had remembered the students in the amphitheater, he said in a lecturer's voice, "While the patient is on the pump, the anesthesia is stopped. Pentothal and Demerol are put into the blood in the pump—only a little, for the patient's blood will be cooled in the pump."

Uneasy silence for a while. Fairchild said with sudden sharpness, "Ready to go on the pump," and in that instant the operating room grew tense, filled with the quiet rustling sounds of many people moving with quick accuracy. With it, there was a sense of change in balance, of its having become the technicians' rather than the surgeons' show. Someone outside the camera's range said,

54

"Blood pressure, one hundred." Someone else said tensely, "Ready to go on. Ready to take off the arterial clamp." Fairchild said, "All ready? One, two, three—*on.*" The pump took possession of the young man's bloodstream.

Fairchild was working fast now, repairing the valve, though Moore could not see what he was doing. The man behind yawned noisily and Moore felt prickles of wrath at his nerve ends. A voice from beyond the camera's range said, "Venous return is twenty-four hundred. Falling off." Then, "Venous pressure, two thousand —I'm losing my level. No, it's picking up . . . still picking up . . . twenty-six hundred. Patient's corrected temperature, thirty-six." Fairchild said, "Can you run your arterial pump any faster?" And the other voice, sounding nervous, said, "Not with the amount of blood I'm getting." Someone who must have been standing by the monitoring screens said sharply, "Pulmonary artery running thirty to forty," and Fairchild replied angrily, "That's very bad. We've got a very weak pulmonary artery here." To Moore all this seemed confusing, but tense; not exciting, but agitating and disturbing. He caught a glimpse of the heart, and imagined its beat had a desperate quality. He half turned in his seat and looked at the door, wishing he could go out. He leaned back and shut his eyes.

He kept them shut until Fairchild's voice said, "We needn't detain the closed-circuit audience any longer. The patient is off the pump. The operation has disclosed that this young man had a slight arterial stenosis which, when I actually saw the heart and arteries, I was inclined to accept as the total problem. In other words, the damage was less than anticipated from the enlargement of the heart and pulmonary artery disclosed by the radiograph. The left ventricle, when I felt it with my finger, appeared to be somewhat tight but not seriously so. The total time on the pump was"—Fairchild turned and appeared to question someone outside the camera's periphery—"Thank you, thirty-eight minutes. Blood pressure, heartbeat and temperature are now all satisfactory. That is all."

The lights went up and Moore experienced that familiar feeling of the shoddiness of the commonplace world that immediately follows all good theater. He rose and stepped out into the aisle, and the voice that had spoken over his shoulder said, "Hardly worth televising, was it?"

55

Indignant to the core, Moore turned to stare at the owner of the voice and saw a type he recognized, the practitioner, usually unsuccessful and a trifle seedy, who likes to hang around hospitals and scrape up acquaintances there. This fellow wore a suit of mustard-brown lightweight tweed, he had a reddish mustache stretched thin by his smile, and topaz-colored eyes that had, Moore thought, a quick-shifting look of unreliability. He was saying, "I mean to say, a simple valvular stenosis—a waste of our time, don't you agree?" To this Moore made no answer but an angry motion of the shoulders.

IV

Dr. David Armstrong entered the Union Club with an air of assurance he did not feel. It was not that the surroundings overawed him, for he had been here before with Adam Fairchild. The uneasiness that he was attempting to conceal by dignity of manner and a slight frown always plagued him when he was forced to meet people in unfamiliar situations. This was not ordinary shyness, for his self-consciousness did not come from a dread of what other people might think of him so much as from a conviction of his own inadequacy where dealings with people were involved. He hated to be self-conscious. He had come to regard this feeling as his greatest handicap, not only because it was a serious barrier between himself and his patients, but also because it interfered with his enjoyment of life.

He gave his hat to the coatroom attendant and braced himself for the meeting with this stranger, Dr. Moore. Short stairs, divided into curving wings, led to the main hall, and as he went reluctantly up them he tried to appear the person he wanted others to believe he really was. The image he wanted to create was of a thoughtful young doctor who took his calling with an extreme seriousness that showed itself in his face and bearing. As he actually was all these things to begin with, the only result of his effort was to produce a hint of the pompous and a slight suggestion of stuffed-shirtiness that, until it wore off as he became at ease, counted somewhat against him.

The hall glittered with good lighting and prosperity, and it was empty. Relieved, he walked over a vast expanse of black-and-cream stone floor to the far end where columns formed a partly separated room. This seemed to him an excellent place to wait concealed in order to allow the two old friends, Fairchild and Moore, to meet without feeling constrained by his presence. There was a fireplace in this room and above it a large painting, which Armstrong went to examine, not because he was interested but because doing so placed him with his back to the hall. An inscription on the painting read: GEORGE WASHINGTON AT THE BATTLE OF PRINCETON, A COPY OF A PAINTING BY CHARLES WILLSON PEALE. Washington had a faraway look, as though his noble thoughts were above the battle raging behind him. Armstrong had seen that look in portraits of surgeons in amphitheaters and he had always thought it exceedingly silly.

There were sounds in the hall that indicated someone, who must be Moore, had arrived and seated himself in one of the red leather chairs on the other side of the column. A few minutes later Fairchild came, and, surreptitiously watching, Armstrong saw Moore rise to greet him, and the tones of their voices vibrated under the high ceiling.

David turned to join them, and when he saw Fairchild's familiar thin, distinguished figure, his mind played a trick on him and he saw instead a memory image of Fairchild's daughter Maryanne. For an instant he saw her as clearly as though she were in the room, tall, hair like a pale gold cloud, light eyes, long-fingered, delicate hands. Her eyes were like her father's, remote, but with a look of wanting something life had not given her. David had seen that look vanish when he and she had first been engaged and watched with anxiety its slow return. He could not feel he had anything to reproach himself with; he could not believe that he had failed her in any way. She had tried to explain to him what she felt. They had long talks about it which ended in tears on her part and in frustration on his. On one of these occasions she had burst out at him, saying, "You'll never make a good doctor, never, unless you learn to understand people better than you do now."

He argued the point with her, trying to remain calm and reasonable. He was quite willing to concede that he didn't "understand people," as she put it. He saw no reason for a surgeon to try, especially as Fairchild, who was his model, did not.

When, three weeks before the wedding, she broke off with him and replaced him with a resident whose "outgoing" personality Armstrong greatly disliked, his sense of her injustice was as strong, almost, as his grief. At the time his feelings were too bruised to allow him to think clearly and it was not until this moment that he saw that he had loved, not herself, but her father's daughter.

This sudden realization gave him an almost physical shock, as though someone had held a piece of ice to the back of his neck, but it also brought him distractedly back to the present. Moore and Fairchild were talking together in lowered tones, and though David felt he was probably being discussed, for once in his life this failed to disturb him, and he went to join them.

Moore, shaking hands, scrutinized him sharply through squinted, unexpectedly blue eyes, but the look was wholly friendly. In the midst of the handshake David felt Moore modify his grasp and guessed that Moore had just experienced the care with which Fairchild guarded his precious hand against strong grips. Fairchild, assuming a role of benevolent good will, said, "Let's have our drinks at the table, shall we?" and walked to the elevator with a friendly hand on Moore's shoulder.

On the third floor they came out into a broad hall hung on both sides with portraits, and Fairchild said, "I want you to see some of these, Ed. We're very proud of our club's picture collection," and he steered his friend by the arm toward a painting of Grant in a blue uniform, looking, it seemed to David, most uncharacteristically well groomed. Moore said, "It's General Grant, isn't it?" and gazed at it in the way people do who are not sure what they are expected to see in a painting or what comment they are expected to make. He said, "Hmm," with great seriousness, and, David thought, tried to conceal his bewilderment by moving quickly on to the next. "Who's this fellow on horseback?"

"Sherman." Fairchild was smiling in a way that irritated Armstrong on Dr. Moore's behalf.

"Horse seems a bit small for him, though he looks to be riding him easily enough." He moved on. "Pershing I recognize, of course. Funny how those World War I tunics made a man's torso look as if it was stuffed by a taxidermist. I've always been sorry we didn't get into that war, Adam."

"I can't say I've regretted it much."

"Did they get you in the next one? I couldn't leave the hospital."

"Only to the extent of making me a consultant to the Surgeon General, which took me to Washington a few times. I didn't like it. Government work is a fine way for a man to lose his identity."

David, his mind still on Moore and the pictures, thought, He's a naïve old boy in some ways and doesn't care who knows it. And as though Moore had read his thoughts, he turned to David, who was lagging behind, and startled that young man by winking at him.

"Pictures aren't much in my line."

Mentally, David substituted the word "unassuming" for "naïve" and felt that he was getting somewhere in his estimate of Moore. They sat at a table and Fairchild said, "What will you drink, Ed?"

"Scotch-and-water—no, by God, I'll have a martini," and he laughed heartily, as though the other two would know why this was funny. Then he subsided into a sort of peacefulness while Fairchild talked, playing the role of good host easily and well. To David it seemed that Fairchild was not being patronizing toward his old friend only because he was too skillful, but that he had made up his mind that the gap between them had grown too great to be bridged by anything but the social amenities. David was not at all sure that Moore was blind to this. He betrayed his own awareness by a slight rigidity of back and a wooden blankness of facial expression.

That Moore did gradually become aware of Fairchild's withdrawal David felt more and more certain. At first he seemed eager to talk, but he was given little opportunity. Fairchild sat back in his chair with easy grace, talking well, holding his drink in the manner of one who drinks only for politeness's sake and from time to time smiling a thin, muscular smile. Moore seemed to draw quietly away. Now and then he glanced around the handsome room, up at the crystal lights and at the cascades of jade-green draperies over the tall windows as though, without lessening his attention, he were finding pleasure in these things. There was a certain dignity in his withdrawal, a mildness about him that put him beyond Fairchild's power to denigrate if denigration were his motive. He had established, without speaking a word, a new relationship with Fairchild, and so subtly, so skillfully, that David was filled with admiration.

Fairchild's able monologue continued. Twice Moore glanced at David, the looks not conveying anything more than placidity faintly colored by humor. And David received the impression that he had made up his mind to enjoy the food and drink, and if he could not find pleasure in one direction he was not going to be deterred from finding it in another.

Moore finished his martini, and set down the empty glass. The instant the glass touched the table Fairchild gestured for another. When it arrived, Moore looked at it as though it had materialized out of thin air, then picked up the small glass in his big hand and seemed to make friends with it.

Fairchild said, "I know the food here, so I'll order," and he did so in consultation with the waiter, holding out the menu and pointing with his thin, long forefinger. David and Moore sat in silence. Then the menu was carried off and just as Fairchild was about to resume, Dr. Moore said, "I want to tell you about my hospital," and leaning forward, began to talk. It was done so smoothly, so adroitly, that David suppressed a smile.

"Naturally," Fairchild said, and leaned back in his chair in a way that suggested judgment reserved.

"I started it twenty-four years ago when Haddon—that's where I practice, Dr. Armstrong—when Haddon needed a hospital badly. The nearest one was—still is—Warwick (he pronounced it Warwick after the Vermont fashion) thirty miles away. Thirty miles is nothing today, of course, except in emergencies. It's too far for those. But roads weren't so good then. And Warwick was just another small country hospital, and closed-staff, so when you sent a patient there he couldn't be your patient any more even if you could take time for the sixty-mile round trip to see him. It still is closed-staff, and country people like to stick with the doctor they're used to. What I'm saying is, we needed a hospital in Haddon."

Cups of soup were put in front of them, and Moore, lost in thought for a moment, began to eat his quickly as though, David thought, he never had time to eat any other way. When he looked up, his expression seemed to reflect the trouble from the past that was occupying his mind.

"I went to the town and asked them to vote the money to build one. Stood up in Town Meeting and made a speech about it, best I knew how. They turned me down."

Fairchild, without shifting his position, said, "Couldn't you have gotten Federal aid?"

"Not in those days."

61

"You implied in your letter that money is a problem. Is it still not possible to get financial help from the government?"

"No, because the hospital is still a private institution, and so long as I own it—"

"You *own* the hospital?" David spoke with real astonishment. "You mean it's really a *private* hospital? I didn't know there were any left."

"Let him tell his story in his own way," Fairchild said irritably.

Moore sighed. "I'd set my heart on that hospital. It seemed like the end of the world. Walking home from the meeting, I made up my mind to leave Haddon. I would have except there were only two of us doctors in town and we needed—still do need—at least three more. About a year later, my wife's father died and left her some money. Then my wife died shortly after. We didn't have any children, so I took the money, about a hundred thousand dollars, and bought a big, old house and turned it into a hospital. We're still there today."

Dr. Moore drew another long sigh. "Everything went pretty well at first. Doctors from around used the hospital. Babies, mostly, and medical cases that couldn't be taken care of at home."

"What about surgery?" David asked.

"Nothing you'd call surgery, then. Fractures, first aid. Kitchen-table surgery in an operating room. We were all GP's. That's what general practitioner means in the country, medicine *and* surgery. I gave the anesthetics—I still do—and when I think of some of the chances I took in those days . . . Well, anyway, about fifteen years ago Dr. Howard Perkins joined us from his surgical residency at a big city hospital in the Middle West. A better man than a country town has any cause to hope for. Perkins put in fifty thousand and we built a new wing, with a good operating room, and so on. I took a four-months course in anesthesiology they were giving at Warwick—"

Fairchild made a startled gesture. "But, good Lord, Ed, anesthesiology's a two-year residency!"

"I know, I know—but we stick to simple techniques. Nitrous oxide, spinals, ether drip. We've never had any accidents. Where was I? Oh, yes—it was during this course that I found out some of the risks I'd been taking."

Moore moved his bulk aside to allow food to be put in front of

62

him, and began to eat mechanically, then looked at his plate with pleased surprise. "We don't get this sort of food up our way." Fairchild laughed and Moore joined in good-naturedly. "Remember the slop we used to eat when we were students, Adam?"

"I do indeed. Which reminds me—what happened to your passionate devotion to psychiatry? Use it much?"

"Psychiatry?" Moore's face took on a puzzled look.

"I thought that was going to be your specialty."

"Where did you get that idea?"

"In the old days you never talked about anything else. You can't have forgotten. You used to drive us all crazy with it, trying to make us read stuff you were reading. It was going to answer everything. I'm not sure you didn't think it could be a substitute for surgery."

In amazement, Dr. Moore contemplated this strange young intern across the years. "I simply don't remember a thing about it," he said wonderingly. "The rough-and-tumble of country practice seems to have knocked it out of my head—so-called scientific psychiatry, that is. No time for anything fancy, and most of my patients couldn't afford it. Common sense and kindness have to do the trick. No, I'd forgotten all about it."

Fairchild, who always ate lightly, very soon pushed his chair back and sat with one hand touching his temple, the other resting on his crossed knee. It was a position Armstrong knew well from a portrait that hung in the Fairchild house, but whether the artist had caught a favorite pose, or whether the pose had become a habit after the portrait was painted, David did not know. There was a frown, exaggerated in the portrait, a thin, sharp, dartlike line between his eyes, and he was gazing at a remote corner of the room with an expression rather like Washington's in the painting downstairs. David said, "I'd like to hear more about the hospital," and Fairchild, bringing the gaze to rest on him, almost imperceptibly shook his head. He meant, it seemed clear enough, that David would be well advised to take no personal interest in the medical affairs of Haddon.

Moore said, "Money isn't the only problem. Not even the most serious." And Fairchild said, "No?" with a lack of interest that implied that they had heard all that was necessary. Moore was too deep in his subject to notice the intended discouragement.

63

"You know, Adam, this trip has been a good thing because, for the first time in years, I've had time to think. When I got the hospital going, I was sure the medical needs of the town were fixed up—and they were—so I just carried on, day to day, without realizing changes were going on in those medical needs that I should have been aware of. Then yesterday I got a jolt, a bad one. It was a shock, but it opened my eyes. And I can see, now that I've had time to get things in perspective, that they needed opening."

Fairchild said, not unkindly, "What happened, Ed?"

"It's too long to go into. The gist of it is that I now realize that the hospital isn't really fulfilling its function in meeting medical needs. I don't mean just that the hospital should be modernized—which it should . . ."

He paused to smile, and the smile's quality increased David's liking for him.

"It's my own thinking that's needed modernizing."

Fairchild answered the smile with a slow and partial one of his own that acknowledged this attempt at humor and dismissed it. David's expression showed deepened interest.

"I've suddenly come to and discovered that though the hospital hasn't changed, the demands on us have. And I never realized it. Not long ago we were really a town hospital working for the people of the town. That's how we thought of ourselves, though we had some patients from the country round about, and from other towns. We didn't concern ourselves with the nature of their problems very much. We were geared to *Haddon's* needs. But now I can see that the needs round about us have become as great as Haddon's—and I can't get over that I've just waked up to it. What's been happening is like the shifting of a balance scale."

Armstrong said, "What has made the difference? Better roads? Increase in population?"

"The first is a factor, of course. The second to a lesser degree, and Haddon itself has grown very little. The big difference is, as I now see it, that people in general want to use hospitals more— farm people, and especially workers in unionized plants."

"Why should that be, Doctor?"

"Better understanding of health matters. But chiefly hospital insurance and the size of the health benefits the manufacturing companies are beginning to give their men."

64

Fairchild said, "That's been going on for quite a while, Ed."

"I tell you, I've been asleep. I've been living in my medical bag. Any way you want to put it. I knew about the rise in insured medical care, certainly. What I didn't see—was too damn busy to see—is the effect it should be having on the hospital. And I've just come to and found myself—and the hospital, which is damn near the same thing—right on the edge of a crisis."

"But, Ed." Fairchild picked up his water glass, looked into it, put it down, and turned his pale eyes on Moore. "Excuse me if I say I don't really see what the problem is. More patients—more money for running the hospital. If you need to, then expand your facilities. It's happening to every hospital in the country."

"That's part of it, but not all of it. I wish it was. Sure I want to modernize, and I intend to." The blue eyes gave Dr. Armstrong a brief, intense glance. "But there's a faction—I only found out about it yesterday, so I don't fully know what it amounts to— that thinks the hospital should be located in a town in which the manufacturing plants are practically the whole community. That would make it company-dominated, and—well, no need to go into all that."

"Your point is clear. But I shouldn't think the town of Haddon would go along with that. Isn't there something else involved?"

"Yes, there is—or seems to be. As I say, this is all new to me. But there appears to be a feeling that the hospital shouldn't be privately owned."

Fairchild said, "A-a-a-h," drawing the sound out long and softly. The implication of this brought sudden color to Moore's face. He struck the edge of the table with his fist.

"Damn it, the only reason I own that hospital is because thirty years ago Haddon wasn't farsighted enough to understand they were going to have to have one."

"Wouldn't you consent to its becoming a voluntary or a public hospital? Let the town buy you out, perhaps?"

"No, I wouldn't. It's *my* hospital. It's become my life, if you want to be dramatic about it. Today, the people of Haddon— except this one faction, and maybe that's only one man—know they do need the hospital. If it comes to a showdown, and it just might, it's *me* they'll support. Me and my hospital. What outsider could possibly know as much as I do about the needs of the town?

65

I'm going to get young men in—a new medical generation to succeed Perkins and me. I'm going to modernize. Don't ask me how, but I'm going to. The people of Haddon are proud of the hospital now. I can promise them they'll be still prouder of it in the future."

There was a silence, and in it Moore became aware that he alone had not finished his dinner. He began to eat rapidly while Fairchild watched him and David frowned with the absorption of his thoughts. In a moment Moore laid down his knife and fork with emphasis, and a lurking waiter instantly removed his plate.

Fairchild said, "You've been very frank about it, Ed, but I wish you'd clear up one point. Do I understand that you've been meeting the deficit each year out of your own pocket?"

"That's what it amounts to, with bank loans and mortgages and so on." Moore turned away from Fairchild and spoke directly to Armstrong. "It's not easy to describe a complicated thing like this so as to give you a true picture. Why don't you come up and look us over? See the hospital and the town, go on some house calls with me. You might have a pretty different impression of things than I'm giving you. A hospital like ours is very close to the life of the community in ways you probably couldn't imagine."

David nervously picked up his coffee cup and set it down again. "I assume that Dr. Fairchild told you that I am looking for a post only for a year before deciding on something permanent? I feel I lack clinical experience. I believe it's a weakness of medical education today, especially in surgery. I want a year of working in close touch with patients . . ."

"I haven't had a chance to tell Dr. Moore anything about you," Fairchild said shortly, and in a manner that made it clear that the amount of clinical experience a surgeon should have was a point of disagreement between Armstrong and himself.

Moore looked at Armstrong thoughtfully for a moment, but instead of pursuing this subject he turned in his chair to face Fairchild squarely and resumed the talk where he had left off. "Now, I have an inducement to offer a young man you couldn't match, Adam. That is that a young surgeon in a hospital like ours would have a chance to do major surgery on his own much sooner than he could hope to in the city." He glanced at David to see if his words had affected him, the glance producing in David a sense of involvement in the blueness and intensity of Moore's narrowed eyes.

Glass dishes of dessert were put in front of them and Moore ate a little of his, then put his spoon down. "And there's another thing. There's a lot going on in country medicine that's new these days. I've been too busy to pay much attention, but change is in the air, so strong you can feel it. You might say it's like a pot that's getting ready to boil—a feeling of suspense and something big about to happen. I don't know if you have the sort of temperament that would find that interesting, but if I were younger . . . Haddon hasn't kept up with progress, I'm afraid. A young man might be an influence along those lines."

Moore put both hands on the table and leaned back in his chair, as though he had said all he could. David raised his eyes and found Moore looking directly at him. For a moment they continued to look at each other; then Moore said, in a voice that was gentle and without urgency, "Why don't you just come up and take a look at us, Doc?"

Armstrong nodded, paused a moment and said, "All right." Moore picked up his spoon and finished his dessert rapidly, all of it, scraping the bottom of the dish.

V

On the mountain airstrip rain had turned the surfacing of the runways dark and muted the colors of the surrounding hills. Moore, collar turned up, came down the steps of the plane as fast as his bulk would let him, and was greeted in loud, friendly tones by the airport attendant called Henry.

"Hi, Doc. No coat? Go on inside and I'll bring your bag to you."

The small wooden building smelled of damp clothing and of the rain-filled wind carrying scents of fields and woods. A handful of dispirited-looking passengers stood about, also waiting in morose silence. In a little while Henry entered noisily, his slicker glistening with wet.

"Here's your bag, Doc. We need this rain mighty bad." Then in a lowered voice, not wanting to be overheard, he said, "I'm sorry about what happened. Maybe I should have called the plane back. I could have, but I didn't think to tell Miss Judson so, and she didn't say there weren't no other doctors. I guess she didn't know herself, then, maybe."

"I don't understand, Henry. Edna Judson called you?"

"Oh gosh. You don't know? I thought you would by this time. There was a man fell out of a window—something like that—in one of the Silver Springs plants, and they couldn't get a doctor. They took him to your hospital and Miss Judson was trying to get you. You heard the phone ringing yourself."

"What happened, Henry?" Moore, looking grave, put his bag down and gave this his full attention.

"Why, the man died. I guess Miss Judson, she done what she could. Don't you worry about it, Doc. He'd have died anyway, most like. That's what most people are saying . . ."

Moore, who had ceased to listen, was looking about for a telephone. He saw one in a booth in the corner, crammed himself inside, hesitated, and then called Howard Perkins. Dr. Perkins's office was a spacious one in a wing of his house and he answered the telephone at its first ring, the loud, confident voice causing Moore to remove the phone a little way from his ear.

"Howard, I just got in. I'm out at the airport. What's this—"

"I gather you've heard about it. Just one of those unforeseeable things. Unfortunate. And there's hell to pay. I didn't call you in New York because there wasn't anything you could do about it there, and no use spoiling your trip."

"The man died?"

"Yes. On the table in the emergency room. Edna first-aided him and gave him fluids. No morphine, because she thought he might have a head injury, which he probably had. I went over every detail of what she did with her. It was all right, and I don't see what more she could have done. She even called some surgeon in Warwick to confirm what she did. But she's feeling pretty bad about it. I got hold of next-of-kin, and that was a job, because it turned out to be a daughter on the other side of the state. She hadn't been in touch with her father for years, but she had screaming hysterics over the phone. I asked her to agree to sign an autopsy permission, and when she found the old boy would be buried at company expense she was so relieved she agreed. It's being done at Warwick. Report's not in yet, of course, but when we get it I'm certain it will show that ten doctors couldn't have saved him."

"That isn't the point, Howard."

"What? Oh. No doctor available. You're right, of course. But if he would have died anyway, nobody could blame us."

Moore, suddenly aware of the damp stuffiness of the booth, opened the door a wide crack to give himself air.

Perkins said sharply, "Ed, are you still there?"

"Yes, I'm here. I was thinking about it, Howard. It shouldn't be possible for a thing like that to happen."

"We'll have to take some sort of action to prevent its happening in the future."

"Just leaving word where we're going isn't going to be enough. How is the town taking it?"

"Pretty wrought up about it, as you can imagine. They're not blaming any one of us singly so much as the lot of us collectively."

"We're going to have to find time to talk this out."

"That's certain. I'll get in touch with you today or tomorrow morning. We are all three summoned to meet with the selectmen at eight tomorrow night."

"That's inevitable, I suppose."

"Yes, but it's not going to be pleasant. We should have some sort of plan to give them, but I'm damned if I know what. Think of something, if you can."

"This is a serious business, Howard."

"For Christ sake, are you telling me? Years of good doctoring for the Goddamn town and something goes wrong, and they're on our necks. I'm the one who's getting the brunt of the ill will. You were leaving for New York. Ladd's so old people excuse him. I'm the one, and if they come down hard on me, I tell you I'm going to fight back."

Moore started to protest, suddenly felt Howard Perkins to be an additional and very heavy burden, and sighed wearily. "Howard," he said, "there's a young fellow coming up to look us over tomorrow. A Dr. Armstrong."

"Couldn't have picked a worse time. Can't you head him off?"

"I don't think so. He'd hear about it, anyway."

There were various mechanical noises in the telephone and an operator's voice said, "Twenty cents, please."

"All right, Ed. Glad you're back. I'll call you."

Moore wiped rain from the seat of the jeep with a rag he kept in the back, thought about putting up the curtain, and decided he would rather get a little damp. On the long drive home the tires on the wet roadway made a sound like the tearing of an endless strip of linen, a continuously urgent sound that was like the feeling of urgency to which his nerves were keyed. Tension infinitely prolonged. He felt the strong need for thinking coherently and constructively and found his thoughts merging meaninglessly with the ribbon of sound. He tried to put the death with its problems out of his mind, and found that he could not accomplish that either. As a result, he arrived worried and fretful.

He turned into his own driveway, squelching and bumping through the potholes that he had honestly meant to fix this summer, not with pleasure at being home again but with a feeling of many pressing duties waiting to be done.

At the top of the wooden front steps he paused, trying to put these duties in some sort of order in his mind, staring unseeingly at the fallen maple leaves plastered wetly against the gray paint of the porch. Lunch first, and then the office. . . . He glanced at his watch. Patients would already be waiting. Telephone calls to make, the hospital, as many house calls as he could find time for, a hamburger at the bar and grill down the street for dinner, evening office hours, and more house calls if he could. Always more than he could compass, the day's work never quite completed, always something remaining that must be added to the next day's work. Moving quickly, he grasped the latch of the never-locked front door and went inside.

He dropped his bag on a chair, and went on without stopping through a short, dark hall, toward the kitchen at the back, his heavy steps on the broad floorboards echoing through the empty house. In the old-fashioned kitchen he brushed wetness off his sleeves and shoulders—Edna had been right; he should have taken a coat—and ran a pocket comb through his thick gray hair. Then he began rapidly, and with characteristic economy of motion, to get himself a lunch. The process was so familiar as to need no conscious thought. He broke three eggs into a frying pan, and while they cooked poured maple syrup over some pieces of biscuit and ate them with a spoon, standing beside the stove. When the eggs were done, he slid them out on a plate, sat down at the kitchen table and ate them rapidly. Then he piled the dishes he had used in the sink and was searching for his raincoat when he heard the kitchen door open and his cleaning woman's voice called, "Is that you, Doctor?"

"Yes. Where the devil's my raincoat, Ellie?"

"In the shed. You left it there when you got it so wet last time you used it. I'll get it." Her voice was high-pitched and harsh with an unmeaning note of belligerence in it, a voice, he thought, that was the unlovely product of a lifetime's need to defend herself. Ellie was one of those unfortunates whom others, instinctively, picked on.

In a moment she came through the kitchen door carrying the

raincoat, a small, thin woman in a bright much-washed cotton print dress and a striped apron with a triangular tear in it. The cheap, garish print must, he thought, be evidence that this downtrodden creature had sometime felt a brief ray of hopefulness about her life.

This hopefulness, which he knew to be wholly unwarranted, depressed him. Hardship was Ellie's lot. That she had largely brought it on herself by taking the wrong turn at each of life's crossroads only added irritation to the feelings of depression she forced on him. She meant so well, tried so hard to please. The irritation gave him a sense of guilt, and that, in turn, made him resentful. And she was a compulsive talker. She could talk your ear off. If you closed your mind to the words, then the unspoken appeal that underlay them, the desperate effort to get right with life that was the cause of them, was all the more apparent. He forced himself to listen.

". . . and I been kind of worryin' all mornin'." She pronounced it "more-nin" in the Vermont way that still seemed ridiculous to him. "This ain't no weather to fly, and when I saw the jeep, why then I come right over."

"It's perfectly safe." He gave himself the luxury of sounding cross, and enjoyed it.

"What I say is, when the birds stop flyin', then humans should—"

"Ellie, can you get the spare room into shape?"

"The *spare* room?" Surprise stopped the flow of talk.

"Yes. Open it, fix it up."

"Sure. Why, sure I can." The wonder of it seemed to strike her anew. "You goin' to have some company, Doc?"

"Yes, there's—"

"My, you ain't had no company—"

"Ellie!"

"Well, I'm glad, Doctor. But surprised! In all the years I've done for you, you ain't never . . . Who is it?"

"That's what I'm trying to tell you. A young doctor from New York is coming to look us over. He might stay and practice here. I want to be sure things are fixed so he'll be comfortable."

"That would be a good thing, weren't it, Doc? Since about that man what fell—"

72

"I don't want to discuss it, Ellie."

"Just to get the curtains up and the bed made is all it needs. I gave it a good reddin' out a while ago. I did what I felt to. Would you like to go up and take a look?"

Without waiting for an answer, she went past him and started to climb the steep and narrow stairs. He sighed and followed, disliking the rear view of her, the end of hair fastened with an elastic band that had worked loose from the knot at the back of her head, the edge of slip showing, the wrinkled stockings on the skinny legs. Disliking (and taking grim pleasure doing so) her proprietary pride in his house and in "doin' for" the doctor.

Going up the stairs, treading heavily, trying to keep out of range of the stale odor that came from her, he thought that he felt not pity but dislike of her because she had only once been as much as thirty miles from home, never more, and that in an old, battered logging truck her husband owned. She had never ridden on a bus or a train, never seen a play or read a book, never lived in a house with a flush toilet or a furnace. What one should feel in the presence of such poverty of life's goods and life's good was compassion. Sometimes he did. More often than not, he was unable to free himself from poverty's reproach, and resenting the injustice of this, he thought that what the underprivileged really made one feel, if one were honest about it, was irritation.

He knew perfectly well that being irritable with Ellie was his secret vice, his secret indulgence. He said, giving his crossness free rein, "I suppose Pierre didn't get those apples picked off the tree out back?" Pierre was Ellie's worthless French Canadian husband.

"Got 'em myself."

"I told you to tell Pierre to get them."

They were walking down a hall that sloped like the deck of a ship at sea. Ellie put her hand on a door latch and turned to answer him. "You know he won't do no work till loggin' starts. No bit of use askin' him."

That was probably true enough. The no-good French Canadian rascal was one of Ellie's more disastrous wrong turnings.

The latch, released, made a sharp click and he followed her through the doorway. The room was a large one over the kitchen, darkened by a great hemlock that grew against the windows at the back. Rain tapped on the tin roof and ran in irregular channels down the window glass. The broad floorboards had been painted brown, and the opening of the fireplace had been covered with a sheet of metal. The air in the room was damp and chill, and Moore went quickly to a register set in the floor and kicked it open. A shaft of warmer air rose from the kitchen below. He went to the old and slightly sagging bed that had a mound of folded bedding on it covered with a sheet. Ellie watched him with bright, anxious eyes. With a vague idea of doing what he should, he prodded the mattress.

"Doctor, the curtains is under the sheet. Don't you muss them."

"I doubt if I did them any harm."

"Think he'll like it?"

"I hope so. I'll have to get along."

She followed him out into the hall. "I made a pie out of some of them apples. I'll leave it on the kitchen table . . ."

She was still talking from the top of the stairs when he let himself out of the house.

The door of the building on Maple Street where Dr. Moore had his office shut behind him with a familiar clash, a sound that had punctuated his life for nearly thirty years. Walking fast, he started down the hall, past the rooms occupied by a real estate broker, toward his office at the back. He knew exactly the scene that would be waiting for him—two or three lamps turned on, lighting drab furniture and torn magazines. Tired people waiting in the shadows for what of himself he was able to give them. To his surprise, the door was shut, with a small sign fastened to it. Then he remembered that he himself had put the sign there saying, because he was not certain when he would be back, that there would be no afternoon hours that day.

Angry with himself for forgetting, and a little disturbed by it, he got out the keys he carried at the end of a long chain, unlocked the door and went inside. There was a pile of mail on the floor below the slot in the door, and he stooped to scoop it up. The dark room was filled with the sound of the Little Torrent River rushing past below the windows, loud and swollen with rain. He went around the room, turning on the lamps. These little forgettings were surely growing more frequent. He had begun to keep track of them, in a way, adding them up into a sort of sum.

Nothing serious so far, and not likely to be, but a premonition of age nevertheless, a warning that the brain was, just perceptibly, starting its decline. Not only the brain, but the whole organism. At night he had begun to listen to his heartbeat, lying in the darkness, his attention sharpened to detect the faintest irregularity until, good sense returning, he recognized this morbid interest as itself a symptom, and turned on his right side and went to sleep. He was not sure how long ago this habit of watching himself had begun, but he knew that it was incurable, that he would never be free of it again.

He went on through the waiting room into his own office, which was dim and gloomy in the darkling afternoon. He dropped the mail on the top of his old-fashioned rolltop desk and turned on the gooseneck lamp. The pool of brightness on the desk deepened the surrounding dusk. He crossed the room to hang up his coat, lowered himself into his desk chair, and allowed himself to feel satisfaction in his unanticipated freedom. His thoughts turned to young David Armstrong. There would have to be an office for him. They could share the waiting room and surgery. . . . Nice to have a young fellow around, someone to talk over cases with at night, with a drink by the fire. . . . There was an urge to pass on, if one could, the kind of knowledge that comes only from living, and the desire to see the new medical generation safely established. and he thought, *You goddam old fool, you don't know he'll want to stay.* Nevertheless, a pleasant feeling of peace came over him. Sighing, he let his chair tip back to its utmost and closed his eyes, and at that moment his telephone rang.

Ianthe Norton's deep voice never ceased to surprise and please him. She was saying, "Oh, so you *are* back, Ed. I know you don't have office hours, but I want to talk to you if you can spare the time, and I thought perhaps if you *did* get home . . ."

"Come on over now, if you want to," he said.

But in the moment of the telephone's ringing he had thought of something and, disconnecting, he stood up. The continuity of the medical generation—he had a feeling that, long ago, he had taken an oath to preserve it. His mind presented to him a picture of two hundred earnest young men, standing and saying with one voice, not unlike the roar of the sea, "I swear by Apollo . . ."

The Hippocratic oath, and he could not now remember one

75

more word. He went to the untidy bookcase and began pulling down books, riffling through their pages until he found what he wanted. He carried the book back to his chair and opened it on his knees.

"I swear by Apollo, the physician, and Aesculapius, and Hygeia, and Panacea, and all the gods and goddesses, that, according to my ability and judgment, I will keep this oath and this stipulation— to reckon him who taught me this art equally dear to me as my parents; to share my substance with him, and relieve his necessities if required . . ."

Incredulous that he had ever sworn to such archaic nonsense, Moore went back to the beginning and read it again. Then, dismayed, he continued:

". . . to look upon his offspring as my own brothers, and to teach them this art, if they shall wish to learn it, without fee or stipulation; and that by precept, lecture, and every other mode of instruction I will impart a knowledge of this art to my own sons . . ."

That must, he thought, have been what he had so inaccurately remembered. Hurriedly, he scanned the rest of it, and found he had sworn not to poison any of his patients (he sincerely hoped he hadn't) and to leave kidney stones to be dealt with by surgeons. (His conscience was clear on that one.) Or to produce abortions (well, he never had, though tempted more than once). He had sworn to abstain from the seduction of females (guilty!) or males (*not* guilty) and not to gossip (about that, the record wasn't very clear). He shut the book with a slam and tossed it on the desk. So the oath he remembered, the true oath and dedication, had been in his mind, not in this preposterous verbiage.

He did not hear Ianthe's step above the sound of the river, for she moved with surprising lightness for a woman of her amplitude, almost with delicacy, and when she spoke she startled him. He whirled his chair around and saw her standing in the doorway, her tan raincoat hanging open, one ungloved hand holding her black leather bag, the other holding to the framework of the doorway. She had a fine carriage, and a part of his mind admired it now as he rose to meet her. She stood erect, chin high, but there was in this unconscious attitude none of the self-valuing, the imposition of self and of will, that such a carriage usually implies. Rather it suggested, at least to Edward Moore, a directness in facing life, a simplicity that put no reliance on the usual feminine resort to deviousness or subterfuge or emotional complications. She had what amounted to a talent, or at least so it seemed to him, for going directly to the heart of the matter in hand without becoming distracted by side issues or details. She carried this attitude into every phase of daily life, and this to Moore's admiring amusement, who liked to watch her unconsciously displaying it in even so simple a task as the making of a cup of coffee. Sometimes people, especially women, found this arrow-to-the-bull's-eye quality disconcerting, but it made her an asset when anything must be accomplished. She was much sought after to head committees of town charities. She would have been a good executive in any sort of work, and possibly a good judge, though not a good lawyer, for the tortuous expediencies to which the law is prone would certainly distress her.

She said now, in that strange, deep voice, "Ed, I've come to talk about Nathaniel."

"Sit down, Ianthe."

He found he used fewer words in talking to her than would be customary with other people, and this, too, Moore regarded as an asset. He held out his hands to take her coat, but she gave her head a shake, and he placed a chair for her facing his own. When he sat down he found himself being regarded with a steady look from her soft brown eyes. The eyes had always fascinated him, for in their depths were flecks of light, like motes moving in a sunbeam. She sat quietly and erect, her hands clasped around the bag in her lap. For a moment they were silent, sitting almost knee to knee, each regarding the other with a look that was oddly similar, direct, honest, experienced, and sad. Then Ianthe said, "You told me once, Ed, if Nathaniel's cancer reappeared in some other part of his body, that it would be a bad sign, that this would mean it had gone out of control."

"Yes, roughly that. We call it metastasis. It indicates that lymph nodes have become involved and that the cancer cells are more or less free to travel. It's not invariably hopeless. Let's say it's not good news."

She lowered her head and her hands moved nervously. Then

they tightened and she lifted her head and looked directly at him. When she spoke, it was as if she did not have enough breath to carry her words.

"The cancer has appeared again, hasn't it, Ed?"

He turned his chair with an abrupt motion toward his desk, picked up the book he had left there, put it down again, shoved at a pile of papers, and said with his back half turned to her, "The pathologist's report isn't back yet, or at least I don't think so. It would go to Howard. Let's wait for that, Ianthe."

"But you don't have much doubt, do you?"

He turned his chair back to face her and saw at once that in spite of what her mind must have told her, she had been clinging to a thread of hope. His hands tightened on the arms of his chair and his lips moved as he struggled with the problem, never resolved in all these years, of what words to use to say that there is no hope. Then he knew that his silence had told her. He saw her hands clutch each other. She began to breathe as though she could not draw enough air into her lungs. He watched her grow rigid with her effort to force control on herself. She never took her eyes off him. Then something inside her let go all at once and he saw her eyes fill and begin to glisten. Two tears ran down her face, slowly, as though they came from melting ice. The slow tears followed each other and she made no attempt to hide them.

He sat and waited, watching her. After a while she closed her eyes and drew a deep, wavering breath.

"I haven't been good enough to him all these years."

"You would always think that, Ianthe, no matter what. As marriages go, I believe yours has been a happy one."

He saw her fumbling in search of a handkerchief, her eyes still shut, tears still clinging to her lashes. He drew his own handkerchief out of his pocket and put it into her hand. She held it against her eyes and her whole body shook with one convulsive sob. Then she dropped her hands to her lap, pulling at the handkerchief with quick, nervous fingers, but once more she gave him her direct look. Her eyes were deep and tragic, but they were steady.

"Nat and I were never really close, Ed. That troubles me now. I don't mean either of us has been really unhappy, but I know I never gave him what he wanted. I love him, but not in the way he needs, not in the way he wants to love me. The thing that seems

78

to me so tragic now is"—her hands shut convulsively over the handkerchief and she had to struggle for control—"that he's lonely. I think he has been lonely all the years of our marriage. Maybe I've always known it, in a way, but it's taken this to bring it home to me, to make me realize fully. . . . I want to make it up to him, Ed. . . ."

He saw that she had not finished, that there was something more she was trying to bring herself to say. It seemed to him indecent to watch her struggle with herself. He rose and began to pace back and forth in the little office. She sat with her head bowed over her clasped hands, the poplin raincoat falling in loose folds around her. In the stillness the sound of the river seemed to him to have grown louder, and its ceaseless rush conveyed to him large, half-formed thoughts about the continuity of life. He did not try to grasp them, for they were like a reminder of something he had long known but never formulated, concerning, in some way, the unimportance of individual life, and in this vague concept he found strength for the present.

Passing her chair, he looked down on Ianthe's bowed head and saw that the soft, tumbled hair had grown grayer since he had last noticed it. The sight of it hurt him. He said, "I wish I could help you, Ianthe, or that I could honestly give you any reassurance."

She seemed not to hear him, and he stood still, a little way behind her chair, and waited. The dim light in the room, the voice of the river, and the weight of Ianthe's sorrow filled him with a sense of the uselessness of his own effort. It worked like a drug in him. He straightened his shoulders to throw it off, then gave it up. Drowsiness overwhelmed him.

Then Ianthe spoke, still almost in a whisper, and he stepped quickly forward to listen. "How long does he have, Ed?"

"It's not easy to say, at this point. The troublemaking cells are loose in the bloodstream now. We don't know where or when they'll strike again. Not more than a year, I should think. More likely less."

She made no reply, and Moore had just begun to pace again when she picked up her handbag and rose, as though there were no time to lose and she must hurry. "I must get back to him."

"Did you walk over?"

"What? Yes, I walked."

"Then I'll drive you home. You don't want to meet anyone just now."

He went to the coatrack for his hat and raincoat, put them on, looked around for his medical bag, and remembered that he had left it at the hospital when he went to take the plane. Ianthe was standing still, lost again. She was staring into space with wide eyes, as though she were struck with horror at what her mind saw, and he knew that she was facing a full realization of life's cruelty. It was a knowledge he had acquired so long ago that he was filled with wonder that Ianthe, a mature woman, had never been truly aware of it until now.

He said without either kindliness or roughness in his tone, "Nathaniel has had a good life, Ianthe."

She turned blank eyes on him, her lips parted, not seeing him, but standing as though she were facing an enemy. He saw awareness of himself and her surroundings come back to her. She raised a hand and plucked at the neck of her dress as though she were suffocating. Then she turned and walked quickly out.

He paused to turn off the lights and snap the spring lock on the office door. She waited for him at the end of the hall, and as he opened the outer door for her, she pressed her hand on her breast and said, "It's so strange, Ed. I can't believe any of this is happening. I can't believe it's real."

He made an inarticulate sound of sympathy and stood back to let her precede him through the doorway. This sense of unreality in times of stress was familiar to him. He recognized in it nature's anesthesia when grief becomes too great to bear, and as a doctor he welcomed it always. In the jeep Ianthe sat with bowed head, and as he drove along the familiar street he made no effort to talk to her, knowing she was numbed by emotion. He hoped she would stay in this condition for at least a time, but he also knew that her greatest difficulty was not in the shock of being told, but in the hours ahead when she would be alone with a clear mind.

He turned the jeep into the uncared-for driveway between tall white gateposts topped by carved pineapples, and stopped beside the kitchen porch at the side of the big house. A lilac, weighed down with moisture, brushed the top of the jeep, and a shower of drops was released on them. He shut off the engine and was reaching for the door when something occurred to him and he sat back again. "Would it make you feel any easier to hear what some-one else thinks—get another opinion from someone at Warwick Clinic?"

"I don't think so, Ed."

He got out and helped her to the ground. "I'm not built for a jeep," she said, and smiled a watery smile.

"Take one of Nat's sleeping pills tonight." He held the screen door open for her.

"If I did I might not hear him call. I'm not going to tell him I talked to you."

"I think that's wise. Call me if you need anything, Ianthe."

As he went down the steps he thought how strongly habits of speech reflect what is normal in life. Nathaniel Norton, with vocal cords cut away, would never "call" again.

He had reached the driveway when Ianthe spoke to him and came quickly out. "Ed, I forgot. How could I? This dreadful busi-ness of that man falling off the roof, and no doctors in the town. I'm so sorry for you, my dear."

"It was a dreadful thing. We've got to prevent its happening in the future, think up some way. . . . Our old system of just telling Edna where we're going to be isn't good enough. The selectmen have called all three of us to a meeting tomorrow night—to give us hell, I suppose. I'm afraid we deserve it."

"Oh, Ed, I'm sorry."

"Don't be, if some good for the town comes out of it."

Dr. Moore sighed heavily and got into the jeep, leaving her standing there gazing at him with sad, compassionate eyes. He backed cautiously out of the narrow driveway. As he swung into the street, his thoughts swung, with almost equally practiced ease, away from Ianthe and to the next of the duties crowding on him.

= VI

D<small>R. M</small>OORE HURTLED THE JEEP into the hospital parking lot with the effect of bobtailed flourish characteristic of that tough-minded little vehicle. Climbing out, he looked down the line of cars that stood nosed into the bushes along the margin, hoping to see Howard Perkins's Cadillac. This was a time of day when Perkins, who did not keep afternoon office hours, would be likely to make hospital rounds, and it seemed to Moore that since he himself was unexpectedly free of office routine, they might discuss Truelove's death and the unpleasant purpose of the meeting with the town's selectmen. The Cadillac was not there. Moore experienced the slight uneasiness he always felt when Perkins was not where he might be expected to be.

He shied away, so to speak, from this uneasiness and then reluctantly forced himself to return and face it squarely, and this cost him considerable effort of will. About most things Moore was frank with himself, but there was a whole area, and a large one, about which he was not frank with himself at all, where he would not meet the issues involved, and where general feeling and sentiment substituted for realistic thought. This area comprised the hospital and more especially the serious state of hospital finances. It included, also, misgivings about Perkins that, in spite of Moore's resistance to them, were growing more acute.

The plain fact was that Perkins was drinking, though Moore still pretended to himself that he could be mistaken about this. He had never found Perkins in a state that could be called drunken, never, in the operating room, noticed the slightest lessening of sureness and skill. He had, in fact, nothing concrete on which to base his suspicions, which made it all the easier to tell himself that they were groundless. Chiefly, there were unexplained absences, bursts of bad temper, a look about the eyes, and sometimes an evasiveness on the part of Adele, his wife, when Perkins could not be located. Moore, reluctantly approaching this large question in his thoughts, admitted to himself for the first time that if there was not now a problem, there was almost certain to be one in the not distant future. As he thought about this, crossing the parking lot, a look of resignation came into Moore's eyes.

In the gray light of the rainy afternoon the tall narrowness of the old part of the hospital, the part that had been the sort of private house that was called a "mansion," seemed to Moore to have taken on an aspiring look. This, together with its appearance of stoic and enduring dignity, he felt would be fine indeed except for the meaningless, stubby turret that hung on one side of the second story. But for lack of funds he would have had this architectural tumor excised long ago, along with the narrow porch that crossed the front and curved lopsidedly along one side of the building. The porch added considerably to the building's upkeep—a painter could spend days on the intricacies of posts and railing—and was good for nothing but the storage of the three or four oxygen tanks out in the open because the building was not kept strictly fireproof. They were there now, their color showing the special brilliance that greens acquire when the atmosphere is full of dampness. He noted this and also that someone had forgotten to turn off the light over the hospital sign hanging on an arm from a post planted in the lawn. These things seemed to him welcoming. He came here with a sense of being integral with the hospital, with a feeling of expansion and a warmth of satisfaction that his own home had not given him for some years. The hospital was his life's work and, in his own mind, the principal justification for his existing at all.

The enormity of enjoying anything at all in view of what lay ahead of him cut the satisfaction short. Sunk in gloom as sudden as his pleasure, he moved on toward the steps, his mind turning to the more immediate problem of Edna. She had been left to cope alone with a responsibility that should not have been forced on her. She had handled it to the best of her ability in a way that was courageous and enterprising; and that she had no choice but to do what she could did not, in his view, undermine these values in the least. But the man had died. And if he knew her as he thought he did, she would be convinced that the blame must in some way be hers.

He hurried up the steps, feeling guilty because he had left her so long without reassurance. Edna was at her desk, bent over some papers, not working but sitting very still and staring down at them. He thought she did not see them nor had she heard the opening of the front door. There was a look on her face that he had never seen before, a look that made her seem as though life had at last dealt her a blow from which she felt she had not the strength to recover. Deeply remorseful, he saw that he had been right in thinking she would take the blame to herself. He thought, She's old; why, she's old. . . . Edna's an old woman . . . Edna? And he thought he could not stand the hurt of it, for her or for himself. Then she was the Edna he knew, rising to stand behind her desk, disciplining herself, as always, to his presence. He went over to her and saw that she was trembling. He said, "Well, Edna," and cleared his throat and didn't try to say any more.

"I did what I could, Dr. Moore."

Not looking at her, he put his hand over hers and pressed it. Then he turned his back on her, and walking quickly, he went into his office and shut the door.

When, later, Dr. Moore was leaving the hospital, Edna had left her desk. He heard her voice from somewhere near the top of the stairs, and though he could not hear what she was saying, he paused to listen critically to the tone. It was quiet but strong and steady; she was at least outwardly herself again, directing the hospital safely and perhaps happily under his authority. Reassured, and very greatly relieved, he went on his way. The rain had stopped and the air was still. Beyond the far end of the town, long streamers of mist were rising from the dark slopes of Mount Adamant, and on the tip of each bronzed leaf of Boston ivy there hung a water drop. Halfway across the parking lot the low-hanging sun came out and the wet world began to sparkle.

Moore drove through this glittering atmosphere into the center of the town. There he parked the jeep, and carrying his bag, he climbed a steep flight of wooden stairs that led upward from the sidewalk between a dress shop and an appliance store. At the top of the stairs there was a landing and a varnished door to which was thumbtacked a hand-lettered card that read MAY TURNER. Dr. Moore knocked lightly, turned the china doorknob without waiting for an answer, and called, "May?"

A light, breathy voice answered him. "Oh, Uncle Ed—come in."

He pushed the door open, frowning, for her cheerful voice was dear to him and he heard traces of pain in it.

"I suppose it's all right leaving your door open like this in the daytime, but you lock it at night, don't you?"

"Yes, of course. Don't fuss, Uncle Ed."

She was laughing at him and it made him feel foolish and pleased and, consequently, inclined to fuss some more. As he crossed the big, sparsely furnished room toward the studio couch where she was lying, he said, "What have you got the shades pulled down for? You should let some light in."

"It made me feel so dismal, watching the rain."

"Nonsense. It's not raining now." He dropped his bag on a chair, bent over the couch, kissed her and patted her cheek. "How are you?"

"All right."

He gave her a sharp, doubting look through squinted eyes and went to pull up the shades.

"It's not good for you to be alone like this."

She smiled feebly as though this were something they had been over so many times that it was not worth answering. He stood beside the couch looking down at her, silently brooding, but on another level of his mind enjoying her prettiness. She had curly black hair, cut short, eyes of a deeper, intenser blue than his own, and a translucent skin that was beginning to lose its rosy flush. Under his gaze she lowered her eyes, the black lashes lying like smudges on her cheeks.

"Don't worry about me, Uncle Ed. I don't mind being laid up."

"That's just what worries me. Now let's have a look at how those bruises are getting along."

He brought a chair beside the couch, and sitting forward on the edge of it, he pushed aside the quilt and the flowered robe she was wearing. He bent over to study two broad, blackish-colored bruises across both legs a little above both knees. He put his hand

85

gently over one and then over the other, feeling their angry heat. She lay back against her pillows, trusting him, almost literally putting her suffering into his hands, and feeling comforted.

This trust, and the ease it brought, was as familiar to him as any aspect of his medical practice. He saw it every day in young and old, more especially in the old. He had never grown accustomed to it, or accepted it, for he was aware that what the patients relied on was a power he did not have.

Uncomfortably conscious of all this now, he glanced up at her with a faintly reproachful expression, and meeting the blue eyes watching him confidently and peacefully, he looked hastily down again. He said in a preoccupied way, "Still having a good deal of pain?"

"Yes, when I move. Especially when I stand up."

"And still, more in the right leg than the left?"

"Yes."

Thought of the pain made her close her eyes, the dark lashes lying on the pale cheeks and her mouth partly open, the curve of the upper lip so childishly lovely that he felt a constriction of tenderness in his chest. Speaking a little gruffly because of it, he said, "It's lucky you didn't get both legs broken."

She pulled herself up against the pillows. "It's very much better, Uncle Ed. Really it is."

He made a sound as though to repudiate the untruth of this, then glanced at her keenly. There was a contradiction here that he did not understand—a perfectly normal desire to believe herself "better," opposed to a reluctance he did not understand to come out of the seclusion that her accident had brought about. In a minute, he thought, he must try to bring these feelings of hers out into the open and persuade her to look at them honestly. He turned back to his examination of her damaged leg, becoming businesslike again. He wrapped his hand over the instep of her left foot, then over the right, thinking that the right felt discernibly cooler under his palm. He felt below her instep for the pulse of the dorsalis pedis artery, first on one foot, then the other, comparing them slowly and carefully. He was almost certain that the pulse in the left was stronger than in the right. He sought for the posterior tibial artery by the anklebone, went through the same procedure attentively, as though he were listening with his fingertips, and received the same impression of a weaker pulse in the right leg.

She said, "What are you doing that for, Uncle Ed?" and he gave her the secretive smile of the doctor who intends to keep his own counsel. He got to his feet, bent over her and felt with his fingertips above the bruise on her right leg for the pulse of the great femoral artery that carries the blood downward into the leg. He pressed hard, knowing he hurt her, and when she cried out he ceased instantly, but he had felt the artery pulsing full and strong.

He arranged her robe and pulled up the quilt. Then he set the chair to face her more squarely, and sitting down again, he studied her in silence. He was debating with himself whether he ought to tell her that he thought there might be a blood clot that had formed in the artery under the bruise in her right leg, partially blocking the circulation. Such a clot might form if the artery had been injured in the accident, and it would account for the lesser pulse below the bruise in that leg. He knew very little about such things, though he thought clots could be removed surgically. The mental state she was in bothered him and he did not fully understand it.

She was gazing a steady question at him. He said, "There's a young doctor coming in on the plane tomorrow to look us over. I hope he'll decide to practice here a while. I want him to have a look at your right leg."

"Oh no, please. I don't want him to. It's better. Really it is."

"I want you to see him." He said it in a tone of firm authority that was seldom unsuccessful in gaining him his own way.

"I don't want anyone else. I just want you."

"I want you to see him, May."

"But why, Uncle Ed? I just won't see him unless you tell me why."

He sighed and remained thoughtfully silent.

"Is it something worse than a bruise?"

"That's just it—I don't know, May. I think perhaps there's a blood clot under that bruise on your right leg, and that's why you're having all this pain."

"But that's nothing, is it? Won't it just go away?"

"I'm not even sure that's it, but maybe it should be removed.

87

It's something I don't know much about, and this young man does."

"Uncle Ed, you're not going to try to send me to a hospital, are you? Because I just won't go. I won't have an operation. I'd rather lie here all the rest of my life than go into a hospital ever again."

"I know you weren't happy there in training, but this would be different."

"No it wouldn't. I just won't, that's all."

"Calm down, May. There's no need to get so excited. Let's wait and see what Dr. Armstrong thinks." He reached for her hand. "May, you're trembling."

"I just won't go into a hospital no matter what he says. I'd rather die."

"Now, now. I won't press you. It may not be necessary. If it is, I won't press you until you yourself are ready."

Her rigidity left her and she let herself drop back against her pillows. Two tears slipped out from under her closed lids and ran down her cheeks. "Here," he said, and pulled a tissue out of the box on the table and gave it to her. He watched her while she wiped the tears away. "May, my dear," he said with sudden urgency, "why don't you come and stay at my house? I don't like your being here all alone."

"I'm all right, Uncle Ed."

"I suppose you are, but my place has seemed kind of lonely sometimes since your Aunt Matilda died. It would be nice to have you there."

"I've told you—I'd rather be independent."

"I thought perhaps you'd come just till you got well . . ."

"I'd rather not, Uncle Ed. *Please* stop nagging me. I've got to lead my own life, and I don't want to be babied. I was grown up when I came to Haddon three years ago, and I'm twenty-five now. I'm old enough to look after myself, and I *want* to. So please— let's just drop it."

He sat without speaking, his hands spread out on his knees, gazing sadly at a spot on the floor. After a moment she said, "I'm sorry. I didn't mean to be cross."

"Well . . . I just hoped . . ." He rose. "I must be getting on."

He hesitated, then bent to kiss her cheek, and she straightened up to meet him.

"Uncle Ed, you're a regular old mother hen."

"You're all I have, you know." He patted the cheek awkwardly. "Be a good girl now and take care of that leg, will you?"

"Of course."

"All right, then."

She had a look on her face that he saw on other faces each day, the desire not to have the doctor's visit end, the fear of the return of anxiety. This look always touched him, even when he was anxious to escape from a difficult patient, and for this reason he had developed a knack of appearing unhurried, of seeming to give to his patients all the time they wanted. It was often the best medicine he had in his power to provide.

May held out her hand to him. "Uncle Ed . . ."

"Yes, my dear."

"About what happened after you had left for New York . . ."

He looked away from her earnest, troubled eyes.

"Everyone knows it wasn't your fault."

"Then everyone's wrong, May. All three of us are to blame. Me, perhaps, more than the others." He gave her hand a slight pressure and released it. "We'll have to see what can be done. Don't you worry about it."

He shrugged into his coat, picked up his bag, gave her a faint, inconclusive smile, and left.

On his way down the stairs he looked at his watch again, and decided that he would have time for a quick call at Beaver Floods to see old Alice Henderson, provided he had a sandwich for dinner, or none at all, and let himself be a little late for evening office hours. He drove fast, his mind wholly occupied with the meeting with the selectmen of the town. He was glad of this opportunity to do what he told himself would be "some constructive thinking" about medical problems in Haddon, but by the time he arrived at Beaver Floods, the hamlet near where Alice lived, he had thought of nothing serviceable. The selectmen would have to receive the solemn assurance of all three medical men that the town would never again be without a doctor, but he could not see how anything more positive or binding than that could be arranged.

Alice lived in a squat old house, gray as the rocks on the hill behind it from a generation without paint. He did not knock, for he thought it unlikely that Alice would hear him, but before he went in, he drew a deep breath of fresh air, knowing it would be his last until he came out again. He pushed the door open and looked around the cluttered, unlovely room so like others he visited on these back roads. A cheap white stove, a chipped sink with a shelf above it, a table with a bright plastic cloth, a hideous linoleum on the floor. No television here. The familiar smell of dirt and poverty rose like a wall in front of the partly open door.

"Alice?" he said loudly.

A sound came from what he had taken for a pile of dark old quilts on a chair by the far window, an inhuman sound like a spit and a smothered yowl. His skin prickling, he came reluctantly into the room, leaving the door open behind him for what good it might do the overburdened atmosphere of the room. Out of the dark mass on the chair, Alice's beady black eyes were watching him, her incredibly tiny wrinkled face half hidden by what he realized were not quilts but clothing bundled on her. As he stared back at her, trying to adjust himself to this disturbing scene, a yellow cat, gaunt and dusty-looking, came out from behind her chair and walked disdainfully away, and for a distracted instant he wondered if it had been the cat and not the old woman who had made that unpleasant sound.

Trying to seem brisk and cheery, he came closer, and she cried shrilly at him, "I ain't goin' to live very long. I tell you, I ain't goin' to live very long."

"Now, Alice . . ." He swung a wooden chair around and sat down facing her, wondering if the sight of him had put her in mind of her sister's death, so that in her blurred brain this scene was a continuation of that other by the bedside, the intervening time now lost to her consciousness. Her thin body inside her bulky garments made him think of the cat, for she had the look of a cat dressed up by children in old clothing.

He said loudly, "How are you, Alice?"

"I just got through tellin' you."

Her scrawny hands trembled with palsy, but there was a fire of malevolence in her jetty eyes and a faint tinge of pink in her cheeks. Moore noted these things with approval, as signs of vitality, and quite possibly as indications that Alice was enjoying her first independence from her sister's tyranny. He reached out toward her hand to take her pulse, and with startling quickness she jerked it away from him, the movement stirring up a mingled smell of old clothes and old woman. He said, "Now, Alice," with reproving mildness, but he made no attempt to force her. Instead, he sat with his hands on his knees and took her pulse by counting the jerks of the artery in her neck and glancing down at his watch.

After that, he just sat and studied her thoughtfully, and she gazed back at him, blinking slowly, but her eyes showing no more feeling for him than if he were any moving object. Long ago he had seen that same look in the eyes of caged animals in the pathology building of his hospital. It represented ego as untempered by any considerations outside self as in a predatory wild animal or an insane human being. Of all unlovely ways to grow old (and Moore thought them all unlovely), this losing of that which is normal in relationships with others, he felt, was the worst. But not, he reminded himself, for the person who was so aging. Old Alice, for example, was cut off from all unhappiness except her own, all tearings of the heart with sympathy or pity for others. He thought she was right, that without her sister and the stimulation of their incessant quarreling, she probably would not live long. The thing to do, as he saw it, was not to pester her too much with doctoring that might or might not prolong her life a little bit, but to feed her hungry ego with what food he could provide, make her as happy as he could, and let nature take its course.

A faint sound like a puff of wind came from her lips. He brought his wandering thoughts to focus on her and saw that her head was bent forward, her eyes closed, and that she seemed to have collapsed gently into her mass of clothing. Alice slept. He rose and quietly put his chair back in place; then he went to the refrigerator and took out a carton of milk, sniffed it and poured a liberal amount in a bowl that stood on the floor beside the stove. The yellow cat, hearing him shut the refrigerator, came out from under the curtain of a doorway, and trotted up to the bowl, purring loudly. Moore let himself out and closed the door.

On the path by the broken picket fence he met and greeted a neighbor woman whom he knew. "Going in to see old Alice, are you?"

"Yes, Doctor, to fix a mite of supper for her. She don't eat more'n a bird."

"That's all right. Her system doesn't need much food."

"And now's you're here, Dr. Moore, I may's well tell you, she won't wash herself, or let me touch a thing in the house but the dirty dishes, not even to make her bed. My guess is she's adoin' it to spite her dead sister who was always so partickler. That, or she's crazy, but somehow I don't think it's her wits."

"Let her be for a bit and see if she gets over it. The dirt won't hurt her as much as being crossed right now. She's her own boss for the first time in her life and it's probably no wonder if it's gone to her head a little. It's good of you to keep an eye on her."

"Well . . . 'tain't nothin' much. We all gotta git old sometime."

"Yes, I'm afraid we do."

Aware that his remark had sounded more feeling than he intended, Moore climbed into the jeep and drove back to town.

Finding that he had a choice between a sandwich and keeping office hours on time, he chose the former, and was punished for it by an unusually heavy influx of patients, every one of whom wanted to take up extra time to talk about Truelove's death and the absence of doctors. When the last one had left, he discovered without surprise that he was very tired.

He snapped off lights, picked up his bag (night calls were always possible) and left the office, and the rattling glass of the front door put a period to another day. The cold, to be expected after rain, was sweeping down from the mountains on long, restless gusts of wind, and the stars were out. There would be frost before morning.

He stood at the top of the steps, looking up and down the nearly empty village street, liking the feel of the cold, fresh air on his face. He remembered then that he and Howard Perkins had not yet had time for the talk they had planned. He looked at his watch, thinking that he would drive by the Perkinses' house on his way home.

As he went down the steps, he saw a light in the alley next to the Republic House, that seemed to be coming from the back window of the liquor store. That would be Joe and Martha Bridges working late at stocktaking. It reminded him that there was no liquor in the house with which to welcome David Armstrong, not even any of the cheap stuff he bought for his own occasional use. The idea of getting something really good to honor the young doctor so pleased him that he crossed the street and rattled the handle of the door until Joe pulled up the shade that said CLOSED on it, and peered out to see who was there. When he saw Dr. Moore, he opened the door wide.

"Hi, Doc. Come on in. We're checking stock. Something we can do for you?"

"I thought I'd pick up some Scotch. I'd like to look 'em over. All right?"

"Sure, sure, go ahead."

Moore liked handling bottles by their long necks and reading the labels. He wandered around behind the counter while Joe and Martha went on with their work, and finally selected the most expensive brand of Scotch they had.

While Joe, a thin, efficient young man, was wrapping up the Scotch, he said, "Terrible thing that happened while you were gone, Doc."

"Yes it was, Joe."

"Makes you pretty uneasy to think there might not be a doctor in the town when you needed one. Suppose something happened to one of the kids."

"We're going to make sure it doesn't happen again."

"That's something you'll have to do, all right. The whole town's upset. They're not blaming you, Doc. They're not really blaming anybody, but they're pretty upset, all right. I guess you know that."

"I guessed it."

Joe handed the package to Moore, and Martha came out of the back to stand beside her husband.

"There's talk that they're going to build a hospital at Silver Springs and that you're going to close yours. I hope that isn't true, Dr. Moore. It isn't, is it?"

Moore felt the ends of his fingers prickle. The clairvoyant quality of small-town gossip frequently startled him, but this was a good deal too close to home. "No, of course my hospital isn't going to close," he said crossly. "You might tell anyone who talks about it that I said so."

The wind was blowing down the dark village street, and he lowered his head against its buffeting and wondered with exasperation how that talk had started. Not Stoner . . . unless for his own purposes . . . a most unpleasant thought. About there being no doctors in town, people were right to be concerned. It had been his experience that people expected three things of a doctor—skill, understanding and availability. No two of these would satisfy. Doctors must be ready to supply all three. Within his memory, country people had thought themselves lucky if there was any sort of doctor within call. Nowadays people thought these three things their right, as inalienable and far more immediate than their rights to education, worship, or the protection of the law. To put it as no doubt the people of the town now were doing—you want a doctor, you want a good one that's got some sympathy for what ails you, and you want him quick. Basically, the desire to make these requirements secure was what the move toward socialized medicine was all about. . . . Moore put his package carefully in the back of the jeep, climbed in and drove away.

The door of the Perkinses' house was answered by Adele Perkins, a slim, thoroughbred, discontented-looking young woman in her early forties, in whose presence Moore never felt quite comfortable. She said, "Hullo. Come in. Howard's in the study," and left him to find his own way there. He seldom came to this house, and when he did it was not for social reasons. It was larger than his own house, not old, and furnished—though this Moore did not appreciate—in the sort of conventional good taste that indicates a background of a certain social standing of a sort not familiar in Haddon.

The study was a small room with a large desk in it, behind which Dr. Perkins was sitting. Newspapers were laid open on the desk top and on them were a disassembled gun, some oily rags and a tall highball glass, nearly full. Perkins rose when Moore came in.

"Hullo, Ed. Have a drink?"

"Well . . . All right, a light one." Perkins went to a small bar in the corner of the room and started to pour. "Hold it, Howard. My God . . ."

Moore took the drink and gazed with dissatisfaction at it, and Perkins, going back to his chair behind the desk, picked up one of the gun parts. The metal was black and glossy with oil.

"Did you come to talk about the meeting the selectmen are going to have about us doctors, or about that bastard, Stoner?"

"Stoner?" Moore was startled but, remembering Joe and Martha, realized that he shouldn't be. No doubt the town was already taking sides.

94

"I met him coming out of Rotary lunch. He told me about the talk he had with you. Ed, he's got you."

"What do you mean, he's got me? Who is he to say this town doesn't need a hospital? Howard, I tell you . . ."

Perkins laughed, put the gun part down and picked up his glass. "Who is he? He's the source of the money you need to run on. Come out of the clouds, Ed. He's the source of the money, remember, and in the long run that's what's going to get you. And speaking of money, when the breakup comes, let's not overlook the fifty thousand I anted in."

Moore stared in silence at the glass in his hand and abruptly, as though he could bear the sight of it no longer, reached out and put it on a table. He clasped his hands and looked at Perkins silently.

Perkins said, "All right. It's early to talk about that now. But listen, Ed." Perkins put his own glass down and the oily fingerprints on it glistened in the light of the desk lamp. "I have to assume that sooner or later it will be necessary to close the hospital. I know this will be tough on you because it's your creation. But you'll get on all right professionally, because you don't absolutely need a hospital to keep on practicing. A surgeon is another matter. A surgeon can't function without a hospital."

"What are you getting at, Howard?"

Perkins did not reply at once. He opened a can of wax, smeared some on a rag and began to polish the gunstock. Without taking his eyes off what he was doing, he said, "I hate to tell you this, Ed, but there's a teaching job at Warwick Medical School—first-year surgery. It carries staff privileges at the Clinic, so whoever gets it could continue doing surgery on the side. It will be open next fall. I'm going after it."

Moore started to speak, moved uneasily in his chair, and said nothing.

"I know what you're thinking, Ed, but that business is so far in the past I don't believe it will count against me. And Adele would like it. She hates it here in Haddon."

"I hope you won't be precipitate about this. I intend to save the hospital by reorganizing it with the needs of the enlarged community in mind. Silver Springs. And do it in a way that will answer all criticisms."

95

"That would take a lot of money."

"I'll find the money. And it's to your interest financially not to let the hospital fold."

Perkins stopped rubbing the gunstock and for a moment he was thoughtful. When he looked up he was half smiling. "Drink your drink, Ed. I'll do what I can to help you—to help us. I don't think this battle can be won, but I'll enjoy the fight. I just don't intend to go down in the crash."

"I really came to talk about this meeting the selectmen have summoned us to."

"Yes. I thought you probably had. I wish you'd leave the bastards to me."

"That's just what I don't think it would be wise to do."

Perkins laughed with one of his sudden switches to affability that were so startling and went so far toward making him, in spite of other traits, a thoroughly likable person to those who knew him more than superficially. "Don't trust me not to blast their tails off? I guess you're right. All right—you lead and I'll back you. It can be your show. But if it comes to a real row, then you get out of my way. You're not tough enough. I'll do the infighting."

"That's fair enough." Moore reached for his drink, finished half of it, put it back on the table and stood up. "We'll talk about the hospital business another time, when it isn't so late."

Perkins went to the front door with him and, as he was leaving, put a hand on his shoulder. "You're not tough enough."

Moore made a sound not unlike a groan, and went out into the night. The wind had gone and the cold felt active and menacing. A frost, and a cruel one, was moving in. With the porch light still to guide him, Moore wedged himself into the jeep, remembering with wonder that this interminable day now ending had begun in New York.

VII

DR. MOORE WANDERED slowly around Nathaniel Norton's sunny bedroom examining various objects. This was something he often did when visiting patients, to keep them from feeling scrutinized, but he felt that Norton, watching from his wing chair, knew quite well that this was a technique. Norton's head, in silhouette against the window, showed strongly the taut, bird-of-prey lines of chin and neck. A patch of gauze lay like a tuft of white feathers at the base of his throat, and his hands, resting on the chair arms, were so thin as to seem skeletonized. Moore, uncomfortably aware of Norton's sardonic gaze, came back to the bay window and sat down in a chair opposite Norton's.

"You're pretty comfortable on the whole, aren't you, Nat?"

Norton's reply was a wheezing breath. It moved the gauze covering the tracheotomy opening that had been made in his throat when cancerous larynx and vocal cords had been removed. The unnatural sound was, in some ways, a dreadful one. Moore decided to take it for simple assent. A knitting bag belonging to Ianthe hung over the arm of his chair, and he thrust his hand into it, kneading the soft wool, thinking how he could make what he had to say as little of a burden to Norton as possible.

"Nat, you should get out more. Go driving with Ianthe. Drive yourself, for that matter. No need to stay cooped up here. Get out of that damn bathrobe once in a while."

Norton shifted himself in the wing chair, pulled from beside him a slate with a pencil attached, and wrote. Moore felt a shudder go down his spine in response to the scratch of the pencil.

Norton held out the slate. In big, sprawling letters he had written, "Don't want to," looked at Moore with a glare, saw that he had forgotten his own question, snatched the pencil and added, "go driving."

"Why don't you go down in the study, then? It would be easier for Ianthe not to have to climb the stairs."

Nat took a piece of damp cloth out of a saucer on the table beside him, wiped the slate, wrote on it and held it out. It said, "Ianthe doesn't mind."

"I'm sure she doesn't, Nat, but just the same, for both your sakes, I wish you would get out of this room more."

This time Norton wrote angrily, with windy breaths whistling from his throat, "What is the use?"

He barely gave Moore time to read what he had written before jerking the slate back, and wrote, "Lab report. Must be back. What is it!?" Both exclamation point and question mark were attenuated and as forceful as the slate pencil would make them. Still holding the slate out, he pulled back the open neck of his shirt to show, just below the collarbone, a short, partly healed scar.

Moore suppressed a sigh and said with an air of casualness, "Fatty tumor, like Howard told you."

Norton wiped the slate and slowly wrote "No." But he left the slate resting on his knee and turned to meet Moore's eyes with a steady, serious look in which there was none of his customary mockery. Moore saw hardihood in the brown eyes and, most strangely, beauty. They were sad, and something of the spirit, in which the beauty lay, shone in their depths. Their eyes held for a moment and then Moore, deeply moved, and feeling that he must hide his emotion, rose and crossed the room to the table that held the vase of dried weeds. With his back to Norton he rustled them with a finger and at once drew his hand back, disturbed because the sound brought with it the desolation of windswept fields dying at the season's end.

He turned back to Norton, feeling closer to him than he ever had, and wanting to give this some expression. He was about to put a hand on Norton's shoulder when he saw that there had been a change in him. Whatever had been there between them a moment before was gone, and Norton was his old self once more. Head held high, mutilated neck stretched thin. He had an air about him now—incredibly but unmistakably—of satisfaction.

Outraged and rebuffed, Moore stood there helplessly and thought, satisfaction for what, in heaven's name? For being smart enough to catch me in a lie? Or for being able in the face of death to preserve the old ironical, cantankerous independence? Suddenly Moore was tired out, discouraged and beset almost beyond endurance by the complications of the medical ideal he strove to serve. He stood looking down at Norton, feeling all his old dislike, but wearily, passively, as though the vitality had gone out of it and of him too. Becoming aware that the pause was growing too long, he said, "I must go, Nat," and as an afterthought he held out his hand. Norton half rose to take it and gave it a slight, indifferent pressure. Then, a little awkwardly, Moore went out of the room, leaving Norton pulling at the cord of his bathrobe, tying it tightly around him with jerky, hostile motions.

Dr. Armstrong had never seen a mountain airstrip, and he looked with interest out of the window of the plane. This was a high, breezy place that seemed remote from anywhere. A shack with a big sign on it saying AIRPORT, which he thought self-evident, a wire fence, a short line of parked cars, six or eight people standing by an opening in the fence. Armstrong looked to see if Moore was among them. He did not remember too clearly what Moore looked like, for it was one of the by-products of his difficulty with people that he did not always remember faces. This was true even of the patients he saw in the office, and sometimes he could recall every visual aspect of an operation and not the appearance of the person on whom it had been performed. When he met people whom he thought perhaps he ought to know, this uncertainty often made his manner a little odd, as though his thoughts were somewhere else, and gave the unintentional impression that he was cold, indifferent and perhaps something of a snob.

He had no chance to test his memory of Moore, for the plane swung around and the people by the fence were hidden from view. He very much hoped Moore had not come to meet him, but coming down the steps, Armstrong saw him and wondered how he had thought he might not remember that massive, stoop-shouldered, blue-eyed man. Moore, coming toward the plane, seemed to Armstrong to walk with more confidence than he had in New York, a man on home ground, and then Armstrong knew by the sudden smile of welcome that he had been seen and recognized.

Armstrong himself did not smile, for a warm greeting was not in his nature, but he let himself yield inwardly to Moore's friendliness. Moore's hand was out and he was saying, "Glad to see you, Doctor. I've been looking forward to this." Armstrong took the hand cautiously and received a carefully light pressure.

"Thank you, sir. You're right in the midst of the mountains here, aren't you?"

"The leaves are kind of pretty. Begun to turn early this year on account of the drought."

"In the city—New York—they just turn brown and fall off. I'd forgotten there could be a show like this."

"Not at their height for a month yet, or nearly. . . . We have to wait for them to take your bag off."

For Armstrong, a wait in the company of a stranger was a matter of constraint. He found nothing to say, and neither did Moore, though this seemed not to trouble him. Armstrong studied him, and of this, too, Moore seemed unaware, looking around with more interest in the activities of the little airport than Armstrong felt they merited.

When at last a cart with luggage on it was pulled up near them, Moore said cheerfully, "Here you are, David, take your pick." The easy use of his first name startled Armstrong, but he found it agreeable. Moore seemed to him to have a comfortable, happy disposition that must make life easier for both himself and his patients. Examining this thought as they walked toward the line of parked cars, he wondered if a thoroughly bright and cheerful disposition was wholly desirable equipment for a medical man. Glancing sidewise at Moore to confirm this estimate, he was mildly startled to discover something quite contradictory in Moore's unguarded face —a look of troubled sadness that the lightness of his manner may have been intended to conceal.

He was still thinking about this when, to Armstrong's surprise, they stopped beside a dirty red jeep. When Armstrong's bag was stowed in the back (along with a spade, Moore's medical bag, and a small, portable oxygen tank that looked as though it resided there permanently), Moore seemed in no hurry to get on his way.

He sat for a long moment motionless, his hands on the wheel. Then he reached down and turned the ignition key.

"There's something that's happened in Haddon that I guess you'd better know about before we get there. As I told you, there are three of us doctors in the town . . ."

Talking, Moore gave a glance over his shoulder at the roadway behind them where departing cars were passing—altogether too casual a glance, it seemed to David—and, still talking, backed the jeep violently into the midst of them. David braced himself for the inevitable crash. Nothing happened. Feeling prickles in his scalp, he said, "I'm sorry, sir. What did you say?"

"I said there weren't any doctors there when it happened."

"Weren't any doctors?" Armstrong was aware of sounding foolish. "But how would that be possible?"

Moore began his explanation at the same time they began their descent from the airport, which, to Armstrong's inexperienced eye, seemed to be located on a full-scale mountain. He saw at once that the road was steep, unpaved, and in the process of being reconstructed by some monster pieces of machinery that, with much noise and activity, and oblivious of everything but their own purposes, blocked their way. At least they seemed to Armstrong to block the way, but Moore appeared to take a different view, for he plunged recklessly among the yellow monsters. The drivers of the great things yelled at him, but though their words were inaudible above the tumult, the purport seemed surprisingly to be good-natured greeting. The jeep slewed and bumped and now and then teetered on the edge of a ditch; Armstrong clutched the edge of his seat, and Moore never stopped his explanation of what had happened in Haddon on that fatal day. But when they came at last to the bottom of the hill and sailed out onto the calm of a paved highway, Armstrong had grasped only the salient facts that there had been an accident, that no doctor could be reached, and that, quite possibly for this reason, the man had died.

But now that the going was perfectly safe except for their breakneck speed, Moore seemed to have nothing more to say. He brooded silently as they rushed across a bridge and through a town and out on the broad highway once more. Finally Armstrong, trying not to be hypnotized by the needle of the speedometer and to make some sense out of what had been told him, said, "I don't see why your telephone answering service couldn't keep track of your movements."

"We don't have a telephone answering service—or secretaries, or office nurses, for that matter."

"Then how . . . ?"

"Oh, Edna looks after mine—Edna Judson, my head nurse at the hospital. Perkins and Ladd have their offices in their homes, so their wives take calls when they aren't there. The thing is, a few of the back-country places still don't have phones, though these are getting fewer, and I happened to be going to one of them."

"You need a central answering service for all three of you."

"Yes, we do, though I doubt if Ladd would go along with it. He's eighty-some, and he still thinks the way country doctors used to when there were fewer patients and each doctor kept away from every other doctor for fear one or two of his precious patients would get weaned away. I imagine that a central answering service, or something of the sort, will be discussed at the meeting tonight. I didn't tell you about the meeting. . . . Wait a minute."

Behind them a siren sounded, short and sharp, and subsided into an angry growl. Armstrong thought, well, naturally! and relaxed for the first moment of comfort he had known since the drive began. Then he discovered that Moore, who had barely slackened his speed, was laughing.

Before he could interpret this incomprehensible mirth, a car shot like an arrow from behind them and drew alongside, keeping pace with them. Two men in state trooper uniforms leaned toward them, broad smiles on their handsome, stereotyped young faces. They both yelled, "Hi, Doc," and the nearest one said loudly, "We'll haul you in one of these days, Doc, that's for sure."

This seemed to delight all three of them, and as the state car shot ahead with a departing derisive yowl from the siren, Moore said, "Nice young fellows. What was I saying?"

"About a meeting, I think."

"Oh, yes. The selectmen—there are three of them and they run the town—they're putting us three doctors on the carpet tonight. Sorry it had to be on your first night here. And that reminds me— I've got it fixed up at my house for you to stay. Nothing very fancy, I'm afraid. I'm a widower, and I keep living simple, but you'll be comfortable. I've been looking forward to having you."

Armstrong answered him quickly. "I made a reservation at the hotel—the Republic House, is it? Thanks just the same."

"You'll be more comfortable with me."

"Thanks, I'd better stick to the original plan."

"Sure?"

Moore turned toward him and Armstrong was surprised to see unmistakable disappointment in his face. "Thanks just the same," he said, and felt obscurely remorseful. "What do you expect the outcome of the meeting to be?"

"Oh—in the end, nothing. We'll be severely censured, and we deserve it. We'll be asked what assurances we can give for the future, but what can we say beyond promising that it won't happen again? I'd like to have something more definite for them."

"There's the telephone answering service."

"Yes, there's that. I'll talk about it to Perkins and Ladd before the meeting."

To David's surprise, a little while later, Moore suddenly slowed the jeep to an almost reasonable speed. "This is Haddon." They looked down a long and tree-shaded street of ample houses among which small businesses and a gas station or two had taken root. In the distance, the street divided around a green, and at the far end a white church spire rose slim and lovely against the backdrop of a mountain slope.

Armstrong saw all this with pleasure while he listened to Moore, who was saying, "I'd appreciate it if you could find time to make a professional call on a niece of mine while you're here. Her name's May Turner. Her father was my brother, and he practiced medicine in southern Illinois. He died about three years ago; his wife a few years earlier. May came here to Haddon. I wanted her to live with me—I thought she'd sort of brighten things up—but she had an idea she wanted to be independent, so she got a little apartment in the village where she is now. Then she decided she wanted to train as a nurse, though she's a little old for it and not temperamentally . . . Well, never mind that. She was training at Warwick Clinic, the biggest hospital near us, and a couple of weeks ago, or a little more, she happened to be alone in Emergency for a few minutes when an ambulance came in. She went out to see if she could help, and was standing back of the ambulance. The drive slopes there, and the brake didn't hold. She was pushed against the wall and crushed hard above the knees on both legs."

"Fractures?"

"No, surprisingly enough. The bruises have begun to clear up, but there's something more than that wrong with the right leg. I suspect she's damaged the femoral artery, maybe a blood clot—a thrombus—partly blocking the artery . . ."

"Traumatic arterial thrombosis with partial occlusion . . ."

Moore smiled slightly. "That's more or less what I suspect."

"Have you had an arteriogram?"

"No, just the original X-ray. There's something else I haven't told you. Something happened to her while she was in the hospital —not the accident, some kind of shock. She was leaving for good the next day—only staying her week out. . . . Here we are, here's the Republic House. If you don't mind a minute more, let's just sit here and I'll finish telling you . . ."

They had stopped along the curb, and Armstrong, looking to his right, saw a brick building, by no means large, with white columns and a porch. On the porch was a row of rocking chairs, some of them occupied, and all the occupants seemed greatly interested in the new arrival. It was then that David noticed, as he was to notice many times again in the days that followed, Moore's adroitness in not meeting eyes. And he realized, as he never had before, that in a small town where the doctor is known to everyone, some such technique is necessary or every appearance on the street would require an endless number of greetings.

Moore was saying, "I can't get her to talk about her nursing experience. She wasn't cut out for it . . ."

Made slightly uncomfortable by the watchers on the porch, David turned as much of his back on them as he could and settled himself to listen. Although the location was odd, this was a consultation. He did not know that his mien had become slightly portentous, or that he was frowning.

"I wouldn't care to attempt a diagnosis without an arteriogram."

"We can't do it in the hospital here, and as things stand now, you couldn't get her to go back to Warwick even for that. She's running away from life for some reason I don't know, and this accident is her excuse for it."

Armstrong repeated, "I would certainly feel an arteriogram would be necessary."

Having reached an impasse, they were both silent; then Moore sighed and said, "I'm afraid we sometimes have to make compromises with diagnostic techniques here in the country. You'll examine her anyway, as a first step, won't you? I wish you'd do that. Then we'll see what next, but she's developed an extreme fear of hospitals. She wouldn't stay in Warwick Hospital after her accident, and I'd have a time getting her to go back for any reason at all."

"Do you have office hours in the afternoon, sir?"

"Yes, one-thirty on."

Armstrong looked at his watch. "Good Lord, it's that now. What about your lunch?"

"The dairy bar will send me a sandwich. I'll pick you up for dinner. We'll have a look at the hospital tomorrow."

Armstrong was halfway out of the jeep. "I'm sorry, what did you say your niece's name is? And where do I find her?"

Moore was suddenly cheerful. "May Turner. Lives right around the corner, up a flight of stairs between the appliance store and a dress shop."

"I didn't bring a medical bag."

"You can take mine. I shan't be needing it during office hours. Drop over to the office—it's right across the street—and I'll give it to you. Thanks."

On the steps of the Republic House, traveling bag in hand, Armstrong paused to watch Moore make a bold U-turn around a traffic stanchion that bore a sign saying NO U-TURNS. Smiling, but resolved to keep out of the doctor's jeep as much as he could in future, he went on into the hotel.

The business section of Haddon was in the shape of an L, but so short in both directions that all of it could easily be seen from the corner. Looking back down Maple Street directly opposite the hotel, Armstrong saw an old building with a sign fastened to the bricks saying DR. EDWARD MOORE. At one side of this building was a shoe store, and at the other a small river flowed, to disappear under a stone bridge, the sound of the water audible above the traffic. The other branch of the L he found without surprise to be called Main Street, and here, on the side on which he was standing, was the white Vermont marble front of the bank. He assumed it to be the only bank, and did not even look for another. The face at least was new and modern in design, and walking toward it, Armstrong thought that, unlike every other building in the town, it was not country, but city-in-miniature, and he pushed open the glass door with some curiosity to see if this pretension would be consistent on the inside.

He was interested to learn, when he inquired at a teller's window, that the bank's president was named Timothy Stoner, a name that seemed to him to have a pleasantly authentic New England sound. And when Stoner appeared, tall, thin, sharp-featured, with dark-rimmed glasses resting on his high-bridged nose, Armstrong's first thought was that here was a stock character, so like the fiction concept of a country banker as to seem to be playing the part. His next was that this was entirely mistaken and that he could fill any role that required cold, shrewd intelligence.

"Mr. Stoner? I'm Dr. Armstrong."

"Glad to meet you. I heard you were coming to town. Come in, Doctor."

He led the way to his office, motioned to a chair beside his desk, sat down himself and swung his chair so that they were face to face. "What can I do for you?"

David began explaining the purpose of this call, aware that he was doing it badly and that while Stoner was listening he was thoughtfully sizing him up.

Armstrong having brought the preliminaries to a rather feeble halt, Stoner said, "I should be interested to know, Doctor, why you are considering the possibility of spending a year with us in Haddon. I do not mean to appear to pry into personal matters, but I should like to hear anything you would care to tell me."

"Some of the reasons are professional, some personal. I've felt, for one thing, that I was deficient in clinical experience and ability. Personally not good in my relations with patients, I mean."

Stoner rocked his swivel chair. "I suppose a surgeon tends to think of himself as having a one-time relationship with his patients —the one or two or three hours spent with him in the operating room and a few visits. Would you say that was true?"

"A good many tend to take that attitude, yes, but not all."

"And when they visit a patient in his room, they are checking up on their work, not on the patient." Stoner gave David his thin smile. "You see, I had an operation once. My surgeon clearly thought that, as a person, I was the responsibility of the medical man. You don't subscribe to that?"

"I'm not sure. I honestly don't know. One of the things I want to think out is just that—and as I say, I'm handicapped by not having had a great deal of clinical experience, compared to students of medicine. I thought perhaps a year in a country town, where, I assume, the doctor-patient relationship is closer than in a city, might not be amiss."

"I have a fancy—it's no more than that—that the character traits of a surgeon are not those to bring him close to his fellow men. I know, of course, that surgeons differ greatly in personality, but don't they, more or less, have this in common?"

"Perhaps you're right."

"I believe I was told you were specializing in vascular surgery?"

"Yes." David had come here for information, and so far he had been giving, not receiving, though it pleased him to think that he had not yielded very much.

Stoner swung his chair as though to indicate a break in the conversation at this point. When he turned back again he was smiling slightly.

"You came to talk chiefly about the hospital, I assume?"

David admitted this was so, and the smile, having served its purpose, vanished.

"Let me start by saying that in respect to medical matters, Haddon is not keeping up with the times. I don't know to what extent you are aware of the great changes taking place in country medicine . . ."

"I'm wholly ignorant of them, I'm afraid. Greater than in the city?"

"I believe so—greater and different in character. Rural medicine is becoming quite different from what it was a short time ago. You can't appreciate what is happening in rural medicine and Haddon's relation to it unless you know a little about what country medicine was in the past."

"The days of the horse-and-buggy doctor?"

"That's a phrase belonging to sixty, seventy years ago. I'm thinking of times closer to our own—say, when Moore began to practice."

Stoner was thoughtfully silent for a moment; then he said, "Excuse me," and leaning over his desk, spoke into a little black box. "I don't want to be disturbed for a little while. Please don't put any calls through." The box made sounds impossible for the human voice, and Stoner said, "Thank you."

When he turned back Stoner took his glasses off, paused to think, then turned his dim sight on Armstrong. "The old-time doctor, and by that I mean the kind of man who was already established when Moore came to town, saw his patients through all their ills, no matter what they were, and without regard to how well he was qualified to manage them. He was medical man and surgeon too—most country doctors still are to an extent. He had an office by himself, away from other doctors, and he worked alone, mostly, not consulting other doctors or referring his patients to anyone else. That was because a doctor earned less in those days, and he kept his patients to himself for fear some other doctor would get them.

"The old-timer didn't know much medicine—not nearly as much as Moore did when he came to town. He—the old-timer—diagnosed measles and typhoid by the smell, set fractures by feel and could tell scarlet fever from German measles for sure only if the soles of the feet peeled while the patient was getting well. Such laboratory work as he needed done—and he thought he needed very little—he did himself. He sent his patients to a hospital only as a last resort.

"Compared to doctoring like that, young Moore was modern and scientific—some thought needlessly so. Then, Warwick Clinic was a hospital the size Moore's is today. In those days, the road from here to Warwick wasn't paved, and if you wanted to get there at times of year when the mud was deep, you had to use a horse. A fair speed for a horse on good roads is six miles an hour, but when the roads weren't good you could get out of him maybe three—four at most. Warwick is thirty miles away. Moore thought Haddon had to have a hospital, and in those days he was right. But the town didn't see it that way, so he fixed one up himself. I suppose you've heard that part of the story?"

Armstrong nodded and shifted himself to a more relaxed position in his chair. Then he realized by Stoner's continued questioning look that the nod had not been seen, and said, "Dr. Moore told me about it."

"Times began to change. Better economic conditions at the back of it. Good roads, telephones even in remote farms, improved central laboratory facilities, a more active public health service, and so on. The younger men and the more limber-minded ones like Moore took full advantage of the changes as they came along —until change began to get too swift and too intricate for them to keep up. But most of them went on being solitary workers. Moore is essentially that today in spite of having associated himself with Perkins. He still handles all sorts of medical problems, including obstetrics. Doesn't send his patients to specialists very much, though I think his way of practicing medicine is more habit than anything else.

"But now some of the towns around us are getting a new set of young men, city-trained mostly, and with very different ideas. They are demanding still better hospitals and laboratories and greater differentiation in medical practice, and they're getting these things. They are so busy they don't have to compete for patients, and they don't have that habit of mind, anyway. They band together into town medical groups, health centers. They consult each other. They not only have their offices together; they buy equipment as a group that not one of them could afford singly."

Stoner paused to review his train of thought, and David said, "In the city—in New York, anyway—I think that patients make more demand on doctors than they used to."

"I believe that is even more true in the country and in towns like this. Not many years back, people around here didn't consult a doctor unless they couldn't possibly doctor themselves. Exceptions, of course, but that was the general way of doing things. Prosperity is at the bottom of the change. More people can afford a doctor and they see him oftener. Television and magazine articles have made them health-conscious, so to speak. They know more about the subject than they did, and they demand more. No, the revolution in rural medicine isn't confined to the doctors."

"I gather you think the changes aren't confined to rural Vermont."

"By no means. To the best of my knowledge, something like it is going on in rural communities all over the country."

"About the hospital . . ."

Stoner swerved his chair sharply toward the desk and groped on its top for his glasses. Finding them, he put them on with a swift, almost peremptory gesture, and the look he turned on David was once more sharp, judgmatic and cold. "The hospital has passed its usefulness," he said.

"I assume you mean in its present condition. Dr. Moore intimated financial difficulties and the need to modernize . . ."

"I mean that under present conditions, Haddon has no need for a hospital. There is no justification for having one with Warwick so near, and the sooner it ceases to exist, the better for the town."

David felt roused by an instinctive, unfounded and surprisingly violent opposition to this view. Stoner said, "You've visited the hospital?" and David confined himself to shaking his head.

"We can talk about it more intelligently when you have. The point I am making is that this town would be better off with no hospital than one that is becoming progressively antiquated and second-rate. It is blocking medical progress."

David, still feeling a need to control himself, said, "If it weren't a privately owned hospital—if it were taken over by the town . . . I don't know how such things are managed . . ."

"It might come to a vote at Town Meeting, when Moore is finally convinced he can't run it any more. I would oppose such a move. Haddon doesn't need and shouldn't have a hospital."

Armstrong, feeling a pressure to say many things, drew a deep breath, saw the present uselessness of saying any of them, left them unsaid, and stated the feeble residue of his ideas, to the effect that he supposed the death of his hospital would break Moore's heart.

"The town owes Moore a great deal. I admire him. I'm even personally fond of him. But he is getting old. Ladd is old. Perkins isn't young, especially for a surgeon. But I know you are thinking about yourself in relation to this question of the hospital."

David, who had not gone so far in his thoughts, took a hasty mental leap and nodded. "A surgeon has to have a hospital to work in. When do you—"

"You are thinking in terms of a stay of no more than a year, I hear. The hospital would survive that long, though conceivably not much longer. I don't think that phase of it need trouble you. But you ought to know some of the background I've been describing before you commit yourself."

Stoner brought both hands down on the arms of his chair, and Armstrong, recognizing this as the classic signal that an interview has ended, got to his feet.

"I'm afraid I have taken up a great deal of your time."

"Not at all. These are matters of great concern to the community. I have spent so much time giving you the medical background of Haddon that I have not said that I sincerely hope that you will see your way clear to coming to Haddon. Come in again— any time you like."

David clasped the long-fingered, slightly damp hand that was held out to him and self-consciously departed.

VIII

DAVID FOUND DR. MOORE'S OFFICE in the old brick building, behind the offices of a real estate firm. A dark hall led to the waiting room, where a number of people were silently sitting, all with expressions of introspective patience that their interest in David's arrival did not wholly dissipate. The light in the room, that came from tall, narrow windows, was dim, the furnishings old and shabby but comfortable, and with the look of having served so long that they had conformed wholly to their purpose. The sound of the river, flowing against the foundations of the building just below the windows, was loud. David looked around for a nurse, or an office girl, remembered that Moore had said that there was neither, and was about to sit down to wait when the door to the inner office opened and Moore appeared.

When he saw David, Moore smiled, his tired face lighting with pleasure. He spoke, not to David but to the other waiting people.

"This is Dr. Armstrong, the young fellow I'm trying to persuade to come here to practice. He wants to borrow my bag—it won't take a minute. Come in, Dave."

There was a responsive stir, and an old fellow with a leathery face and woodsmen's boots said something in a voice gruff with shyness. David made a stiff, self-conscious bow and followed Moore into his office.

The inner office seemed to him about what might be expected from the appearance of the waiting room. There was one window, open to the voice of the river, an old rolltop desk, a bookcase full of untidily placed books, dating—by the looks of them—from Moore's medical-school days. Through a partly open door there was a view of a small surgery beyond. The place seemed to David to fit Moore like the clothes he wore, comfortably and untidily.

He was saying with an air of pleased proprietorship. "I've had this place for more than thirty years. There's a room the other side of the surgery that I've been thinking we could fix up for you. Bigger than this one. The real estate people are using it to store records in, but I'm pretty sure they'd let us have it."

He took his bag off the seat of a chair and interrupted David's thanks by saying, "All right," laid a hand on his shoulder and good-naturedly propelled him toward the door.

The medical bag was worn, bulging, and so heavy that it seemed Moore must carry half his medical equipment around with him. Carrying it down the street made Armstrong feel self-conscious, the more so since he felt that everyone he passed recognized it as Moore's. In his own practice he had little use for a bag, since he seldom made house calls, but nevertheless he had one. It was not a bag in the traditional sense but an attaché case like a Madison Avenue executive's, and he had designed the fittings himself. When he carried it, he was indistinguishable from hundreds of other preoccupied young men on the streets of New York, which was exactly what he had intended.

At this hour of day the town was crowded with people, hurrying as though they were afraid they could not buy all they wanted before closing time. Prosperity was in the air. Among the tightly packed cars nosed in to the curb there was scarcely one that was more than five years old; the store windows were filled with merchandise that looked expensive, and citified.

In a vacant space he came on a large bulletin board headed TOWN EVENTS, and, struck by the curious mixture of rural and sophisticated in all he had so far seen, he stopped to read the carefully chalked announcements. A bake sale by the ladies of the Congregational Church to be held (how odd!) in the shoe store. A supper at the Beaver Meadow Grange to raise money for the local fire department. A concert by the Haddon High School band. The arrival of the Bloodmobile on Thursday. . . . A country community in transition, on the way to becoming, not suburban, like the areas that surround and live on big cities, but something unprecedented in the American scene. Producing unique problems in the course of the change, he had no doubt, and among them unique and very interesting problems in medical care. . . .

Quite suddenly he discovered the improbability of being where he was—walking along an unfamiliar street, carrying a medical bag not his own, bound on an errand that had only a remote relation to his familiar life. And he experienced one of those uncomfortable moments of self-realization such as came to him sometimes at a concert or in a medical lecture, that had nothing to do with what was going on, but in which he would be overwhelmed by a strong sense of his own being. It was unpleasant in the extreme, and it made his nerves tingle.

With relief he found he had arrived at the flight of stairs that led to May Turner's apartment.

The stairs, though wide, were steep and dark, and he took them in a rush until, halfway up, he heard music and slowed down to listen. The music was coming from above, with something in the tone quality that made him sure it was coming from a radio, and he recognized the closing pages of the César Franck D-Minor Symphony. This was music that, to his mind, had been worn threadbare with too much repetition, but here, heard unexpectedly in the semidarkness of the stairs, it had renewed its beauty. On the landing at the top he stood still to listen. He waited for the final note, and waited a moment longer for the echo in his mind to fade; then he knocked on the varnished door.

A light voice answered him, and putting down a sudden shyness, he turned the doorknob and went in. May was on the couch, her hand still on the small radio on the table beside her, and she smiled at him in the disarming way of those rare people who expect every stranger to be friendly. He smiled too, without thinking about it, and came into the room with sudden assurance. She made an attractive picture with the Renoir-like lighting from the windows on her dark curls, the flowering house plants on the windowsill beside her, and the bright colors of the coverlet, but he was careful to keep from betraying his appreciation by the tone of his voice.

"I'm Dr. Armstrong, Miss Turner. Dr. Moore asked me to come in and see you."

To his own ears his manner of saying this sounded stilted. It was the old difficulty, the old inability to meet people halfway, and he thought he saw something in her that had been advancing to meet him come to a halt. She looked down and said with constraint, "Yes, Uncle Ed told me you were coming."

He said, "Was the music coming from the radio?" and was at once ashamed of the inanity of that remark.

"There's a station in Boston that plays good music every day at this time. Won't you take your coat off, Doctor?"

He threw his coat over the back of a chair, gave a quick look around the neat, sparsely furnished room and brought another chair to the side of the couch. He would have liked to say something light and pleasant that would make her smile again, but nothing occurred to him. She gave him no help, watching him with her head tilted to one side, alert and a little wary. He abandoned the effort and said with a slight frown, "Dr. Moore told me that the bumper of an ambulance struck you when the brakes gave way."

"Not the bumper. It was an old, high ambulance from one of the small towns and it had a sort of step that you pulled down when the door opened. It came out farther than the bumper."

"Then that explains why you were injured above the knees and not below. I couldn't visualize it."

"Yes, and the driveway sloped, so when the brakes didn't hold it caught me."

"And you went out to help because you were the student nurse on duty and there was no orderly or doctor in Emergency at the time?"

"Yes. There's supposed to be an orderly there all the time, but he was needed in X-ray, so I was there alone. I called in to have the doctor paged, then I went to see what I could do, and it happened."

Armstrong thought about this a moment, puzzling over the scene that was in his mind, wanting to see exactly what had happened.

"Let's have a look at that injury," he said in a most professional tone, and he made an ineffectual effort to arrange the quilt and her flowered housecoat.

She helped him without embarrassment, and exposed the ugly bruises. As he bent over to examine them, she said, "They're better, really they are," and he heard, as Dr. Moore had, not her assurance but her anxiety.

As Dr. Moore had done, he felt for the pulses of the arteries in

115

her feet, comparing them. In her right leg he found the popliteal artery that is the extension below the knee of the femoral artery, pressed it with his thumb and compared it with the pulse in the other leg. He pressed with his fingertips on the femoral artery in the groin where its pulsation is most easily felt, taking care to distinguish between the lifting throb of the artery and the more diffuse beat of his own pulse. In the end he suspected, as Moore did, that a thrombus or blood clot, attached to the inner wall of the artery, was impeding the flow of blood to the lower part of the leg. He felt certain that an arteriogram should be made, and that the rapid series of pictures, made while a dye flowed through the artery, would show the clot, its size and its location. With that information, the removal of the clot would not be difficult. He pulled the covers back in place and faced the anxiety in her eyes, hoping she would see and believe in the perfect candor in his own.

"This is nothing that can't be fixed up all right, with some co-operation from you. I'll have a talk with Dr. Moore. Now I want to give you a quick general check-over."

He saw he had not lessened her anxiety. She was clutching the edge of the quilt in both hands, and her eyes were dark with fright—far more fright than was warranted, he felt—but she said nothing.

He opened Moore's bag and, to his surprise, found the contents well organized. He made his examination swiftly, with practiced care, and repacked the bag. Then he sat down in the chair by the couch.

"You've always been pretty healthy, haven't you?"

"Oh, yes."

"You still are, as far as I can see." He remembered that Moore had said that she was using this accident in some sense as an escape from life. Thinking about this, he studied her thoughtfully. Under his steady, impersonal gaze her eyes fell, he saw a flush color her face, and she began with the tip of one finger to trace the pattern of stitching on the quilt. He thought he could feel the disturbance, the near panic of her emotions. At a loss, he continued to watch her in silence, the feeling of his own inadequacy growing stronger as he sought for a question that might give him a clue to what it was that she was hiding. Finally he asked the only one he could think of.

"Why did you want to be a nurse?"

She gravely considered his question as though it were one she had never asked herself.

"I suppose because Father and Uncle Ed were doctors. I guess it wasn't a very good reason."

"When you get this leg fixed up, you could go back and finish your training."

"Oh, *no!*"

He waited, and after a moment she said, "I couldn't go on being a nurse. I simply couldn't. It was all a mistake. Before I got hurt it was all settled that I was to leave—the next day, actually."

"But why?"

"I don't want to talk about it. I don't want to see the inside of a hospital ever again." She was silent for a moment, leaning back against the pillows with her eyes shut. Abruptly she sat up and stared at him with wide, terrified eyes. "You and Uncle Ed aren't thinking that you're going to send me to a hospital about this leg, are you? Because I won't go. I won't."

"Don't you want to get well again?"

"You *are* going to try to send me to a hospital. I won't go to one —not even to Uncle Ed's . . ." She covered her face with her hands and burst into tears.

He sat and watched her for some minutes, feeling extreme discomfiture. Finally he said, "Has Dr. Moore suggested it?"

She shook her head.

"Then don't you think you'd better wait to get upset until he does?"

She took her hands away from her face. Tears still filled her eyes, and her lashes were stuck together in points. She rubbed them with the sides of her fingers in a way that made her seem to him very young and vulnerable.

"I'm sorry. I shouldn't have . . ."

"I didn't mean to upset you. Can I get you something? A glass of water?"

"Oh—could you make us some coffee?"

Her tone was pleased and eager. Astonished by the suddenness of her change of mood, he stared at her. Then he laughed.

"Sure. Coming up." He stood up with alacrity.

"There's some you could warm up, unless you're very particular."

"I'm not. You know the kind of coffee that usually falls to a doctor's lot."

The kitchenette was small, but well ordered and very clean, and while he assembled things on a painted tray, waiting for the coffee to show signs of warmth, he thought about her. The blood clot must be removed as soon as possible, and any tendency on her part to resist, to use this injury as a means of withdrawing from life, must be overridden. Moore's job. And there came between him and the flowers on the coffee cups an ugly vision of what she would certainly be in a few years if she were allowed to hide herself away: lines of pain cut deeply into a sallow face . . . irritable with suffering, voice thin and querulous . . . all the instincts of a naturally warm and eager nature leached away . . . her only interest outside herself perhaps her plants on the windowsill; in his mind's eye he saw them as large-leaved, overnurtured, noxious, her thin hands moving anxiously among them.

Oppressed by the vividness of this picture, he did not feel inclined to talk, and he drank his coffee almost in silence with occasional glances at her to reassure himself. The silence seemed not to trouble her. In fact, while they sat there raising their cups slowly from time to time, exchanging scarcely a word, a curious thing was happening to them both. They seemed to be progressing with great speed toward a common feeling of ease and fellowship, of understanding and even of regard. To such an extent was this true that when, later, he looked at his watch and began gathering up the coffee things, he was aware that they had dispensed with much that normally impedes the first stages of a friendship.

While he was rinsing the cups and setting them to drain, he paused a moment to be surprised and pleased with himself that something so uncharacteristic could happen to him. Offhand, he would have said that she was not "his type" at all, emotional, quickly changing in her moods, a vitality that seemed equally strong in all of them. And he let his thoughts dwell on the contrast of all this to the delicate bleached style of Maryanne.

When he went back, May was running a comb through her short black curls. Standing beside the couch, looking down at her, he said, "I'll report to Dr. Moore. We must get you fixed up without any more delay," and he frowned at her because he meant this so emphatically.

She laid down the comb and held out her hand. "Thank you for coming."

As he went down the stairs, the heavy bag bumping against his leg, he thought she knew quite well that he would like to be asked to come again, and that it was from an impulse of sheer mischief that she had not suggested it.

IX

THE UPSTAIRS ROOMS of the Republic House were old-fashioned, unlovely, and clean. But Armstrong was untroubled by the unattractiveness of his room, for, like so many people interested in music, decor had little meaning for him. While he was hurriedly making himself ready to meet Dr. Moore, he scarcely saw his surroundings, for he was preoccupied with the varied events of this long day and in reviewing the report he intended to make about May Turner's condition.

These thoughts were interrupted, however, by the minor difficulty of fitting the plug of his electric razor into the socket, which was part of an old-fashioned light fixture high above the washbowl. And the moment he achieved this he found that while he was occupied in this way an idea had moved in. He was sufficiently startled by this phenomenon to examine it even before he turned to the idea itself. "Moved in," he thought, was just the term to describe what had happened, as though his subconscious mind had evolved this idea and matured it while his conscious thoughts were elsewhere occupied. Then, at the first moment when his thinking slackened—while he was jabbing at the socket with the prongs of the razor plug—his subconscious shoved the idea into the light of day.

"I'll be damned," he said, staring at his image in the glass and seeing instead May Turner restored to health, her living room equipped with the paraphernalia of a doctors' telephone answering service. The equipment might be installed right away, to be operated from her couch, and the feeling of being useful might help Moore to convince her that she must have the clot removed. "Perfect!" he said, and turned on the razor. He instantly shut it off again as he realized that he had not appreciated the real quality of the job his subconscious had been doing for him. What he found himself considering, and with great astonishment, was, in addition to the answering service, a two-way radio connection between May Turner's room and the doctors' cars, a radio telephone on which she could talk to them or they to her within whatever radius such things could be made to operate.

With a buoyant spirit, he began to shave, the industrious buzz of the razor a pleasant accompaniment to his thoughts. She needed something to occupy her mind. This could be it. She wanted to be part of her family's medical tradition. Again, this could be it—and at the same time keep her free of actual contact with illness and suffering for which her nature did not fit her.

More pleased with himself than was warranted, since he had not in any real sense "thought" this up, he hurried through his dressing. Five minutes later he rattled the door key in the loose old-fashioned lock, thrust it in his pocket and made for the stairs.

Dr. Moore, turning over battered magazines on the lobby table, heard Armstrong's precipitate descent of the uncarpeted stairs and looked up, thinking that this was not such an old-young man as he strove to be. At the thought the lines of strain in his face softened with pleasure.

"Hi, Dave."

"I'm sorry to be late, sir. I've been to see May Turner."

"Tell me about it while we eat. The meeting's at eight so we don't have to hurry, but we don't want to waste time."

Moore propelled him toward the dining room. David was aware that everyone in the vicinity was watching with expressions of intense curiosity on their faces, from which he judged that these people, and perhaps the whole town, knew about the meeting. The big dining room was almost full, and while they were waiting to be shown their places by a young woman wearing the same kind of hostess smile that can be seen in eating places all over America, he thought he would not like living so in the public eye as a country doctor seemed to do. Moore too seemed to be aware that they were being watched by people from other tables, for he said in a low voice, "Fifteen years ago—ten even—there wouldn't have been this agitation about there being no doctors in town. They'd have accepted it as part of the general hardship of their lot. People's attitudes toward doctors have changed—more demanding, more knowledgeable. . . . She's got a table for us over there. Let's go."

When they were seated and the hostess had moved away, he said, "What about May Turner? What did you think? Has she got a blood clot in there?"

"I wouldn't want to say without an arteriogram, but it looks like it."

"I'm not up on such things. You open up the artery and take it out, I suppose."

"Yes, and patch the artery where you go in, either with plastic or a graft taken from a vein."

"How long can we delay operating?"

"There's no reason for delay, is there? The sooner the better. The clot turns to fibrous tissue after a while and when that's happened you cut away all you can. Taking out a thrombus of long standing is something fairly new, but I've assisted Fairchild at two or three of them. However, no point in waiting. She's having a certain amount of pain and the leg isn't getting the circulation it should."

"Nevertheless, I think it should be postponed as long as possible."

"Why?" Aware that he had spoken more peremptorily than a junior should speak to a senior, he softened his question. "Why do you want to delay?"

Armstrong's opinion of Moore's professional standing was not based on what he had seen of Moore himself but on the whole category, country doctor. The belief that country doctors were inferior to city men in skill and knowledge—that by the nature of things this had to be so—was deeply imbedded in his mind. He never questioned it, but he believed in maintaining the forms of politeness under all circumstances. He thought this the only attitude that stood any chance of surviving the strain of working with one's fellow men, and so after a second's thought he softened his question still further. "I'd be interested to know, sir."

"Her nurse's training was a traumatic experience. She should never have forced herself to stay with it as long as she did, but she has plenty of willpower—too much for her emotional makeup to support. The trauma—whatever it was—has had the effect of making her willing to be an invalid. Or that's the way it looks to me, anyway."

"Why not fix up her physical disability and treat her withdrawal as a separate psychiatric problem?"

"I'm pretty sure that if she's left alone she'll recover her emotional balance in her own way. If we were to force an operation on her in the emotional state she's in, I think she might have a breakdown she'd never recover from. No, I don't want to force her."

"To me it seems that the better sequence would be to get her well physically, and let the rest follow—naturally, if possible, if not by therapy. Or put her in touch with a psychiatrist right now."

"That last's not practicable. It's financially out of reach for her or for me, and anyway, there isn't a trained psychiatrist nearer than Warwick. No, if you think postponing the operation for a year or a year and a half would be feasible—even if you don't think it desirable—I believe that's what we should do."

Armstrong started to protest again, realized he had pressed the matter as far as, under the circumstances, he could, and gave his attention to the soup. It was the same noontime soup grown slightly richer as it neared the bottom of the pot, but he was hungry and uncritical. After leaving a decent interval for traces of their disagreement to vanish, he told Moore about his great idea. Moore was interested and delighted.

"It would give her something to do," he said, "and be a real benefit to us. Also, she's a real favorite in the town. It would be good public relations for us doctors. Do you have any idea what those gadgets cost—the two-way radiophones, or whatever you call them?"

"No, but they must be expensive. At a guess, a thousand dollars, maybe."

Moore's face clouded, and David remembered the eternal struggle he had to keep the hospital above water financially.

"That seems like a lot of money, but I suppose you're right." Then he brightened. "Maybe, the mood the selectmen are in, they'd agree to the town paying part of it. Maybe all the cost of installation. Dave, I think you've had you a real thought, and now I can face those old fellows with something constructive to offer. Good boy!"

For the rest of the meal Moore chatted cheerfully enough. At the end, when he laid his napkin on the table and pushed back his chair, he said, "I've got a young fellow coming over from Warwick to cover for us while the meeting's going on. Office hours are canceled, of course, but just in case of emergency—"

"But you'll all be right here in town, won't you?"

"I'm leaning over backward in case one of those three cantankerous so-and-sos . . . We serve the town for damn near all our professional lives, and then . . . Well, never mind."

"I'd have been glad to help out."

"I never thought of it. But it would have been kind of an imposition, your first night here. This young doctor's name is Ted Barlow, and he's finishing up his residency in medicine at Warwick, and when he's through I hope he'll come and settle here. If you haven't anything else to do tonight, why don't you come to the office and meet him?"

Moore was about to stand up and Armstrong was preparing to follow him when Moore gestured him back in his seat. "Wait a minute. Those are the selectmen. Let's let them leave ahead of us, the bastards."

Three men had risen from a table at the far end of the dining room and were coming down the narrow strip of carpeting toward them. Moore had turned in his chair and was pretending not to see them, but Armstrong looked at them with a good deal of curiosity. Two of them were short, wizened men of any age past fifty, who looked like brothers. They had worn, bitter faces with skin the color and texture of too-long-stored apples, and the business suits they wore seemed not quite right on them, as though they wore them only for funerals and important occasions such as this.

The third wore his clothes more naturally and seemed as though he might be the owner of a store. His thin face had the look of a sardonic eagle. Collectively, these men appeared tenacious and morally strong; individually, they gave the impression of finding life a hard and crusty business.

To Armstrong's surprise the first of them, who had a toothpick in his mouth, made remote acknowledgment of his presence, a slight motion of the head, a slight, soundless movement of the lips, no warming of the eyes. The second and then the third did the same, and by this time Armstrong was half standing, clutch-

124

ing his napkin, confused by the force turned on him, and surprised by his own instinctive reaction of respect. They passed and he sat down again. As Moore had said, bastards undoubtedly, but there was also a curious feeling that took him some moments to analyze and that in the end came to him as a conviction which, oddly, gave him personal satisfaction. It was that, in this Vermont town, government of the people, by the people, and for the people had not perished.

He remembered that these were the men who would preside over the Town Meeting if at some future time the fate of the hospital were to be decided there. Now that he had seen them, the whole question became more real and immediate. He was still thinking about them and about his growing perception of the town's personality when, a few moments later, he and Moore crossed the street on the way to Moore's office.

The door to the waiting room, which had a sign on it saying NO OFFICE HOURS TONIGHT, was open, and inside three men were standing—three as widely different men, Armstrong thought, as he could well imagine. Moore introduced the oldest first, Dr. Ladd, a tall, carefully dressed man who Armstrong remembered hearing was in his eighties and still actively in practice. He must long ago have acquired the doctor's ability to seem to pay attention while his thoughts were busy elsewhere, and his attitude still expressed this. But he seemed not to care to make the pretense any more, and after the first word or two, which he received in silence, his thoughts visibly wandered.

The second was Dr. Perkins, who was clearly angry and who said "Hullo" with a carry-over of belligerence in it and at once turned to Moore without bothering to shake hands with David.

"The more I think about this outrage, Ed, the madder I get. If these three bastards start anything, I'm going to ask them where they think the town would be without us two—us three—looking after their blasted little ills."

"I hope you won't take that tone, Howard."

"Why not? I tell you, Ed—"

"We agreed you wouldn't—remember?"

Armstrong, embarrassed, moved tactfully out of hearing toward the fourth man, who had also withdrawn some distance.

"Dr. Barlow? I'm David Armstrong."

"Oh, yes. I heard you were here. I'm glad to meet you."

Dr. Barlow was a young man to whom all the trite phrases used to describe promising young medical men amply applied. He was clean-cut, serious, studious-looking, and with the stamp of a good medical school visibly on him. Armstrong, recognizing these indicators of fellowship with approval, liked him on sight. They shook hands, and—Barlow having much the same reaction to Armstrong —a good deal of cordiality and meaning went into the handshake on both sides.

They walked, as though by agreement, to the window, where both stood with their hands in their pockets gazing out into the falling darkness. Moore, looking around to see what had become of them, thought that, from the rear, they looked amusingly alike. Both of a height which could not be called tall, Barlow slightly broader across the shoulders, both in dark, well-pressed suits, with well-disciplined hair, well-polished shoes. And well-polished minds to match, Moore thought with a smile.

A moment later the three older doctors left, three big men tramping heavily out in silence. Turning to watch them go, Barlow sang under his breath, "Onward, Christian soldiers," and David laughed, instantly felt guilty and said, "It's a shame. I hope they'll make out all right."

"Oh, they will, but it won't be pleasant. Let's go in the other room near the telephone."

With the older doctors gone, there was a feeling of lifted constraint. Barlow tried the top light in Moore's office, found the glare unpleasant and switched it off in favor of the gooseneck lamp on the desk that threw a circle of radiance on the telephone as though to enshrine it. Barlow dropped into Moore's swivel chair, tipped it back and put his feet on the desk.

"I hear you're considering practice here?"

Armstrong seated himself more decorously. "Considering, yes, but only for a year. Rural medicine is different from anything I expected. I don't really know what I expected, but nothing like the reality."

"Don't take Haddon as typical. They're behind the times here."

"So I understand. Moore told me you're finishing your medical residency at Warwick. Do you intend to practice in the country?"

"Yes. That's why I chose Warwick, as a matter of fact. I went to Harvard Med . . ."

David almost said aloud, "I thought so."

". . . interned at Mass. General. I'm married, and my wife and I didn't want to raise a family in the city on what I'd make starting out. We haven't begun the family yet, but I finish my residency in June."

"I should think you'd find getting started in the country considerably harder financially than in the city. I gather your fees would be four dollars an office visit and five dollars a house call. Right?"

"Right, but remember the number of patients you're likely to have because of the doctor shortage—say twenty, thirty a day, if you're any good, and even if you're not. Vermont doctors pay the second highest income tax in the country. And all your expenses are less. You don't have to keep up the same standard of appearances as in the city. You don't have to have a swank office, or dress as well, or drive so good a car. In fact, you'd better not. You live in a house with lots of grounds for the children instead of a small apartment. The schools are better and there isn't the delinquency problem."

"All things I haven't thought about. I'm not married."

Barlow pulled a crumpled pack of cigarettes out of his pocket. "Being a surgeon, you don't smoke, I suppose?" David shook his head. Barlow lit one, then held it up and looked at it.

"I figure cancer's my own problem. There's a pathologist at Warwick who says, 'Send me a piece of lung tissue and I'll tell you whether the donor smokes or not.' I just try not to inhale. Now, another thing about rural practice. By tradition the doctor is an important man in the town. He's respected and listened to. He has real influence, even as a young man. How many city doctors ever get to have that sort of position in their city?"

"None, I guess. But the thing that bothers me most about country practice is the thought that you might have to see thirty patients a day. How can you do a good job medically on so many? You can't. It's impossible."

"Look at it this way." Barlow's feet came off the desk and he leaned forward earnestly. "Most of those patients wouldn't get any

127

care to speak of if there weren't a doctor doing the best he could. You just have to figure out ways to spread yourself out thinner. All the doctors in a town should form a group, make a clinic out of it, buy equipment like X-ray and fluoroscope in common, one office nurse, one billing system."

"Group medicine was a dirty word not so long ago."

"It's the only answer to the doctor shortage."

The telephone rang, startling them both. Armstrong listened to the tones of a woman's voice, strident with anxiety, and to Barlow explaining in a kind, interested way that if little Tom had eaten six doughnuts and a glass of chocolate milk, fried fish, fried potatoes and cold baked beans for supper, and then thrown them up, it was simply nature taking her revenge. Hanging up, he said, "Country kids simply aren't what they used to be."

"What do you suppose is going on at that meeting?"

"The doctors are having it rough, you can be sure of that. And in a way, they deserve it."

"I suppose so, but I hate to think of Moore taking a beating. If ever there was a conscientious man, I'd say he's it."

"You like him, don't you?"

"Enormously."

"He needs the help of someone like you."

"Or you."

"Or should we say, *and* me?"

"If there were two of us we might get something done."

"But you're only thinking about a year and I'm not through at Warwick until June."

"Where is this damn meeting? The Town Hall?"

"No, in a vacant room up over the hardware store just down the street."

"There's a dairy bar open at the corner. Why don't I get us some coffee?"

"I could use it."

The large room over the hardware store was unfurnished except for a battered table and a stack of wooden folding chairs against the wall. One of the three selectmen was picking up the chairs, opening them and setting them down at random. His name was Jake Miller, he was proprietor of the store below, and the racket he was making in the process of opening the chairs reverberated in the empty room.

In a corner, a radiator, just turned on, was pounding loudly.

Under cover of the noise, Perkins said to Moore, "Clever of the bastards to have the meeting here instead of the Town Hall, so it's unofficial and doesn't have to go on the record."

Moore nodded without replying. Selectman Miller put a chair by the table, sat down, and looked all around the room as though an audience filled the empty spaces. Perkins said, "Evening, Jake," and laughed. The laugh startled Moore until he remembered that Miller was scheduled with Perkins for a small but intimate piece of surgical repair. Miller gave Perkins a look of hatred, and put some papers on the table. The two other selectmen, Lund and Whittacker, put chairs to left and right of the table, and Miller watched them as though what they were doing was of importance. They were the only ones present who had taken off their coats, for the room was cold. Moore sat down facing the table and Perkins moved around restlessly, his hand in his pockets. Ladd took a chair, very slowly carried it away from the others and put it down by the wall, as though he wanted to imply that he had not the same relation to the proceedings as the others. Everyone watched the old man, waiting, and Moore thought, he shouldn't have been made to come here tonight. He's too old. He's outlived his medical generation. He's history.

Ladd settled on his chair with a sigh, spread his delicate old hands on his knees and fixed his gaze on space. Miller ceased to watch him and said, "Well, I guess we don't need to consider like this was a formal meeting, so we'll just begin. I don't aim to mince words. On the morning of Wednesday, September twenty-third, a workman, a janitor, I believe, of the Silver Springs Machine Tool Company, fell—I'm not sure how—"

Perkins said, "The damn fool had crawled out a fifth-floor window, as I heard it, and was trying to sit on a flagpole!"

"Doesn't matter how he fell," the selectman named Whittacker said, and shut his mouth in a way that reminded Moore of a large turtle he had once carried to the side of a road to save from the wheels of passing cars.

Miller said reprovingly, "It's important to get these things straight. Now, he fell off this flagpole out a fifth—"

Outside, on the wooden stairway, there were the sounds of rapid, emphatic steps coming up the stairs, and as all eyes but Ladd's turned in that direction, Perkins said sharply, "Who the hell is that?"

"I asked Mr. Moriseau, president of the plant, to be present, since he has an interest in the medical setup here."

Moore said, "I'm not sure that was wise, Jake," and the door was opened by a man in his early fifties who nodded to Moore and Miller, and looked around as though preparing himself to take the situation in hand. Moore knew him only slightly, for though the hospital cared for the plant's employees, Moriseau took his personal ills to the doctors at Warwick. Moore had long ago put him in the numerous category of those who, having discovered in the war the usefulness of a military manner, carried it over into civilian life.

"Sorry to be late," he said in a hearty voice that carried no suggestion of regret. "Glad to see you didn't wait for me."

He went up to the table and held his hand out to Miller, not quite as other men shake hands, but as though the hand were an object of value. Miller rose to take it, and Lund and Whittacker, when their turns came, also rose. Moriseau turned to the doctors.

"Hullo, Moore." He offered his hand in a different way, man-to-man. "Good evening, Dr. Perkins." He glanced at Ladd, who had shut his eyes and was sitting motionless except for the slight rise and fall of the gold watch chain across his vest, and said in a louder voice, intended to wake him if he were sleeping, "I don't believe I've ever had the pleasure of meeting Dr. Ladd." The old man opened his eyes and said, "Evening." He pronounced it in the Vermont way that was not native to him, "Eve-*nin*," and the corner of Moore's mouth twitched with a suppressed smile.

"Well, where were you?" Moriseau said with a sort of generalized affability.

He swung a chair around in a way that put it a little in advance of Moore's, sat down, dragged up another chair and rested his feet on a rung. "It's cold in here."

"I have just stated that a man—I believe his name is—was—Truelove?"

"That's right. Janitor."

"Fell from the fifth floor and was seriously injured."

"Came hurtling down right past my manager's window. Tree broke his fall so he wasn't killed right then, but he was a bloody mess. I wasn't in the plant at the time, thank God."

"And your manager telephoned to Dr. Moore, who had left for the airport on the way to New York."

"Phoned the hospital and got the head nurse. I don't know her name—the one built like a slat with a bit of plaster sticking to it."

"Edna Judson," Moore put in.

Miller leaned forward and made an effort to regain control of the meeting. "Edna Judson seems to have done all she could. Everything she could. I believe I speak for the three of us when I say we think no blame should attach to her." Miller turned to Whittacker and Lund and they both nodded. "Dr. Perkins went over with her everything she did and I got a written report covering it from him."

Moore, in surprise, turned to look at Perkins who was standing, hands in coat pockets, a little behind, and Perkins made a slight affirmative motion of his head. Miller went on speaking.

"I have the report here." He laid his hand, fingers spread out, on the papers in front of him. "I myself took this report to Dr. Perry, chief surgeon at Warwick, for his opinion. He said that Edna— Edna Judson—had done everything a trained nurse could do, considering she was not a doctor, so . . ."

"So," Moriseau said, "we can leave her out of it and get on with this business." He took a bunch of keys on a chain out of his pocket and began twirling the chain around his finger and untwirling it. The clatter of the keys was like a projection of everyone's jangled nerves, and Miller stared at them reproachfully, sighed and resumed.

"Edna's first act was to—"

Moriseau kicked away the chair in front of him and stood up, the key chain hanging by his side.

"Look here, Miller, excuse me, but let's cut this short. O.K.? We came here to discuss one thing—why there weren't any doctors who could be reached when a man was dying, and what kind of guarantee you doctors can give that the same thing won't happen again." He gave Miller a hard look and began pacing up and down behind Moore's chair, the bunch of keys clicking with each step. Miller too rose and leaned his hands on the table.

"All right, Mr. Moriseau." He looked at the three doctors slowly, one after the other, and said, "Well—why?"

Perkins came a few steps forward. "Why what? Why did the man die, or why couldn't we be reached?"

The selectman named Lund began to move his jaw as though he had a chew of tobacco in his mouth, and Ladd wearily leaned his head back against the wall and shut his eyes. Moore said "Howard" under his breath, deprecatingly.

Miller said, "You know what I mean, Doc, and you know it damn well. You three have got the health of the people, the well-being of the community, in your hands. You're the town doctors, and—"

"What is this you're talking about?" Perkins said. "Socialized medicine at the town level? Well, I'm not having any. And another thing I'm not having is interference by three . . ."

He left his sentence incomplete and looked from one to the other of the selectmen with contempt. Moore said "Howard" again.

"I've been here fifteen years, Ed Moore around thirty, Ladd . . ."

Perkins looked toward Dr. Ladd who opened his eyes, said, "Never figured it up," and closed them again.

"During that time none of us has ever turned away a patient. Most of our days off we work. In all the time we've been here we've not one of us had a real vacation."

Moore looked up at him. "I took four days off when I was married. Went to a medical convention with my wife. And I could have cut this New York trip shorter by maybe half a day. Howard, nobody's accusing us of not working hard enough."

"They've come to take us for granted. Apparently they have to be reminded what they're getting. Not one of us, including Dr. Ladd, who isn't young—"

"Eighty-four come March."

"—has ever failed to answer a night call. We each of us take care of quite a few charity cases, and do it free because we don't have time to do the Goddam paper work to collect from the government. Now what happens? Ed is on his way to New York, Dr. Ladd was way off in the country at an unusual hour for him, and I had an emergency call at a time I'm usually in my office, so this thing happens and we can't be reached. Did it ever happen before? Is it ever likely to happen again? No! And I refuse to be treated like a criminal because, unfortunately, it did happen just once." Perkins opened his coat, pulled a folded paper out of his pocket, and walking up to the table, slapped it down. "There's the autopsy report on Truelove. Came in the afternoon mail. You won't be able to read the medical language, but it means no doctor on earth could have saved him. It's a miracle he lived to get to the hospital, and if you ask me, it's too damned bad he did."

Perkins kicked viciously at the chair Moriseau had been using, turned his back and went to join Moriseau where he was sitting in the shadows behind Moore. For a moment there was silence. Miller said, "Dr. Moore," and Moore moved his bulk uneasily on the inadequate chair.

"Dr. Moore, the town has always regarded you as head of medical concerns in Haddon, maybe because you've been here a long time, maybe because you own the hospital, maybe because you've always been interested in the medical welfare of the town as a whole. Anyway, that's the way the town feels—that you're the head."

Moore put his arm along the back of the empty chair next to him. "I don't think any one of us is any more interested in town welfare than another. We all are. And I don't think any one of us should be considered 'head.'"

Lund broke his long silence. "It's a fact, though, and you can't escape it."

Moore turned his intense, blue-eyed gaze on him. "I'm not trying to escape anything. I think the doctors are to blame for what happened. If you think I'm more to blame than the others, then let's have it that way."

Miller said, "The town feels that the doctors as a group are responsible. They regard you as the leader of the group." Moore gave him a swift, keen look, then bowed his head and let his hands hang between his spread knees, listening passively. "The doctors are responsible for this terrible thing that happened. Dr. Perkins says this report shows he would have died anyway. That's beside the point. You could have been the cause of his death. Out of carelessness. Because you didn't take the precaution to set up a system that would prevent a situation like this. You've failed as doctors and you've failed the town."

133

From Dr. Ladd, sitting apart against the wall, there came a sound, wordless, but full of hurt, an inarticulate and anguished expression of defeat. Silenced by it, everyone turned to look at him. The old head was raised; the faded eyes looked back at them, but as though they were a long way off. When he spoke his voice shook.

"I don't know what people have come to. I don't know what this town has come to either. . . . When I first came here to practice, people thought it was a privilege to have a doctor in the town. A privilege, I tell you. Now they think it's their right. They used to be grateful when you got to see them. Now they're indignant if you don't get there within the hour. I don't know, I tell you. I don't know. It ain't the same atmosphere I used to practice medicine in. It ain't the same town. I don't know as I like doing it any more."

In the pause that followed he pulled a watch out of his pocket and looked at it, and it came to Moore that his slow, precise movements were meant to conceal the tremors of age. Moore watched him make an effort to rise and checked an impulse to go to his assistance. Ladd tried again, and was on his feet. For a moment he stood there, head lowered, brooding at the floor, holding himself stiffly as though his old body must resist the downward pull of the earth.

They all watched him, and after a moment he raised his head and said loudly, "*I don't know as I like it.*" He turned his back on them and, heavy and slow but dogged with purpose, went out the door.

For a long time no one spoke. Miller sat down and said in a voice from which the belligerence had gone, "The town has never interfered in medical matters before. We don't want to tell you how to run things even now, after what's happened. But we've some suggestions to make, and we feel you doctors should take them pretty seriously."

Miller looked to left and right at the other selectmen, who nodded solemnly. Moore saw that they were uncomfortable and embarrassed by all that was being said, and he was faintly amused.

"The first suggestion is that you doctors make a general review of medical needs both here and in Silver Springs. Work up a sort of definition of them. That strike you right, Mr. Moriseau?"

134

"That's right. We should be included." Moriseau spoke from behind Moore, where he and Perkins were sitting together out of the direct light.

"We also think you should consider the whole question of the hospital and its status. This is too big a subject to go into now, but there's lots of feeling about it in the town. We suggest that after you've had time to think and talk, we meet informally—say dinner at the Republic House—and talk it all over. Can you see your way to doing that?"

Moore said, "Yes, certainly." Perkins did not reply.

"And another thing we want to see done. We want Haddon to have a health center, like other towns where all the doctors have offices together. A girl to keep track of things, act as receptionist, send out bills. The kind of equipment not one of you could afford alone. A clinic, in effect, with two or three younger men in addition to yourselves. Then, even if Haddon should find itself without a hospital—"

Moore said, "It won't," and Perkins said, "Who's going to pay for this health center?"

"Popular subscription—a drive. You'll find the town will respond. We thought Ianthe Norton might head it up. She's good at such things."

"Don't ask her just at present," Moore said.

"Nat kind of bad these days?"

"Yes."

"Sorry to hear it. Well . . . I guess that's all, unless you doctors, or you, Mr. Moriseau, 's got something to say."

Moore said, "We're setting up a telephone answering service for the doctors. That ought to include a two-way radio setup so we could call the service and receive calls in our cars, on the road."

"That's a good, constructive idea. Isn't it?" Again Miller turned to left and right and again Whittacker's and Lund's heads nodded like marionettes on strings.

"The radio setup costs a lot of money. We thought the town treasury might be willing to contribute that."

"Might be. Yes, might be. Well, is this meeting ready to sugar off? Don't think we need to adjourn formally . . ."

●　　●　　●

135

In Dr. Moore's office the two young doctors pried the lids off paper cups of coffee that had been brought in from the dairy bar. David took a cautious sip of his, feeling the steam as dampness on his face.

"Do you, by any chance, know a girl named May Turner who was a student nurse at Warwick not so long ago?"

"Dark blue eyes, curly black hair, very pretty, and had an accident? Yes, I do, and I've been meaning to find out about her. Do you know her?"

"Well, not exactly. Dr. Moore asked me to have a look at her. It looks to me as though it's a thrombosis—partial occlusion of the artery. Should be taken out, but the thing is she seems to be in something of a mental state, withdrawal in a way. Doesn't want the operation, doesn't want to get well. Moore doesn't understand why, but he thinks she may have had some sort of shock, and it just occurred to me that you might be able to throw some light on it."

"Well—maybe I could." Barlow let the swivel chair tip back and gazed thoughtfully into his coffee for a moment. "But I don't think it was any one thing. No traumatic experience while she was at the hospital, unless there was something about the accident itself I don't know about. I'd say the trouble was she wasn't cut out to be a nurse, but she had too much character to quit. Forced herself, and after a while it got her. She kept at it for more than a year, and then she had a kind of breakdown. She didn't tell you or Moore about that?"

"No, she doesn't want to talk about her hospital experiences at all."

"I was in on it, as a matter of fact. She was on GYN-OB at the time. Somebody's baby died and she had to wash it, and I guess it was that on top of a lot of other things. She got through the job all right; then one of the nurses found her in the linen room having an attack of hysterical weeping. It got so bad the floor nurses couldn't cope with it, and I happened along and I went into the linen room to see what I could do. She's a damn pretty girl, even with her cap all cockeyed and her face all smeared up with tears."

"She's pretty, all right—incredible eyes."

"I got her quieted down after a while and sent her back to the nurses' home with another student. But I sort of couldn't get her off my mind. She is damn pretty . . ." Barlow smiled a little sheepishly and drank coffee. "I phoned Emily, my wife—she's got a degree in psychology—and she went around to the nurses' home and got May and took her home to dinner. I was on duty so I wasn't there, but after dinner May went to pieces again, but good. The hold she'd been keeping on herself all that time only made it worse, of course. Emily was having more than she could handle. When I got home I gave May a shot and phoned the nursing office and squared it to keep her overnight with us. Next day I had a talk with Miss Terry, superintendent of nurses. . . . This coffee isn't bad, by the way."

"Moore will be interested in all this. Go on—what happened?"

"Miss Terry said she had been worried about May for some time. She'd even had a talk with her about whether she ought not to give up her training, but May didn't want to give up and Miss Terry let her go on. Miss Terry liked her, and so did Emily and I. The girl's got something . . ."

"Blue eyes, for one thing."

Barlow laughed. "More than that. Well, anyway. Miss Terry called her in again and told her she'd have to quit. She was going to leave at the end of the week, and this accident happened just the day before."

"Do you think her state of mind had anything to do with the accident? Gave her a reason for quitting other than just failing at the job?"

Barlow considered, tipping his chair back and forth. He set the empty cup down on Moore's desk and said, "How can you know? I've never understood how the psychiatry lads feel so sure of themselves. My guess is it was a real accident, and she didn't have time to get out of the way. But as I say, how do you know? I should think what's the matter now is that she hasn't got over the effects of forcing herself all that long time to do a job she wasn't fit for. That, and a feeling of having failed. She probably just doesn't feel up to tackling the big, cruel world again. Listen . . . Wasn't that the outside door? It must be Moore." Barlow picked up his empty coffee container, dropped it in the scrap basket, and both doctors stood up.

X

The next morning at seven Armstrong had a telephone call from Dr. Moore, asking if he would like to look at the hospital at about ten-thirty or eleven o'clock. "I'm at the hospital now. I'm giving an anesthetic this morning, but it doesn't amount to much, and I should be finished by that time. I'll come and pick you up."

The bell in the church at the far end of the green was just striking eleven as the red jeep pulled into the hospital parking lot. The two curtained doors opened like wings and the two doctors climbed out. The morning was clear and bright, a mountain morning, and the sound of the bell came through the thin air with perfect purity. Armstrong, struck by the unusual beauty of the tone, stood still to listen to the final notes, and Moore, waiting, watched him. When the sound died, Armstrong said, "I never heard a bell like it."

"It's a Revere bell. The town is very proud of it."

"No wonder. I'm surprised I didn't hear it before."

"Carries on a clear day like this."

Armstrong walked beside Moore toward the hospital, receiving his first impression of the ugly dignity of the old building. In the clear air every detail stood out as though with an added dimension, the outline sharply defined with an effect of being more real than reality. But that such a building could actually be a hospital struck him with something of a shock, and before he had gone ten feet the impossibility of even considering practice in such a place made him turn involuntarily toward Moore. In doing that, he failed to see a light truck that had swerved into the parking lot and was coming at them.

Moore took him quickly by the arm to hold him back, and the

138

old and shabby truck came to a palsied halt in front of them. The open body of the truck was loaded with farm produce, baskets of red apples, tomatoes, squash, pumpkins and some vegetables that David could not have named, and from them rose a rich aroma. The driver, a young man with the type of good looks that seems so exclusively American, shouted over the noise of his throbbing engine, "Hi, Doc."

"Hi, Bob."

"You're doing pretty good this year, Doc. This is my third load this morning."

"I'm glad to hear it. Keep it up."

"Sure thing."

The truck lurched and moved off, and they could speak in normal tones again.

Moore said, "This is Donation Day and I forgot all about it."

"Donation Day?"

"It's the day on which people all through the countryside, and the stores in town, donate what they can for the use of the hospital. Last year we got pretty near enough bed linen and cleaning things and winter vegetables to see us through. Some money, but it's easier for a town like this to give produce and merchandise."

"They give these things even though it's a privately owned hospital? That seems to me extraordinary."

"I don't suppose it could happen anywhere but in Vermont, or one of the other New England states. People are grateful to us. They are well aware that the hospital needs help, and they figure that, in one way or another, they stand to gain by helping to keep us going. There's a close but intricate relationship between the doctors and a town like this that probably isn't remotely like anything in your experience. I don't believe I could explain it to you if I tried. Part of it is that we doctors are the servants of the town —not of people, of the *town*. There's a very important distinction there. We belong to the town, and so does the hospital, and the fact that it's privately owned doesn't make much difference."

"That's a point of view I'd have some difficulty understanding."

"Last night was an example of how it works."

They were going up the steps, wooden steps in need of paint, and David again tried to imagine himself working here, and failed. He glanced at Moore and saw a glow of pleasure on his face, and with a feeling of dismay he realized how much his coming here must mean to the old doctor. A little ashamed, he said, "How many beds do you have here, sir?"

"Thirty—not counting five cradles and an incubator. I have some telephoning to do. If you don't mind, I'll turn you over to our head nurse, Edna Judson, and she'll take you on the grand tour. I'll come and find you when I'm through."

Edna Judson acknowledged the introduction while David tried to keep his fascinated gaze from resting too openly on her amazing cap.

"We're glad to see you here, Dr. Armstrong. I'll be pleased to show you around."

He met the steady eyes and looked away. There had been other formidable head nurses in his career who had the power which she possessed to make him feel like an intern again, but he had not expected to find one here. He shook the feeling off and found that he really wanted to see this hospital.

Following her, he realized that she wanted him to understand more than his eyes saw, though she did not attempt to explain anything. "This is the men's surgical ward, Doctor, though Dr. Moore does not like to have it called a ward. It was the parlor in the old house. We are proud of our old mantelpieces. This is the narcotics cupboard. If you will come this way I'll show you the men's medical . . ."

She spoke in a monotonous voice, a little hard to hear, as though she were preoccupied with matters quite different from those she was talking about. She seemed quite uninterested in him, and this piqued him in spite of himself.

They went up the broad staircase past three private rooms, which seemed to be all there were, past a cramped nursing station and a children's room. Armstrong had begun to suspect that in some ways she understood the workings of the hospital better than Dr. Moore. About one thing in particular he was curious and he decided to ask her.

"Do you have many charity patients here?"

She stood still to answer him. "A few. We call them 'welfare cases.' "

"It's a slightly better phrase."

"And you know, Doctor, they don't stand out as they used to."

"Why is that?"

"Well, we get a good many patients from the Silver Springs plants. They don't pay either. The company benefits usually cover medical costs for the employee and his family too. Then there are various government health programs—Social Security, Kerr-Mills, and so on. And Blue Cross and Blue Shield. Almost everyone nowadays has part, if not all, of his medical expenses paid. This can't be anything new to you, Doctor, but perhaps we see how it works more clearly here than you would in a big hospital in the city."

"I never thought of it in just that way before."

They moved on into what appeared to be a new wing, and she said, "Here is the operating room," and stepped back to let him enter by himself.

Operating rooms not in use disturbed him, though for what reason he could not say; and though he was curious about this one, he went in with a slight reluctance. At first glance, though some of the equipment seemed old, none of it was antiquated, and in general the place seemed a good deal more up-to-date than the rest of the hospital, and his mind presented him with a quick memory picture of Perkins, assertive, dynamic—the kind of man to get what he wanted in spite of a crippled budget.

Armstrong began to make a sort of mental inventory. Operating table, old but serviceable; lights, good; anesthesia equipment—under covers—for both nitrous oxide and Halothane, modern. He stopped by the cabinet of the Bovie, the electric cautery that seals off small blood vessels with a touch of its burning point—vessels that would otherwise have to be laboriously tied off by hand. The cautery seemed to be the oldest piece of equipment in the room. Someone had left a copy of *Standard Nomenclature of Diseases* on top of the cabinet, and he raised the cover to see "Edw. Moore" written inside in a reasonably legible hand that looked, more than anything else, purposeful and hurried.

He looked around for Miss Judson and found that she had left him alone here, probably for reasons of her own. And as though the complicated room were pulling at him, convincing him that he could work here (which he felt he could), he suddenly wanted to escape in precisely the way something in him had wanted to escape every commitment he had ever made. He went out quickly without again looking around.

She was waiting for him outside, ready to lead him farther into the wing. Almost at once he was aware of noise, and when she opened a door, a blast of radio music, talk and laughter burst out. Over it all, a caged canary was singing, making him think of a prima donna determined not to let the orchestra get the better of her. A cheerful, vital, sunny place.

"The maternity ward," Miss Judson said—unnecessarily, for the smell of the place had already reached him. A smell of women and babies and, faintly, of something else that he remembered from his months as an intern on GYN-OB. A thick, sweetish smell that seemed to cling to him and that no shower could quite wash away, so that he seemed to live with it, eat with it, wake with it around him in the morning, and for a while it had made the thought of women distasteful. Here, it was little more than a memory, but enough to make him hang back.

At sight of Edna Judson, the six young women sitting or lying on their beds let out a joyous shout. She said, "Now girls, stop it, behave yourselves. I've brought a visitor, Dr. Armstrong, to see you."

They were silent instantly, staring at him, drawing their blowsy wrappers around them, smiling shyly. One of them ventured a feeble "Hi, Doc," and he said "Hullo there" to the room at large and to his intense exasperation felt his face growing red.

When they left and Edna was shutting the door behind them, she was smiling. "Having a baby is the only vacation a lot of them ever get."

He thought the tour must be over, but to his surprise she led him through a narrow door and up some steep stairs into an attic over the old part of the building, where the hospital smell was replaced by the odor of ancient beams and broad floorboards. There was nothing to see here but some well-filled storage shelves, and he guessed that she had brought him here only because she liked the place. Here the old house still held its own in stillness and peace remote from the hospital activity on the floors below.

Without a word Edna Judson led him to the front of the attic where a band of sunlight came slanting downward through a small round window. The shaft was as clean-cut in outline as a solid beam, and they stood beside it looking down at the motes swimming in it. She put her hand into the light, and the motes, disturbed, swam in frantic circles around it. She took her hand away, nodded, and led the way in silence to the stairs. He was not sure what she had meant to convey to him or even if she had meant to convey anything at all, but he found he liked this austere, silent woman.

At the bottom of the stairs she turned toward the new wing, saying over her shoulder, "I saw the elevator on this floor so I'll take you down that way, though mainly we use it only when we have to because it costs so much to run. It's the only one in town."

At the back of the floor below they went into a large room where, surprisingly, there were mounds of produce and vegetables, and six or eight women in smocks moving among them, taking inventory.

One of the women, ample in figure but tall enough to carry it with dignity, made her way toward them, and Edna said to her, "Ianthe, this is Dr. Armstrong. Mrs. Norton, Doctor, chairman of the Donation Day volunteers." Armstrong liked the warmth of her smile, and her brown eyes had real beauty, but under the smile her face seemed careworn and in their depths the eyes seemed sad. Her voice was deep and gentle, and Armstrong, sensitive always to sound, listened with pleasure. She was saying, "We're having a good day, Edna. People are sending us really useful things. Some years, Doctor, it seems as though people were just cleaning out their attics."

Miss Judson was looking around the room, searching, he thought, for someone. She said to Mrs. Norton, in a lowered voice, "Where's Adele Perkins?"

"She's not here. You didn't really expect her to be, did you?"

"Well—no, but she ought to be."

"We've just sent the apples down cellar, Edna. They're a pretty sight. You'd better show them to Dr. Armstrong."

The stairs to the cellar were precipitous and Edna said, "Watch your head, Doctor. It's a typical old Vermont cellar with a stringer beam just where it could do the most harm." He ducked just in time, and then felt the cool air of the cellar around him, and there was something that he, city-bred, had never encountered before, the wonderful aroma of hundreds of ripe apples. Baskets of them stood everywhere on the hard-packed dirt floor, red McIntoshes, for the most part, Edna told him, a whole winter's supply. "And all those wires and cables over your head are for the X-ray machine, Doctor."

It was here that Dr. Moore found them, and David saw at once that something had pleased him, for he was smiling and his face had a smoothed-out look. He spoke quickly to Edna.

"Mrs. Newberry's tumor isn't cancer, Edna."

"I'm very glad to hear that, Doctor."

"The report's on my desk. You might phone her and tell her I said so, and give the report to Perkins when you see him. Have an apple, Doc?"

Before David realized what was happening, a red apple came flying through the air and he caught it just in time, smack in the palm of his hand.

They ate their apples, bending over to keep the juice from running down their chins. Moore said, with his mouth full, "You wouldn't be doing anything like this in a big city hospital, Dave." And Armstrong said, "No, I sure wouldn't," and started to laugh. They were laughing together; the moment was a fine one, and it was important that it had happened, though why these things were true he did not know. Then it was over and he was wondering what to do with the core of his apple and settled it by dropping it into an old florist's basket.

Moore led the way through a door marked X-RAY into a small room that must once have been a pantry. Where the sink had been there was a table with an X-ray backlight on it, a film and a piece of paper with crabbed writing resting on the glass. Moore turned a switch and they stood looking down at ghostly diseased pelvic bones.

Moore said, "A doctor comes from Burlington once a week to read our films for us." He stooped to read the writing on the paper, and for the first time Armstrong noticed that he had no need of glasses. " 'Osteoarticular tuberculosis. Anteroposterior view of pelvis shows hypoplasia of right femoral shaft and hemipelvis. Acetabulum is poorly developed.' Medical language has gotten a lot more technical since I was a student. Patient of Howard's. Fifty-eight years old, been lame since he was four. Abscesses recently. Penicillin-resistant staph. aureus. Seems like whatever we do, the bugs can keep a jump ahead of us. Let's go in here where I guess we can talk without being interrupted."

They went into the next room, that was largely filled with the X-ray table and apparatus. Moore hoisted himself to sit on the table's edge, and David, looking around for a place where he himself could sit, found only a white metal stool, which he dragged out from the wall. He said, "I'd like to ask you why, in the face of a growing deficit, and with a hospital like Warwick so near, you feel it worth while to carry on here."

"Two main reasons," Moore answered with the affability that seemed to be his working attitude toward whatever faced him. "You've seen that people around here think of this as their own hospital where they get taken care of by their own doctors. Warwick is 'closed-staff,' which of course means that outside doctors like myself can't take care of patients there. We have to turn them over to doctors they've probably never seen before. That, and the impersonal atmosphere of a big hospital, and the distance from home, upsets a lot of them. I don't like it. An unhappy patient isn't easily cured."

Moore fell silent, apparently brooding over a problem that, David thought, must be of frequent occurrence among the patients who came from the back country. When this silence continued, David said, "The second reason?" and Moore looked at him as though for a moment he had lost the thread of their discussion.

"Simply this. How are you going to get good doctors to practice in a town without a hospital? Close this one and Perkins would leave tomorrow. He's already talking about a teaching job at Warwick Medical School. Ladd would stay, I'd stay, but only because we're too old not to. And we'd have an even tougher time getting younger men than we're having now."

"I'm a surgeon, and a surgeon has to have a hospital."

"Exactly. And another thing. There's a town called Silver Springs eight miles from here where there are some manufacturing plants. They use us for industrial accidents, medical benefits, and so on. That's thirty-eight miles from Warwick, which is just too far."

"I realize you need another doctor here—probably two of them. But would my coming for a year do you any real good? Shouldn't you be looking for a man who would be here permanently?"

"What I'd gain by your coming would be time. That's all I need to get things straightened out. Time. Your being here would convince the town and the Accreditation Board that I don't intend to let the hospital go downhill. That will take a lot of the heat off and give me time to get new staff and to work out the financial problems."

"I don't feel at all sure my being here would do all you say."

"It would, believe me. It has to. I hope to God you'll come."

The door opened and Moore looked up. "Yes, Edna?" David turned to see the head nurse standing like a thin white shaft in the doorway.

"Dr. Moore, did you make an appointment with Stella Thayer here at the hospital? She's here and she says you did."

"Oh Lord, yes, I forgot." Dr. Moore slid off the X-ray table. "What are your plans, David?"

"I thought I might catch the two o'clock plane to New York. I'll walk back to the hotel from here—it isn't so far."

"Tell Stella to wait a minute, Edna."

They walked slowly out into the hall and toward the front door. Dr. Moore was all concern. "I don't suppose you've made up your mind yet, about coming here?"

"I'll let you know from New York. Promptly."

Moore made no reply though the air seemed thick with his unspoken thoughts.

Going through the door, Moore put his hand on David's shoulder and patted it much as he might have patted a favorite dog. They shook hands warmly.

"It's been interesting being here. Thank you."

"It's been fine having you."

When Armstrong reached the street, he knew that Dr. Moore was standing at the top of the steps looking after him, looking as he often must when he thought no one was watching him—alone, tired, and a trifle wistful. The feeling was so strong that David felt compelled to turn around. Dr. Moore was not there.

THE WOMAN BEHIND THE DESK at the Republic House smiled at Dr. Armstrong because she liked him, though he seemed to take life so seriously. She felt he did the hotel more credit than the traveling men. "A message, Doctor. Mr. Stoner phoned from the bank and said he wanted you to lunch with him. He said to tell you he was most anxious to see you."

"I was planning to get the two o'clock plane to New York."

"There's another, gets you in at eight. I'll phone the airport and get you on it, if you like."

"Well . . . all right, thanks."

"Mr. Stoner said twelve-thirty. It's almost that now."

At twelve-thirty precisely Stoner came into the Republic House with another man. David, mildly surprised at this, gave them time to hang their coats on the rack by the dining room door, before advancing on them from across the lobby. Stoner said, "Good morning, Doctor," and closed his faintly moist hand over David's reluctant one. "This is Mr. Whitall of the Public Health Service. Dr. Armstrong."

Whitall was a thin, hollow-chested man in his forties, with a big chin that drooped rather than jutted, and straight, darkish hair that seemed to have been combed with no particular direction in mind. He said, "Glad to meet you, Doctor," in a twanging voice, shook hands in slow motion, and rocked back on his heels as though against the support of some invisible wall.

Stoner steered them through the door of the dining room and nodded to the hostess who came brightly toward them. "Put us over there in the corner by the window, Mary, so we can talk." The three chairs on the wooden floor made a great deal of noise as they were adjusted to the table, and Stoner raised his voice. "Mr.

Whitall and I have been spending some time together this morning. He is naturally interested in the medical problems of Haddon."

Whitall said, "Naturally," and seemed to wait with some complacency for Stoner to continue.

"He is especially interested in our community problem of the hospital. But let's order, shall we, and get that out of the way? The chicken potpie is always good here."

As Whitall unfolded his napkin, the glitter of a Phi Beta Kappa key, hung on a watch chain across his vest, caught David's eye.

"I am in charge of hospital area planning for the state, Doctor" —Stoner, ordering, kept a nervous eye on him as though watchful not to lose his leadership—"I'll send you a copy of my report when it's ready, if you like."

"Thank you."

Whitall, in his curious, slow-motion manner, pulled a small black notebook out of his pocket and made a brief notation in it while Armstrong reflected that he could not possibly know where to send this report. Stoner watched him with the intensified keenness of gaze his glasses produced. Whitall shut his notebook with a snap.

"The title of my report will be 'Area Planning Plan Number . . .' the number slips my mind, for the moment, for of course we have a great many reports, all numbered—"

Stoner cut in crisply, "The point is, the report will recommend abolishing Moore's hosp—"

"Let's say, rather, it will not recommend its continuance."

"In other words, the Public Health Area Plan does not include Moore's hospital and it will be closed by that authority."

"I *wish* you wouldn't express it like that, Mr. Stoner."

David, startled, said, "But how could you do that? It's private property. Dr. Moore's personal property!"

Stoner turned his sharpened gaze on Armstrong. "You saw, of course, that the greater part of the hospital building is not wholly fireproof?"

"But . . ." The wider implications of what had been said struck him and he was silent.

Stoner said sharply, "Let's not get off on questions of government control in medicine. The reason why I asked you to join us at lunch, Doctor, is that I thought you ought to hear the alternative plans to having no hospital at all in Haddon."

"This chicken pie *is* good," Whitall said.

David pushed his plate away, his pie partly eaten, for this conversation made him slightly sick. "Is this alternative plan the government's?"

"Oh, no," Whitall said. "Well, not exactly. I take it you're not familiar with how government agencies move in situations like this."

"No, I'm certainly not."

"We explore; you might say we probe. We study the picture in its larger aspects. We recommend, we advise. We are extremely slow to take any action."

"What *are* the alternative plans?"

Whitall picked up a spoon, captured the last juices of the pie, sat back slowly, drew from his pocket a large, underslung pipe. All this was plainly a ritual preliminary to speech from which he derived much pleasure, but it was ill timed, for Stoner took advantage of the delay.

"One plan would be to build a small, modern hospital, constructed with expansion in mind, to replace Dr. Moore's obsolete one. This would cost . . . what would you say, Whitall? Around six hundred thousand . . ."

"New hospitals of this type are being built all over the country, and—"

Stoner held up an arresting hand, and Whitall, silenced, gave the bowl of his pipe three slow, expressive taps.

"The usual procedure in such a case is for the town to raise half the money and the Federal government to contribute half, in return for which certain controls and restrictions are imposed. No need to go into that."

"This is a practical and highly desirable form—"

"Mr. Whitall—please! I am against this alternative, Doctor, for several reasons. One of them is that the town of Haddon couldn't possibly raise such a sum. I mention it only to give you a complete picture. The other alternative, and the one that I shall back, is to have a hospital at Silver Springs. There would be no trouble with the financing, because the plants could be expected to contribute heavily. Also, this plan would have the bank's backing."

Whitall waved a long, pale hand at them. "My choice would be a modern hospital in Haddon for the simple reason that the government, as a partner, could work more easily with representatives of a town than with representatives of corporations."

Stoner said sharply, "It's not to be considered. The town couldn't raise the money, and the bank's stand would be against it."

Whitall began to draw noisily on his pipe, and David, glancing at it reproachfully, said, "What becomes of Dr. Moore and his investment in his hospital?"

Stoner waved his hand and let it drop heavily to the table. For a moment no one said anything. Stoner took his glasses off and polished them with a corner of his napkin, and David, watching him, was struck again by the change in personality their absence seemed to bring about. Stoner put them on again and turned to David.

"The purpose of telling you all this, Doctor, is that I presume you would be more likely to decide to come to Haddon if you thought the medical situation here were not completely static, that change is at least contemplated. Or I assume you would feel that way, though little could actually be accomplished in the year you would plan to be here."

"You've told me considerably more than you did in your office."

Stoner's facial muscles became involved in a movement somewhat resembling a smile. "Perhaps, Doctor, we were both feeling our way during that interview. Taking each other's measure, so to speak."

Whitall lit a large match with his ragged thumbnail, and the small explosive sound made David's nerves jump. Whitall held the match to his pipe and sucked and looked at David over the flame. Stoner put his glasses on and the waitress put down a saucer of pale green ice cream which David stared at remotely. He said, speaking slowly, "I haven't made up my mind yet. I'm going back to New York this afternoon in any event."

"And during your year with us," Stoner said, "you might be of considerable help and influence in establishing new medical standards for Haddon."

Whitall, holding his pipe in abeyance in his left hand, clicked his spoon against his dish. "You get good food here." He put the

150

spoon in his mouth and slowly and sensuously drew it out again.

While David and Stoner and Whitall were getting up from the lunch table, Dr. Moore, across the street, was fitting his key into his inner office door. Six or eight patients were already waiting for him.

"With you in a minute," he said, going toward the inner office and taking off his coat. At that moment the telephone began to ring.

He dropped into the desk chair, and picked it up. "Dr. Moore speaking."

The voice that replied was urgent and anxious. "Dr. Moore, this is Helen at the hospital. The examiners from the Accreditation Board are here."

"Oh, good Lord!"

"Edna's going round with them. They're going into everything. They even looked down the linen chute. They looked at all the charts in the nursing station, and Edna overheard them say the wiring for the X-ray is too near the wooden beams."

"They've passed that every other year."

"They want to talk to you, Dr. Moore."

"Is it the same three men as other years?"

"Yes."

"Then they know I have afternoon office hours."

"They said they'd meet you at the Republic House bar between five and six."

"All right. Thanks, Helen. Don't worry about it."

Moore put the telephone down, sighed deeply, and pushed himself out of his chair. His face showed the tight lines of worry. He opened the door and looked out into the waiting room. "Who's first?"

The bar of the Republic House was in the basement, a large, dimly lit room with booths along the walls. A jukebox, now mercifully silent, stood at one end. The booths had rigid wooden backs and the seats were too narrow for comfort. Moore hated the place.

When he came in, he saw that the only customers were the three examiners, sitting at a table with a candle on it, and when they saw him, they rose as well as they could in the restricted space, and Moore shook hands all around. Their voices were a little loud, which meant they had all had at least one drink before he came. Moore sat down uncomfortably, and one of the men across the table from him, a man named Brown whom Moore had always thought the friendliest of the lot, said, "What will you have, Doc?"

"Bitter Lemon, I guess."

They all laughed as though this were very funny, and Brown said, "What will it really be?"

"I've got a call to make before evening office hours." He looked up at the elderly, gray-haired woman who was, so improbably, both waitress and barkeep of this underground place. "Bitter Lemon, please, Mabel."

One of the other men said, "He's just trying to impress us," and they all laughed loudly again. There was a little constraint and a little nervousness in the laugh, and when it was over there was an uncomfortable silence. Moore said, "Well, how did you find things?"

The man beside Moore, the oldest of the three, named Zimback, lit a cigarette and shook out the match. "About as usual. Well run, clean, in need of having quite a bit of money spent for both plant and equipment."

"I hope you're going to give me full accreditation again."

"You know we can't tell you what we decide before the formal report is prepared."

Brown said, "How is your financing for the year ahead?"

"All right." His own statement sounded a little sparse to Moore and he added, "I fixed it up with Stoner the other day." Then he glanced quickly at the two men across the table, for he had a strong impression they already possessed this information.

There was another pause, and in it Moore became more and more acutely aware that there was something in all their minds not yet in the open, but some important, some crucial thing. His drink came and he said, "Thanks" and sat there with his hand around it, staring into the candle flame, waiting. He knew the wait could not be long, but suddenly it was filled with intolerable suspense, for he thought that within the next minute or two he would have the clue to whether the hospital would be allowed to live. Sweat came out on his forehead and on the palms of his hands. He stared at the candle flame and everything else vanished in luminous mist. Then he raised his eyes and looked toward Brown, not seeing him because of the afterimage of the flame, and not knowing how much of his anxiety was in his face.

Brown leaned forward, smiling a little. "How much truth is there in the rumor that Dr. Perkins is leaving you to go to the Warwick Medical School?"

"How did you know about that?"

"It's our business to know. Obviously, a hospital without a surgeon couldn't be given even provisional accreditation under present-day standards."

Moore picked up the candle holder and set it forcefully to one side. He folded his arms on the table and leaned on them. "The first I heard of it was less than a week ago. He told me that he was going to apply for that teaching post. I don't know that he's done anything about it."

"He has."

Moore received this blow thoughtfully. "He should have told me. But applying isn't to say he'll be accepted. There must be others wanting the job."

"Dr. Greer for one."

"What?"

"Greer," Zimback said. "He's after it."

"Harlan Greer—here in Haddon? Are you sure? He's a rich man and he's retired. I know he lectures there sometimes, but what you're talking about is a full-time job, or nearly. It's hard to see why he'd want it."

"Bored with retirement, I guess."

Brown said, still in the friendly tone, "Warwick won't decide until the new year, which is much too late for our report. But what about the young surgeon who was up here from New York looking you over?"

"Anyway," the third man said, "he's not a general surgeon. Specializes in something, I heard."

"He would expect to do general surgery with us. His training's been the best."

"Yes, but is he coming here? That's the real question."

"I don't know yet."

"Any guess?"

153

"No, I just don't know."

Brown raised his arm to signal for the check. "We've got a long drive ahead of us. We'd better get going." Moore, for politeness' sake, drank a little of the Bitter Lemon and they all rose.

Brown, paying the check, detained Moore until the others were out of earshot. "It's like this. We're under pressure—I won't say from where—to make this report unfriendly to you. I don't like pressure, and I don't propose to be influenced by it. Also, it's not our business to get into this hassle about whether the town needs a hospital or not. As you know, all we do is pass on the hospital's fitness. I'll say this much, because you probably know it anyway. Your hospital has got several bad black marks against it, and the uncertainty about Perkins is probably the worst of the lot. I don't say it would make all of the difference if we knew positively this young surgeon was coming, but it would make an important difference. You expect to know pretty soon?"

"I hope so. I believe so. A week, maybe."

"Let me know, will you? As soon as you can. Don't delay it. Perhaps you could pressure him a little."

"Perhaps. I'll let you know as soon as I do."

"I saw Whitall from the Public Health Service in town this morning. Do you happen to have any idea what he's here for?"

"No, not the slightest. You're the one who should know."

"One of the characteristics of government, state or Federal, is confusion, I'm afraid. I'll find out when I get back to Montpelier. I'd better join the others or they'll wonder what we're talking about. Nice to have seen you."

"Same to you. And thanks." Moore held out his hand.

When David reached La Guardia he ate a brief, unpleasing dinner and took a taxi to his small apartment on Seventy-sixth Street, just east of Madison. He felt tired beyond reason by the extraordinary pressures produced during his first experience with small-town life. As he put his key in the lock, his feeling was that he would be glad never to see Haddon again. The apartment seemed to him unwelcoming, and as though it had been empty for a long time, and after taking a few things out of his bag he did something he had never done before; he put his coat back on and went out to the Carlyle bar to have a drink.

154

He had some idea that this might be a way to begin to think things out, but in the restful semidarkness of the bar, with a highball in his hand, the conviction came to him that nothing needed thinking out, and that his relief at being home was all the indication he needed that New York was where he belonged. He slowly drank his highball, enjoying the feeling of peace. Presently he made the discovery that the Haddon interlude had served at least one good purpose, for it had come between himself and the immediacy of his distress concerning Maryanne. That unhappy affair, he found, had receded from his mind and heart, leaving pain, but pain that was endurable and not entirely free of a certain morbid enjoyment.

When he returned to his apartment the telephone was ringing. He hurried into the bedroom and sat on the bed to answer it, but all he heard was the steady singing of the dial tone. With the telephone still on his lap, he thought about calling Fairchild, and decided the hour was too late. Then he found himself seriously considering putting in a call to May Turner, and was shocked by the fantasy of this idea. He put the telephone decisively back on the table, saw that his alarm was set, as always, for six o'clock, and began to get ready to go to bed.

At the hospital the next morning the feeling of having been away for a long time persisted, and to such an extent that he felt himself almost a stranger. His locker in the doctors' room on the OR floor seemed not as he remembered it, and the contents were like things rediscovered from the past. He dressed himself in smock and cap and went out of the doctors' room, intending to stop at the nursing station to find out what Fairchild's operating schedule for that day might be, but in the corridor he met Fairchild himself.

Fairchild nodded gravely. "So you're back." It was a bare statement that carried no bias of feeling at all, and Fairchild did not slow his rapid walk. Rather awkwardly, David fell into step beside him.

"I got in too late last night to call you. I haven't seen the schedule yet. What have we got this morning?"

Fairchild said, "A stenotic mitral first. Since you didn't tell me when you were coming back, I'm having Mike assist."

David, taken aback, did not at once reply. Mike Foley was chief surgical resident, the position David himself had held up to the previous June, when, his residency completed, he had entered Fairchild's office. Mike Foley was the man Maryanne was to marry. David had never before heard Fairchild, who was punctilious about such things while in the hospital, make use of Mike's first name. They walked on in a silence David did not know how to break. In his mind he formed the words "I'm back to stay, you know," and imagined them being received in silence with a stare of the cold, light eyes. It came to him then that Fairchild had all along been angry and resentful at David's plan to take a year's absence, and had characteristically waited to show it until a moment when he could cause extreme discomfort. When he thought about this planned, concealed anger, of which he had not been aware, David felt a slight, unpleasant tingling of his nerves.

They came to the operating suite that Fairchild used, and Fairchild, his hand on one of the double swing doors, said, "Having told Dr. Foley to assist, I can't, of course, change now." David, knowing this was not true and that he was being offered an insult, grew red in the face. Fairchild saw it, and a shadow of his cold, muscular smile appeared. "If you care to act as second assistant, you may, though for a mitral it's hardly necessary, of course."

Fairchild pushed the door open and went in. David hesitated for a fraction of a second, and then he slammed the other door hard with his palm and followed.

Mike Foley was already scrubbing, standing at the sink to the right of Fairchild that was the one David usually used. Foley was the same general type of surgeon as Dr. Perkins, big, loud-voiced and confident, but lacking Perkins's inner hardness. The quality that in Perkins was force in Mike more nearly resembled bluster. David, who had never liked this extrovert personally, did not quite trust him as a surgeon, not as a result of any experience but from an instinctive feeling that he might not prove adequate in an emergency.

Mike's foot was on the pedal; a stream of water was running over his hands. He half turned, saw David and said "Hi" loudly. David, his tone low and controlled, said "Hullo," and went to the side of the room to stand on the platform of a piece of mechanism that looked like a weighing scale and would indicate on a dial the amount of static electricity carried by his body and clothing. Rather to his surprise, he found this to be well within the normal range. He stood on the platform a moment longer than necessary, watching Mike, and noting with pleasure that Mike was suffering a degree of embarrassment. Then he went to the sink next to Mike's and began to scrub.

Out of the corner of his eye he saw that Mike, big hands dripping, had turned to Fairchild for guidance in this unusual situation, much, David thought grimly, as a big dog turns questioningly to its master. Fairchild said, "Dr. Armstrong is going to assist *you.*" Without looking at Mike, David was aware that he was suppressing a smile and expanding with satisfaction. Big slob, he thought passionately, and glanced up at the clock to time his scrubbing.

When he had finished, though he was still angry, he had grown calm enough to think clearly. The result was amazement at his own thickheadedness in not realizing that by going to Haddon he had given Fairchild the opportunity that, probably, he had been waiting for. Mike would finish his residency in June, Mike would then marry Maryanne, and if David's place in Fairchild's office were then vacant, what more appropriate than that Mike should step into it?

In an excess of exasperation at his own blindness, David threw the sterile towel he had been using viciously at the used linen container. It was entirely characteristic of Fairchild not to come out in the open, but to gain his ends in this devious manner. Illogically, since the idea of leaving had, in the first instance, been his own, he felt unfairly treated. The nurse was holding out a gown for him. He thrust his arms into the sleeves and turned around to let her fasten it in the back.

Usually, when the morning's operating was finished, Fairchild would suggest to David that they lunch together in the huge doctors' dining room in the basement. This day he simply departed without saying anything, and later David saw him eating at a table by himself with a medical journal open by his plate. David carried his own tray of food to the opposite side of the dining room and ate his lunch, brooding on the dilemma of having decided against going to Haddon only to discover that he was no longer wanted here. The dining room was filled with white-coated figures, and in

157

the noise of talk and cutlery the paging system droned monotonously, calling doctors' names. David came out of his thoughts abruptly to hear the disembodied voice saying, "Dr. Armstrong, Dr. David Armstrong, Dr. Armstrong . . ." He put his napkin down and rose.

The telephones stood in a row on a shelf and he picked one up and asked for the paging service.

"Dr. Armstrong. You've got a call for me?"

"A long-distance, Doctor. Hold on, please."

There was a pause filled with a sense of space and distance, and then Moore's voice, surprisingly strong and clear, said, "Hullo. David, are you there?"

"Yes, sir. How are you?"

"Fine. Fine. I didn't get a chance to say a proper good-bye, so I thought I'd call. I don't suppose you've had time to think things out yet?"

"Not yet." To shut out noise David put his free hand over his ear and turned his back on the dining room. "I'll let you know, of course, as soon as I do."

"I'd appreciate that."

Something in Moore's tone caught David's attention. "Is there any special reason why you'd like to know immediately?"

"Well . . . the inspectors from the Hospital Accreditation Board were here. It's going to be a near thing whether the hospital gets by. I gather your coming might make considerable difference."

"Oh Lord . . . Well, I tell you, I had about made up my mind not to, but since being back here . . . No need to go into that. I'll let you know tomorrow. Will that be all right?"

"Yes, that will be all right. I hope very much your decision will be to come. Nice to talk to you."

Thoughtfully, David went back to his cold lunch.

In Dr. Fairchild's private office, David occupied a small room across the hall from Fairchild's much larger one. It was there, in the afternoons, that they saw patients, the two doctors working more or less together. This afternoon, however, Fairchild worked alone while David sat morosely in his office, waiting to be called. He saw three of his own patients and after that there was nothing to do, no mail to be answered, and the telephone did not ring.

When Fairchild's door opened he could hear voices, but otherwise his isolation was complete.

Toward four o'clock he went out into the waiting room, gathered up a collection of magazines, and took them back to his office. He settled down with his feet on his desk to read them and found that nothing in them held his attention. Finally he gave it up and concentrated on his own problem. Obviously, the situation in which he found himself was impossible and could not continue. The more he thought about it the plainer it became that he and Fairchild would have to have a talk. David took his feet off the desk, got up and began to pace back and forth in the office, planning what he would say.

A little after five, when he thought the last patient had gone, he went across the hall and knocked on Fairchild's door. Something in the way Fairchild said "Come in" told David that Fairchild was expecting, and perhaps waiting for, this scene. He was sitting with his desk chair turned toward the door, his thin hands on the arms, his long white coat buttoned down the front. He said "Well?" without looking at David squarely and made no suggestion that he should sit down.

"I thought we should have a talk, Dr. Fairchild."

"I hardly think it's necessary. When a man has shown signs of being discontented, I believe he should make other arrangements. I would not want to hold him."

David made no attempt to answer what was so clearly a subterfuge to push him aside and make room for Mike Foley. Instead, he put his hands in his pockets and stared down at Fairchild, wondering almost dispassionately at what point the scheme to dislodge him had entered his dissembling mind. Quite possibly before he went to Haddon, perhaps as soon as Maryanne had made clear her preference for Mike.

Strangely, this thought did not anger him. Instead, a feeling of emancipation took hold of him and grew stronger. Still staring straight at Fairchild's pale, secretive eyes, he began to jingle coins in his pocket.

"Don't do that," Fairchild said sharply.

David smiled. "When would it be convenient for me to leave?"

The telephone rang and Fairchild answered without taking his eyes from David's face. After a moment he turned his chair to face his desk and, talking into the telephone, picked up a pencil, pulled a scrap of paper toward him, and wrote on it. Still talking into the telephone, he held the paper out to David. He had written in large letters, "Any time!" David crumpled it, threw it in the scrap basket, and went out of the office.

XII

FOUR DAYS LATER David arrived at the Republic House in an arthritic vehicle labeled RAY'S TAXI. He asked for, and was given, the same room as before, and there was something proprietary in the way he threw his bag on the bed, something practiced in the way he handled the too-short telephone wire when he called Dr. Moore.

"I'm here, sir. I just got in."

Dr. Moore's grave voice lightened to cheerfulness. "That's fine. Welcome to Haddon. We didn't dare let you know before, but we're going to work your ass off, Doc. Have you applied for your Vermont license?"

"I wrote for it from New York."

"Good. It shouldn't take so long—a week and a half, two weeks. I got that office for you near mine. I'll see you get an invitation to the Rotary lunch so you can get to know people. Rules are, you can't join in less than a year's residence, but you ought to be taken in on some sort of basis."

David was about to protest, thought that this was not just the moment to do so, and said instead, "I guess there'll be plenty to keep me busy until my license comes. I'll have to find a place to live, get a car . . ."

"I'd be glad to have you stay with me, but I suppose you'd feel more free on your own." Again Armstrong thought he detected a note of wistfulness. "Well, I'll be seeing you. It's fine you're here, Dave."

The problem of finding a place to live was uppermost in Armstrong's mind, and with some vague idea of taking steps he wandered out onto the street. The town, just before time for the stores to close, seemed full of good-natured activity, so different from the five-thirty struggle in the city that he stopped on the corner to take it in, and almost at once found himself watching instead a young woman coming toward him on the other side of the street. She was moving rapidly with long, easy strides, her brown tweed coat open, her brown-gray hair blowing back from her face. She was tall, and at that age when slim grace would shortly become thin boniness. Not a native, he thought, though she greeted the people she met with a quick, curt motion of her head. She gave an oddly strong impression of holding herself aloof, of having an objective attitude toward her surroundings, though what it was about her that gave him this conviction he had no idea.

At that moment she swung to the curb and began to cross the street at a long angle that would bring her near him. Conscious that he had been staring at her, he turned his back and walked slowly away, looking into store windows as he passed, like any loiterer, but aware, by a heightening of the atmosphere that seemed to be one of her qualities, that she was in the vicinity. And a moment later when a strong, clear voice said, "Aren't you Dr. Armstrong?" he knew before he turned around that it was she who was speaking to him.

She had stopped with an effect of motion only temporarily arrested. Hazel eyes were looking at him, bright, compelling, intelligent—curious rather than friendly.

"Yes, I am," he said, a little on the defensive against that confident gaze.

"I thought you must be. I'm Adele Perkins, Howard Perkins's wife."

She held out a thin, tanned hand to him—all her movements seemed to be quick and graceful—and taking it he felt nervous tension in the fingers that closed lightly over his. Her features were clear-cut, but at the same time delicate, as though of a substance hard enough to take the finest detail. There was sensitivity, even a too-acute sensitivity, in her face, but if there were inner warmth it did not strike one. If his own self-consciousness at meeting a stranger had not made a muddle of his thoughts, he might have perceived that she was concerned with whether he would please her rather than the opposite. The sensitivity was to her own feelings, as is the way with a strong and demanding ego, and the hardness was for those who would not comply.

Not any of this reached him as coherent thought, for he was distractedly searching for something to say. The best he could manage was "I've just been looking around the town. What I've seen of it seems to be very pretty."

"Oh, it is, but it's becoming too self-conscious about it."

"Why should that be?"

He thought his guess that she wasn't a native must be right, for no native would have so objective a view.

"Well, for one thing, not any of the fine old houses except one, the Nortons', belong to native Vermonters any more. They've been bought by people with money who think there is some special virtue in living in New England. They are set on 'preserving' the Vermont 'atmosphere and traditions' without realizing that they themselves have destroyed them. The result is something completely phony. I hate them for it—not that I'm so fond of pure Vermont either. But enough of that." With her thin hand she brushed her hair impatiently away from the side of her face. "I'm on my way home and Howard told me he has just no more than met you. Would you like to come with me and have a cocktail with us?"

"Thank you. Yes. That's most kind."

"Good. I don't have the car, so we'll have to walk, but it isn't far."

She set out with her swift stride down the street that edged one side of the long oval of the green, past beautiful houses with lights already showing behind the fans above broad doorways. She rustled through the early fallen leaves, a Diana in tweed, her short hair keeping the rhythm of her steps with an airy jounce. Self-possessed, she seemed untroubled by their silence, though it disturbed him to the point of uneasiness. Finally, after discarding several opening remarks, he glanced cautiously at the chiseled profile and said, "But surely, you wouldn't rather live in the city than in such a lovely place as this?"

She made a swift half turn of her head toward him and spoke with a vehemence that startled him. " 'Better fifty years of Europe than a cycle of Cathay.' "

He failed to recognize the quotation and it forced him to search for a reply. About small talk she seemed to please herself without taking the trouble to make it easy for the other person. And with a liking, he thought, for the startling and the bizarre.

"But is it the town or the people that you don't like?"

"Oh, the people!"

"Are they really so bad?"

"I hate them." She stood still and turned to face him. To his amazement, he saw that she was breathing in quick, shallow breaths, clenched hands thrust into her coat pocket. She reminded him of that moment of trembling incandescence before the breaking out of flames. "*I can't stand them!*"

He walked on and she went with him readily enough. After a moment he said, "Who are these people you don't like? Surely it isn't that you 'can't stand' everyone in the town."

Surprisingly, she laughed, but nervously, and she repeated the gesture of brushing her hair away from her face, but some of the tension seemed to go out of her.

"Oh, mostly the people I was talking about earlier. And the Vermonters, who live and work here, though in a different way. Not the tourists or summer people—they don't count. The outsiders who have come here to live are the tightest group, and they never break out of it, no matter how long they live here. They have money, or they wouldn't be here. They go to town meetings and try to feel they belong there. They work for what they call the 'improvement' of the town, by which they mean things like flower boxes on the storefronts. You can see it's really the women I'm talking about. They're forever giving parties to which they ask a native or two just to prove they really do belong—the Episcopalian rector, perhaps, or a lawyer."

Armstrong laughed. "No Catholics? No Methodists?"

"Oh, no, or storekeepers or teachers or real farmers."

Armstrong was still amused. "How about doctors?"

"Well, Howard and I are asked, and patronized. Oh, how patronizing the women can be. And how they gossip!"

"Don't people everywhere?"

"You can escape it in the city. Here it's avid, it's cruel, it's fanatic, and it controls your life. They're dedicated to it, these women—the dedicated, backbiting sisterhood of the mediocre. Oh, God, how I hate this place."

164

"What about the natives—the people who really belong here?" He was amused and interested. "Don't you fit in there either?"

"With the women, you mean? In a place like this they're all that count with another woman. They're a tight amalgam of defensiveness and righteousness—meaning, of course, they've not accepted me either. I'm not their type."

He thought he detected both resentment and self-satisfaction in her tone, and this intrigued him. He said, "I wish you'd explain."

"They've evolved an attitude, a behavior pattern to which they all conform because, though as individuals they're weak, collectively they're strong. Then, having conformed, they force conformity on everyone else. To enforce it they use gossip, disapproval and the threat of exclusion. These are powerful pressures which the women themselves have, for the most part, neither the intelligence nor the self-confidence to defy. This is the base on which small-town morality rests. For those who conform, being socially obedient is synonymous with being good. The good have such hate for the clever . . ."

"And the clever such scorn for the good?"

She laughed. "I talk too much, don't I? Implying I think I'm clever. But it's something I've thought a lot about. I've had to. If you don't accept these women's standards—and accept them without question—if you're more intellectually restless, or just more attractive—if you're different in any way at all, then they shut you out. The key word is 'different.' If you're different from themselves, they don't trust you; they fear you and they shut you out of their group in exactly the way that animals drive out one that isn't like the rest of the pack. I've been shut out, and once that happens the door is never, never opened."

David kept silent, for he was feeling the emotional undercurrents too strongly and he hoped for a change of subject. Presently she said, "It's a relief to talk to somebody to whom I can say what I think. I hope we're going to be friends."

"I hope so . . ."

"Here's where we turn—over this bridge."

As they stepped on the planking of the old bridge, the ironwork overhead, skeletonlike against the fading sky, rattled faintly. She said, "It's quite safe really. It's just always made this noise. We hear it at our house, only we don't hear it, we're so used to it. But we always hear when the ice goes out in the spring. That's the way they say it here—'the ice goes out'—and it goes with a roar, and when it's gone the winter silence has gone too and the river has a voice again. Let's watch the water for a moment, shall we?"

She turned to the rail and leaned over it, and he, beside her, grasped the rail, feeling it still warm from the departed sun. The dark water below flowed swiftly with a rushing sound that, as his attention focused on it, grew into a roar. On the surface white crests of foam appeared, were swept away, and reappeared. The breath of the river rose damp and chill around them. She leaned far out watching the water, so far that, alarmed, he put out a hand ready to steady her.

With one of her quick, and to him unpredictable, movements she drew herself back and faced him.

"Dr. Armstrong, go away from this town. Leave it while you can. Don't stay in this dreadful place. Just go away."

He made a heavy-handed attempt at a light reply, and regretted it at once. "It sounds as though you should be the one to go away."

"I can't. I can't. Howard's in a trap here and so am I." She shivered and drew in a sharp breath. "I'm cold. Let's go on. . . . There's just one hope that we might go. . . . A teaching post will be open at the new Warwick Medical School next fall . . . I don't dare let myself think about it . . ."

After a few steps she said in an ordinary, casual tone, "I'm sorry. I've said a lot of things I shouldn't have, haven't I? That's our house facing the bridge. Howard's car is there, so he's home."

They walked up a path with steps in it, and up onto a porch. She opened the front door and called, "Howard, are you there?" Through the arch that opened from the hall into the living room he saw Dr. Perkins sitting by the lighted fire, an open newspaper in his hands and a drink in a tall glass on the floor beside him.

"Howard, I've brought Dr. Armstrong home for a drink."

Perkins dropped his newspaper on the floor, picked up his glass with his fingers over the rim, and rose without hurrying. He came partway to meet them and stood there swinging his glass.

"Hullo, Doctor. I heard you had arrived."

His manner was cordial, but with enough reserve to suggest that

166

he was not altogether pleased by this intrusion, and he left Armstrong to look around for a place to deposit his coat. He gave his wife a look that Armstrong could not interpret but made him think that unexpected guests were not usual in this house.

"Have a good flight up? What's your drink? Scotch? A martini? I make a good one. Bourbon? You want the usual martini, I suppose, Adele. Come in, won't you?"

This last was said with a touch of irritation, as though the indeterminate way they were standing just inside the room offended a mind that did not want to tolerate vagueness.

"If Mrs. Perkins is going to have a martini, I'll have one too."

"Good." Perkins went to a table where glasses and bottles were set out. Adele threw herself with a show of petulance into a chair opposite the one Dr. Perkins had been using, and thrust her long legs out in front of her. David was left to find a chair, which he drew up to face the fire, and she said, "I'm sorry," leaving him in doubt whether she was perfunctorily sorry about his having to drag up his own chair or about something more generalized in the atmosphere of this house. She made a lovely picture, slim and graceful, her long hands hanging over the arms of the chair. She had withdrawn into her thoughts as completely as though she were alone in the room, and they sat in a silence that gave a false importance to the tinkling sounds of glass and ice from the table where Perkins was stirring the drinks.

In a moment he came back to the fire carrying two stemmed martini glasses filled to the very brim. One he put on a table beside Adele, who glanced at it and turned her brooding gaze back to the fire. The other he held out with a perfectly steady hand to Armstrong, who rose to receive it, awkwardly, because the glass was too full and because he felt himself physically dominated by Perkins's proximity. When Perkins returned to the table to fetch his own drink, David seized this moment of not being observed to take a hasty sip from his and, to his annoyance, spilled a little.

Perkins came back with his own glass replenished and deep amber in color and sat in his chair nursing it in both hands while Armstrong experienced something like panic because he was sitting in silence with two complete strangers and could think of nothing to say. His wits seemed to have deserted him and he sat on his uncomfortable chair with every muscle cramped. Nevertheless, when Perkins broke this silence, he was so startled that he was in danger of spilling his drink again and took a hasty gulp.

"What did you think of our hospital, Doctor? Not exactly what you're used to, I imagine."

"It seems to have all the essentials for a hospital of its size."

"All the essentials but funds to run on."

"But I understand you're always full, that more people want to use the hospital than you have room for, and that if it weren't for rising costs . . ."

"That's true, but those costs make it uneconomic to run a small hospital. Moore is convinced we have to expand or go under."

Adele stirred, gave Perkins a look of reproach, and sighed. Perkins said, "She hates talk about the hospital," and smiled. She flushed with anger, opened the delicate, hard mouth to speak, thought better of it, shrugged slightly and turned a little more toward the fire. This silent show of temper seemed to please Perkins, for he watched her closely, smiling.

Absorbed in this byplay, though unable to follow its meaning, David was unprepared for Perkins's next remark.

"I've a hysterectomy scheduled for tomorrow. Perhaps you'd like to be there."

"Very much, if Dr. Moore hasn't any plans for me."

"He won't have. He's giving the anesthetic."

"Then I'd be delighted."

"Good. . . . You hear, Adele? He'd be delighted. That calls for another drink. Bottoms up!"

He stood up and drained his half-filled glass, and Adele said, "Howard," in a tired voice, as though she knew that protest would be useless.

When Perkins went off to the table that held the bottles and ice, she turned in her chair to face David. "He'll be brilliant, you'll see. He always is, especially when there's someone to watch him. He's really a first-class surgeon."

Perkins brought the shaker and filled her glass, though she had scarcely touched her first drink. He stood beside Armstrong's chair and said, "Go on, finish it, Doctor," and when Armstrong, not wanting to, drained his glass and held it out, Perkins filled it to the brim. He was laughing, though David could see no cause for it, and something about the laugh made him flush.

"It's quite an event—isn't it, Adele?—to get a new doctor in Haddon, and one, Moore seems to think, with a simon-pure record. No blemishes, by God. Not a single one." He went to the bar and came back with a full glass in which the liquor was as dark as before. "Well, here's to Dr. Parsifal!"

David, in distress and wondering how best he might make his escape, glanced toward Adele and saw her watching her husband with bright, hostile eyes, her breath coming quickly, her body rigid as when she had burst out with her hatred of the women of Haddon.

Perkins said, "Our surgical work, by the way, is mostly with farm people, and low-income town people and workers and their families from the Silver Springs mills. The rich outsiders haven't discovered that now they can get careful, modern surgery done in the country, and they take their problems to Boston or New York where it costs them more and isn't any better. What I'm leading up to is this. You'll hear that I do more hysterectomies than any surgeon in the state, and it's true. This is why. Some farm woman comes to me with trouble with her uterus. Maybe it doesn't amount to much and I might be able to carry her along for years. But she'd have to keep doctoring and paying bills for it and worrying and probably not be able to do the work she should. So I take her uterus out right off without waiting, and save her all that. Sound procedure, I think, though some don't agree with me. By the way, do you hunt, Doctor?"

David said vaguely, still watching Adele, "Hunt?"

"Deer season coming up."

"Oh, I see. No, I don't hunt."

Adele made the now familiar gesture of brushing the hair from the side of her face, and he found he had been expecting that. And he returned his attention to Perkins with a certain amount of hostility in his own attitude.

Dr. Perkins, drink half lifted, was listening. A door slammed, and Adele raised her head to listen too. There were scrabbling noises, then the sound of someone walking in the back of the house, and he had an impression of her face and Dr. Perkins's hardening into oddly similar expressions that had no meaning for him but that he felt might be habitual to them. At the far end of the room a door burst open, and a youth who looked to be about seventeen came in precipitately, saw an unexpected stranger there, and came to an awkward and self-conscious halt.

He stood there blinking as though a spotlight were on him. He was tall and spindly as an undernourished weed. He wore a bulky sweater, open in front, sagging and not very clean. Blue jeans covered his long legs to a point above his anklebone and on his feet were dirty sneakers. Under his arm he carried a pile of books which he clutched nervously to him, and while the three around the fire still stared at him in silence, he dropped one of them. The motion with which he stooped to pick it up was quick and furtive as an animal's, but Armstrong saw that the hand stretched out was well-proportioned and smooth—a fine, honest-looking hand that made him at once think better of this miserable, shy boy.

Adele was the first to speak, saying in a voice too high and loud, "My son, Dr. Armstrong. Howard Manville Perkins, Junior, 'Howie' for short, who, if you can believe it, is destined for the medical profession. His sartorial standards are those of the local high school. I might add that he doesn't want to be a doctor."

Though her voice was clear and steady, Armstrong thought she was not very far from tears. Howie looked as though he had received a blow which made him shrink but caused him no surprise. He continued to stand there as though he did not know how to do otherwise, so plainly expecting to be struck again that, shocked, Armstrong looked to see how his parents might be taking this. Adele was sitting very straight, her feet drawn under her chair, her head held high, looking, Armstrong thought—clinically watching a pulse beating swiftly against the taut skin of her neck—as though she too had received a blow. Perkins, shaking his glass to make the ice rattle, was staring at his son with cold contempt. Armstrong, embarrassed and angry almost beyond endurance with both Perkins and Adele, said the only thing he could think of.

"The fact is that I'm not at all familiar with hysterectomy procedures. I've only seen four of them—as an intern when I was on GYN-OB on rotating service."

Both parents had turned blank faces toward him, and from

Howie he heard a sigh of relief like wind in autumn leaves, and knew that the boy had escaped to a chair in a corner and was opening one of his books. Armstrong plunged on.

"I brought a few books with me so I could put in some time studying before I actually get started, because I suspect two-thirds of what I'll be doing here will be new to me. I'll have a good look at Zollinger and Cutler's *Atlas of Surgical Operations* tonight so I'll have a fair idea of what you're doing tomorrow. And now I think I'd better be getting on. . . ."

The front door was closed behind him almost before his back was turned, and the porch light went out when he reached the bottom of the steps. He stood still a moment to let himself grow used to the darkness. Behind his eyes he felt a dull fullness that meant the beginning of a headache, and he drew in deep breaths of the cool, pure air. The dim glow of a streetlight barely showed him his path, and on the bridge there was no light at all. He made his way toward it feeling as though he were alone at the end of the earth.

As soon as the door shut behind Armstrong, Dr. Perkins returned to the living room, leaving Adele to turn out the porch light. He went directly to the table that held the ice and bottles and poured himself another drink, saying over his shoulder, "Why the hell did you have to drag him here with you?"

"He's a stranger in town, for one thing. And he'll be working with you. I thought it was the polite and civilized thing to do."

"Polite and civilized! That's you all over, isn't it?"

Perkins came back and threw himself heavily into the chair by the fire. Some of his drink slopped over onto the carpet and he stared at it unseeingly.

Adele was standing by the fire, her elbow on the mantel shelf, looking down at him with an expressionless, fixed stare. He raised his glass and drank. She drew a long sigh. "Oh, Howard . . ."

He set his glass down hard on the table beside him. "Once for all, will you keep out of my affairs?"

She stared at him a moment longer, then she tossed her head back and walked with quick, staccato steps toward the kitchen. There she found Howie standing by the open door of the refrigerator, a glass of milk in one hand and two pieces of bread, from which a large bite had been taken, clamped together in the other hand.

"Howie, put that down. You'll spoil your appetite for dinner."

"I'd rather eat like this, Mom. I don't want to sit at the table and eat a regular dinner. I'm not hungry anyway. I'd just rather eat like this." And his eyes shifted toward the living room where Perkins was sitting with his drink.

"I said put that down, and shut the refrigerator door."

Howie shoved the door shut with his shoulder and went to the sink. There, with his back to his mother, he took a swallow of milk and a large bite from the bread before he put them down and, with his mouth full, turned to face her. She was tying an apron around her waist.

"And another thing, young man. When we have company, don't just stand there letting your charm overwhelm them. . . . Oh God, if I could only be proud of you . . ."

From the living room there was a sound of breaking glass, then heavy footsteps. Adele turned her head toward the wall that divided the living room from the kitchen, listening. Howie drew his shoulders in, and his face slowly and painfully reddened. After a moment they heard the slam of the front door.

Adele, her hands still on the tie of her apron behind her back, stood very still. A car motor started into life, the sound sharp and precise in the clear night air. There was a crunch of gravel, and the throb of the engine dying away in the distance, then silence. For a moment more Adele stood without moving; then she threw herself into a chair by the kitchen table, covered her face with her hands and burst into tears.

Howie stood for a moment looking down at her, his face twisted, his thin body shaking. With a convulsive movement he took a step toward her. He made an effort to speak, and the words turned into a strangled swallow that made the Adam's apple jump in his taut throat. He flung his arms out in a wild gesture of helpless desperation, and turning his back on his mother, he grabbed the glass of milk, drained it and set it back on the sink. Moving furtively, his soft shoes making no noise, he went to the back door, opened it and slipped out into the night.

172

XIII

At seven o'clock on a frosty morning Dr. Armstrong was sitting at the golden-oak table that had been somebody's gift to the nurses' dining room, listening to something of no greater importance than the clatter of dishes in the adjacent kitchen. In the morning thickness of atmosphere these sounds were loud and dull. At noontime they would be sharp and rapid, at suppertime slow, irregular and quiet. The same pots and pans and dishes, yet all the difference in the world. . . . He lifted his own half-filled coffee cup and set it down hard in the saucer. The result was an unrewarding thump of heavy crockery, and, suddenly bored with the whole business, he reached for the percolator and filled the cup to the brim.

Across the table Dr. Moore was lost in thought, his cup empty and on his plate a powdering of sugar where there had been a doughnut. He had been sitting there like that when Armstrong arrived, had sent him a shaftlike glance, said a pleasant "Good morning," and withdrawn again into his thoughts. He was already in a white scrub suit like the one David himself was wearing. The ill-fitting, belted smock made his body seem more massive than usual. The thickness of his gray hair pushed up his cap, which he wore back on his head, exposing his forehead. He was relaxed on his hard chair as though he had learned, as an old dog does, to use every possible moment for rest. Feeling David's scrutiny, he came with an effort out of his brown study.

"See Perkins's car out there? A big, black Cadillac."

Turning to look out of the window toward the parking lot, David remembered that, as Moore did not wear glasses for close work, he probably could not see well at a distance.

"There's a car down at the other end that might be it."

"Good."

The way Moore straightened his shoulders seemed to indicate relief.

"I was thinking about a woman who came to the office the other day complaining about pains in the abdomen. She'd seen two doctors in her own town. They both said appendicitis. She'd heard of this hospital so she came to see me. I put her on the table and I could feel the trouble easy."

"Not appendicitis?"

"Cancer. I could feel it had spread all over everywhere—feel it easy. The thing is, neither of those damn-fool doctors had touched her, didn't put a hand on her. Just leaned back in their chairs and said, 'Appendicitis,' just like that. There ought to be some way to get at those birds. My God."

"What did you do?"

"Had Perkins look at her. He didn't want any part of it—the thing had gone too far—so we sent her to Warwick. The operating surgeon phoned to say her appendix was small and clean as your finger, but the cancer was all around everywhere. They just sewed her up again. But can you imagine those doctors not taking the trouble to—"

An elderly nurse in a scrub smock and cap appeared in the doorway. "Excuse me, Doctors, we're ready when you are."

With a start David recognized Edna Judson. Because she was without the towering Punch-and-Judy cap and her hair was hidden, he was fully aware for the first time of her features. She looked worn fine, like a too often washed piece of linen; her lips were thin and bluish. The gray, tired eyes looked at them from some remote standpoint of her own, and her skin seemed on the point of quivering, as though nerves lay just under the surface. She hardly seemed the same woman.

She left them quickly and the two men rose, Moore as though he felt the weight of his own body. Going through the door he put his arm across David's shoulders. "Let's use the damn elevator, shall we?"

As they came to the operating room, Edna—this strange new Edna in surgical dress—came out of a doorway guiding a wheeled cart. A woman wearing a flowered wrapper over a crinkled hospital gown was lying on the cart. Moore smiled at her.

174

"Hullo, Addie."

"Hullo, Dr. Moore." The reply was quavering, the voice thickened by sedation.

"This is Dr. Armstrong, Addie, who's going to watch us and see we do right by you."

"Hullo, Doctor."

Through the fog of her sedation she was trying to manage herself, trying to be adequate, and, it seemed to David, doing a good job of it. Her body was thick and short. "Stalwart" was the word that came to his mind, and he thought he could easily picture her standing, thick legs apart, lifting a full pitchfork of hay. Her short, nondescript hair was stringy and dried by too much sun and wind, and the fingernails of the hand that clutched the edge of the cart showed lines of black too deeply imbedded to be scrubbed away.

David and Moore stood aside while Edna and Addie went slowly past and around the screen into the operating room, and then they followed. The operating lights were on, the familiar glareless, shadowless illumination that gave David a feeling of being in his own element. An instrument nurse gowned in green, her mask in place, was rapidly sorting instruments and barely paused to acknowledge Moore's introduction of David. Edna was taking off Addie's flowered wrapper. Moore said to her in a sharp undertone, "Perkins here?" and she answered in the same way, "Yes, sir."

"Addie, we've got to get you over on the table." He pushed her gently, then put his arms under her, grunted and lifted her. She sat up for a moment, dazed, then carefully stretched herself out on her back, pulling her short gown down with both hands. She lay there holding on to the sides of the table, her legs shaking. Moore bent over her.

"What kind of anesthetic do you want us to use, Addie?"

She stared up at him, wide-eyed, saw he was joking and managed a weak smile. "Whatever you say."

"I always think a piece of lead pipe with some gauze around it is pretty good, don't you, Dr. Armstrong?"

Her smile grew firmer. "Go on now, Doc."

Edna began vigorously pulling off her gown and Addie, naked, put both hands over her shaved *mons Veneris* and turned her head away. "Edna."

"Here, dear."

Edna pushed a towel under the hands and Addie clutched it and pressed it to her body.

"I'm cold, Edna."

"No you're not. That's just nerves. Be a good girl, now."

David wandered off to the stand that held the anesthetic materials and picked up Addie's chart. "Addison Day," he read. "Age forty-three. Heavy periods for ten years. Pap smear negative. Fibroids and uterine bleeding." The anesthesia record, still to be filled in, lay on the table, and bending over to read it, he saw that the anesthesia was to be spinal-block, and that in preparation for the operation she had been given Nembutal. He looked toward the table where Addie, under the influence of the Nembutal, seemed to have gone to sleep.

Moore came to the anesthetic table and began to prepare a spinal needle. "See many spinals these days, Doc?"

"Not many—in the kind of surgery I do. They were in disfavor for a while with our staff. Now they're coming back again to an extent. Used a lot in obstetrics, of course."

"They've been popular in the country ever since they got to be safe, for if a surgeon has to, he can pretty near do the whole show himself."

Moore held up the needle and looked at it critically, and the instrument nurse said suddenly, "Addie, do you feel like urinating? Because if you do . . ."

Addie stirred and said thickly, "Is that you, Helen?"

"Yes it is. Do you . . ."

"No, I don't."

"You better be sure, Addie, because we don't want to be mopping up."

Dr. Moore seemed to be dissatisfied with the spinal needle he was about to use, and while he fussed with it, there was quiet in the operating room. Then Addie said loudly, "I feel fine. I think I'll go home," and everyone laughed. David was growing accustomed to Miss Judson's different appearance, as he might to the appearance of a stranger, but without fusing the two images of her in his mind. She seemed older, sadder, but in perfect accord with her surroundings, watching Dr. Moore with experienced eyes.

"Are you all ready, Dr. Moore?"

176

"Yes, all ready now."

Edna put a hand on Addie's shoulder and another on her hip and turned her on her side with her back to Dr. Moore, who had laid the spinal needle down and was standing by the table. Addie clutched her towel. Perkins came in wearing a scrub suit and cap, his air of being larger than life undiminished by this clothing. His skin was sallow, his eyes a little bloodshot, and the lines of his face looked as though they had been drawn in heavily with a blunt pencil, and it came to David with an unpleasant shock that the man must have gone on drinking after he had left the Perkinses' house the evening before.

Perkins stopped by the table and looked around. "For Christ sake, aren't you folks ready yet?"

Addie opened her eyes and giggled. "I'm going home."

Perkins looked down at her without any change of expression and went out, saying over his shoulder in a tone of sarcasm, "Take your time," and after he had gone David thought he felt a slight rigidity in everyone's attitude, including his own. Moore was swabbing the spot on Addie's back, below her waist, where the needle would go in, using a gauze sponge that had been dipped in antiseptic, and David found a stool by the wall where he could watch and be out of the way. He was feeling a little taken aback by the informality of all that had been going on, not sure how it could be otherwise when all those present knew each other so well, but disturbed by it, thinking of it as something to which he would have to grow accustomed.

Addie, realizing suddenly that her time had come, cried out in fright. "Edna, are you there?"

"I'm right here beside you, dear. Now arch your back. Pretend you're a cat who has just seen a dog."

Moore was feeling the spaces between her vertebrae with the fingers of his left hand, holding the spinal needle with his right. "I can't do it like this. Edna, can you sit her up?"

Edna held the naked woman, an arm around her, a hand on the back of Addie's head, pressing it down on her shoulder. The towel slipped to the floor and Addie put her arms around Edna's waist. And unexpectedly to himself David was deeply moved by this scene. There was a quality here in this country operating room that was wholly new to him, though he was not sure if it had any

177

relation to surgery, valuable or otherwise, or even precisely what this quality was. Compassion, perhaps. Yes, certainly compassion, and also trust. All these people trusted each other out of long, shared experience.

The support given to the patient by such warmth and friendliness would, he thought, be impossible in any but a small community hospital.

He had been so absorbed in watching Edna caring for Addie that he had missed the actual administering of the spinal anesthetic and now Moore was saying, "That's it, Addie," and patting her back. "Now you can leave the rest to us."

Edna, her hand still holding the back of Addie's head, bent over and laid her on the table, her arms under Addie's shoulders and legs. Addie was crying. Helen held out a piece of gauze and Edna took it and wiped Addie's eyes. "Don't cry now, Addie, we're all here looking after you."

A moment later Perkins was standing in the doorway of the scrub room, saying, "You better get off that stool and scrub, Doctor."

Startled, Armstrong rose. "I won't be able to scrub with you, Dr. Perkins—my Vermont license hasn't come through."

"Never mind about that."

"I really don't think I should."

"Look, I've done hysterectomies alone in my time, but I'm not going to do this one. What the hell do you think we hired you for?"

"Dr. Perkins, I'd be glad to assist, naturally. It's one of the things I'm here for, but until my license—"

Moore was around at the anesthetist's station at the head of the table with a protective hand on Addie's shoulder to keep her from being alarmed by their raised voices. "I thought you'd fixed up for one of the Warwick residents to come and assist, Howard. Where is he?"

"I called him off. Dr. Armstrong—fan your ass to the scrub room, *stat.*"

Armstrong, fighting down anger, looked toward Moore and found Moore watching him with troubled eyes. "The laws says, Dave, that you have to have a license except in case of an emergency. At least, that's what I think it says. Come to think of it, I've never read it. I guess we'll have to call this an emergency. I'll take the responsibility, but I don't believe anyone's going to hear about it. Go along and scrub."

Armstrong stood in front of the sink next to the one Perkins was about to use, and waited for him to take a mask from one of the two boxes on the shelf above. The mask Perkins chose was made of a greenish composition, molded to fit over the mouth and nose, and, in place, it looked outlandishly like an animal snout. Armstrong, who did not think these composition masks fitted tightly enough, took a gauze one from the other box, and the two doctors each tied his own set of double tapes in silence.

Armstrong looked on the shelf for a timer to set for the requisite five minutes of scrubbing and found instead an hourglass that, he assumed, was filled with five minutes' worth of sand. The hourglass appeared to be as old as the hospital. Amused, he upended it, waited for Perkins to finish using the bottle of antiseptic detergent, and poured it liberally on his forearms. He scrubbed them thoroughly and continued on to the backs of his hands, the palms, the fingers, inside and then outside.

He was rinsing before beginning to repeat the whole process when Miss Judson looked in the door.

"Glove size, please, Dr. Armstrong?"

"Seven and a half. Thank you."

On with the scrubbing. Perkins, at the next sink, arms raised and bent, was letting antiseptic solution drip off his elbows. The drops on his arms ran a zigzag downward obstacle course among the black, wiry hairs. Out of the corner of his eye he was watching every move that David was making. Annoyed by this surveillance— as though he were an intern scrubbing for the first time—David felt the beads of perspiration coming out on his upper lip, making his mask feel damp and clammy. Dipping his arms in a basin of antiseptic, he ignored Perkins insofar as he could.

A few minutes later, gowned in green and gloved, they stood at their appointed sides of the operating table and Armstrong began to swab the site of the abdominal incision, with Perkins still watching him closely.

"Get a move on, Doc."

179

Armstrong glanced up and moved just perceptibly faster. When he had finished, he went out for a second quick scrub. As he left he heard Perkins say, "O.K., Ed?"

And Moore replied, "O.K., Howard. Aren't we, Addie?"

"I guess so." Her voice sounded feeble and forlorn.

Returning, Armstrong found that the first part of the incision had been made. Perkins was wholly concentrated on what he was doing. Armstrong saw at once that he worked with impressive sureness and at a speed to which Armstrong was not accustomed. Holding retractors and clamps, he had the feeling of being always just a little behind and he realized that he was going to have to change some deeply rooted habits. Perkins was tying down on bleeders with a speed that made it impossible to follow his motions, but the sutures were expertly knotted. Twice Armstrong's hand got in the way and when he said, "Sorry," Perkins replied with a grunt. The thought crossed Armstrong's mind that Perkins might be showing off, but when he glanced at him suspiciously he saw that Perkins was too committed to his work for this to be true.

The abdominal packs brought the uterus into view, and Perkins said, "Self-retaining retractor, Helen," and received an instrument that, in place, held the incision open in a diamond shape, freeing the surgeon's hands. Perkins pulled the uterus where Armstrong held it with a fork-shaped clamp, while Perkins with toothed forceps in his left hand picked up the loose layer of the peritoneum and with scissors in his right hand made a transverse cut in it close to its attachment to the uterus. That done, he paused to examine the uterus, which was unhealthy-looking and half again its normal size.

"Nasty-looking organ, isn't it?"

At the head of the table Moore stepped up on a riser to see.

"No question about that having to come out."

"None at all. Addie, can you hear me?"

"Is that . . . It's Dr. Perkins, isn't it?"

Her voice sounded as though she had awakened from a deep sleep.

"Yes. You feel anything, Addie?"

"I can feel you boys pawing around down there, but it doesn't hurt. I think I'll go to sleep."

"Good, you do that."

Perkins's hands were resting lightly on the rim of the retractor, and David noticed irrelevantly that the black hairs on their backs showed through the yellow gloves. When the hands moved, the hairs moved with a different motion as though they were separately alive. Repelled by this sight, he looked away.

"Doctor!"

Armstrong started and met a challenging stare from the bloodshot eyes.

"Daydreaming?"

"No, sir."

"All right, then. Take over."

"What?"

"I said, take over. Deliver the uterus. Take it out, Doctor. Let's see what you can do."

At the head of the table, Moore, who was sitting down again, raised his head to listen.

"I don't understand, Dr. Perkins. Are you asking me to finish the operation?"

"Yes. Alone. Without assistance. You're going to start being a country doctor right now."

Addie said in a thick-tongued, frightened voice, "What's going on, Dr. Moore? What's going on?"

"It's all right, Addie. They're just talking. Nothing to do with you."

Out of the corner of his eye David saw Moore pick up a hypodermic, guessed he was going to give Addie an injection of Pentothal and was glad.

Perkins said, "Come on, Doc, are you going to leave that uterus in there all day?" and Armstrong realized he was still holding the uterus in its pulled-upward position.

"Dr. Perkins, I've only seen four hysterectomies—when I was an intern. I told you that. I'm not competent."

"I thought you were going to read up on it."

"I did, but—"

"A country doctor has to do lots of things he isn't experienced in doing. You'd better find out what it feels like."

Moore was standing up again. "Howard, you can't ask him to do that. He isn't licensed in Vermont yet."

"He was assisting, wasn't he?"

"That's somewhat different, Howard."

Perkins leaned over the operating table almost into David's face, the black hairs under his gloves moving in their unpleasant way as he laid his hands on the rim of the retractor.

"Dr. Armstrong, who's the boss in an operating room? By law, Doctor?"

"The head surgeon."

"All right, Doctor, deliver the uterus."

Armstrong looked toward Moore, who said, "Can you?" But before he could answer Perkins said, "I'm not going to walk out, Ed. I'll be right here watching every move. I just want to see what kind of a surgeon you got us."

Armstrong, as angry as he had ever been, looked down at the work waiting for him and concentrated on steadying himself. Trying hard to remember his reading of the night before, he thought that his first move should be to isolate the round ligaments and the Fallopian tubes, and realized he was in trouble before he started. With one finger under the Fallopian tubes and the other hand holding the instrument that was keeping the uterus in place, he was unable to make any move at all.

Perkins started to laugh and Armstrong grew red with anger. Then Helen's gloved hand appeared and took the handle of the instrument from him, holding the uterus as he had been doing. He looked up to meet serious, sympathetic brown eyes and knew by the way her mask moved that she was smiling encouragement at him. Then he went around to take up his position at the operator's side of the table and Perkins moved to the assistant's place.

Perkins was still laughing. "You see, Doc, you've already learned the first two lessons of country surgery—self-retaining retractors and a willing scrub nurse." He laughed loudly again and David glanced nervously toward the head of the table. Under the injection of Sodium Pentothal Addie was sleeping peacefully.

What followed had the quality of a very interesting nightmare, but he became so absorbed in what he was doing that most of the time he forgot Perkins. Step by step he repeated to himself what he remembered.

Slip a loose gauze sponge into Douglas's pouch to keep any intestine from coming down into the operating field.

As though he had spoken aloud, Helen held out a sponge clamped in forceps.

Watch out with the Ochsner clamps. Don't point them downward for fear of damaging the ureters.

He hesitated over this, and when he directed the first clamp correctly, Perkins said, "Good."

Watch out for the arteries . . . use a half clamp higher up when the uterus is as large as this one.

A resident in GYN had let an artery get away from him and in half a second the field was flooded with blood and the resident was groping wildly in it for the end of the severed artery. By good luck, he had found it quickly. David had not been present, but he heard about it, and remembering, he took extra care to secure the arteries before he cut them.

He took no account of time, and again and again he stopped to figure out how some procedure could be done single-handed or with the help of Helen, leaning down from her platform by the instrument stand. At last the uterus came clear and was lifted to a waiting basin. Perkins watched it, grinning, and David, seeing the quality of the grin, hoped with sudden vehemence that he wouldn't say what was in his mind.

With the uterus on the first stage of its journey to the pathology laboratory, Armstrong took time to straighten up for a moment's relief from physical strain. The back of his neck ached and the corners of his eyes were full of sweat. He drew one deep breath and bent over his work again.

The operation was by no means finished. He worked on, placing sutures with care, inspecting for bleeding, insuring support from the round ligament for the empty vaginal vault, bringing the bladder flap over it and anchoring it to the uterosacral ligaments. These steps would insure that Addie, in her farm work, would not be hampered by any structural weakness.

Perkins, to Armstrong's surprise, helped him with the closing, keeping to the assistant's side of the table and confining himself to the assistant's role, not crowding Armstrong, allowing him to work at his own pace.

When they had finished, Armstrong nodded gravely to Helen and said, "Thank you," hoping she would realize how truly grateful he felt. He waited while she untied Perkins's gown, and when she untied his own he said, "You helped a lot," and saw the serious brown eyes above her mask grow soft as velvet with pleasure.

In the scrub room, pulling off his gown and throwing it at the used-garment hamper, he stood with his back to Perkins, but his anger had vanished during his absorption in his work and he was too tired now to fan it into life.

The two doctors washed side by side in silence, David too exhausted to think about anything but his longing for the shower he intended to take when he got to the locker room. Perkins was the first to finish and he went to the door, still without breaking the silence. But with his hand around the edge of the door he turned back for a minute and stood there watching David drying his hands. Then he said, "It took you damn near all day, but it was a good job, Doctor."

=== **XIV**

Aʀᴍsᴛʀᴏɴɢ's ʟɪᴄᴇɴsᴇ to practice medicine in Vermont took longer to arrive (like all such things) than it was reasonable to believe. But in this period of waiting he was far from idle, and he discovered what sort of things can be done quickly in Vermont and what other things, for no clear reason, take an interminable time. He took a test for a driver's license, which consumed an entire morning and was a good deal more rigorous than he expected. He bought a car, which was simple.

About the car he had consulted Moore. "Should I get a jeep, sir?"

"I wouldn't, Dave. This country gets pretty rough in winter, but the state is pretty good about keeping the highways and secondary roads open except during blizzards, maybe. I've a few patients in families that have sort of been pushed back into the hills by progress, and sometimes those roads are pretty bad. There are fewer of those people every year, but they're the reason why I drive a jeep. You can always use mine if you need to. Perkins doesn't have that kind of practice, and he only keeps a jeep to get up to a cabin he has on top of Mount Adamant."

The car David bought was small, gray, and had, as he discovered when he knew this country better, the architectural lines of a beaver house. He drove it with characteristic circumspection.

The renting of an apartment was also easy, though that, he suspected, was largely luck. It was located over the shoe store, on the same side of Maple Street as Moore's office, about three doors away. It consisted of two rooms and a small kitchen, and it was reached by a flight of wooden stairs up from the street. He liked it because the building was old and solid and there was a fireplace that the landlord claimed was in workable condition.

The furnishings were another matter. He chose what he thought he would need, an austere collection from the floor samples at the furniture and undertaking establishment on Main Street. The salesman didn't "rightly know" when the pieces could be gotten out of the warehouse, which was in another town, and could not be persuaded to name even an approximate delivery time. "Soon's we can, Doc" was all he would say.

Dishes, a few pans and a percolator he bought in the dime store, and the buying of them took him a little further in his acquaintance with small-town life. He happened to be the only customer and when it was discovered what he had come for, the manager and three women clerks gathered around to help. They discussed his needs as though this were a purchase of great importance and took the decisions out of his hands, for which he was grateful.

One day, in the midst of all these varied activities, it occurred to him to wonder how, when the time came, he would be able to leave his work long enough to go back to New York to vote. That thought gave rise to another, which was that if he were to become a citizen of Vermont there would be no problem. The idea had an unexpected appeal for him, and after some thought he brought it up in a talk with Dr. Moore. They were in Moore's Maple Street office, and when Moore heard about it he swung back in his swivel chair in a way that David had come to know as a sign that something had given him unexpected pleasure.

"Why not, Dave? It's simple enough, and people would be bound to hear about it and they'd like it."

"What do I do?"

"You go to the town clerk, take the Freeman's Oath, pay your poll tax, and that's it."

The town clerk's office turned out to be a partitioned-off space at the back of a dusty and dark hardware store. The clerk was an old man—in his nineties, David thought. He was sitting at a roll-top desk in surroundings that must have been unchanged during his fifty years of office. When David came to the door, the old man laid a knotted, blue-veined hand on a pile of papers, looked up over his glasses, and startled him by saying, "Morning, Doc."

"Good morning, sir. I was thinking about becoming a citizen of this state and I'm told you're the man to see."

186

"Just thinkin', or made up your mind? If it's just thinkin', I'm not agoin' to help you. It's somethin' a man has to do what he feels to about, and he needs to take counsel with himself good before he decides."

David started to smile, and thought better of it. "My mind's made up."

"All right, then, young fella, come in."

There was a chair by the desk, but since it was not offered, David remained standing, and the old man scrutinized him with severity. After a moment, he nodded his head and made a sucking noise with his lips that David interpreted as satisfaction.

"All right, then, I'll read you the Freeman's Oath, and you listen careful."

The old man slowly and carefully began the painful process of getting to his feet, and David, shocked at the effort this involved, put out a hand to assist. "Must you get up, sir?"

The hand was waved away with the peevishness of extreme age. "The Oath's somethin' you stands on your feet to read, Doctor."

He stooped over the desk, pulled a loose-leaf book from a pigeon-hole where it lay by itself, and opened it at a marker. Then he straightened himself in ceremonious preparation. David, uncertain of what was expected of him, started to raise his right hand and the old clerk fretfully motioned it down.

"No, not yet. I read it first, and you listen good. Then, if you think you can do as it says, I read it again, and you put your hand up and says, 'I do.'"

"*You solemnly swear that*"—the quavering voice grew unexpectedly strong and steady, and it was apparent that the Clerk did not need to look at the book in his hands—"*whenever you give your Vote or Suffrage, touching any matter that concerns the State of Vermont, you will do it so as in your conscience you shall judge will most conduce to the best good of the same, as established by the Constitution, without fear or favor of any person.*"

He lowered the book and gave David a searching look, and David nodded thoughtfully.

"There's another piece, Doc, for them who, like yourself, comes from out the state."

"*You do solemnly swear that you will be true and faithful to the*

State of Vermont, and that you will not, directly or indirectly, do any act or thing injurious to the Constitution or Government thereof. So Help You God."

He read this with the same solemn emphasis, and at the end David said, "I can swear to that, sir."

"Well, then. Raise your right hand." The old man lifted the book and took a deep breath, but this time he made no pretense of reading. Over his glasses his eyes held David's, bright, sharp and knowledgeable. And at the end, the old man cocked his head on the side to listen as though not to let a shade of the quality of David's tone escape him. After that he let David help him back into his chair and waved a hand at the chair that stood beside his desk.

"Sit down, young man, while I put you in the Town Records. Then there's a bit I want to say to you."

He made a careful entry in another very fat book, doing it, surprisingly, with a ballpoint pen. When he had finished he swung his chair to face David.

"The way I look at it, the Oath means something special in your case, you being a doctor."

"Yes?"

"Like this, seems like. You ain't been here long enough to know, maybe, that doctors here are something they ain't in the city—they're public servants. Public servants. That's a big responsibility you take on right on top of your responsibility as a citizen and to your patients. You know what I'm gettin' at?"

"I'm not sure."

"Well, listen now. What was your responsibility as a doctor back in the city?"

"To do the best I could by my patients. I owed something to my chief, Dr. Fairchild, of course, and in a sort of general way to the hospital."

"I thought that was about it. Well, here, you—along with every other doctor—are responsible for the level of health in the state. The government's sort of tried to take it over through the Public Health Service. That doesn't lessen your responsibility one bit. You see something you think's not just right, you come to Town Meeting and say so. We got a town health officer who ain't a doctor. He'll be coming to you and Moore as he does to Perkins, and even Ladd sometimes, for advice. You give it to him in the best interests of the town. Then there's another thing. Medicine's changing awfully fast. I suppose you've run into that?"

"I certainly have."

"Now, what I'm saying's important. It's up to you doctors to see that we get these improvements so country people can have the advantage of them. I don't say the doctors in the state haven't been doing it pretty well, maybe, but it ain't a job any of you can lay down on. Now, that's all, excepting you pay the poll tax. Four-fifty."

David put the money into the Clerk's thin, dry hand, and waiting for a receipt, feeling in some dim way that he would like to remember every detail of this experience, he looked around him. Over the desk were several framed documents; one of them surprisingly (or perhaps not so surprisingly) was a diploma granting a B.A. degree from Harvard long ago. Beside it was a faded photograph of a building that looked like a courthouse, and beyond that a stuffed trout mounted on a board. On a shelf by the unshaded window stood a dusty row of old-fashioned seals such as notaries used. Against the wall opposite the desk was a long row of filing cabinets, some old wooden ones, some modern metal. On top was a large, evil-looking stuffed bird with wings spread that, David thought, not being an eagle might be a hawk.

The clerk said, "Here you are, young man," and with a start David saw he was holding out the receipt and that he was showing the preliminary signs of being about to rise.

"Don't get up, sir." David himself rose, pocketing the receipt.

"If you'll excuse me, I won't. Nice to have you in town. Someday I'll come in and see you—see if you can do any better about this rheumatism than Doc Moore's been doin'."

David went back to the hotel to put in an hour or two of study, which was a thing he did in every moment of leisure he could find. Now that he was committed to this year in Haddon, he was, perhaps belatedly, appalled at the many things he would have to know that he did not, and since his practice would be about sixty percent medical, the books he was studying were textbooks on medicine.

His unpreparedness for a general practice was brought home to him uncomfortably one day, when he went on a house call with Dr. Moore. The patient was a boy about seven years old whose face and chest were covered with sores. A strange, unpleasant smell filled the room where the boy lay, and Moore's first action was to open a window. The lad's condition looked serious enough to David, though Moore seemed to take it lightly. Moore gave the boy a stern lecture about not scratching the sores, and rummaged in his bag for some medicine which he gave to the boy's mother. While Moore was talking to the woman, David made his escape to the fresh outside air.

When they were driving away, David said in his solemn way, "What was your diagnosis, sir?"

"What?"

"The skin eruption—what do you think is causing it?"

Moore stared at him in astonishment; then he burst into a shout of laughter. "Chicken pox, Dave. Chicken pox. Wrong time of year, but chicken pox. I knew what it was by the smell as soon as we went in the house. Haven't you ever seen a case before?"

"No, as a matter of fact, I haven't."

Moore thought about this in silence for a while as they drove. Then he said slowly, "I can see how that might happen. So much basic science a medical student has to learn today that there's not the time there was for simple symptoms. And chicken pox isn't something that gets into a big city hospital."

"Just the same, it's pretty serious my not knowing . . ."

"Don't be too bothered by that. More than half the medicine I learned, I learned after I was in practice, largely from the older doctors round about. Nowadays we don't think of learning from the older men as standard educational procedure, but actually it is. I imagine you've picked up quite a bit from Adam Fairchild, haven't you?"

"I have indeed."

"Same thing in a general country practice, only more so, probably. Don't let it bother you, Dave."

This humiliating experience drove David to work even harder at his books. He studied late at night; he propped a book open on the dresser and read while he tied his tie. He took his book to meals.

One day, on his way to breakfast with his book under his arm, he stopped at the desk to see if the morning mail contained the license he was waiting for, and found instead an invitation to be a guest at a Rotary Club luncheon, which he threw away, and a note from Moore hastily written on two pages torn from a prescription pad. The note asked him if he could go to Beaver Floods sometime that day to see how old Alice Henderson was getting on. It need not, Moore said, be a professional call, but as he had not been able to see the old woman for some time, he would like to know that she was all right. There followed some confused lines and scratches that were a map of the roads that led there.

David started out as the Revere bell was striking ten. Once out of town he drove slowly, for never in his life had he seen a day like this. The sun, still low in the sky, was filling the chilly air with a pale gold glitter. Mist rose from the streams, the trees were a blaze of color, and the meadows were white with hoarfrost. The frost was a miracle such as he had never seen. Every blade of grass, every roadside weed, was covered with it and transformed into white, lacelike beauty. From the chimneys of the farmhouses pale blue wisps of woodsmoke rose. In the gardens, finished for the season, a few heads of bluish-gray cabbage still remained, a few tomato vines blackened by frost, and here and there a pumpkin. Along the dirt road David was following, patches of ice, that would be puddles when the sun rose higher, splintered and crackled as the wheels of the car passed slowly over them.

Bemused by this strange world, David had been driving for a half hour, Moore's map on the seat beside him, when he came to a steep hill with an open pasture at the top. Some level ground had been enclosed by a rail fence, and in the middle there was a horse jump from which the two top bars had been removed. At the far end of the enclosure he caught sight of a horse and rider, saw that the rider was a woman and that she was about to take her horse over the jump. He stopped his car and silenced the engine in time to hear the thudding of hoofs on the hard ground, and his pulse quickened at the rhythmic sound.

Horse and rider came on headlong, or so it seemed to him, and he saw that the woman was Adele Perkins, that she was tense but sure, and that the horse was young and frightened. He had no time to sort out these impressions before they were at the jump. Then everything happened too fast for thought. The horse stopped just short of the jump, forefeet planted, long head thrust out, nostrils flared and eyes wild with panic.

David was opening the car door as he saw Adele rise in the saddle. Expecting disaster, he leaped to the road. Horse and rider had miraculously become one again. The horse, with nervous, dancelike steps, was moving sideways away from the hurdle, and Adele, riding him easily, was bending forward talking to him and patting his neck. The horse, calmer now but still skittish, tossed his head, making his bit chains rattle.

There was no doubt in Armstrong's mind that he had just watched through a moment of great danger. Shocked, and a little angered by the recklessness, he jumped the ditch at the side of the road, feeling the grass crisp with frost, and cautiously approached the fence. He stood there, uncertain what to do but convinced of the need to do something, and afraid to call out for fear of exciting the neurotic-looking animal still more.

Occupied with the horse, she did not see him standing there, and then, to his distress he saw that she was urging the beast back to the starting point. She wheeled him round and he stood still, quivering. She spoke to him and moved the reins, and they were off on that wild flight toward the jump. David gripped the fence rail hard.

They came on, and he was intensely aware of Adele's willing the horse to go over the jump and that the horse, young, rebellious, and unsure, was resisting her. She seemed to hold him on his course. The bars were in front of them. There was a pause, a fraction of a second only. The long neck reached out; there was a thrust of the hindquarters and they rose. He saw them rise to the jump as clearly as though they were immobile there, Adele bent forward, the horse's front legs curved inward. They sailed; then the forelegs thrust out to meet the ground, the hindquarters wonderfully drawn up; they landed.

David let go a long sigh of relief, and felt his breath, turned to mist in the chill air, damp against his face. The momentum of the jump had taken horse and rider some distance away, but now she turned to come back, saw him, and raised a hand in greeting. They made a pretty sight against the background of dark hemlock and brilliant maple, their breaths rising in white clouds. He almost laughed, for the horse was coming so sedately, with a great show of good-mannered style, pleased with himself as though the achieving of the jump had been his doing alone.

When they were near she said, "Hullo, Doctor," as though it were not surprising to find him in this remote spot.

"That's too dangerous a business to be doing out here all alone."

She smiled at him—pityingly, he thought. "That's not a high jump. Didn't you see the top two bars are off? This fellow is a novice—he's just made his first jump."

"He's a beauty."

"Isn't he? He's not mine, but I wish he were. I'm just training him for some people I know. But he's sweating from jitters, so I can't keep him standing still, and anyway I want to take him over a couple more times so he won't forget he knows how."

"I'll stay here until you finish, then."

They went off at a trot, and for the first time David became aware that there was another horse in the enclosure and that, while he and Adele had been talking, this horse had been slowly coming closer. He too looked like a youngster, a beautiful chestnut color that shone in the sun. He had been approaching step by slow step, drawn by sociability, deterred by uncertainty. He stopped a little way off and turned his head to watch Adele and her horse going away. He seemed so disappointed, so sad, that David laughed. The youngster turned back to regard him with soft, doubtful, judgmatic eyes, sharp ears cautiously pointed forward. Neither man nor horse moved, and for David it was a moment of suspense, as though much of importance depended on the horse's estimate of him. The brown head pushed forward tentatively; the nostrils flared and quivered. Everything hung in the balance. Then a delicate, slim leg came forward, a ripple of muscles along the shining flank, a sound of breath in the wide nostrils, and he had come one step closer.

David could smell him now, rich horse odor, warm in the chilly air. Another step and another, and David did not dare to stir. The long neck stretched out slowly, with wonderful grace, and David felt warm breath on his hand. Then he was touched lightly and it was like nothing he had ever felt before, velvety and alive. The head lifted and the touch was on his face. David shut his eyes, afraid but not moving. The soft, prehensile lip explored his cheek, his ear, the side of his nose, and breath blown at him stirred his hair. Then it was over and David opened his eyes to see the beautiful creature, communication established, standing contentedly. He had never felt this nearness to any animal before. He thought, He likes me! I'll be damned if he doesn't like me! He felt oddly stirred and very greatly pleased.

That was all. The horse—in possession of new knowledge and something more, and with something more than curiosity satisfied —moved slowly off, and the strong horse odor receded with him. He was indifferent now, all horse, no longer wanting any contact with a world not his own. He lowered his head and began to crop grass, and David, watching, felt both sad and happy.

A moment later Adele rode up, patting the neck of her horse, saying, "Open the gate, will you? This fellow has had enough." The young chestnut went on cropping grass, moving away, his tail switching. David unfastened the gate.

In the road Adele dismounted to lead her horse by the reins. "Come with me while I take his saddle off and rub him down. The barn is just behind those trees."

"I mustn't. I have a call to make. I hear a car. Will the horse be all right?"

"I don't know. Stand clear."

She shifted her hold to the bridle just above the bit chain.

"May I help you?"

"No—" The car was coming at them. The horse backed, dragging her with him, then lifted his forefeet, thrashing the air. "Stand *clear!*"

He leaped away and saw her dragging at the bridle, the thrashing hoofs inches from her. The big car was beside them. It slowed, leaped forward, and went fast away from them. David said, "That was your husband," realized he had not said it aloud, and was glad. She, wholly occupied with the horse, had not seen.

The horse was not rearing now but quivering with fright, nostrils blown wide, eyes white with terror. She was talking to him, gentling him. "It's all right now, it's all right . . ." David found he was standing half in the ditch and got himself back into the road.

"I'll walk with you as far as this barn, wherever it is. But I honestly don't think you should ride that horse, and certainly not alone."

They walked up the road side by side, the horse docile now and willing to be led. David was silent, thinking about Perkins, who must have seen the difficulty she was in and yet had driven on.

By the time David reached the Henderson farm, the hoarfrost had vanished under the slowly strengthening sun. He stopped the car by a path that led through tall weeds to crooked steps and gazed with astonishment at the desolation. If the house had ever been painted, all traces of it had vanished long ago. A ragged lilac with dead, broken branches at its base grew by the rotting porch, and at the side of the house was a patch of what had once been vegetable garden, grown up now with weeds, the soil unturned for a year or more.

It seemed hardly credible to him that anyone was living here, but as he walked up the path he saw a strip of curtain at a window and a spindly house plant, leaves pressed flat against the panes of glass. No one answered his knock, and he stood listening to the uneasy stillness before he knocked again. There was no change in the quiet, but the feeling grew on him that someone was there. He depressed the latch, found the door opened under his hand, and went in.

A yellow cat came out from behind the stove and walked stiff-legged, tail held high, out of the room. And then he thought he heard a peevish cry, like the thin cry of a fretful baby. He went in the direction it seemed to have come from, pushed aside a skimpy cretonne curtain that hung in a doorway, and found himself in a bedroom so small that the cheap metal bed filled almost all the space. An old woman lay in the untidy bed staring at him with malignant faded eyes. He controlled disgust, breathing the foul air shallowly.

"Are you Miss Alice Henderson?"

"Yes, I be. Who are you, young fellow?"

"I'm the new doctor in Haddon. Dr. Armstrong. Dr. Moore asked me to stop by and see how you are feeling."

"Don't want to talk to you. Why didn't Moore come hisself?"

"Dr. Moore is very busy, Miss Henderson. I'm sure he'll come one day soon."

195

She turned her head away from him, so all he could see was straggly gray hair with patches of pink scalp showing through. He raised his eyes from this unlovely sight and saw a battered mirror hanging on the wall opposite him. It hung tilted forward, and with a shock he saw reflected dimly in its dusty, silvered depths the old woman's face. She was like an apparition, a trick of the mind. And then he saw that her face was contorted into a look of helplessness and misery and that she was crying.

"Miss Henderson," he said, and heard in his own voice more expostulation than pity. He came out of the doorway and stood at the foot of the bed, grasping it with both hands. Her crying was silent, and with both parchment-colored hands she pulled the sheet against her open mouth. She and her suffering seemed to him so little human that they appeared to him abstract. He was not moved by her in the slightest degree.

"Miss Henderson," he began again, "I'm sorry Dr. Moore couldn't come, but since I'm here don't you think you'd better tell me if there's anything I can do for you?"

"They ain't nothin'."

"But surely you're not alone here?"

She had stopped crying though she still lay with her face turned away from him, and she had begun to shake. He watched her intently.

"Alone enough. Woman down the road comes and does for me, time her own chores is done."

"But wouldn't you rather be in a nice home with other people you could talk to? I'm sure there must be such a thing in Vermont, and Dr. Moore could fix it up for you."

She gazed at him with the bright, hostile eyes until all of a sudden she seemed to realize what he had said to her.

"*You leave me be.*" It was a shriek and a piercing one. He gripped the foot of the bed tighter. The frail old body was trembling all over, shaking uncontrollably.

He said, "Are you cold?"

No reply. He came around to the side of the bed and stood there looking down at her. She seemed to have gone away into a world of her own that was, perhaps, gray and full of terrors, for her eyes were wide and staring. He had not brought his bag, since this was not to be a professional visit, but he would have liked his

196

stethoscope. He reached for her wrist to feel her pulse and thought she did not know that he was touching her. The pulse was light and uncertain, her skin was clammy and the wrist so thin that he could feel the articulation of the joint as accurately as though he touched the bones themselves.

He laid her arm back on the bed, frowning. He knew without looking that there would be no telephone in this place, but there was no doubt in his mind that she should be moved out of here and into a hospital as fast as possible. The dilemma was that she should not be left alone for the time it would take him to find a telephone. Worried, he looked down at her and discovered with an unpleasant prickling of his nerves that she had been watching him with her former malignant animosity.

She said something inaudible and he bent down to hear. "I'm sorry, I didn't understand that."

This time she spoke with a shrillness that made him jump.

"I said, *medicine.*"

It took him a minute to realize that Moore had probably left her some. A bureau with an incredible clutter on its top seemed the most likely place to look. He found not one but two druggists' bottles, both with prescription numbers and Dr. Moore's name, but the tablets they contained were not identified on the labels. Doubtfully, he turned to the bed with them and held them on his palm for her to see, wondering if her vision would let her distinguish between them.

"Which one?"

She pointed a shaky finger, barely lifting her hand.

"Are you absolutely sure? You wouldn't want to make a mistake . . ."

Her hand darted out; she snatched it from him with surprising vigor and hid it under the bedclothes. Her eyes were squeezed shut and he stood looking down at her, wishing for his own former hospital where the nurses took the brunt of this sort of thing. He sighed and went to get her a glass of water. Holding her up while she drank it, he thought that her poor, thin, worn-out body felt like a bag of loose bones. When she had swallowed, she pushed the glass aside and tipped her head to look up at him.

"Go away."

There seemed nothing else to do. She appeared to be stronger now. This was brought about in her, he thought, not so much by her own desire to surmount her illness as by nature's indomitable drive for survival. *Vis medicatrix naturae*, the will to prevail over the ills and damages a living organism sustains. He had seen before the incredible vitality with which so often the old cling to life.

"I'll leave you now, Miss Henderson," he said, and received no reply.

In the doorway, holding the curtain aside, he looked back at her, saw the yellow cat come out from under the bed and leap up and curl herself against old Alice's back.

There was nothing in David's new apartment but packing boxes from New York, for his furniture had not yet been delivered. When he found that the morning's mail contained no license, but only another invitation to a Rotary luncheon, which he threw away, he went across the street to see if he could find his record player in one of the boxes. By the time he had located it and opened a carton of recordings, the floor was littered with packing material. He was about to ignore the litter and listen to some music when, to his surprise, someone knocked on his door and he opened it to find Adele Perkins standing there.

She said, "I heard you were moving in, so I thought I'd come and help. My God, what a mess."

"I was just going to clean up a little," he said untruthfully, but he said it to her back, for she was already stooping to pick up papers from the floor.

"Here, let me do that."

She paid no attention and he began to help her. When her arms were full of crumpled paper she turned to face him.

"I didn't really come to help you unpack, and I'm in no mood to pretend I did."

"Let me take that packing stuff," he said. He was holding a much smaller bundle of papers.

She turned away from him and carried her load to the fireplace, where she dumped it. She felt in her pocket, brought out a cigarette lighter and, before he knew what she was going to do, lit it and held it to the papers. They caught with a great burst of flame that alarmed him.

"Is that safe? I don't know anything about the condition of that chimney."

"Oh, I should think so." She laughed. "If it isn't, we'll soon find out. But they built these old chimneys pretty well, and this building dates from about eighteen-forty or -fifty, I should think. You're a cautious person, aren't you?"

"Perhaps. Do you think that's bad?"

"It's your way, that's all. I like to be reckless."

"I saw that yesterday when you were riding that untrained horse."

"Oh, that wasn't dangerous. Besides, I'm much too good a horsewoman to be reckless when I ride. Daring, maybe—not reckless. There's a big difference."

"I suppose so. It seems a very slight difference to me."

"Maybe. Here, give me those papers and you collect some of the boards from the boxes and we'll have a good fire."

Flames were still rushing up the chimney with a roaring sound. She took his armload of papers from him, and he stayed to watch until he saw that she was not going to put them on the fire all at once. Then he went to pry off some packing-box boards, doing it cautiously so as not to damage his hands. He brought the boards back and put them on the floor beside the hearth. She was sitting on the floor with her back against a box of books, and he let himself down beside her.

"Recklessness is some sort of defiance, isn't it?"

"Oh yes, of course, though the way you choose to be reckless doesn't always have any relation to what makes you want to be reckless. I don't usually go in for the physical sort. I prefer something more like coming here."

"Coming here?" he said, bewildered.

"Yes. It would shock the cackling old hens of this town to know that I was up here alone with you like this. The real reason I came is that I met Ianthe Norton just now and she gave me a lecture in her irritatingly sweet way about my not having gone to the hospital to help the other women on Donation Day."

"I met her there, I think. A large woman with brown hair turning gray? And so you came here to defy her on principle?"

He laughed and she joined in. "Yes, and all her kind. As I told you, I don't like the town women, and I'm not one of them. I feel like being more reckless still, so let's have a drink and then we can get some sandwiches from the dairy bar for lunch and eat them here. Is there any liquor in this place?"

"No, I'm afraid not. But I'll offer you lunch at the Republic House, if you like."

"It would be all over town that I was lunching with you before we'd finished eating. Of course I'd love that, but it's nicer here. Besides, we'd have to eat in the coffee shop because the Rotary lunch is in the dining room. I'm surprised you're not there. No, you go to the liquor store—we want gin and vermouth for martinis, don't we?—and I'll get the sandwiches. It will be fun. Come on."

They sat side by side on the floor with their backs against the box and the pitcher of martinis within reach. They ate their sandwiches from plates he had bought at the ten-cent store, and when they had finished there was still some martini left in the pitcher. She held it toward him ready to pour.

"Let's finish this ice water."

He took a sip from his filled glass and set it down on the floor. She held hers and gazed in silence at the fire.

The rooms seemed to be growing darker and he looked at his watch. Two o'clock. She moved restlessly, as though she resented his interest in the time, but she made no comment. He turned to look out of the high, uncurtained windows and saw black clouds scudding across the sky. He said, "It's going to rain," and saw her quiver as though his breaking of their silence were an unfeeling act of clumsiness.

The darkness in the room deepened and there was a sudden sharp tapping on the windowpanes. Hail, not rain. He tensed a little, leaned forward and tossed another crate board on the fire. Adele did not move or speak. The hail gave place to rain, and the grayness in the room, halfway between light and darkness, was bleak. In it the fire seemed full of consequence.

She stirred, sighed, leaned toward him with a sudden, fierce movement, pulled him toward her and kissed him. He held her by her arms, at first lightly, then with a fierce, hard grip. The kiss lasted a long time. When he released her she gave a little cry and pressed against him. His arms went around her and he held her to him tightly. Her body strained against him, trembling. He put his hand on her breast and she moaned softly.

And then the telephone rang, the sound in the almost empty room shrill and nerve-shattering. Her body jerked and tensed and his muscles tightened. He said *"Christ!"* with vehemence, and struggling to his feet, he saw her smile. The room reeled around him and the telephone rang again, dismaying his nerves, but bringing him nearer to command of himself.

He plunged across the room, sat down on a packing box and stooped to pick the instrument up off the floor. "Dr. Armstrong speaking."

His voice seemed to him choked and unnatural. He cleared his throat and was about to repeat himself when the telephone said, "This is Miss Judson at the hospital, Doctor."

"Yes, Miss Judson."

His head was still reeling and he fought to bring this conversation into normal focus. His back was deliberately turned toward Adele, but some part of his mind was dimly conscious that she had risen and was going out of the room. He made an effort to put his attention on what Miss Judson was saying.

"We've just admitted a patient of Dr. Moore's, and Dr. Moore asked me to call you and ask you if you could get the work-up started and he'll be along as soon as office hours are over. And he asked me to tell you your license has finally come. One of the boys at the post office guessed what it was from the envelope and he thought you might be anxious to get it, so he brought it along in his lunch hour."

"Thank you. I'll be there right away."

"No special hurry, Doctor. The patient just got here."

He was wholly himself again. He got to his feet and put the telephone down on the packing case. Adele seemed to be in the kitchen, for a rattle of dishes came from there. She called to him in her clear, high voice, "I'm making us some coffee." She seemed to have quite fully returned to normal, and, illogically, this made him a little resentful. He drew a packing case toward the fire— there would be no more sitting in close, unwise proximity on the floor—then bethought himself and pulled forward another one for her. He sat down to wait, and then, with a shock that was as much a wave of physical sensation as thought, he realized the full enormity of what had so nearly happened. He spared himself no blame and he thought perhaps it was the most foolish—the most utterly witless—thing he had ever done, or nearly done, in his life. But what really disturbed him almost to the point of horror was that his self-discipline, so carefully and for so long a time built up, should vanish at the first writhing of desire. And not desire for this woman, but merely desire. He had never felt this intensity of physical wanting for Maryanne. He asked himself if it were not precisely the fact that Adele Perkins was almost a stranger . . . He had no liking for the implications of this thought, and he was struggling to shut his mind to it when she returned.

She came back carrying two full cups, walking carefully, her eyes on the cups. He watched her come, coldly and with solid indifference. She looked up, saw his expression, and quickly looked down again. A deep and painful flush slowly colored the skin of her neck and face. She held out a cup to him, tipping her head sidewise and downward to let her hair slip forward to curtain and protect her. She sat down on the packing case, hunched over her coffee, shoulders bent, legs drawn in and awkwardly to the side. Twice she drew a quick, sharp breath as though she were about to speak, and gave it up. He sat in silence, feeling no impulse to help her. Finally she said in a barely audible voice, "I'm sorry. It's just that I need someone so much. But not that way—a friend. I need a friend, and I don't know how to go about it. Everything's a mess—my whole life. I just can't stand it any more."

The cup jerked in her hand, spilling coffee. He reached out and took it from her, putting it on the floor, and she covered her face with her hands.

After a moment he realized that she was crying, the tears wrung out of her in silent agony. He said in the tone he might use to a patient, a tone of serious attention and seriously attempted sympathy while his mind analyzed, "Don't you think you'd better tell me about it?"

And she answered him like a patient, knowing his true purpose to be analysis but needing the sympathy so much that she could pretend to herself that his was real.

"Howard was drinking again last night. Howie came home and found him drinking, and Howard went for him . . . Yelled at him, and Howie didn't reply and that infuriated him and he hit him.

He's never done that before. And instead of standing up to him—
he never does, and that makes Howard wild—Howie cringed in a
corner and just let Howard hit him. Then he got away and ran out
of the house and never came back all night. He went up to Howard's cabin on the mountain, I suppose. He must have gone
straight to school in the morning, for I haven't seen him since."

"Are you worried about him?"

"Yes, rather. There's no need to be really, for he knows how to
take care of himself. He loves the woods and he's often gone off by
himself, but never all night before. He's a queer boy. He likes to be
alone and you never know what he's thinking about. He wants to
study to be a veterinarian, and his father despises him for it."

"Can't you phone the school and find out if he's there?"

"Not without starting talk. I don't want to direct attention to
our family affairs, for if people ever begin to suspect that Howard
is drinking we'll be finished here in Haddon. If Howie doesn't
show up after school, then we'll have to do something. I don't
know what. He isn't like other boys. He hates his home."

There was a long pause, and when it had grown intolerable to
David he said very carefully, "Is this trouble about Howie the real
cause of your husband's drinking, do you think?"

"Does anyone really know why a person drinks? I think dissatisfaction with Howie is the biggest part of it. He wanted Howie
to have the distinguished surgical career that he himself failed to
achieve. Well, obviously Howie's not going to. Then another
thing. Howard's too good for this place and he feels it. You've
seen him operate. You must have seen that he's a truly able
surgeon."

"Yes, I saw that."

There was a pause and she seemed to have forgotten what she
was saying; she sat staring into the fire, not moving, but the visible
pulse in her throat was beating too rapidly. David wanted to get
away to the hospital, though there was no real need for hurry, but
he felt he should not leave her in this emotional state. He rose
and said, "I'm going to get you some more coffee. This is cold.
And get myself some too—then I have to go. No, sit still. I'll get
it."

When he came back, she had tidied her hair and was putting
lipstick on. Her shapely legs were stretched out toward the dead

fire, her tweed skirt well above her knees. He thought she did not deliberately make these physical displays of herself, but nevertheless she made them, and he found himself wondering if this were a symptom of her discontent and whether it might not be a factor in her lack of popularity among the women of the town. He held out her coffee cup and she took it from him as though grateful for being waited on. He sat down on a packing case a distance away.

"How did you happen to come to Haddon in the first place?"

She gave him a swift look and was silent. He was thinking that there was some mystery here and that she was not going to answer his question, when she said, "I might as well tell you. I want to tell you, because if we're going to be friends I'd like you to know what there is to know about me. It's something that happened fifteen years ago, and nobody in Haddon knows anything about it but Dr. Moore and a retired surgeon named Greer. Howard was finishing his residency at a big hospital, Midtown Central in Cleveland. He was chief surgical resident. Everyone was certain he would be a very successful surgeon. He was sure of himself, a bit overbearing, I'm afraid, and impatient with stupidity, but he was good. Dr. Harlan Greer was head of the department."

"The same Dr. Greer who lives in Haddon now?"

"The same. Howard was a great protégé of his. I had inherited a little money from my parents. We were married after he started his residency, and at the time I'm talking about Howie was two years old. One day Howard was assisting one of the attendings and he got an idea about how he thought that kind of operation—I don't think I ever heard what it was—could be done better. He decided not to say anything to anybody, which is like him, but to practice until he had it perfected and then just do it someday when he was operating on his own. He could have arranged with Pathology to let him experiment, but that way he couldn't keep what he was doing a secret and he might have had to wait. He's impatient. He gets an idea and he has to act on it.

"That night he went down to the hospital morgue to do his experimenting on one of the bodies . . ."

"But that's against the law, and for a resident, mandatory dismissal."

"Yes. Well, there was a body that wasn't frozen. Howard got it onto a table and he was doing his operation when someone saw the light under the door."

"So he wasn't allowed to finish his residency."

"Not only that, but of course he hadn't a chance of forming any future connections with a first-class hospital. But Greer had always thought highly of Howard's ability. Greer's father was a Vermont country doctor and Greer used to vacation in the old family house where he's living now. He got Howard taken on at Moore's hospital. Really Howard bought his way in with what was left of the money I inherited."

"The new wing."

"Yes. And Haddon is a life sentence. I hate it. I simply hate it and I'll have to live here till I die. Howard thinks we might escape, at least to Warwick. I don't believe it. I don't believe there's anything in life for us because of what he did. I should have left him then. I wish I had. . . . No, I don't mean that. He was wonderful when we first were married—but then his career being wrecked, and now his disappointment in Howie . . . it's changed him so, and come between us. . . . And Howie . . . I feel so alone. You'll be my friend, won't you?"

"Of course, Adele."

She looked at him in silence, her expression troubled, as though she knew that his reply was perfunctory and that the friendship she wanted could not be had by asking for it. After a while his attention strayed away from her and he discovered that while they had been talking the room had lightened and the rain had stopped. And as though this strange interlude had ended with the ending of the storm, he found himself feeling impatient to get on with the business of the day. He suppressed a sigh and surreptitiously tipped his arm enough to look at his watch. A few minutes later she too seemed to grow aware of the change in mood, for she rose, tossed back her hair and carefully not looking at him said, "I must go now. Thank you for listening, David." Then she walked quickly to the door.

He listened to her going down the echoing wooden stairs, thinking that it would be wise to wait a few minutes before leaving himself. Hands in pockets, he walked idly to the window. Gray clouds, torn and wispy, were sailing rapidly across a lightening sky. A wind that sounded sharp with cold rattled the window, and across the street at the Republic House someone was hauling down the Rotary flag. The flag, heavy with rainwater, came down on the lanyards in heavy jerks. And then he saw her crossing the street with her long stride, her hair lifted by the wind. Her head was raised as though she liked the ice-water feel of the air on her face. In a mood of complete apathy he watched her out of sight.

═══ XVI

D<small>R</small>. M<small>OORE</small> <small>HELPED</small> a thin, perturbed woman down off the examining table and watched her rearranging her clothing—like a hen, he thought, shaking its feathers into place. She was plainly angry and dissatisfied.

"I don't think you understand, Doctor, how bad these pains is. Every month, like I tell you, they has me just in knots. There *must* be somethin' wrong and you just ain't found it."

There was something wrong, all right, but not with the female organs she was so concerned about. The trouble was with a no-good, roistering husband and the blonde that kept bar in the tavern out on Route 14. Her bodily complaints were an invention, malice and martyrdom combined, and ever since the discovery of the blonde she had been playing them for all they were worth. And he knew she would not let up until she got what she wanted —talked herself into the hospital to get her uterus taken out. "Spite hysterectomies," Moore called such operations. Strange what a woman's emotions would do, and the symptoms real enough to fool anyone. You had to know the background, and when you did, there was usually nothing you could do about it but try to keep her from figuratively throwing her uterus in her husband's face. . . .

"You keep on taking that medicine I gave you, Clara."

"It don't do no good."

"Take it anyway. Give it a fair trial."

He propelled her toward the door and, shutting it, sighed over the complications and need for keen judgment that cases like Clara's demanded. Then he sighed again for the good old days when women didn't complain to a doctor unless there was something really the matter with them, and going to the hand basin, he started to wash his hands. He dried them slowly to cleanse his mind of irritation and rest himself a little before seeing the next patient.

From beyond the door that led from the small surgery to the room that would shortly become David's office there came various sounds indicating that David was there. Moore listened with pleasure, thinking that he was a likable young fellow, though his reticence had so far stood in the way of the close relationship that Moore had hoped for. He had not volunteered any information about himself, and Moore, thinking about this with the damp paper towel between his hands, realized that he did not know where David's home was, or if he had living parents, or any means outside of what he earned, though on this point the evidence seemed to be that he had. The medical profession was like the religious life in that it divorced a man from his background. By the time a doctor had finished his training there was a new stamp on him; different habits of mind had been implemented in him. He would never again look at people or at life in the old way. . . .

Moore threw his paper towel in the general direction of the trash basket. In David's office a book dropped with a thud, and the sound was followed by a distinctly audible and vigorous swearword. Moore's eyes lighted with merriment. He went to the connecting door and opened it.

"Hullo, Doc. I guess we're going to have to soundproof this door if you're going to use language like that."

"Hullo, sir. I'm getting settled."

"So I see—and hear."

"My things have come from New York. They're up in the apartment. I thought I'd bring the medical books down here to fill up the shelves the real estate people left."

Moore looked around the otherwise bare room. "Your furniture coming pretty soon?"

"I certainly hope so. Dr. Moore, I went out to see Miss Henderson, and I want to talk to you about her as soon as you can spare a minute."

"All right. As soon as I finish with those people out there. Every time I look in that waiting room some more of 'em have come in." The expression of pleasure faded from Moore's face. He sighed and went out, shutting the door behind himself.

• • •

Nearly two hours later David, sitting in a chair borrowed from the waiting room, was reading an old textbook by the fast-fading light, when Moore again opened the door.

"Well, that's it for this afternoon. Something special wrong with old Alice? Want to come into my office and tell me about it?"

David shut his book and rose. In Moore's cluttered office the overhead light and the desk lamp were on, and Moore went to the switch to turn one off. In the harsh glare the lines in his face looked deep and taut; his eyes, in shadow, seemed intent to the point of fierceness. For an instant before Moore pressed down the switch, David had the impression of seeing beyond the features a glimpse of a harassed but strong and determined spirit. Then the overhead light went out, and Moore, once more the tired, mild-mannered doctor he normally appeared to be, went to his swivel chair and sat down, motioning David into the patient's chair facing him.

"I think the youngest Parker boy's showing signs of being epileptic. Know anything about it?"

"Epilepsy? No, except that it isn't always easy to be sure of your diagnosis. Why?"

"His teacher called me up about it and got his mother to bring him in. The mother doesn't want to believe there's anything wrong with him. I put him on Dilantin and phenobarb and we'll see what that will do."

"You're going to have an EEG, aren't you? Surely—"

"Not first off. Not if the Dilantin and pheno do all right. Did you have something on your mind about Alice Henderson?"

"But, Dr. Moore—excuse me, but I can't believe you're going to guess at your diagnosis and treat a disorder like epilepsy by trial and error, when . . . There must be a qualified neurologist at War-wick. If not, shouldn't the boy be taken to Boston?"

"The Parkers aren't rich, and they aren't poor enough to qualify for free medical care. They're in the income group that has it tough when it comes to medical expenses, even if they come under some health insurance plan. Case like theirs, I try what I can do first. That shocks you, does it?"

"Very much. I wouldn't do what you're doing."

"Maybe you will when you've been here longer. And bear in mind that what I'm doing can't do any harm and may solve the whole problem."

"What I'm shocked at is that you're willing to guess. I'd feel I had to know. I don't think any other considerations could be as important as that."

Dr. Moore studied him for a moment in silence. When he spoke there was no shadow of feeling in his tone. "Let's get back to Alice Henderson, shall we?"

"I think she's in a pretty bad way. I wanted to suggest she be got into the hospital as soon as possible."

"Temperature?"

"I didn't have a medical bag with me, but I shouldn't think so. But she's obviously got a lot of things wrong with her that some tests would show up."

"I know pretty well what's wrong with her. She's old, and she's wearing out—heart, kidneys, everything. Just how worn-out doesn't matter, since there isn't much that can be done about it."

David jumped up and, hands in pockets, began to pace across the narrow space between the hat rack and the waiting room door. Once he turned to face Moore, started to speak, thought better of it, and went back to his pacing. Moore, leaning back in his chair with his hands around the arms, watched him. The noise of the river filled the room with a muted tumult of sound, and the circle of light from the desk lamp deepened by contrast the surrounding shadows. Moore said, "Come and sit down, David," and reluctantly David went back to his chair.

"I know you don't like this way of doing things."

"No, I don't. The Henderson woman is your patient, of course, but there's a principle involved that disturbs me very much."

"You're used to working in a big hospital where your patients are, so to speak, captive. You see them in your office sometimes, maybe, but almost never in their homes. You make a certain attempt to find out about their backgrounds by asking a few questions, but you can't get very far that way. It's natural for you to put a good deal of emphasis on the hospital and a good deal of reliance on its facilities. What you don't realize about old Alice is that to her the hospital is where you go to die. The poor old thing would be terrified and maybe she would die. It would be cruel, and all you'd have gained would be a little detail about the extent to which her worn-out old body had deteriorated."

"Didn't I hear that you had her sister in the hospital?"

"She developed pneumonia. I had no choice. I pray it doesn't happen to Alice."

"In spite of what you say, I don't think she should be left in that place."

"Then there's not much use my saying anything, is there?"

David made no reply, and in the silence each gave the other a long, steady look. Then David rose and walked rapidly out of the office. Moore, his hands tightening around the arms of his chair, looked after him.

Anger toward Moore, self-righteous and burning, propelled David out of the office. He paused only for his coat, and slammed shut the outside door, the violent rattling of the glass giving him a vicious satisfaction. He walked fast without the least idea where he was going, and at the corner he crossed the street for no other reason than that the traffic light had turned green. But instead of charging straight on, he let what he would have called blind impulse steer him to the right so that his arrival at the foot of the stairs that led up to May Turner's apartment was, so far as he was aware, entirely unpremeditated.

The fact of being there made him pause, and the slight mental jolt allowed the beginning of a suspicion to enter his mind that his anger with Moore was out of proportion to the cause and very much against his ideals of behavior. That thought having entered, another put a foot in the door of his mind. It was that his anger with Moore was an excuse not to feel legitimate anger with himself for letting himself become involved in small-town medicine. By the time he had successfully repudiated these thoughts and restored his anger, he was halfway up the stairs.

Above him, May's door opened and a young man came out. He was carrying a long mechanic's box, and over his arm there was a coil of what looked like telephone wire. He grinned and said, "Hi, Doc," and David, who was not yet used to having everyone in town know who he was, said "Hullo" as cordially as he could.

He found May radiant, her black curls tumbled, the arch of her

212

upper lip giving her face a piquancy and charm that diverted his thoughts at once from his troubles.

"Oh, David, come and see."

She was blushing, he thought, because of her unthinking, eager use of his first name. It was charming.

"See what? Oh—the telephone answering equipment. They've put it in."

"They just now finished. Do come and look."

She was patting, as though with affection, the box that had levers, and buttons, and a telephone hanging from it on a hook.

"Does it really work?" It was, he thought, a silly thing to say, but there was a feeling of being aware of each other on another level that made what they were saying of little importance.

"Of course it works. Only it hasn't yet. But it could any minute, if someone called."

"You talk as though it were almost human."

"I feel that way. Imagine—when it's all installed, I'll be able to talk to you in your car when you are way off somewhere."

"It's not exactly a new invention."

"I know, but do come and see."

"Such a fuss over a tan box and a row of buttons. May I take off my coat first?"

"Oh yes, of course."

They smiled at each other as he crossed the room toward her, still communicating on that other plane.

"All right now, let me see it."

"Come and sit here and I'll show you."

She made room for him to sit beside her on the couch, forgetting, in her excitement, to be careful. Pain contorted her face. He stopped and looked down at her seriously.

"I don't like that at all, May. You can't go on having pain like that. We've got to get you fixed up quickly."

"Don't let's talk about that now."

"All right. . . . Do you know how to work it?"

"Certainly I do. The man showed me."

The buttons were neatly labeled MOORE and PERKINS and ARM-STRONG. Two buttons at the end of the row had no labels.

"What are those two for?" He was frowning, though he did

213

not know it, in his effort to keep his mind on what they were talking about.

"One's for Dr. Ladd, only he says he won't. One's for if we get another doctor in Haddon."

"Suppose someone calls me—what happens?"

"The button with your name lights up, and something buzzes, and I pick up the phone. And you've told me where you are, and then I call you and tell you whatever it is. It isn't complicated, and I'm going to love it."

"But you can't call me while I'm in my car with that equipment."

"Not yet. That's to be a separate thing. Because it's radio, we have to get permission to use a wavelength."

"Won't that take time? The mills of government grind slowly."

"Mr. Miller—he's a selectman—knows the Governor and he'll push it. He thinks it won't be long because of the tragedy that we had here. Do you know it will cost nearly a thousand dollars just for the radio part I will have in this room?"

An unimaginable sum to her, obviously. "You know the town is going to pay half."

"I do know, but I hate to think of Uncle Ed's having any more expense."

"The doctors should share. I'll pay my part."

There was no excuse to prolong this proximity, no excuse for not getting up and sitting in a chair, but he was very reluctant to put that much distance between them. He sighed, smiled at her, and rose. The chair had to be placed in just a certain way, or, when she leaned back on her pillows, the tan box would partly hide her.

"May, you're sure you don't mind my dropping in like this?"

"Oh no, it's lonely sometimes."

They were silent for a long, contented interval. Then she turned toward him, the concern caused by a sudden thought plainly showing on her face.

"David, is something troubling you?"

He gave her a quick, startled look. "Well, yes. That is . . . Haddon is quite a change from what I'm used to, and I didn't fully recognize the difficulties of that before I came."

214

"I can imagine how that might be, but won't you get used to it?"

"I don't believe so. I honestly don't believe so, May. The difference is so fundamental. It's as though Dr. Moore thought that preserving a patient's comfort and happiness should come before everything else."

"He's kind and understanding, always."

"That's not a doctor's first duty, May. It's something a doctor does if he can, but it shouldn't interfere. Dr. Moore tends to treat the patient, not the disease . . ."

"And you want to treat the disease, not the patient."

"Those are overstatements. I only mean—"

"Have you and Uncle Ed quarreled about this?"

"Well, no, not exactly."

"Was it about a particular patient?"

"Yes."

"About *me?* Because you think Uncle Ed isn't putting pressure on me to go back to the hospital and see if there is something really wrong with my leg?"

"It wasn't you. It was an old woman I think should go to the hospital for an accurate diagnosis, and he doesn't want to send her there. I think he should. He says the hospital would frighten her, but I can't help wondering if there isn't another reason."

"What would it be?"

In New York there was always someone to talk to about any worry—everyone talked, in the doctors' room, the cafeteria, the hallways. In Haddon—no one, so that worries could build up pressure like a growing tumor pressing against the skull. And May— so ready with anxious understanding, and an intelligence more like instinct than a process of the mind.

"I have to say I wondered if his real reason might not be that he didn't want the financial burden of an old woman who couldn't pay to fall on the hospital."

"Oh, how can you . . . how hateful of you!"

"Please don't be angry. It's a thought that naturally would occur. Don't, please."

"You don't know anything about him, do you? I should think anyone—anyone, however blind—could see the sort of man . . ."

215

"I wouldn't want to misjudge Dr. Moore."

"But you have. Dreadfully. He would give his last cent . . ."

"But the hospital is nearly broke. I don't see how he could take charity cases even if he wanted to. I didn't mean to imply he's hard-hearted. As I've just been saying, he's too much the other way."

"Don't you know how it works? Taking care of poor people, I mean."

"No, I don't. Not in a private hospital in the country."

"Then I'll tell you, for you most certainly ought to know . . . Oh!"

A buzzing as of a giant bee was coming from the tan box. When he leaned forward, David saw that Dr. Perkins's button was glowing brightly. She reached for the telephone and covered the speaking part with the palm of her hand.

"David—quick, what do I say?"

"Say 'Doctor's office.' "

"Doctor's office."

With a vague idea of its being politer not to seem to listen, he got up and wandered to the other end of the room. She was saying, "This is an answering service. . . . Yes, it *is* May Turner—it's my job now. All calls come to me first. I'll have Dr. Perkins call you right away. 'Bye, now."

On a table he saw stacks of printed cards, and, curious, he picked one up. It was a form that read, "I pledge the sum of $_____ toward the building and equipment of the Haddon Health Center. Signed _____." So they were working on it, and no time lost, and May helping. . . . He dropped the card on its pile, and listened to the sound of the dial spinning. May, talking to Perkins, was pleasant and businesslike, and Perkins's voice sounded loud and hollow. When the brief conversation was over, David went back to his chair.

"May, I'm sorry. I should have been more careful about what I said. I didn't mean anything against Moore personally. You were going to tell me how charity patients are handled. I'd really like to know. Let's say, this old woman."

"A state social worker would visit her. She would want to know how much money she had, and ask to see her bankbook, and if she owned land and if it was mortgaged, and if she had relatives who could pay her hospital bills. It would be so humiliating for her, David, but if you're poor you don't have any right to privacy, it seems. Then there's lots of paper work. Edna does it. And after a while the state sends Uncle Ed money, though never quite as much as it costs him."

"But it wasn't always done that way?"

"No. Uncle Ed just sent the bill to the selectmen at the end of the year, and the town paid. The total was always in the printed report they give you at Town Meeting. But now, because it isn't the town who pays, lots of people think it's free, but of course it isn't, really."

"And it works the same way for poor people Moore sees in his office?"

"It could, only there's so much paper work for each one that the doctors just don't bother. They can't spend that much time on forms. . . . David?"

"What, May?"

"You're going to help about the hospital, aren't you?"

"How do you mean?"

"Don't you know that some people are saying that Uncle Ed's hospital is too old and run-down and that it should be closed?"

"It's old and run-down, all right. What I can't understand is why a man of his age should care. I should think he would be glad not to have the responsibility. And who's to run it after he retires? You'd never find anyone who would make the sacrifices to keep it going that he apparently has. And if there were a hospital at Silver Springs that the Haddon doctors could use, a good modern one . . . No, I should think he would really welcome an excuse to close up."

"Oh! If you're the good doctor everyone says you are, how can you be so insensitive? It's his life work. It's something great that he's done for the town. He believes the town needs it, and it does. He wants it to live after him."

"I'm not at all sure that so personal an attitude behind a hospital that is meant to serve the public is really wholesome."

"Then why did you come here?"

"I've been wondering that myself. May . . ."

"What?"

"I don't want to quarrel with you."

"But you don't even try to understand."

"It's difficult. To me it looks like a simple question of economics —Moore is going to run out of money, and Stoner, as president of the bank, won't give him any more. There couldn't be a drive for funds, as apparently there is to be for the Health Center, because it's a private hospital. And yet I gather public opinion is very much aroused and beginning to take sides."

"Public opinion is what runs a town like this. Didn't you know that? It's going to be Stoner and the people who want more industry at Silver Springs on one side, and on the other people who want a hospital here. People will love my uncle."

"I still don't see how public opinion can prevail."

"You will. At Town Meeting you will."

"And when is that?"

"In February, always. Before sugaring starts. . . ."

"You're tired."

"Yes, suddenly." Her head on the pillow was turned sideways. The black lashes flickered and came to rest on the pale cheeks, and the prettiness seemed suddenly so fragile.

"Please forgive me." He saw the upward sweep of the lashes and the look in the eyes coming from so far within. "I've put too much on you, but you've told me so much I ought to know. . . . I shouldn't have come, May, but I wanted to talk to you."

"I want to be friends."

"So do I!"

She smiled briefly.

"Well, then . . ."

At an hour that was late for Haddon, Ianthe Norton was moving without much purpose around her big, dimly lit kitchen when she heard a car brushing under the branches of the old lilac bush. She glanced at the clock, saw that it was almost eleven, and going to open the door, she smiled at the sound of Moore's heavy footsteps coming up on the porch.

"I saw your light," he said. "I thought I'd stop by . . ." He left the sentence hanging, his tone half an apology, half a plea for welcome.

"I'm glad you did, Ed. Come in."

218

"Office hours lasted late. Seems like people want more doctoring all the time."

"Ed, did you eat any supper tonight?"

"I didn't have time to go home, but I had a sandwich at the dairy bar."

"Hang up your coat, and I'll fry you some eggs—no, really, I'm not tired. I'd like your company for a little while. The house seems so big and empty now that Nat's upstairs all the time."

"I'll have to phone May to tell her where I am."

"Is your telephone answering service really working, then?"

"The equipment's come. Just came this afternoon. She phoned to tell me. The radiophones on our cars will take a while because we have to clear it with some communications commission to use the wavelength, or some such thing. But it's a bright idea Dave had."

Moore hung his coat on a peg by the cellar door and disappeared into the hall to telephone. When he came back Ianthe was laying long strips of bacon in a pan. He came to stand beside her, smiling.

"Woke her up, I think, but she didn't seem to mind. This job's a fine thing for her. How is Nat, Ianthe?"

"There's been a change, Ed. Just the last two days. I want to talk to you about it. This won't take long."

Moore sat down at the table between the windows and watched her with enjoyment. The warmth of the kitchen, the steady sizzling of the bacon, soothed him and he slipped into a half-dreaming state in which the sadness spread out to encompass everything in his life. He rested in it, letting it sap his will and dull his need to struggle. When Ianthe came to the table bringing eggs and bacon and coffee, he had to make an effort to rouse himself and, rising to help her, felt as though his arms and legs were weighted. He swallowed coffee and forced his mind to take hold of the present. "About Nat," he said. "What sort of change is there?"

"It's hard to describe. He seems dulled, not so alert, and indifferent."

"That doesn't necessarily have any meaning. Anyone who's tired feels that way." And Moore thought how nearly he himself had drowned in a mood a moment ago.

"This is different. He seems to have given up being himself. He's drifting. He sleeps a lot."

"He's sleeping now, I suppose."

"He was a little while ago. Ed, what does this mean?"

"I don't know. Maybe nothing. I'll stop by in the morning and have a look at him."

Ianthe rested her forehead on her hand and traced a red square on the tablecloth with a fingertip. After a moment she sighed and got up to bring another coffee cup. "I think I'll have some too. I don't sleep much these days anyway." She poured coffee into their cups and pushed cream and sugar toward him. "Ed, I can't reconcile myself to this."

"I don't know how to help you, Ianthe. I wish I did. I felt that way when Matilda went. He isn't suffering physically, you know."

"But, Ed . . ." She stopped and her eyes filled with tears. She found a handkerchief and wiped them. "It doesn't do any good to talk about it, I guess. Tell me, Ed, how is your new young man working out?"

"Dave Armstrong? He'll be all right, give him time. He's got a lot to learn and a lot to unlearn before he makes a good country doctor."

"I thought he'd had such a good education."

"He has. A lot better than I had when I started out. Perkins calls him the educated fool."

"That sounds like something Howard would say."

"I sent him out to see how old Alice Henderson is getting along, and he came back all in a swivet wanting to get her right into the hospital and start all sorts of tests."

"What good would that do? The poor old thing would die of fright."

"Precisely. I guess he wants her to die scientifically. I don't see why Alice shouldn't die peacefully in her own bed. Dave just happened in when she was having one of what the neighbor woman, Tillie, calls her spells. My guess is she was having a take of missing Sister Ila and feeling sorry for herself."

"But mightn't she be really sick and all alone?"

"Tillie goes over there three, four times a day, and her oldest girl, fourteen I think, sleeps there nights. She'd let me know if anything didn't seem just right. I phoned her after I had the talk with Dave and she said she'd just been over there. Found Alice up and dressed and cherky as you please, boiling hot dogs on the stove. Jabbing at them with a fork 'real vicious,' was the way Tillie put it."

Ianthe laughed and filled Moore's cup with hot coffee. He drew it toward him, frowning at his own thoughts. "The thing is, these new young men are too dependent on laboratories. That's fine when you're making your diagnosis. But it looks to me as though they tend to plan their management of cases on laboratory findings without paying enough attention to the patient as an individual. That's a fault, as I see it, primarily of city medicine. Perhaps we're too much the other way in these rural communities. But with these changes coming in as fast as they are, I'm afraid the patient as a person may get lost. We wound up, Dave and I, with a bit of coolness between us."

"That's too bad, Ed."

"It will blow over. He didn't say so, but I suspect he's worried about the size of a country practice—doesn't see how a doctor can do a good job with so many patients. According to his standards, that's true, but I don't know what any of us can do about it. You make the best fried eggs I ever ate, Ianthe."

"I could show you how."

"It wouldn't be the same."

He pushed his chair back and started to rise. She put her hand on his sleeve. "Ed, do you have a minute more? There's a lot of talk around town that you might be going to give up the hospital. That isn't true, is it?"

"No!"

She considered this for a moment. "The trouble is money, isn't it?"

He put his elbow on the table and rubbed his open hand over his face as though he could rub out his troubles. Then he reached for the coffeepot and emptied it into his cup.

"I could make you more coffee, Ed."

He shook his head. "Had too much already. I'm sure of enough money for close to a year. Stoner won't carry me beyond that."

"I don't like Tim Stoner and I never did. I think perhaps it's his great handicap that nobody really does. It turns him in on himself, and emotions he'd normally work off on other people corrode him. That's not being very charitable, is it? I'm sure he's lonely—he was lonely even when he was a boy and we were in school together. He couldn't play games because of his glasses and he was more intelligent than anybody else, so in class he made the rest of us look stupid, which isn't the way to win popularity in school or out. I think he always wanted to be—planned how to be—the most important man in town as a sort of compensation, and maybe as revenge on the rest of us."

"He's doing what he thinks is right. He thinks Haddon doesn't need a hospital but that there should be one for the plants at Silver Springs."

"And I can just picture what that would be like. An institution run by a committee for the benefit of the workers—like something in Russia. Doctors and nurses from anywhere. They wouldn't want people like us in Haddon—probably wouldn't be equipped to take care of us. Ed, no. For heaven's sake, no. We want the hospital we have. Your hospital."

"I'm not so sure if it came to a showdown that people generally would feel the way you do."

"How can you say that? Think of what happens on hospital Donation Day."

"There's something else involved in all this—a trend in modern life. I'm just beginning to realize how immense it is in the field of medicine. It's the trend toward government participation and control. To people who believe in that it doesn't make any difference that my hospital is well run and fills the needs of the community. They want to destroy it just because it's a private hospital, owned by an individual."

"You'll find a lot of people who don't feel that way."

"I'm not sure of it. That's just it. I'm not sure of it."

"And I think people in the town should understand what the issue is. I can't do much as things are with Nat, but I can do something, and I will."

Moore thought about this, his folded arms resting on the table. After a moment he gave Ianthe a swift, alert look that had behind it a great deal of force and vitality, and seeing it she smiled. He said, "You must understand this, Ianthe. The crux of the matter is money. Stoner refuses me any more loans. I have to find someone who will lend me money and enough of it so I can expand and modernize enough to put an end to criticism. I can't make a public appeal for money because I'm a private hospital, so all I would accomplish by getting public opinion on my side would be to create a favorable atmosphere for a loan."

"Where would the loan come from?"

"I don't know. I just don't know, and believe me, I haven't thought about much else. From here and there, I suppose. Small sums from lots of sources, perhaps. Banks in other towns. Harlan Greer is a rich man. I've thought of asking him."

Ianthe, deep in thought, picked up the edge of the tablecloth that was lying on her lap, and examined the hem, first one side, then the other, seeming to give it her whole attention. She laid it on the table in front of her and smoothed it out with the flat of her hands, and Moore, watching her, was thinking that he had never really noticed her hands before. They were small and compact, and the nails, short and neat, were without polish. Seeing these details, he felt he understood her more intimately. And then he was seized by an impulse to put one of his hands over hers. This so horrified him that he shoved his chair abruptly back from the table, his guilty hands clutching the edge of the seat.

At his movement, she looked up and smiled mistily, from a distance, so that he realized with immense relief that she did not know what antic thought had been in his mind. With a quick gesture, she pushed the edge of the tablecloth back in her lap.

"Ed, do you remember that my father wrote several textbooks?"

Moore, not quite back on his mental feet, said, "The professor? No, I'd forgotten."

"They made quite a bit of money. Nat never wanted us to use my money, so it's still there—principal and most of the interest. By Haddon standards, I'm a rich woman, Ed."

Moore made a sound that had no meaning and watched her warily.

"What I'm getting at is this: You can have the money, and I don't care whether I get it back or not."

"Ianthe!"

"I mean it, Ed."

"It's too great a risk. It's not a safe investment."

"I tell you, I don't care. It's about fifty thousand dollars. That would help, wouldn't it?"

"Of course it would help, but, Ianthe, I can't . . ."

Pressed by emotion into action, Moore jumped to his feet, and stood, head bent, staring at the floor. When he looked up, Ianthe's smile had grown in warmth and light.

"I don't want to talk about it any more, Ed. I just want you to think about it." She too rose. "It's late. I think you should go home now." She crossed the kitchen and got his coat and held it it out to him. He shrugged into it and put his hands in his pockets. One of them came out again holding a crumpled scrap of paper. He looked at it vaguely and shoved it back again.

"Ianthe, I can't begin to say—"

"Don't, Ed. I won't listen. Go along home."

Suddenly he laughed. "By God, you make a man feel good. Thanks for the eggs. I'll be in to see Nat in the morning."

XVII

DURING THE FEW WEEKS he had been practicing in Haddon, David had formed the habit of using the front stairs of the hospital, perhaps because the elevator was Perkins's choice. Against the outmoded grandeur of the staircase he was a conspicuous figure in his long white coat with his looped stethoscope protruding from a pocket—the more so since neither of the other doctors wore coats like his. Before he had come down more than a few steps, he realized that something unusual was going on in the hall below, for Edna was standing, leaning over her desk and staring at the closed door of Moore's office. Through the door came the sound of angry voices, the loudest of them Moore's. David ran down the rest of the stairs.

"Miss Judson, what in heaven's name is going on?"

"It's two men from the Veterans' Administration, Doctor. There are three veterans who were once patients at the Veterans' Hospital that Dr. Moore has been treating free for the last two years. There are two inspectors in there with him threatening to have him into court for doing it."

"But, do you mean to say—"

The office door was thrown violently open by Moore, who stood just inside, shouting, "Now get the hell out. Nobody is ever going to tell me I can't see someone who comes to me for help, and nobody is going to tell me to send a bill if I don't want to. Tell those damn fools if they want to haul me into court to go right ahead. By God, I'd *enjoy* it. Now *get out!*"

Two men emerged, mild-looking men with briefcases, wearing identical smiles made up of self-consciousness and amusement. They looked at David curiously, both nodded, and one said almost in a whisper, "It's sometimes hard to make these old boys understand." The other, passing Edna's desk, winked at her. She brought the palm of her hand down on the desk with a hard slap that made the man who had winked give her a broad grin.

The front door closed behind them, and Moore said, "*God Almighty*," and came over to where David was standing. "And this is the free and sovereign state of Vermont, U.S.A.—would you believe it? People say we're going to get socialized medicine. Hell, it's here. And look at the result. A fine and noble idea, like free medical care for veterans, gets put in force at the top, and this is the sort of thing that comes out at the bottom of the bureaucratic hopper. Well, it's not those birds' fault. They were just doing their job, but I couldn't help blowing off at them. What the hell time is it? My watch is being cleaned."

"Twelve-fifteen, sir."

"You're going to the Rotary lunch, aren't you? It's time to get going."

"I don't think I'll go. That's not just my line."

"Now look here—I know you're not much in a mood to take advice from me these days, but going to Rotary lunch is something that, in a small town, you have to do."

"Have to?"

"You'll suffer for it in various ways if you don't."

"Somebody drag me into court for it?"

Dr. Moore looked startled, then he grinned. "All right. All right. This is different. It's *government* I don't want to be pushed around by. But you really should come—shouldn't he, Edna?"

"Yes, Doctor, you really should."

David, to whom the term "Rotarian" meant a special and unfamiliar type, saw the moment he and Moore entered the dining room that he was wrong. These men were no different from any cross section—perhaps more cheerful than a group of doctors, less impressive than a group of bankers, and more standardized in appearance than men engaged in the arts or their promotion. A mixture, a blend of average men. Once inside the door, he felt he merged with them in a way quite satisfactory to himself. By a table in the middle of the floor Dr. Perkins was standing, motioning to them, and as they worked their way through the crowd, David saw that Perkins had turned up chairs for them.

"Well, I see you finally made it." He gave David a slap on the back that David took without change of expression, and laughed as though some special joke were involved.

There was a fourth man already seated at the table and Moore was saying to him, "Dr. Greer, I don't believe you've met our new staff member, Dr. Armstrong. David, this is Dr. Harlan Greer."

David found himself bowing to a tall, thin man who had watchful, judgmatic eyes.

"I'd heard about you, sir, before I came here."

Greer—neurosurgeon who had once had a reputation for brilliant risk-taking. Greer made no move to shake hands. His long fingers were making small movements, like exercises—pointless, but oddly delicate and precise. His eyes held David's for a moment; then he looked away as though he had seen all and more than he wanted to.

Perkins talked loudly above the general din, for the morning of operating, that had tired David, seemed to have had the opposite effect on him. David thought he saw in Perkins's manner toward Greer a slight restraint, and then thought he might be imagining it because he had heard their past history from Adele.

The canned fruit salad yielded place to ham. The noise in the room died down a little at this more serious business, and David, who did not think he should remain wholly tongue-tied, said to Greer, "Are you practicing at all these days, sir?"

Greer examined the piece of ham on his fork in a finicky nervous manner, put it back on his plate, cut another.

"No, not at all. Those days are past. Now I write. I'm at present reading proof on what is really a book of neurological essays, the most important being a discussion of postmortem angiography of the cerebral vascular system. I find the writer's is a life of toil. I think I shall try a little teaching to keep my mind from rusting. There will be a teaching post open at the Warwick Medical School—first-year surgery—a restfully simple subject. You may be interested to know that I have applied for it, and"— Greer smiled at them all, including them in his little joke—"I rather think they will give it to me, don't you?"

Perkins laid down his knife and fork with elaborate precision, his face expressionless. Moore hitched his chair forward sharply, but neither made any comment and Greer seemed not to expect an answer. A waitress took Perkins's plate and put a dish of pale green ice cream in front of him. He said, "*Christ!*" and pushed it away. David gazed at him, not troubling to conceal his dislike, and withdrew behind a barrier of disapproval.

After three hours of keeping Perkins's rapid pace in the operating room, David did not feel like making an effort to understand the undercurrents of unexplained emotion that seemed to be an inescapable part of life in Haddon. He sat, arms folded on the table, head bowed and his mind as nearly free of thought as mind can be. Awareness of his surroundings began to slip away from him. He no longer heard the clatter of the crowded dining room or thought about his companions, and his feelings began to swell with boredom, lassitude and a false sense of peace. In this condition nothing mattered to him, nothing seemed worth struggling for. He vaguely felt he had found at last the perfect, the only, workable attitude toward life. From this tumescent apathy he was aroused by Moore, who was touching his arm.

"Better listen to this, David."

The room filled with the noise of chairs being scraped and bumped into new positions. At the long head table the president was standing with the gavel in his hand, and David was astonished to see that he was Mr. Beatty who owned the local plumbing and heating business. The gavel came down.

"Folks . . . it isn't often the town gets a chance to welcome a new doctor."

David quickly looked down at his plate and Moore grinned at his discomfort.

"Last one came here was Dr. Perkins. That was about fifteen years ago, wasn't it, Doc?"

"About." Perkins spoke without raising his eyes.

"Well, as I guess everybody knows, we got a new one now. Dr. David Armstrong. Stand up, Doc, and git your welcome."

There was a roar of applause and calls of "Welcome, Doc." Seriously, and a little red in the face, David half rose, sat down again and gave his whole attention to turning a spoon over and over, the flush deepening as the applause continued.

The gavel came down again. "That's enough, folks. I guess he's got the idea. But that ain't all there is to it. This is the *first* time

Doc Armstrong's been to one of our meetings, though he's been invited before. I know, because I sent the two notices myself."

Beatty was grinning, and all around men were beginning to laugh. David leaned over and said to Moore, "What's this about?"

"Wait and see."

Beatty was saying, "You all know you have to have lived in town for a year to be a member. But Doc Armstrong don't plan to stay with us more than a year, so we thought we'd treat him like he was a member. Nothing in the bylaws against that as I know of. Now, you know the rule—though maybe our new doc doesn't— about what happens when you miss a certain number of meetings."

There was another burst of laughter, and David tried to keep a smile on his face in spite of growing uneasiness about what was coming.

"The fact is, our new doc gets the rabbit."

Someone beside the president reached down behind the speaker's table and came up holding a cage. In it was a large brown rabbit, placid and undismayed by the new outburst of noise.

"What's this?" David said to Moore, and Moore shook his head, laughing at the desperation in David's face.

"I got stuck with him myself, three times."

"Doc Armstrong . . ."

"Get up, Dave, get up." David rose slowly to his feet.

"This here is the Rotary rabbit. Name's Harry. When a man misses two lunches straight, he gets to keep Harry till the next meeting, to sort of remind him he'd better come. He's a mighty fine rabbit. Come and get him, Doc. He's all yours for a week."

Perkins, enjoying this, hitched his chair up to let David pass. Greer said, "Don't look so serious, my boy. Smile." And David, wedging himself past chairs, trying his best to display an amusement he did not feel, heard Perkins say to Greer, "A good surgeon, but a bit of a stuffed shirt."

At the speaker's table he was handed the cage, and then found he was expected to clutch the awkward thing to him with one hand and shake hands right and left with the other. At the end of this ordeal he looked down at his burden. The rabbit sat with slack indifference to his fate, long ears laid back, eyes shut, a shred of lettuce hanging from his mouth. The effect was of amicable raffishness, and David smiled; then, feeling fine, he laughed. "Hullo, Harry," he said, and, still laughing, turned to face the room. There was a great deal of noise, and in it all David was conscious only of good nature and friendliness surging around him.

Moore, arrested by something unusual he saw in David's face, stopped clapping to study him. David, it seemed, was showing to the whole room of strangers something that Moore had never seen before, something boyish that had to do with the difficult business of enjoying life. By the time David reached the table and Moore had moved his chair to make room for the cage, the mask was almost back in place again.

The gavel was pounding once more, and a thick-set, dark man at the back of the room was standing to be recognized. David leaned toward Perkins. "Who's that?"

"Zovick. Joe Zovick. Runs the hardware store and belongs in the category of slob."

Zovick was moving clumsily into an open space and Moore said, "He's exaggerating his limp for our benefit."

"Yeah." Perkins turned to David. "He was in an accident, broke his pelvis, his tibia and his ankle, then had the nerve to sue us because he walked with a limp. Case was thrown out of court, but he's had it in for us ever since. He's always making trouble of some sort. That's why Beatty's trying to ignore him."

Zovick was calling loudly, "Hey, I got something to say."

The president said, "All right, Joe." He said it reluctantly and the room quieted down to listen.

"I been thinkin' that since we ain't got no special program today —that's right, ain't it?"

"That's right, Joe."

"Well, since there ain't no program and since we got the doctors here—"

Moore said, "Good Lord," under his breath, and gave Zovick his full attention.

"—there's something the town's pretty much wrought up about. That's about the hospital."

Perkins said loudly, "Sit down, you damn fool," and Beatty pounded his gavel.

"I ain't goin' to sit down. This is somethin' that concerns all of us. We got a hospital here—it's a lousy hospital and it darn near

230

done for me. What I mean to say is, it's run-down, and it's broke, or so I hear. I hear Doc Moore's going to shut it up and quit—"

Moore said in a loud voice, "I'm not shutting up, and I'm not quitting. And this isn't the place to discuss it."

"Sure it's the place to discuss it. Everybody hear Doc Moore? He says he's not going to shut the hospital up. Now, I'm not just sure he ain't got to, and that what you might call circumstances may maybe git too much for him. What I say is, that whether or not Haddon has a hospital concerns all of us here. It concerns us as family men and it concerns us as businessmen. "

Someone called out, "Shut up, Joe."

"I won't shut up till I've finished my say. My say is that this is a matter that concerns all the people. I see Mr. Stoner over there in the corner. If Doc Moore won't discuss it, maybe Mr. Stoner will."

Beatty had his gavel raised with the clear intention of bringing this scene to an end. At mention of Mr. Stoner he paused with the gavel in the air and waited to see what Stoner would do. Stoner was slowly rising from his chair. Sunlight from the window glittered on his glasses, so that nothing of his expression was visible but the thin, straight mouth.

Stoner paused to insure silence and attention from everyone in the room. He spoke without raising his voice, but his sharp, incisive words could be clearly heard.

"You have just heard Joe Zovick say that the continuance or discontinuance of the hospital is a matter that concerns all the people."

A soft sound beside him made David glance down. Harry had jumped to the front of his cage and thrust a quivering nose upward. Absently, David put a finger through the wire mesh and scratched behind an ear.

"Joe Zovick is wrong. It is no concern of the people at all."

All over the room there was a murmur of dissent.

"I say, no concern at all, and I will tell you why." He took a step forward and his manner became sharp and incisive. "The reason is that the hospital is private property. Dr. Moore owns it. It's nobody's business but his what he does with it. The town has no voice whatsoever in the matter. He can do exactly what he pleases or what the 'circumstances' to which our friend Joe referred may force him to do, and the town has no more to say than if he decided to sell his house or his car."

Perkins said, "*Bastard!*" in a voice that made men at nearby tables turn to look at him. Stoner shifted his position, and his glasses glittered as though making their independent comment on Perkins's word.

"Whether the private ownership of a hospital is desirable in this instance or any other is another question. But—and in this I agree with Dr. Moore—this is not the place for such discussion."

He sat down and the room was completely silent. After a moment Beatty cleared his throat, gulped some water, and leaned on his gavel. "Well, folks, that seems to have concluded that. So now we might as well get on to—"

Dr. Moore moved so suddenly that David was taken by surprise. Standing up, he looked massive. "Now *I've* got something to say." His voice was controlled and strong.

"Tim Stoner is right. I do own the hospital, but only because, thirty years ago, the town didn't know its own needs well enough to know that what were then the advances in medicine made a hospital essential. I don't profit by ownership of the hospital."

There was a general laugh, and Moore looked surprised that he had caused it. Then he smiled.

"I don't know as I've consciously made an effort to run the hospital in the interests of the town, but I have tried to have it meet medical needs as I see them, which works out to about the same thing."

There was an outbreak of applause and Moore put up his hand to stop it. "Now, I don't agree with Tim Stoner that it isn't anybody's business but my own whether I close the hospital or not. I think it's the concern of the whole town. I said a while ago that this isn't the place to discuss it, and I think that's true, because, however well we think of ourselves here in Rotary, we're not the whole town.

"Now, I have a proposition to make. I want to ask the Town Meeting in February if the town of Haddon still wants a hospital and let the meeting discuss it."

A voice of peculiar raspiness behind David's shoulder said, "Yer can't do that, Doc. 'Tain't accordin' to parliamentary." David turned around and saw that the speaker was one of the three selectmen he had first seen here in this same room. Beatty said, "Is Jake Miller here? How about that, Jake?"

Toward the front another of the selectmen half rose from his chair, the one that David had thought might be a businessman.

"It's nothing you could take a vote on. But it would be proper to ask for intention. 'Is it the intention of this meeting that there should be a hospital in the town?' Something like that would be inside the rules, I guess."

Moore looked all around the room as though to include everyone in what he was saying. "All right. I want it put up to Town Meeting whether the people want a hospital. If they do, I'll modernize and enlarge, and the hospital will take its place in current medical advances."

Stoner's voice from over by the window said a single, sharp word: "How?" And David, watching Moore turn his head in that direction, thought his eyes had never seemed so full of blueness and life.

"I don't know how. At the moment, I don't have the least idea how. I didn't know how I was going to start a hospital all those years ago, but I did it. If it turns out that the town wants a hospital, I give you my pledge to do everything I can to see that there is one and an adequate one. And I shall take whatever steps are necessary to insure that I have an able successor."

During the outbreak of applause, Moore stood with his head bowed, and David thought that he was realizing that the applause might well be for him personally and nothing more. From the back, Zovick's unpleasant voice said, "And what about if the town don't want a hospital, Doc?"

For a moment Moore was silent. Then he drew in a long breath and let it out again. "If the town doesn't want a hospital, I shall begin closing it at once. You realize, of course, that Howard Perkins, being a surgeon, could not continue to practice here. I myself have been accustomed to the facilities of a hospital too long to learn to practice without them. I should retire."

As the tumult broke out, Moore sat down, covered his ears with his hands, and stared at the tablecloth. David wanted intensely to say something, anything, and found neither voice nor words at his command. He saw Perkins staring at Moore as though he felt he had never quite seen him before. Greer put his hand on Moore's

233

sleeve and said something inaudible. David thought the words were *"Don't retire."* A man behind Moore turned around and slapped him on the back, and though Moore's shoulders jounced with the blows, he paid no attention. The rasping voice of the selectman behind David said loudly, "Wal, that's saucered and blown it all right, and fixed it ready so's the town can drink right up!" The sound of the gavel began to invade David's consciousness, and at the same time the room slowly quieted down. Beatty said "Well, folks . . ." and waited for the last sounds to die away.

"Well, folks, that's the kind of personal ovation any man might be proud to get from this group . . ."

And David thought, It's just that—a personal ovation and nothing to do with how these people feel about the hospital.

Beatty was saying, "I don't know's I ever heard anything like it before. But now time's getting on and we'll all have to get back to work, but there are just one or two little matters first. Now—about the flagpole sockets in the sidewalks along Main and Pleasant that Rotary's paying for . . ." David ceased to listen.

A few minutes later the meeting was breaking up and they were all going toward the door. Perkins made his separate way there, a look of black anger on his face that took David's mind back to the early part of the meeting. Greer vanished, and David, holding Harry's cage awkwardly against his chest, followed Moore. Many people were stopping Moore to speak to him, and Moore was saying over and over again, "I don't want to talk about it now." Then they were out on the porch of the Republic House and people ceased to crowd them.

Moore said, "Well, David. Office hours—remember? What time is it? Damned inconvenient having no watch."

"Two-oh-five."

"They started five minutes ago. What are you going to do with that thing?"

David looked down at the cage in his arms and his face grew red. "I almost forgot I had it. I'll take it up to my room and be right over."

He put the cage down in a patch of sunlight from the window, and watched Harry hopping around his restricted space as though in search of something. He knew little about animals, and what the wants of this furry ball might be he had no idea. A thought occurred to him and he carried an ashtray into the bathroom, filled it with water and, squatting beside the cage, opened the wire door and put it inside. Then he smiled. "There you are, Harry old fellow, saucered and blown and ready to drink!"

═══ XVIII

OCTOBER FLAMED with colored leaves, and the wayside ferns made a bright filigree of golds and rusts and browns. Then there came a day and night of wind and driving rain, and after that the trees were bare, except for the larches that stood like slim, gold spires against the dark background of pine and hemlock. Here the season seemed to pause before making the final change into winter. Days went by when the air was still, the sun shone palely and haze hung over the mountains. The damp chill had weight and a settled feeling, as though further change had been indefinitely postponed.

As Moore turned the jeep between the white gateposts of the Norton driveway, he was thinking that all this that had been taking place in nature was not unlike what had been going on in Nathaniel's dying body. The first struggle with his enemy had left him gaunt and wasted, but the sharp, sardonic mind had not suffered. Then the mind, without clouding, had changed subtly, softening in its relation to life. In this phase he seemed to see, without greatly caring, aspects of the world that had never before attracted his attention. He seemed to be reviewing life much as he might turn the pages of a book that filled him with vague wonder, but did not truly concern him.

This was the change that Ianthe had seen in him, and once established, it seemed as likely to continue indefinitely as the bleak fall weather. The enemy in him rested. He grew no better but neither did he seem to grow any worse, but to Moore's practiced eye this phase had lasted overlong. He had begun to watch closely for the slightest sign that it was coming to an end.

He left the jeep under the lilac bush and knocked lightly on the kitchen door, thinking that if Ianthe had gone upstairs to be with Nathaniel, there was no need to call her down. She was looking too worn and strained these days for his liking, and much more would be demanded of her before this business came to its inevitable end.

When he found there would be no reply to his knock he turned the doorknob, found the door unlocked, as he expected, and went in. The big house seemed weary and sad. He looked in the study where so often he had found the old professor working at his desk, but the room was empty and had about it an unfamiliar tidiness, a look of little use. A pleasant room with its wall of books, a room in which he had always liked to linger. Knowing the habits of the house, he did not look into the lovely but formal room across the hall, but went quietly up the curving stairway.

The door of Norton's room was open, and from the hall he could see the high four-poster bed in shadow and Norton in his gray dressing gown lying there asleep. Nearby, in an armchair, Ianthe sat staring into space. She did not hear him in the doorway, and for a moment he stood looking at her face, seeing there things he had never seen before as one does in the faces of the sleeping and the dead. Norton moved then and she looked up, and the moment in which he felt himself coming to a new understanding of her was gone.

She saw him and smiled. "Come in, Ed. Nat, here's Ed to see you."

Nat slowly turned his head on the pillow, and as they went to stand by the bed, he looked up at them with eyes dimmed and softened by sleep. A pleasant sleep, Moore thought, from which he had not fully awakened . . . lips forming words that should have been "Hullo, Ed," but the only sound the breathy wheeze . . . and with that the sleep gone, and in the eyes the agony of remembering. . . . If only Ianthe hadn't seen . . .

They were both so moved they did not at once understand what it was that Nat was groping for on the bedside table. The slate. "Is this what you want, Nat?"

A nod of thanks, the eyes still full of misery and bewilderment . . . And as the pencil moved on the slate, Ianthe drew a sharp breath because the sound was a screech the nerves could scarcely endure.

They both leaned close to read, their shoulders touching. On

237

the slate was written, "I dreamed I had my voice again." Sudden tears came into Ianthe's eyes and she made a quick motion of her hand to her mouth.

Moore put his hand on Nat's shoulder and watched Ianthe as she walked across the room, then back to stand by the bed again. "Ianthe, I'm going to look Nat over now. Do you think you could give me a cup of coffee when I come down?"

"Of course, Ed."

"All right, Nat."

His thin, feeble hands were working at the knot of the bathrobe cord. His face wore an expression of weary acquiescence.

The examination was careful, but it did not take long, and at the end of it Moore knew that the almost inevitable had happened. The cancer cells had broken out and planted themselves in Nat's breast and his abdomen, where they could be felt, and perhaps in his lungs and brain. He helped Nat to retie the gray cord, and sat down on the foot of the bed, his back against the post. For a moment they looked at each other in silence. Nat's gaze was steady, and in it Moore read that there was nothing about his condition that Nat had not guessed.

When Moore felt sure of this and of the steadiness of Nat's self-control, he said, "Nat, I want you to go into the hospital now."

Nat's gaze did not shift but his eyes grew deep and sad, so that Moore knew he understood the full implications of this. Then he turned on his side slowly, as though all motion were an effort, and reached for the slate. Moore started to get up to help him, and Nat gestured him away. He wrote on the slate and passed it to Moore.

He had written in the large, bold hand that no longer seemed like his, "Would it be easier for Ianthe?"

Moore lowered the slate to his knee and thought, but he said only, "Yes, Nat, it would." Then he sat and waited, watching Nat.

After a while Nat seemed to remember that Moore was waiting, and he gave him a faint, apologetic smile. His lips formed the word "When?"

Moore rose and put the slate back on the table. Now that he had said these difficult things and Nat had accepted them, he could return to his normal manner. Then he remembered that the things they had not said, but both understood, had made it im-

238

possible for Norton ever to return to a normal life of any sort, and he glanced at him with troubled doubt. Norton gave him the faint half smile again, and Moore, suddenly not able to bear the resignation he saw in it, turned away and walked toward the window, saying over his shoulder, "I should think you might go as soon as possible, Nat. Ianthe's looking a little tired, it seems to me. Why don't I go and phone Edna right now and make sure she's got a room for you?"

He turned around to look toward the bed. Nat nodded, his mouth pulled in tightly. There were tears in his eyes. Moore went quickly out of the room.

A little while later, his arrangements made, he went to the kitchen to look for Ianthe. She was not there, but the room was filled with the odor of fresh coffee, and cups were set out on the table between the windows. Thinking she might be in the garden, he found his coat and went outside. He saw her by the perennial border at the back of the house. She had put on a sagging old gray sweater and gardening gloves, and she was taking pine needles out of a wheelbarrow and scattering them on the flower beds for winter protection. She saw him and came toward him, stripping off her gloves and pushing back her hair with the back of her hand. Ianthe in an old gray sweater came toward him and, his senses overwhelmed, he had to grope like a schoolboy for something to say.

"Isn't it early to put on a winter mulch?"

"Yes, but I thought I'd better get it done because . . ."

For a moment they both stood still and thought about this. Her cheeks were a lovely, clear shell-pink from the cold. A wisp of gray hair slipped down and touched the corner of her mouth and she tucked it back again, and said in a low voice, "because *il faut cultiver son jardin.*"

This came to him only as a murmur, and he began to think about how he should tell her that Nat must be taken away from her to the hospital. "About Nat . . ." he began, and saw that she had turned away from him, listening to sounds of someone crashing through the underbrush.

"Who could that be, Ed?"

They both began to walk quickly toward the back of the garden, where, beyond a line of shrubbery, a tangle of wild blackberries and steeple-top grew on the beginning slope of Mount Adamant. The crashing grew louder, the shrubbery parted and a towheaded youth in a black leather jacket appeared. He staggered a little under the weight of the small, limp body of a fawn he carried in his arms. The fawn's slim legs, the little black cloven hoofs, hung motionless; blood from its mouth had smeared the sleeve of the leather coat.

"Why, Howie Perkins!" Ianthe ran toward him and Moore followed more slowly.

Howie stood still, panting from his exertion. "Gosh, Mrs. Norton, I'm glad you're here. He's hurt, Mrs. Norton. Somebody shot him." The boy's distress was evident, and his words tumbled out high-pitched, his voice almost out of control. "Dr. Moore, you'll do something, won't you? Won't you? He's alive—I can feel his heart beating."

"Calm down, Howie. Take him into the barn. We'll have a look at him."

They all started across the lawn toward the barn. The deer in Howie's arms struggled convulsively and more bright blood appeared.

"Oh, gosh, Dr. Moore . . ."

"Where did you get him, Howie?"

"Up on the mountain. I found him . . . I just happened to find him or he would have died. Nights, it gets awful cold up there."

"Calm down now, Howie. You must have had a hard time carrying him. But calm down now."

"All right, Dr. Moore, but gee, I'm glad you're here. Can you imagine anyone doing anything like that . . . shooting him, I mean?"

"It may have been dogs. We'll see."

The barn, dating from more ample days, housed Ianthe's old car with floor space to spare. Howie, with Moore's help, laid the deer down. It made no more effort to move, but lay with eyes shut, its dappled sides heaving. Moore squatted beside him. When he put a hand on him, the deer quivered.

"He's a very young one. Born too late in the season. Sometimes they don't stand much chance when winter comes."

240

"But imagine anyone's just shooting him, Dr. Moore. It's lucky you're here. I don't have any money to pay a veterinary and I didn't know what I was going to do . . ."

Moore and Ianthe smiled at each other.

"And I didn't dare take him home because Dad wouldn't let me keep him. He'd just call the game warden . . ."

Moore's hands were moving gently over the animal's throat. "And what makes you think we won't call the warden?"

"You wouldn't . . . Oh, gee, I know you wouldn't, or Mrs. Norton either."

"We'll have to report to him, Howie. That's the law. You're not allowed to keep a deer shut up, or to make a pet of one, but I'm sure he wouldn't make you turn this fellow loose in this condition, so don't worry. I'll ask him to let you keep him through hunting season, though he's too young to be shot legally, but hunters get careless sometimes."

"Would you do that, Dr. Moore? Gee, that's swell. Thanks."

"Here it is. Dog bite." Moore exposed some torn perforations in the deer's throat. "Went clean through. Get me my bag, Howie. I left it in the jeep."

"Is he hurt bad?"

"We'll see."

When Howie came back with the bag, he squatted by the deer's head, stroking the reddish hair. Moore put the bag on the floor and rummaged in it. Howie pulled a grubby handkerchief out of the pocket of his leather jacket and gently and carefully wiped blood from the animal's mouth. Ianthe made a small sound of pity, more for the boy than for the deer, and went to stand at a distance.

Moore slipped his hand under the injured throat and the deer jerked convulsively, tried to raise its head, its eyes wide and staring, and sank back again.

"*Oh, gosh.* Don't hurt him, Dr. Moore. Please don't hurt him . . ."

"I'm not going to be able to help it, Howie." He glanced at Ianthe and smiled. "You know it's illegal in the state of Vermont for an M.D. to treat an animal, don't you?"

"No, I didn't, Ed."

Howie was sitting back on his heels, balancing himself with one hand, the other resting on the deer. "That don't seem right, Dr. Moore."

"Don't worry about it. Glad to do what I can. I'll have to report to the game warden. He'll probably come around to have a look, but I'll see he leaves you and this fellow alone. If Mrs. Norton will let you keep him here, that is, which is quite a lot to ask."

"He can stay if you feed him, Howie."

"I'll do that, Mrs. Norton. Sure I'll do that."

Moore had taken out of his bag disinfectant, gauze and a swab. "This has got to hurt him, Howie. If you don't want to watch, maybe you'd better go outside."

For an instant Howie looked torn, then, "I couldn't do that, Dr. Moore. I guess he knows I'm his friend. I couldn't walk out on him."

"All right, then. I'll be quick's I can."

The deer jerked and thrashed and lay still.

"Now the other side. Don't lift him. I'll turn him over by his feet and you turn his head."

When it was finished Ianthe said, "Come in the house and get warm. I have a piece of chocolate cake."

"I just don't think I should leave him for a while, Mrs. Norton. He might get scared in a strange barn."

"All right. Don't get chilled. I'll bring you the cake and some coffee."

As the kitchen door closed behind Moore and Ianthe, she said, "And that's the lad Perkins wants to make into a surgeon."

"He's certainly not cut out for it."

"But you have to say, for all his nerves and anxieties, he's got courage. You want a piece of cake too, Ed?"

"No, thanks. But I want to talk to you a minute when you get back."

She gave him a quick look of alarm, but she said nothing, only hurrying a little as she cut the cake and put the coffee on to warm. When the coffee was ready, she put the pot on a tray with the cake and a cup, and he opened the door for her, going out on the porch ahead of her to hold the screen door open. He watched her walk away toward the barn thinking the screen door shouldn't be up this late in the year—thinking that one of these days soon he'd better find a screwdriver and take it down for her . . . and maybe look around for other chores to do. . . .

When she came back she went to sit by the kitchen table, waiting and not saying anything, the troubled, beautiful eyes watching him. He stood looking down at her, wishing he could reach her with the compassion he felt. Finally he sighed and said, "Nat's trouble has come back again, Ianthe."

He thought that she was going to speak. Her breath came in quick, shallow gasps. Her eyes still on him, she began to take off the gray sweater, her movements swift and jerky, as though she must tear it off at once, with no delay, but it seemed to him she did not realize she was doing this.

He said, "Ianthe," and waited while her thoughts came back to him and he could feel sure that she would understand what he was saying.

"I want Nat in the hospital."

"No, Ed, no."

"It's best for him."

"I know I can take care of him. I can get a nurse to help if I have to. Let him stay in his own home."

"It wouldn't be wise. For your sake . . ."

"Don't think of me . . ."

"This is something you must make up your mind to, Ianthe. There's bound to be some suffering now, and if he's at the hospital we can minimize it."

The telephone rang and Moore said, "I'll answer it. It will be Edna to tell me when the room will be ready."

He went quickly into the hall, and she turned herself toward the table and put her elbows on it and her face in her hands. When Moore came back into the kitchen, she struggled to her feet.

Moore said, "The room's ready now. Let's not wait, Ianthe. You get him ready and drive him to the hospital. I'll meet you there."

She stood still for a moment as though she were trying to grasp the meaning of his words; then she moved toward the hall. As she passed him he touched her shoulder gently. She turned her head and looked at him without stopping and he watched her out of sight. Then he let himself out and got in the jeep and drove away.

Ianthe went upstairs, and standing in the doorway of her husband's room, she saw him bending over an open bureau drawer, taking out a shirt. All her life she would never forget the way he looked then, his old gray robe hanging loose, one tassel lying on the floor, bent over to lift the shirt out of the drawer, moving so slowly.

"Oh, Nat . . ."

She went across the room to him. He put the shirt down and held out his arms to her. She buried her face on his shoulder and he held her close. His cheek rested on her hair; his lips moved soundlessly and moved again, and he put his face down close to hers. She felt him trembling.

After a moment he pushed her away and, keeping his face hidden from her, picked up the shirt and carried it to the bed. He laid it down and unfolded it slowly and uncertainly, as though he was no longer sure how it should be done. She watched him, and inside she was crying but without making any sound. After a moment she said in a small, choked voice, "Let me help you, Nat." He shook his head and gave her a little smile, and she saw that he wanted to do it this last time himself.

He put his shirt on and the rest of his clothes, even his watch, and every movement was an effort for him, so much so that with each new thing he did, it seemed that he could not finish doing it. He did not look around him at the room, even when he was all dressed and ready. He took no last look, but avoided it, avoided seeing anything. He went out as quickly as he could move, and she with him.

Down in the hall he opened the closet under the stairs and got his coat, but he could not quite get into it by himself and she pulled it up over his shoulders for him, her hand feeling how the flesh had gone away from his shoulders. The coat hung on him as though it were a coat that did not belong to him. She saw this and it was terrible to her because it showed her that he had changed even more than she realized. It seemed to her that in not realizing, she had let the distance grow between them again and that again she had failed him. She was still crying inside and it was for this as well as for him. He reached up on the shelf for his hat and put it on. He was still looking only at what he was doing, as though this were no different from other times he had left the house, but she knew he was trying not to see. He put his hat on and he put his arm around her, and they went out. It was he who was leading her.

=== XIX

M<small>R</small>. W<small>HITALL</small>, of the Public Health Service, put his briefcase on the floor of Armstrong's office and kept one hand lovingly on it while with the other hand he took out of his pocket his large, underslung pipe. He looked around the office with a half smile, his lips making small, sensually sampling movements. David, watching him, his feelings halfway between irritation and amusement, thought he looked extraordinarily like Harry, the Rotary rabbit. There was the same blandly ruminating look, the same satisfaction with creature comforts, the same unawareness of the feelings of those around him. Magnify Harry's stolid obtuseness into a factor that had to be dealt with, and might you not have something pretty alarming?

Whitall had an unattractive personality, most certainly, and one that made an instantly unfavorable impression on others. But David, sitting across the desk, studying him, thought there might be something in the man that dislike had made him fail to see before. Intelligence, for one thing. When you looked at him with an open mind, you saw it plainly in his face. But in a personality like this, wouldn't intelligence be thwarted, frustrated, blunted before it could reach its mark, simply by his failure to make people like him? He was pathetic—no, actually tragic—if you thought of it like that. He was pompous and dogmatic, but wasn't he these things because he had to conceal a knowledge that people disliked him and a sense of failure that, most likely, never left him? His reliance on his pipe and the display of the Phi Beta Kappa key as social props with which to give himself an assurance he did not feel would bear out this theory.

This piece of insight took David thoroughly aback, first because his having achieved insight of this sort was in itself unusual enough

246

to be startling and second because he now saw perspectives in Whitall where before there was only a blank wall. Wondering whether the discovery of vistas in Whitall would make him like him any better, and feeling sure it wouldn't, he realized that the man had been talking all the time. "I'm sorry," he said. "Something on my mind. What did you say?"

"I was talking about the probable effect on a practice like Moore's of the increasing role of government in medicine."

"I'm afraid it's something I haven't thought much about. Too busy and too concentrated, I guess."

"We'll talk about it again, sometime. You've got things fixed up fine in here, everything new. I shouldn't have thought it would be worth while for only a year."

"I'd have been glad to furnish it secondhand, but this country's growing so fast there isn't any used office stuff."

"Quite a lot of noise the river makes. Bother you?"

"I don't even hear it any more."

Whitall looked away, gazing for a moment at the window, and then he fixed his eyes on David. Made uncomfortable by it, David said, "Did you want to see me about something special?"

"I've just come from an interview with Dr. Moore. Likable old boy. Doctors of his stamp did lots of good in their day, and their day isn't quite over yet. But he was awfully uncommunicative. I was just trying to find out some minor facts about his hospital."

"I should be interested to know—do you—does the Public Health Service—give this kind of detailed, personal attention to all the small hospitals in the state?"

Exasperatingly, Whitall took time before answering to fill his pipe and tamp down the tobacco. His fingers were long, yellowish, and they had spatula-shaped ends. He brought a kitchen match out of his pocket, and David tensed to endure the striking of it with his thumbnail. There was something vicious in the way he did it, and something unpleasant in the satisfaction it gave him. He took a gurgling drag or two on the pipe. "By no means," he said with the pipe still in his teeth, and David had to think back to remember what they had been talking about.

"By no means. I have a personal sort of interest in this setup here. As it stands, it's somewhat unusual, and the future possibilities are exceedingly interesting from the professional planner's point of view. I'm glad to spend some of my own time studying it. I don't see how you tolerate the sound of that river."

"So you're asking these questions on your own time?"

"Yes, I'm glad to. I want to make an important report. And I feel I may have various things to say out of my experience that will make it worth you doctors' time to talk to me. But I must say, though Moore answered my questions, he did it with nothing to spare. Sat in his swivel chair facing me with his hands on his knees and didn't once look directly at me. Fine old fellow. Lots of these older country doctors are—but he seemed to be all stirred up inside about it all. What I want you to tell me, Doctor, is—what is his real attitude toward the hospital question?"

"I don't think his attitude is hard to explain. He knows you think his hospital should be closed up. He doesn't agree."

"I'm surprised he's been able to keep it open as long as he has. He's no businessman. Do you know, while I was talking to him he did something I guess is typical. We were interrupted by a man who came in for some capsules. Moore shook some—a handful nearly, out of a bottle, put 'em in an envelope and handed 'em over. I took a look at the bottle. It was an antibiotic and I happen to know those capsules cost fifty cents each. When the man had gone, I said, 'Are you *giving* him those?' He pretended he didn't hear me, but that was what he was doing, all right. He should just have written a prescription, and"—David looked at his watch—"I suppose in lots of other ways . . ."

Whitall embarked on one of his long, annoying pauses during which he fingered his Phi Beta Kappa key. He did this in his dreamy way, making the little movements with his lips, and David repressed the rebellion of his nerves as well as he was able.

"Didn't you have anything special that you came in to see me about?"

"Well . . . yes. As a matter of fact I thought we might have dinner together tonight—food's good at the Republic House, I find —and sort of talk about things. I have some ideas I think will interest you."

"I'm sorry, I have an engagement."

David's manner of speaking was curt, and he was at once ashamed of himself. To soften the baldness of the statement, he said, "A Dr. Barlow is coming from Warwick."

"That the Dr. Barlow who is considering practicing here?"

"Yes, but if Haddon is to be without a hospital—"

"I've wanted to talk to him. May I join you?"

"His wife is coming. We're all going to a friend's for a sort of picnic supper."

"Is the friend anyone I know?"

"I don't think you'd know her. Her name is May Turner."

"Oh, the young woman who runs the telephone answering service. If it's just a picnic, I'm sure I could be included without inconvenience. I'd appreciate it mightily if you'd fix it up."

Whitall began to bang out his pipe in an ashtray with slow, heavy blows. David gazed with revulsion at the stinking pyre, sighed with fortitude and reached for the telephone.

The town was in the quiet of dinner hour, and a few flakes of snow were drifting lightly down. David put his gloved hands in his coat pocket and drew in his shoulders. "This is what one of my patients calls black cold."

"Oh, this is nothing. Wait a bit." Whitall wore fuzzy gray woolen gloves that made his long fingers look like caterpillars. Gray, woolly gloves and plaintive brown eyes—somehow, David thought, these made one feel like a heel. He said a vehement though inaudible "Christ," resenting equally the gloves and the feeling. Whitall was speaking with his provoking slowness. "As I was saying, this town doesn't know how far behind the times, medically speaking, it is. The people have no concept of what it could be like in a town like this. Even a well-informed man like Stoner doesn't know—and Moore, because he's too close to it, least of all. Now, as I see it, the town must first be made aware of what is missing. A problem of education, and—"

"We go up these stairs," David said.

They found Dr. Barlow already there when they arrived. "My wife's in the kitchen," he said, receiving from Whitall a woolly handshake with a blank neutrality of expression. To greet May, Whitall removed the glove. She said, "How do you do?" in her light voice, and while he said something overelaborate about his pleasure at being included, she gazed at him with childlike, solemn wonder. Barlow said to David in a low voice, "You can recognize the bureaucrat by his symptoms, the way you would a disease."

Whitall solved the problem of what to do with his coat by handing it to David, drew a chair toward the center of the room, sat on it and waited as though for the party to begin.

At a table in the corner Barlow was mixing drinks with a pleasant rattle of ice in a pitcher.

"Martini, Mr. Whitall?"

"No, Scotch, please."

"Dave, it's your night off . . ."

"Yes, I'll have one. A martini, I mean."

"Here's Emily."

David turned to see a sturdy young woman in an apron who had straight dark hair cut in a bob, with a severe bang over the top of dark-rimmed glasses. He wondered whether this somewhat impenetrable façade might not be deliberate, and decided it probably was, for a closer look showed him a pleasant, gravely intelligent face. She gave the impression of self-possession, but of preferring not to put herself forward. Whitall was saying, "I'm very glad to meet you, little lady," and David laughed aloud, for Emily was holding out a hand to him and on her wrist was a thin gold chain from which hung a Phi Beta Kappa key. A swift, sidewise look showed him that May had seen and was laughing too.

Except for Whitall, and perhaps because of his presence, these comparative strangers were at once a cohesive group, with an understanding that was almost intimacy. Emily took May her martini and sat on the couch beside her. David, seeing the two girls touch their glasses, thought that Emily Barlow was just the kind of girl he would want May to have for a friend, and was unconscious of the possessiveness in this thought.

He came out of his brief reverie to hear Ted Barlow saying to Whitall, ". . . and another advantage a city man has is that he doesn't have evening office hours and so he can have one of these" —he held up his glass—"whenever he likes."

"A point, if it means something to you . . ."

And David thought, My God, he doesn't know Ted's joking!

"But to get back to what we were talking about, Doctor"—the pipe was in Whitall's hand, the stem stabbing the air in Barlow's direction—"I tell you, in ten years the conditions of practice like the one you're contemplating will have almost no resemblance to the way things are today."

David said, "You think so?" and got up to get the martini pitcher. As he filled their glasses, the two girls on the couch smiled at him as a parenthesis in their listening.

"You think of yourselves as practicing medicine as individuals, don't you? Not so isolated as the old-timers like Dr. Ladd, or even as Dr. Moore. More willing to cooperate with each other and to use specialists. Haddon's going to have a health center where you'll all be together in a sort of informal clinic. You can consult with each other or not, just as you please. Well, a lot of self-determination in practice will be taken away from you in ten years' time."

"How so?" To David's alert ear Barlow sounded belligerent, and thought that here might be the medical conservative in pure form.

"You already have a partner in the practice of medicine, and I'm surprised more of you don't realize it. Government. State and Federal government."

"If you mean more controls, limiting our freedom of—"

"I don't mean anything of the sort." Whitall sounded pettishly irritated. "I'm surprised at you. In one minute one of you is going to start talking about the 'creeping socialization of medicine.' "

"Well, that's exactly—"

"No, hear me out. Please." The cracker-barrel voice rose into a higher register, and the pipestem made a sign in the air as though to ward off evil. "Take Dr. Ladd, for example. He's still practicing medicine with the same equipment he had when he started, and most of it he can carry around in his bag. Now, you younger men have been trained to use equipment for both diagnosis and treatment that you can't possibly afford if you practice alone. So you form groups like what the Health Center will be, and all chip in, and the town has some church suppers to raise money and you buy a fluoroscope and X-ray equipment. And that isn't enough. Sometimes you need equipment that's so expensive most small hospitals can't afford it—equipment that takes specially trained doctors to handle. You—and your patients too—are making more and more demand for these facilities."

"I never heard of a patient not getting what he needed." As he spoke, Barlow glanced sidewise at David, and David shrugged slightly to indicate his neutrality.

"But maybe he has to travel miles and maybe there are money problems. What I am getting at is that individual enterprise and charity have done a pretty good job, all things considered, but they have gone about as far as they can in providing these things. The only way from here on to advance and expand is by using Federal grants. That's already operating to a very considerable extent. It will have to be very greatly increased in the near future. That's what I mean when I say every doctor will have government for a partner."

Barlow jumped up and waved his arms, then shoved his hands in his pockets as though to discipline himself. Emily got up unobtrusively and went into the kitchen.

"You make it sound all very fine and progressive. But, damn it, money means control. It always has and it always will. If and when the major share of 'health money,' if you want to call it that, comes from government, then doctors will be working for government. You said that, in effect. What you didn't say is that then a bunch of bureaucrats will be telling me what to do and how to do it. I don't like it and I won't have it. I'll work for my patients—"

"A large percent of whom, in ten years' time, will be paying you through one sort or another of government insurance. It's the wave of the future, Doctor. You can't resist it. You—oh, thank you, Mrs. Barlow. That looks delicious."

Whitall took the plate that Emily was holding out to him, and when she turned away David saw her give May a flicker of a wink. It delighted him.

But Whitall had not had his say, and when he was in full hue and cry after an idea, he had no objection to talking with his mouth full. He also gestured with his fork, back up, making sharp, prodding motions with it. There was something about this gesture that gave David the feeling that he knew a good deal about this man's origins. A poor boy, almost certainly, with a lonely dream of an education he had worked hard for. He had managed it somehow, and one could suppose it had not given him all that he had hoped.

"In a way, Dr. Barlow, it's like what's happened in research. Time was when the greatest medical advances were made by doctors working alone, usually at night, after a full day, with a Bunsen burner, maybe, and a few flasks—Lister, Pasteur, lots of others. This is wonderful food, Mrs. Barlow."

"It's just stew."

"Wonderful! Then research got more complicated and research equipment more costly, until now . . . Did you know, Dr. Barlow, that Federal grants now make up seventy-five percent of all medical research funds?"

"I didn't know it was so much."

"Well, it is." He popped a small potato in his mouth and maneuvered it into his cheek in a way that made David think of a hamster he had once seen in a cage in the pathology department. "And did you ever hear of research men being controlled or restricted in any way?"

"I can't answer that. I don't know."

David said, "I don't think I ever have—it's an interesting thought," and Emily said, "My husband is the old-fashioned type of rugged individualist, Mr. Whitall. You'll never beat him down."

The dark frame of Emily's glasses emphasized the tip of her nose and the generous curve of her lips that struck David with surprise as being seductive and lovely. She had a knack for timely intervention. He carried his plate across the room and asked May if he might sit on the edge of the couch. Here, in the partial privacy created by the telephone equipment and dim light, they whispered together.

"David, he's simply awful, isn't he?"

"That's certainly the first impression he gives. I don't think I'd ever enjoy his company, but when you get past the first impression, you have to admit he's got something."

"Do you agree with what he's been saying?"

"He hasn't said very much, and I agree with it so far, though it seems to have aroused Ted's old New England hackles. It's plain enough he's a medical socialist—or what Ted would call one. The thing I've been chiefly made to realize tonight is that I haven't thought enough about the whole question of government in medicine. I guess I'm not alone in that. I rather think doctors everywhere are beginning to realize they've been caught in an upheaval and that a lot of them, maybe most of them, don't really know what's happening to them."

"Aren't the Barlows nice? Oh, I hope they come here to live."

They talked about this possibility until Emily began to collect plates, when it belatedly occurred to David to help. Cake followed, and Whitall, receiving his, said, "Did you make this, little lady?"

Emily said, "Why, yes," vaguely and went away. After a while sounds of dishwashing came from the kitchen. Whitall scraped his cake plate with the side of his fork, ate the last bit of frosting, and put the plate on the floor. David rose to pick it up and carried it out to be washed.

When he came back, the everlasting pipe was in evidence again, a flaming kitchen match held over the bowl, and Whitall was talking between sucks. "What I . . . don't . . . understand . . . is—"

David said to himself, *God damn it, light the thing.*

"—why you all . . . don't see . . . ah! don't see that Moore's hospital couldn't survive under any circumstances. You all—the whole town—even Timothy Stoner, who's the brightest man in it —think the people have a choice of having Moore's hospital or not having a hospital. That isn't the choice at all. Moore's hospital is dead, it's history. If somebody put a million dollars in it tomorrow, it would still be dead history, though it might go on functioning for a few years."

May said indignantly, "What's destroyed it? I'd like to know."

"The wave of the future, I tell you. The wave of the future. Don't you agree, Dr. Armstrong?"

"I don't know. I don't believe in private hospitals, though I'm willing to concede there may be good ones, and that Moore's, small as it is, is one of them. I can't see that a hospital is really needed here, if there is good first-aid equipment in the Health Center."

"The town has a choice, but not the choice it thinks. The choice is between no hospital or a good, modern hospital meshed in a statewide plan, built in part and maintained in part by Federal funds. Why, just look at Moore's hospital in your mind—a firetrap of an old building never meant to be a hospital, run by a man so old he ought to retire, who never did know anything about hospital administration. Now, contrast that with a fine, low, modern plant of colored tile and glass with plenty of ground—"

"Mr. Whitall!"

May brought both small fists down on the tan telephone box so hard that something inside it jangled, and David grinned.

"Yes, my dear little lady?"

"You're an outsider, Mr. Whitall. You don't belong here. Excuse me, but that's true. You don't know how the town feels. We

254

love Uncle Ed. We want his hospital just as it is. We don't want colored tile and glass and the patients with numbers instead of names and some agency telling us how to be sick according to a government plan. We want our *own* doctors and our *own* hospital, and we don't want any outsiders. That's how we feel about it, Mr. Whitall."

She slid down low on the couch, hidden from them all by the tan box. David rose from his chair to go to her, and saw Emily standing in front of Mr. Whitall saying, "Here's your coffee, Mr. Whitall. Cream and sugar?" Whitall was looking up at her, red in the face, bewildered, and, David saw, hurt.

In the concealment of the tan box David held May's hand until she stopped trembling with the aftermath of her anger. Presently he remarked that Mr. Stoner had once assured him that the question of Haddon's having a new and different hospital was an academic one, even with government aid, since the amount of money the town would be required to contribute was too great. The remark fell like a stone in the silence. Ted had pulled a book out of the bookcase and was turning pages with every sign of absorption.

Whitall was brooding like a man who has found that the language he speaks is unintelligible to those surrounding him. In a little while, subdued and moody, he said he had some work to do, put on his coat, said a constrained good-bye with his hat gripped rather tightly in his hand, and left. They all listened to his heavy footsteps on the wooden stairs.

When they could hear them no longer, Emily said, "I'll get us all more coffee," and Barlow moved his chair closer to May's couch. May pushed her curls back from her forehead in a distracted way that made David smile.

"I suppose I'm hostess, sort of, and I shouldn't have said that to him, but he just made me mad."

Barlow held out his cup for Emily to fill. "There's nothing cockier than a little fellow with a government agency at his back."

"You know . . ." Emily stood in the kitchen doorway with the coffeepot in her hand. "I'm sorry for him."

"Why, for heaven's sake?"

"Poor little man. He's rather horrid, really, and of course nobody loves him and he knows it. He's lonely—just terribly lonely, I imagine. Needing people so much and not knowing how to get on with them, and only his pipe and his key to help him. He's probably going to his room and pull papers out of his briefcase to work on and try to make himself think he'd rather be doing that than anything else."

Barlow ran his fingers through his hair, then carefully smoothed it out again. "I don't know whether I dislike the fellow most for what he is or because I don't like his ideas."

"He's intelligent and he's lonely, as we said. And he's just the type you'd expect to find in the early stages of a reform movement, or a revolution. It's the refuge his type seeks. I'm sure there are lots of others like him in the current revolution in medicine."

May, who was not yet entirely calm, said, "Emily, what on earth do you mean?"

Emily waved the coffeepot. "I mean, society shuns these unappealing people, and so they set about dreaming up a new society, or a segment of society where they think they'd have a place. That's an oversimplification, of course, of motives that are certainly unconscious anyway. But if their dreams are timely enough to appeal to people . . ."

Ted laughed. "I can't see Whitall manning the barricades, if that's what you're talking about."

"Oh, that kind of revolution has its Whitalls too—the dreamers who plan the future utopias. But they're in the background, and they belong to the early stages. When the street fighting starts, the intellectuals get lost sight of—and usually their ideals too. They get pushed aside by a different type with different aims. They'll get submerged as the medical revolution develops—you wait and see. Men like Whitall who gave the new ideals their original form will be replaced by other—"

Barlow said, "Interesting, if true. But explaining him doesn't make me like him any better. Come on, baby—finish washing up the dishes and let's go. We've got a long drive ahead of us."

XX

The front door of the old Greer house should, Dr. Moore supposed, be called a "restoration," except that nothing so fine had been here in the old doctor's day. Then the door had been a bright green, the paint chipped off at the bottom where the old doctor's boots had kicked it. No delicate white paneling, no brass knocker, no fanlight. . . . The door was opened by a squat man whom Dr. Moore had never seen before and who had an air about him of foreignness and servitude.

"I'm Dr. Moore. Is Dr. Greer in?"

"Ya, in study. He expect you, no?"

"He expect me, yes."

Inside, the squat person held out a hand in what looked like a gesture of supplication that confused Moore for a moment until he realized that all the fellow wanted was to receive Moore's hat and coat. Grinning, Moore gave them to him. He was led through a room that Moore remembered as having faded wallpaper and a potbellied stove but that now had exposed beams in the low ceiling and an impressive fireplace. Beyond that, Moore thought, had been the cold pantry, but it was now a book-lined passage. Then came a room with a picture window that had once been the shed with a big pine stump in it that the old doctor used to split his kindling on. Then there was another, very large, room and Moore thought, the barn, by God, and grinned at Greer who was getting up from a large desk by a big window that gave a long view of the mountains.

"Hullo, Moore. Glad to see you. Fritz . . ."

There followed some rapid words that Moore did not understand.

"What language was that?"

257

"German. I told him to bring us some sherry. Let's sit by the fire. I have an idea we're going to disagree about something, and disagreements are never so serious by a good open fire."

Moore let himself down into the corner of a sofa. "What makes you think we're going to disagree?"

"There's an air of determination about you. That, and some of the things you said last time we met. But let's wait until the sherry comes."

"You've made a lot of changes here. How on earth do you heat this room?"

"Jacked up the stringer beams and excavated. It has its own furnace underneath."

"I helped the old Doc, your father, hitch up in here one night when we were going to the same case. Roads were bad and he wouldn't trust the old rattletrap I drove. Must have been the first or second year I was here. Even Ladd was driving a car. I didn't know how to hitch, and your father thought that was disgraceful. He never really had any faith in me as a doctor after that."

"Here's the sherry. It's very dry. I assume that's what you like?"

"The odd fact is, I never tasted sherry."

"Really not? Then you won't know how excellent this is. I bring it from New York. Thank you, Fritz, that's all."

Greer held his glass up to let the firelight shine through it, and Moore did the same. He watched the shifting gleam of the flames in the pale brown-gold; then he took a tentative sip. He could think of quite a few old-fashioned medicines that had a pleasanter taste. Holding the delicate, V-shaped glass carefully, he rested its base on his crossed knee. "You've made the old place pretty comfortable."

"Yes, but I hope I've kept its spirit."

Anything more unlike in spirit the little house that had belonged to old Dr. Greer would, Moore thought, be hard to imagine.

"But it's finished now. And my book is finished. I find myself without any real occupation—and, do you know, I don't like it."

"Is that why you're interested in teaching at Warwick?"

"Yes, I must keep active."

"I should think you'd find it not active but strenuous, going so long a way."

"I'm not feeble, Moore."

"I didn't mean to imply you were. Did you know that Howard Perkins has also applied?"

Greer put his sherry glass down carefully. "No, I didn't. Is that what you came to talk about?"

"One of the things. I merely thought you ought to know."

Greer's knees were crossed, and Moore noted irrelevantly that his foot jerked slightly with the beat of the compressed artery and that it was, perhaps, a little faster than it should be. Greer, as though he read this thought, put both feet on the floor.

"You would be in a pretty bad spot if you lost him, wouldn't you?"

"I'm in a bad spot now."

"Just exactly what did you want to say to me about this, Moore?"

"I doubt if anybody at Warwick knows about that old business when he was dismissed from his residency, and after fifteen years I don't suppose it would count very heavily against him if they did . . ."

"But you're suggesting that it *might* prejudice them against him and as a result you wouldn't lose him?"

"Certainly not." Moore shifted angrily in his seat. "But it's the kind of situation, when a man is under investigation, when things in his record come out. I don't think he'll be offered the post now that you have indicated your interest, but if my hospital goes under he will have to relocate somewhere, and if that old story got around it wouldn't do him any good. You were exceedingly kind to him once. I want to ask you, if you hear that old story coming out, to do what you can to put the lid on again."

Greer stared at the fire, then he sighed. "You're a remarkable man, Ed. I apologize for misinterpreting you just now, but any other man in your position would be likely to use any undercover methods he could to keep his chief surgeon. If you lose him, your chances of saving your hospital, or of keeping any sort of hospital here in Haddon, are almost nil. Any chance that Armstrong would stay permanently?"

"None at all."

They were silent, and Moore, turning over in his mind how best to introduce what he had to say, raised his eyes absently to a large portrait of Greer that hung above the fireplace. Seeing the direction of his look, Greer said, "A good likeness, isn't it?"

"What? Oh, yes." The portrait was of Greer in a long white coat, leaning back against a table, one hand curved around the table's edge to show the sensitive modeling of that hand and to suggest its skill.

"My niece did it. As you can see, she's a painter of some distinction. Now I want to ask you something and I want a frank answer. Suppose the choice for the Warwick post lies between us two. Myself, a surgeon not, I may say, unknown, but retired for some years, and an unknown surgeon, but a good one, skilled in general surgery and knowing the requirements of a country practice. Which of us would they be likely to pick?"

"That's hard to say. You both have important—but very different—qualifications. Your prestige value to the school would be considerable. I should think the choice would fall on you."

"And—I'm a little surprised at myself—I really want it. I don't suppose you've ever had time to be bored, Ed, but I'm bored now. Bored with retirement. When I wake up I think, My God, another day, and what am I going to do to fill it? Potter down to the town to get the New York papers and read everything in them, and then what? And what tomorrow and the day after that? No, I really want that teaching job. But forgive me. Let me fill your glass. And I think you had something else you wanted to talk about, didn't you?"

"Yes, and it might have some bearing on what you're talking about. But first let me ask you a question. At that Rotary lunch where I more or less told 'em off, I don't remember your saying anything much. Are you among those who think there should be a hospital in Haddon?"

"Yes, with qualifications. A hospital at Silver Springs, where there is very little population outside the plant workers, might not meet the needs of the much larger and more varied population of Haddon. If there is to be a hospital in this area, it should be at Haddon."

"Then you are in favor of a hospital in Haddon?"

"On the whole, yes. At present we don't need one as much as Silver Springs, but this part of the state is growing fast. In a few years' time there will be enough people to support a hospital here as well as Warwick."

Moore gave Greer a sharp look, put his glass down and leaned forward. "All I need is money for repairs and some modernization, and there is the hospital that Haddon needs—or the start of it. I thought perhaps you would be willing to put some money in and to associate yourself with the management of the hospital to any extent you cared to."

Greer did not move or change his expression, but the casual relaxation had given place to wariness. He sat like this for a moment, completely encased in himself, and Moore sighed and lowered his eyes to the floor. A log on the fire broke and fell forward in a shower of sparks, and Greer glanced at it with annoyance, rose and set it right with the fire tongs. When he sat down again a little of the inner rigidity had disappeared.

"How much money were you thinking of, Doctor?"

"Well . . . I haven't figured it closely yet."

"But the rough figure you have in mind?"

"A hundred and twenty-five to a hundred and fifty thousand."

Greer sat in silence, his fingers tapping an agile flight of soundless notes on his knees, and Moore, breathing a little heavily, waited. Greer gave him a quick glance.

"I'll go so far as to say the idea interests me. There is a lot to be said against the continuance of your hospital—I don't have to tell you that. But putting it in shape, getting it ready for growth, would be a challenge. But we're two old men—or I am, and you're not so far away. . . . I'm not making much sense, I'm afraid. It interests me, but let me think it over, will you?"

"Yes, certainly. Of course."

"Another glass of sherry?"

"No, thanks. That stuff is stronger than it looks, and I have to get back to the hospital for a few minutes."

"How is young Armstrong working out?"

"I don't think he likes the way we do things very much, but he bears out what I say about the need for expanding—we've both got as many patients as we can handle. Some of the increase is curiosity about the new Doc, of course, but still . . ." Moore pushed himself up out of the sofa corner and Greer rose also. "You think about it, and let me know. I won't hide it from you that your coming in would probably make all the difference in whether the hospital pulls through or not, but . . . You think it over."

•   •   •

261

To Dr. Moore his hospital had never looked more worthy than as he crossed the parking lot from the jeep. There was dignity in the old building and a homely friendliness that, to his way of thinking, no modernistic, functional building could possibly achieve. Even the hideous turret helped to defend the structure against the curse of the institution look. He smiled up at it as though it were a friend.

Edna was at her desk talking to the floor nurse from the maternity unit—a blowsy girl called Molly whom the patients loved and Edna constantly admonished. At sight of Dr. Moore Molly fled and Moore went up to the desk.

"Is Dr. Perkins here, Edna?"

"He left about an hour ago, Doctor."

"Armstrong?"

"Making rounds. Shall I call him?"

"Please. I'll be in my office. I think maybe I have some good news. We could all use a little, couldn't we?"

"That we could!"

His old tweed jacket, when he shrugged into it, gave him an almost sensual satisfaction. Contented good nature rose to its natural place on the surface of his being, and when Armstrong came in, white-coated, solemn, Moore smiled at him in a way he had not done for some time.

"Sit down, Dave. I've been to see Greer and I think perhaps our troubles will be over before long."

When David sat, Moore thought, he never looked relaxed, even leaning back with his knees crossed. He should be taught to find more enjoyment in life.

"You mean about the hospital?"

"That's just what I mean. You know, Greer is generally supposed to be a rich man, and I guess it's true enough. He's also bored with his retirement, and looking for something to give him an interest. Well, I got to thinking—why shouldn't the interest be this hospital, and why shouldn't he put in some of his money? So I went to see him and put it up to him."

"And he agreed? I must say, I'm surprised."

"Why? It's a natural for him when you think about it. As a matter of fact, he didn't agree then and there. He said he'd think it over, but I haven't any doubt of the outcome."

262

"May I ask how much money would be involved?"

"I suggested a hundred and fifty thousand, and his participation in the running of the hospital to any extent he cared to. Mrs. Norton has already offered us fifty thousand—"

"Mrs. *Norton?* You mean Mrs. Ianthe Norton whose husband is in the tower room? I'd no idea she had that kind of money."

"She's always liked to live simply, like lots of other old families that have it. I'd only accept it as a loan, and I wouldn't even consider that without the financial security Greer's money would give us. But the combination would give us nice working capital. Say, five or six thousand for repairs—perhaps seven or eight. Then the new equipment Howard has been ranting about—an autoclave, an electric cautery, perhaps a new operating table. The table alone would be nearly three thousand. New anesthetic equipment—say another fifteen hundred or two thousand. Maybe we could allow as much as fifteen or twenty thousand for equipment like that and still have enough for a building on that property next door."

"It sounds like Christmas."

"Doesn't it? Then, I've been thinking we should have a board of advisers like the trustees of a nonprofit organization. Greer, of course, and Moriseau, and some other operators from Silver Springs. Then they couldn't say we weren't trying to serve everybody's best interests."

"If this really happens, you ought to have someone from the town. Stoner, perhaps?"

"Dave, if this really happens, and it's going to happen, it will give me very special and personal pleasure not to have Tim Stoner on the board."

David laughed, and instantly looked grave. "Will you excuse me, sir, if I make a suggestion?"

"Sure. What is it?"

"Well—you probably wouldn't do it anyway, but don't you think that, until this is settled, the less said about this the better?"

"Oh, certainly. Perkins should hear about it, but that's all, I should think. It wasn't necessary to tell you, but . . . Dave, did you ever see a pail of milk that got left in a barn on a zero day? It gets too big for itself, bulges, and sometimes splits the pail. Way I was feeling, I would have split if I couldn't have told somebody.

You've taken the pressure off. Enough of that. I suppose you looked in on Norton on your rounds?"

"I did. Mrs. Norton wants to talk to you when you have time."

"How long do you give him?"

David thought about this carefully for a moment. "It would be hard for me to say. Of course I've had far less experience than you in this sort of thing. I'd make it a week—not more."

"I think you'll find it longer—two to three, nearer three."

"It's invading his brain, isn't it?"

"Yes, I think so."

"Mrs. Norton doesn't realize that, I take it. She said something about the things he wrote being incoherent occasionally, and I said the medicine would sometimes do that."

"Good. No need for her to know before she has to. He'll be perfectly lucid most of the time, and perhaps it won't really catch up with him before he dies. I'll go up there in a few minutes."

"Then I'll finish my rounds."

David rose and had opened the door when Moore spoke to him again. "How's your chief patient these days, Dave?"

"My chief . . . Oh!"

To Moore's delight, a bright flush came to David's face. Moore swung his swivel chair backward out of sheer exuberance, with a twang of the spring like a note from a giant harp. "All right. All right. She seems to be your patient now, but I'll check up on both of you one of these times."

The door shut with some haste on David's embarrassment, and Moore, righting himself, propelled the chair toward his desk with his feet after the fashion of a boy with a soapbox on wheels. He felt fine. He felt like work, and lots of it. He felt simply fine.

Outside Nathaniel Norton's room Moore looked at his watch and saw himself doomed to dining in his office on sandwiches sent in from the dairy bar—unless Edna was keeping some food warm for him. The thought cheered him immeasurably, and he pushed open the door to the tower room and went in. Norton lay motionless and Ianthe sat in the half circle of windows, lamplight shining on her hair. She smiled at Moore and he felt the beauty of the smile all through him and did not know his face was sad because she looked so tired. On the bed, Norton turned his head slowly, as though Moore's coming, like everything else that happened around him, mattered very little. Then his eyes went to Ianthe and to the door.

She rose. "He wants to talk to you alone," she said. "I'll wait outside."

"Go home and get some dinner, Ianthe."

Norton nodded in agreement. She looked from one to the other, hesitating.

"All right."

When she had gone, Norton groped on the table for his slate, and Moore, handing it to him, took note of how feeble he had grown. The effort to write seemed almost too much for him, and it seemed to Moore, watching him covertly, that he was struggling to remember words. Finally he let the slate drop on the bed and Moore picked it up and read what was written in half-formed, wandering letters. They said, "Hosp—don't let them destroy it, Ed. It's *good*—the fools don't know how good. Fight them and keep it. Keep the govern. out. Ianthe wants to give you money. She told me. Take it. And fight, Ed."

Moore stood with the slate in his hands, looking down on it, too moved to speak, feeling as though Nat had returned from a long absence. After a while he realized the groping skeleton hand was reaching out to shake his and that the bony face was contorted into the only friendly smile he had ever seen there.

Moore sat on until, a moment later, Norton drifted off into apathy. Then he put the slate with its message still on it back on the table, and quietly left the room. At the head of the stairs Ianthe was waiting for him. He said, "I thought you'd gone home for some supper."

"I had something to say to you, Ed. I want to talk to you. Not here. Could you possibly come to the house for a few minutes after office hours?"

"Yes, I'll come. You must go home now. Have you got your car here?"

"No, I walked."

"I'll drive you back."

"But you must eat too. Can't I . . ."

"No, my dear. Thank you."

Good-bye to Edna's hot food. A ham-on-rye and a wedge of

apple pie would have to do, and they would "set," as the Vermonters say, like a piece of rock. . . . He put his hand around Ianthe's arm and they went down the stairs together.

At ten o'clock that night many lights in the houses along the green had been turned out, but light shone from the study windows in the Norton house and faintly through the fan over the front door. Moore had just climbed out of the jeep into the darkness by the kitchen porch when he thought he heard someone moving along the drive from the barn. "Who's there?" he said sharply.

"It's me, Dr. Moore."

"Who's 'me'?"

A tall, thin form materialized in the dim light from the kitchen window. "Oh, Howie. What are you doing here?"

"I was looking after the deer in the barn."

"Deer? Oh yes. You've still got him, have you? How's he doing?"

"He's all right now, and the game warden says I can keep him until after the deer season. I've fixed up a big wire pen for him and he's just fine. He's tame now."

"He's not being a bother for Mrs. Norton, is he?" There was something about young Howie that was disturbing, Moore thought, to one's instinctive desire to have life well ordered, with all the pieces neatly in place. The piece that was Howie didn't fit anywhere, and this at once made one angry with Howard and with Adele. Now he had assumed the quick defensiveness, the whining protest, of one who is constantly being blamed.

"She says he doesn't bother her, Dr. Moore. She says she doesn't mind having him there a bit."

"Well, all right, if that's really so."

"He's awful cute, really he is. He knows to look in my pockets, minute I come in, to see if I've got anything for him. He likes Baby Ruths and that milk kind of Hershey bar just fine."

Moore laughed. "You'll have a deer with a gastrointestinal upset on your hands, if you don't watch out."

"I better be careful, then."

You could like the lad if only he didn't expect you not to. As it was, what he mainly made one feel was annoyance because, obscurely, and altogether unjustly, he made one feel to blame. Here

266

he was, hanging around, talking, not because he wanted to but because he couldn't accomplish the simple act of going away.

"Why don't you study to be a veterinarian, Howie?" An idea with some merit, if only . . .

"Gee, I always wanted to—do you think Dad would ever let me?"

"No, I'm afraid I don't," Moore said, and went on into the house.

Ianthe had made a fire in the study and set out a tray with a glass, ice, and a bottle of Scotch. Moore poured himself a modest drink and brought it to the chair opposite Ianthe's by the fire.

"I don't expect to be called out tonight, but it's always possible."

"Can't David take your night calls for you, Ed?"

"New patients, yes, and some I've shunted off on him. But my regular patients I'll see to myself. What's on your mind, Ianthe?"

"It's about Nat. I realize he's not suffering very much physically, but most of the time his mind is clear and he's suffering mentally. I can see it in his eyes when he doesn't know I'm watching him."

"Nat's a brave man."

"I know, but it's cruel, Ed. It's cruel. Why is life so cruel to us?"

"I don't know, my dear."

She shut her eyes, and her fingers pressed the base of her throat. He waited, watching her, feeling compassion for her. When she spoke it was in a voice thick with unshed tears. He put his glass down on the hearth beside him helplessly.

"I didn't understand you, Ianthe."

"I can't bear it. I can't bear it." The words were a cry, loud and agonized. She rose and went quickly away to the end of the room, standing with her back to him. After a moment she said in a more controlled voice, "It's the waiting that's so hard, Ed."

"I know."

She said nothing more. Her head was bowed and she wept silently. After a moment he went to stand beside her.

"Ianthe."

She brushed at her tears with the back of her hand and looked up at him.

"I must talk about this sensibly . . ."

"Come back and sit down." He took her by the arm and led her back.

267

"It's so strange, Ed. Nat and I are closer now than we've ever been. I feel that now he understands so much and he doesn't mind about any of the troubles we've had, but he'd like so much to live to use this new understanding. It tortures him. Ed, I want you to fix it so he won't think any more. Can't you do that? So he won't be conscious any more . . . not for one minute from now until the end."

"Sit down, Ianthe, and we'll talk about it."

He pushed her gently into the chair and pulled his own closer. Now that she had said what was on her mind, she seemed to feel a great physical weakness. She sat with her hands in her lap and her head down, as though it were too heavy to lift. The reflection of the light of the flames leaped in Moore's glass on the hearth. There was no sound in the room but the fire's whispering and his heavy, distressed breathing. He drew a long, fortifying sigh.

"I can give him drugs that will do what you want . . ."

She turned quickly toward him. "Then do it, Ed. Please do it."

"Are you sure you want it, Ianthe? You said just now you had a new understanding of each other. Are you sure you want to let that go?"

"We've had it, Ed, and from now on, as he grows sicker, it will only grow more dim. He knows that too, I'm sure."

"What about him? Do you know how he would feel?"

"Yes, I know. We haven't talked about it, but I know. He would like so much to live, but since he can't he would like to go now. It would be like going if he didn't have to think or feel any more. He's too proud to ask you, but I know he would want you to, Ed."

After a moment he said, "You're sure?"

"Yes."

They were silent again. She put her hand over her eyes and he saw that her mouth, grim with sorrow, quivered. He stretched out a hand to touch her, and withdrew it again. He gazed at her sadly, feeling how alone she was, and feeling his own aloneness until these feelings mingled in a sadness that was not without its own comfort. After a while she took her hand away from her eyes, and turned and smiled at him faintly. She reached out and put her hand on his sleeve. "Thank you, Ed." He put his hand over hers and took it away again, and she used both of hers to brush her hair back from her face.

"I thought I'd be able to talk to you about this without emotion, but I couldn't."

"It's all right, Ianthe. But there's one thing more."

"What is it?"

"There's a certain amount of risk in doing this. I'd give Nat morphine, but in the quantity I'd have to use, it would tend to repress respiration. It's a risk doctors often take when it's justified, as it is in this case. I'll do it, but I want you to understand."

"Don't think I haven't thought about the meaning of this, Ed. I know it's a grave responsibility both for you and for me. I know it will be the end of his conscious life, and the real end of our life together."

She stood up and went toward the door, and he followed her. She braced herself with a hand against the doorframe. "It will be the real ending of my life, too."

"No, it mustn't be that, Ianthe."

"I want it that way. I've struggled enough with all the anxieties and cruelties and disappointments life brings. I want in the future to live so quietly, so negatively, that I won't ever again feel anything very much."

He stood with his head down, his mind in a tumult of revolt against what she was saying. Then he looked at her almost angrily and started to speak. His lips moved, but he said nothing, overwhelmed by the realization that the vehement protest he wanted to make was personal.

She smiled at him almost in her old way. "It's all right, Ed. Don't worry about me. I shouldn't have said anything about myself. God knows, you have troubles enough."

"Ianthe . . ."

He said no more and she seemed not to expect any more. They stood looking directly at each other in silence. Then he nodded his head once, not knowing what he meant by it, not understanding or trying to understand his own feelings.

When he went out to the jeep he saw that the snow, which had held off for so many weeks, had begun to fall in earnest. In the last hour the town had whitened, its aspect wholly changed. He stood a moment by the jeep, feeling the tiny, insistent touch of the snowflakes on his face, knowing that in some mysterious way the change was also in himself. He did not know why this should be, but he felt that when he got into the jeep and drove away it would be into a life that had changed in the last hour so that nothing in it would ever be quite the same.

He was on his own front porch, stamping snow off his shoes, when the telephone began to ring. He said "Damn" in a loud voice, and bustled inside to answer it. May's voice, sounding a little sleepy, told him she had a call from the Hull farm that Ruth Hull's pains had begun and they were bringing her in to the hospital.

"Did you ask her how fast her pains were coming?"

"She said, kind of irregular, but about every fifteen minutes."

"All right, thanks, May. I'll meet her there. It's her third, so it ought to come out pretty quick."

He hung up, looked at his watch, and saw he could just get the weather report from Mount Washington. He went into the kitchen and turned on a small radio and listened to a voice informing him that the snowfall in New Hampshire and in northern and central Vermont would be heavy before morning. He clicked the radio off and looked at his watch again. It would take the Hulls twenty minutes, half an hour to get in to Haddon. Time enough to get the snow blade on the jeep if he humped himself a little. He opened a heavy drawer filled with an untidy assortment of tools and pawed around in it, looking for a wrench.

XXI

DAY HAD BARELY COME and the sky was an opaque, even white, only a little darker and duller than the snow. David's compact little car came over a rise and he saw in front of him a solitary figure trudging along whom he recognized with surprise as Howie Perkins. The boy had his hands in the pockets of his windbreaker, the hood over his head, and he was walking with a diligence that could only mean he intended to walk all the miles to Haddon. David drew abreast and hailed him. "Want a lift to Haddon?"

"Well, sure, thanks." Howie scrambled in, all legs and arms, and panting like a puppy. He settled down and braced himself as though he expected something to happen to him.

"What on earth are you doing way off here at this hour?"

"Well, I was walking . . ."

"I could see that. Don't you have to go to school today?"

"Yes, but gosh, there's lots of time, especially if I drive back with you."

David, glancing at him, saw that he looked anxious, as though in dread of the whim of an elder, incomprehensible to him, but from which there could be no appeal. His thin shoulders were hunched over and a tic in his eyelid flickered. David had a sudden, strong desire to shout at him to sit up straight and stop looking like a bent coat hanger. He spoke with more severity than he intended because in some obscure way he felt the boy's uneasiness to be a reproach that he resented.

"Do your parents know you're way off here?" He must have got up in the middle of the night to come this far.

"I guess not, maybe."

271

"Howie, you shouldn't worry them. You mustn't behave this way."

"They don't care."

Sullen now, and flinging himself sidewise on the seat, wanting to escape . . .

They drove on for a while in silence, David acutely aware of the isolation of youth. Aware, too, that his own tone had not been a propitious one.

"Don't you have any friends at school, Howie?"

"Oh, sure, yes, I guess I do all right."

A sidewise glance revealed the boy's misery under this questioning, and there came to David the sudden certainty that the boy had been out all night in the cold, like an animal.

"Howie, what is it about the woods that you like so much?"

Silence.

"It's really none of my business, I suppose."

Silence.

"Look here, Howie, Dr. Moore told me I should carry snowshoes in my car just in case, and I don't know how to use them. Could you teach me?"

A look of blank surprise and then a dawning pleasure . . .

"Why, sure, yes, I'd like to, Dr. Armstrong."

"That's settled, then. And thanks, Howie." In the town, an aroma of woodsmoke from morning fires hung in the air. "I'll drop you at the bridge. You'll have time for something to eat before school."

At the bridge Howie got out, and the cold air turned his breath into a plume of vapor. He stood hesitating with the open door in his hand and then spoke with a rush, as though he must get the words out that way or not at all.

"Dr. Armstrong—could you tell me—how do you get to be a veterinary?"

David laughed. "Is that what you want to be?"

"I think so. I think I would."

"You go to a school, like a doctor. I don't know what the requirements are. Someone at the high school could tell you. What gave you the idea you wanted to be a veterinarian, Howie?"

"Well, you see, I found this young deer that had been hurt . . ."

"I heard about that. How is he?"

272

"He got well, and then, after deer season, the game warden's men came and got him and turned him loose. They took him clear across the state to where there's a big tract of woods so he couldn't try to come back and where he'd be away from people until he learned not to be tame. I know that's right, but gosh, I miss him. Now he's gone, I like to go and watch the deer in the evening or early morning when you can see them best. I'm sort of getting to know how deer think."

"I still don't see why you want to spend your life with animals instead of people."

"Animals are so easy to get along with. Everything is so simple between you and them."

"And it's not simple with people?"

"Well . . ."

"Don't answer if you don't want to. It wasn't a fair question. I was just interested in this business of your wanting to be a vet. You better go get something to eat now."

"All right. Thanks for the lift, Dr. Armstrong."

Lights were on in the dairy bar, and David parked, took his bag out of the car and went in. Dr. Moore was sitting at a table in a corner and seeing him, David hesitated. The coolness between them had worn thin largely because David found it difficult to preserve in the face of Moore's failure to see it was there. He looked up, saw him, and beckoned. And suddenly David realized the wrongness of letting any estrangement come between them. Flushing, and hating himself for it, feeling small but freed of a burden, he took the chair opposite Moore's own.

"Been out on an early one, Dave?"

"The Blake boy out on the gulf road. May said you had a delivery on your hands, so I took it. Appendicitis, but it will keep, so I told them you'd be in touch. You're looking pretty tired, sir. Was the delivery a tough one?"

The waitress came and David ordered. Moore pushed his plate away. He had barely touched what was on it, and David, seeing a slight trembling of Moore's hand, said, "Did something go wrong?"

"Baby born dead. Shouldn't have been. The girl had two other children easily enough. It could have been my fault—I don't know. Something I did wrong." He turned his head toward the counter where the waitress was rattling dishes. "Sally, bring me some more coffee, will you? . . . I was thinking just now when you came in that I'm pretty well behind the times in a lot of things, including obstetrics. I was thinking that maybe I should take a refresher course somewhere, and maybe in anesthesiology too."

"My God. I'd be lost if you went away."

"Nothing like as lost as I was when I first came here. You know a lot more than I did then."

"I wouldn't want to put it to the test."

Sally came with toast and eggs and bacon, and David ate in silence, thinking about what Moore had said. The idea of Moore, at sixty-five, going back to learning, so that for the few years he had left he could do a better job, seemed to him very moving. Moore was leaning back in his chair, resting mind and body, his arm lying on the table. His hand, with its pattern of distended veins, was prominent against the table's white top. The ridged nails were short and meticulously clean, the fingers blunt, the cords and muscles prominent, and it came to David that the hand's character had been molded by hardship, skill and strength.

"Dr. Moore, there is something I'd like to ask you about."

Moore looked up and smiled slightly at this classic introduction of the thing that is hard to say.

"Go ahead."

David lowered his voice though no one was near. "I'm aware that Dr. Perkins now and then drinks a good deal . . ."

"Have you seen any sign of it in his operating?" Moore spoke quickly.

"No, I must say I haven't—except for bad temper, which could come from other things."

"That's partly the result of finding out Greer wants—and will probably get—the teaching job at Warwick. Howard wants to sell out and leave Haddon."

"What I'm getting at is this. I picked up Howie this morning way out on the gulf road. I got the impression he'd had a row at home and been out all night."

"Howard has a cabin up on Mount Adamant. He may have been up there and come down on the other side of the mountain."

"It looked to me as though things were in a bad way with him. He's thin and nervous—almost sick, by the look of him. He's obviously unhappy at home. It's not hard to imagine that some tragedy is building up. I was wondering if there were anything you could do to help."

"I've been asked that before. I don't see how."

"But you do agree he's not exactly a well-adjusted boy."

"Well—yes—though I don't go along with the idea that an unhappy childhood and youth is necessarily bad. If a young person has underlying strength of character, a maladjustment is as good equipment for success as I know. My watch has stopped. What time have you, Dave?"

"Just eight."

"Lord, Lord, and I wanted to get to the hospital early." Moore pushed his chair back and stood up.

"I wish you'd give up obstetrics, sir."

"I feel like giving it up, after what happened last night."

When they were standing at the cash register, pocketing their change, David said, "Why don't you let me take over for you this morning and you go home and get some sleep?"

"It's your day off, isn't it?"

"I guess it is. I'd forgotten about it. But that doesn't make any difference."

Moore smiled. "Thanks, there's something special I have to do at the hospital, but I might be able to take an hour around noon. By the way, our radio equipment has come. They put mine in the jeep last night. Leave your car at the garage and they'll hook it up. See you later."

Edna Judson knew the sound of Dr. Moore's footsteps, and so she had risen from her desk when he came in. She glanced quickly at the week's operating room schedule, to assure herself of what she already knew, that there were no operations listed, and so no need for Dr. Moore to be here to give an anesthetic. Her face, when she looked at him, was tight with worry. "Good morning, Doctor. We were all hoping you'd be at home getting a little rest."

He sighed. "Is Ruth all right?"

"She's sleeping."

"Good. I'll see her later."

"Mr. Brown is here, Doctor. I put him in your office."

"Mr. Brown?"

"One of the examiners for the Accreditation Board."

"Oh, of course. Thanks, Edna."

Mr. Brown was looking at the pictures in a medical journal with a layman's pleasurable horror. He put the journal down to rise and shake hands.

"How are you, Doctor?"

"Aren't you about pretty early?"

"The three of us are heading downstate and we spent last night at the Republic House. I wanted to have a private word with you, so I came along."

"What about your report? You've taken long enough about it. Sit down, won't you?"

"The report's in the mail. You should get it today. Otherwise I wouldn't be here."

"What does it say?"

"Provisional accreditation."

For a long moment Moore was silent, then he said, "That's quite a blow."

"When you think about it, there's not much else we could do. You're financed, not too liberally, for only less than a year. The tenure of both your surgeons is uncertain, and there's no one else in sight. We try to be fair, as you know, but, frankly, with your plant and equipment in its present condition, you're lucky we didn't close you up. Are you interested in why we didn't?"

"Yes—of course." Moore spoke dully.

"Your location. Frankly, we'd rather see a hospital at Silver Springs than here, but we feel there should be one closer than Warwick."

"I've got an almost sure chance of getting enough money to put the hospital back in shape and do some building too. Maybe I'll eliminate this old part altogether, though I'm sort of attached to it."

"I wish I could say I'm glad to hear it, but the fact is, private hospitals have seen their day. You wouldn't want to tell me where your money's going to come from, would you?"

"At this point, better not."

"Would you object to a bit of advice?"

"No."

276

"Don't carry your expansion plans too far until you're sure of a staff."

"That's about the first order of business when things get going."

"You may find your chief difficulty right there. By the way, I hear there are plans for a health center here. How far along are they?"

"I don't know. The drive for funds is getting going. There's a church supper next week."

Brown laughed. "You'll have to eat one in every church in town just to be public-spirited. Well, I've got to get going or my colleagues will wonder what's become of me."

He rose and held out his hand and Moore shook it. Moore said with as much cordiality as he could, "Nice of you to come in," but he was not able to keep worry and disappointment out of his voice. When he was sure that Brown had gone, he went heavily out of his office. Edna was looking at him anxiously. He started to tell her about the provisional accreditation and found he had not the fortitude.

She said, "I do hope you're going home now to get a little sleep."

"I'm going up to see Nat. I'll need a hypo of morphine."

He started up the stairs and she followed him. He went to the nursing station where Helen, in a winged cap with a black velvet band on it, was making entries on a record sheet.

" 'Morning, Helen. You got Norton's chart there?"

She turned to a rack behind her, drew out the aluminum-covered chart and laid it on the counter in front of him. Reading it, he felt his pocket for a pen, and wrote. Edna, looking over his shoulder, read "morphine ¼ grain, atropine ⅟₁₀₀," and went quickly away down the hall, the key to the narcotics cupboard in her hand. When she came back she was carrying a tray with a folded towel on it, a hypodermic, two small bottles, alcohol and cotton.

"Do you want me to give it to him, Doctor?"

"No, I'll do it."

Taking the tray, he saw the troubled look in her eyes. "Ianthe's with him," she said.

"At this hour? I thought I'd be ahead of her."

"She's here all the time. I can't get her to rest."

He carried the tray in both hands as he went toward the tower room, as though it were heavy. He saw Ianthe, in the instant before she was aware of the door's being opened, sitting in the armchair, her hands folded in her lap. When she saw him she started to rise. He made a half-audible sound and shook his head, but she went to the side of the bed. Norton, opening his eyes, looked up at her. He had, Moore thought, been in a half-conscious sleep, but when he saw Moore he smiled a little and watched Moore put the tray down on the bedside table. Moore knew without looking that Ianthe had put her hand in Nat's.

Moore kept his eyes on what he was doing, trying not to see anything else, and in his mind giving them what privacy he could for this final hour. He pulled up the sleeve of Norton's gown and swabbed a spot on the pitifully thin arm. He looked once at Norton and swiftly away again. This was involuntary, not intended, and it involved him briefly in a realization of the strange magnification of spirit that is like an aura around the consciously dying. Wishing he had not seen this, but to a degree exalted by it, he busied himself with what he had to do. He did not want to prolong this, but he turned his back, giving them this little time alone. He steadied his thoughts on what he was doing, trying not to be aware of anything else, but knowing without seeing it that Nat had turned his head toward Ianthe and that they were looking at each other. Suddenly he felt very tired, and the hand holding the morphine bottle cramped, the muscles knotting painfully. He set the bottle down and spread his fingers, holding them that way, and the cramp went away. He picked the bottle up and pushed the needle through the top.

Moore knew by the way Nat braced himself for the needle that he had guessed. He knew without looking that Ianthe was holding Nat's hand in both of hers. The rest was over quickly. He jerked the needle out deftly, dropped the hypo on the tray, picked up the tray and went out without looking at them. He carried with him a feeling of their communication with each other and with himself. He did not realize that not a word had been spoken. He left the tray on the counter of the nursing station and went to the doctors' lavatory and washed his hands. He bent over the bowl and threw cold water in his face; then he washed his hands again.

XXII

ADELE LAY IN HER BED and stared at the dim oblong of the window. From the moment she awakened she had listened, though for what she did not know, for she heard nothing but Howard Perkins's heavy breathing in the bed next her own. She had awakened alert and restless, conscious of her own body and that the world outside the window was not sleeping. The night had a luminescence, not from the moon or the stars, but sourceless, diffused, and disturbing. On such a night deer have moved out of the darkness of the woods and have become still, gray shapes standing in the meadows. Night birds fly low and small animals venture stealthily. Adele felt the wakefulness, the urge to move forward into action. She sat up in bed and gazed with wide eyes at the dim objects in the room around her.

She thought of Howie and she felt how a night like this would stir him. She listened now only to hear any sound that he might make. The house was still and there was a feeling, that grew on her, of its emptiness. More and more, she was certain that Howie had gone, that he was out in this strange night, understanding it and belonging to it. She wondered if he might have gone to find his deer, thinking that perhaps he had found it and they were together now. At the thought she felt a strange pang of jealousy. Then she told herself that these were imaginings, that he had been home at dinner time, and that he must be sleeping in his own bed. But the feeling that he had gone persisted.

She pushed her legs over the side of the bed. Her nightdress had slipped up to her waist and off one shoulder, and she shuddered with cold, but she sat there listening. She hated the sound of Howard's steady, loud breathing. She wanted to cry because she was cold and alone, and she made a sound like a sob, but she could not make the tears come. She covered her face with her hands and made herself a mind picture of Howie, out in the night, moving furtively from shadow to shadow. With her bare legs hanging over the edge of the bed she rocked herself in misery because she was alone and no one cared, but she could not make the tears come.

After a while she slid off the bed and stood up barefoot. She found her robe and put it on and tied it. She squatted down and felt for her slippers under the bed and sobbed again because she could not find them. Shivering, she went to the window, pulled it down and imagined that at once the whiskey fumes were stronger in the room. She stared out the window for a moment, feeling the intense quality of the night; then she went to the foot of her husband's bed and stood looking at the mound his body made under the bedclothes. She had given up wanting to ease her loneliness by crying, but that only made her feelings more poignant.

She let herself out into the hall, not taking any particular pains to be quiet, and here she was warmer and the floor was warmer under her bare feet. She opened the door to Howie's room, and in the eerie half-light from the windows she saw the outline of his long body on the bed. She clung to the handle of the door, leaning on it, weak with relief but not quite able to comprehend that her fears were groundless. After a moment anger began to overcome relief, anger the more bitter because there was no occasion for it. She hated him. She hated him for his secretiveness, and for the way his mind always escaped from her, and for the fright he had just given her. She wanted to strike him as Howard sometimes did. Not knowing what she intended to do, she came farther into the room.

She bent over him, outraged that he should sleep so peacefully, and at the same time hurt that he could cause her so much misery and be unconscious of it. Then she saw that the bed was empty and that she had mistaken the ridge of thrown-back covers for his sleeping form. She stood where she was, staring down at the bed. Cold wind came through the open windows, billowing the curtains. She stood in the path of the wind until she was numb in body and mind. When she was half frozen, she moved stiffly to close the windows.

With the wind shut out, the room seemed smaller and safer.

She groped for the chair where Howie threw his clothes at night, and, hand stretched out, she felt his trousers hanging over the back. They were those Howard had sent him upstairs to put on before dinner in place of the dirty jeans he was wearing. She thought he must have put the jeans back on again. Then she thought how cold he must be in the worn-thin old blue jeans, and she drew her robe more tightly around her. She went to the closet to be sure about the jeans and in the darkness felt along the brief line of clothing that hung there. Her fingers found no texture of denim. Shaken by the intimacy of these things he had worn, that were closer to her and more docile than Howie, she searched again, though she knew they were not there. She came out of the closet, passed the bed without looking at it, and went on out into the dark hall.

She did not waken Perkins until she was sitting in her own bed with the covers pulled up over her shoulders and her body was beginning to grow warm. Then she said, "*Howard*," sharply, as though she were still in the first shock of Howie's absence. He came awake, not easily, but with the determination of a doctor long accustomed to calls in the night. He reached for the telephone, and she said, "It's not a call, Howard. Howie's gone again."

"You wake me up for that, for Christ sake? He'll get back all right. He's done it before."

"Only once. But he must be made to stop doing it. He won't be any good at school tomorrow."

"I'll talk to him in the morning. What time is it?"

"Two-thirty."

Perkins pushed himself down in bed with his back to her and pulled the covers up.

"Howard, I've been thinking . . . He's so unhappy all the time—"

"It's his own fault. All he has to do is brace up and get hold of himself. And maybe if you didn't nag him all the time . . ." Angrily, he pushed himself up in bed. "Maybe if you'd lay off him a bit . . ."

"You nag him too. But, Howard, maybe, if it's what he wants so much, we *should* let him be a veterinarian. I'm convinced he'll never make a good doctor."

"Has he been talking to you about it again?"

"Well—yes. And one of his teachers talked to me."

"I've told him, and I've told you—I won't discuss it."

"Then—he's so terribly unhappy all the time—perhaps we should take him to Warwick to see a psychiatrist."

"And have the whole town saying he's even nuttier than they've thought? I should say not."

Suddenly, without warning, Adele put her hands up to her face, bowed her head to her drawn-up knees, and burst into a storm of weeping.

Perkins said, "Oh, Lord!" under his breath and reached for the light. He got heavily out of bed and put on his bathrobe. Then he sat on the edge of the bed facing her. "Look, Adele, we've been all over this before. I'm not any prouder of him than you are, but I haven't given up hope. I'll make something of him yet whether I get any help from you or not."

"It's all because of this horrible town." Her voice was thick with resentment and tears. "If we hadn't had to come and bury ourselves here—if we could have lived the kind of life your wife and your son have every right to expect—if you hadn't done that fool thing—"

"*Shut up!*"

Silence. She sat with her arms wrapped around her legs and her forehead on her knees. Her hair curtained her face, and though she no longer felt the cold, she was trembling.

After a moment Perkins said in a weary voice, "Haven't we quarreled enough? God knows we don't do much else. I'm trying my best to get you out of this town. Now let's forget it and get some sleep."

"You can't leave Howie out there in the night."

"What can I do about it, for Christ sake?"

She turned toward him, brushing her hair back with a violent gesture. "*Find him.* That's what you can do. *Find him.*"

"Where? Do you want me to go rushing all over the state of Vermont at two-thirty in the morning?"

"You know perfectly well where he's gone. He's gone to that cabin of yours where you set him such a good example by drinking yourself blind."

282

He threw the covers back and got out of bed. He stood looking down at her. Then he turned away and started to put his clothes on. She jerked the nightgown into place, slipped down in bed, turned her back to him and pulled up the covers.

The brief thaw had exposed the rutty mountain road in places, though the ground was frozen hard. Under the overhanging hemlock boughs the night was windless, and the jeep climbed upward in the tunnel of brilliance from its headlights. In the stillness the noise of the jeep seemed to travel far, and Perkins, driving into the clearing before the cabin, thought if Howie were there he must have heard. The clearing was surrounded by the wall-like darkness of the forest, and Perkins, leaving the headlights on, took a flashlight and, with little hope of finding Howie, opened the cabin door.

Warmer air surrounded him and he saw the red glow of a dying fire on the stone hearth. He snapped on the flashlight and turned it toward the cot bed that stood against the wall. Howie was sleeping there, blankets over him, his clothes and his quilted parka in a heap on the floor beside him. Perkins moved the light so that it did not shine directly on the boy, and stood looking down at him.

Howie's thin body seemed not so much relaxed in sleep as surrendered to exhaustion. The paleness of the boy's face was a shock, and the features seemed to Perkins strangely delicate. Howie seemed frail, almost ill, and there were marks of suffering in his face that Perkins did not remember having seen before.

Perkins backed away, having seen too much, wanting to defend himself against seeing more. When he spoke to the boy there was none of the usual harshness in his tone.

"Howie."

He saw Howie stir and push himself up on his elbow, slowly waking. The boy looked around, not seeing Perkins as yet. Then Howie's eyes were on him and Perkins saw the look of openness die away and a blank look with something defensive behind it take its place. Suddenly this was unbearable to Perkins and he shouted.

"You God-damned young fool, what do you think you're doing? Get up."

Slowly and reluctantly Howie pushed the blanket back and paused, looking up at his father as though he almost hoped for kindness. Perkins again shouted, "*Get up!*"

While Howie was dressing, Perkins worked at the fire with a poker, scattering the embers, striking at the glowing bits of charred wood again and again until they were all extinguished. Then he moved toward the door, saying over his shoulder, "I'm taking you home. You think you can behave any damn way you like. Well, your mother and I . . ." He held the cabin door open and jerked his head toward the outside. "Come on. Get going. I'm not going to hit you." Howie slunk past him and he slammed the cabin door.

The jeep bumped and jolted under Perkins's rough control. The road, no more than a logging track, was precipitous in places and Howie braced himself, holding on to the edge of the seat with both hands. A night bird flew low in front of them with a weird, wild cry, and Howie turned his head to watch it disappear into the woods. A stream crossed the road, the water in the path of the headlights clear amber with flecks of foam riding the current. Perkins ran the jeep across the ford without slowing, and wings of water curved away on each side of them. They came fast around a curve, and at the same instant they saw a flash of motion at the side of the road. Before either of them could see what it was, a deer leaped in front of them. Howie cried out and Perkins reached for the emergency brake. They hit the deer with a soft thud, but the force of it made the jeep shudder.

There was a moment of frozen stillness while the sounds of the night replaced the noise of the motor that was stalled and silent. The deer lay on its side in the road. Slowly Perkins reached out and turned off the ignition.

"Well, we got him. We'll have to report to the game warden. I hope he didn't damage the jeep."

Howie sat in rigid stillness, staring with fixed, wide eyes at the deer. Perkins glanced at him and sighed. Then the deer moved, lashed out with its forelegs and raised its head. A gush of blood came from its mouth and Howie moaned.

The deer was struggling to rise, the forepart of the body twisted around, head raised, forefeet planted on the ground, the legs in a beautiful arching curve. The hindquarters and the hind legs were motionless. "Back's broken," Perkins said.

284

The headlights were full on him in a merciless white glare. The front part of the creature heaved upward again and sank back. The black hoofs of the front legs beat a fierce, rapid tattoo on the ground. The proud, beautiful head with its crown of antlers was lifted and blood came in a steady drip from the mouth while the rest of the creature still lay as he had fallen. The wild beating of the front legs came again and Howie covered his face with his hands.

Perkins bent forward, groping on the floor, and straightened up with a tire iron in his hand, holding the short, blunt piece of metal like a weapon. He held it out to Howie.

"Here, take this. Get out and kill him."

"I couldn't. Oh, Dad, I couldn't." Howie shrank away, making desperate motions in the air as though to ward off the iron.

"Do you want to see him suffer? Do as I say."

"Can't we do something for him, Dad? Can't we help him?"

"No. His back's broken, I told you. Do as I say."

"I couldn't, oh I couldn't. Please, Dad . . ."

"You damned weakling. Take the iron."

"No, no. I won't. I—"

"You sniveling crybaby. I'm going to make a man of you if it kills you. This is only an animal. Do you understand? Only an animal. Here, take this iron. Do you hear me? *Take this iron.*"

He bent forward, thrusting the iron in Howie's face. Howie, frightened eyes on his father, slowly took the iron. He held the iron weakly, his lips trembled; then he began to tremble all over.

"Now get at it. And do a job of it. Hit him on the forehead. Look out for his hoofs, for Christ sake. Hit him on the middle of the forehead, and hit him hard."

Howie slowly began to move toward the deer, circling the dead hindquarters to reach the head. Perkins grimly watched him. Then with desperation Howie turned back to his father. "Dad . . ." He saw the implacable contempt in his father's face and dragged himself forward. Perkins, watching him, said half aloud, "Christ, he moves like an old man."

Howie by degrees got himself around in front of the deer, and as he came close to the pointed hoofs, Perkins tensed. The deer, when it saw Howie, tossed its head high and drummed the earth with its hoofs. Howie raised the iron slowly and Perkins leaned forward to watch.

"Go on. Damn it, be a man. Give it to him."

Howie turned his head toward his father, then back to the deer. He raised the iron. Suddenly he made a sound that was both a cry and a moan, and the iron fell on the road. He turned and ran, leaped the ditch, scrambled up the steep bank, and as Perkins shouted, he fled into the woods.

Perkins shouted, "Come back here, you . . ." Then he stood still and listened to the sounds of Howie crashing through the woods. He shouted again, "Howie!" And again he listened as the crashing grew fainter. Then he rubbed his hand over his face and went to look at the deer. The mouth was open now, though the blood had stopped flowing. The forelegs were still arched, the hoofs pressed into the earth, and the live front of the body was swaying a little.

Perkins picked up the iron. He raised it; then with a swift, accurate motion he brought it down on the deer's skull and jumped back to avoid the head as it sank to the ground.

He walked quickly back to the jeep and tossed the tire iron on the floor. Then he went back and stood by the deer, looking down on it, wanting to be sure it was dead. He pushed up his sleeves, seized the deer by its forelegs and dragged it to the side of the road. He got into the jeep and sat for a long time looking toward the woods and listening. The woods were black and still. He reached out and turned the ignition key, and the engine started with a roar.

XXIII

IANTHE WOKE EARLY, though there had been little sleep since Howie had come stumbling up onto the kitchen porch just before dawn. Awaking, she had at once a full recollection of the boy's grief and exhaustion and of the tears he had shed as she held him in her arms, and she felt again her own shock at discovering what he had been forced to endure.

She glanced at the clock, saw that the time was a few minutes past seven, and hastily got out of her bed. She found her slippers, wrapped herself in a warm robe, and went quickly but silently out of her room, aware, as she always was when she passed the door of Nat's room, of the emptiness therein. Outside the door of a bedroom at the back she paused to listen. There were no sounds and she pushed the door open a little way. Howie lay sleeping, his face turned toward her, his fine, long-fingered hand resting on the quilt. He seemed to her to look frail, almost ill. Marks of suffering overlay the boyish contours of his face, making him seem at once old and very young, as though there had not yet been time for youth and sorrow to merge into maturity. She breathed a soft sigh of pity and closed the door with care.

She went downstairs feeling the nighttime secret aliveness of the big house, and feeling it retreat before her. She sat down by the telephone, found Dr. Perkins's number in the slim book marked HADDON AND VICINITY, and gave it to the operator, speaking softly because of the sleeping boy. May's sleepy voice said, "Doctor's office."

"May, good morning. This is Ianthe Norton. I want to talk to Adele Perkins and I don't have the private number."

"I'll ask her to call you."

Ianthe waited with her hand on the telephone and lifted it instantly when the bell began to ring. She said, "Hullo, Adele?"

"Yes." There was something anxious and guarded in the single word.

"I'm sorry to bother you so early in the morning, but I thought you might be concerned about Howie and I thought I'd better tell you he's here with me."

There was a long silence before Adele said, "Thank you. Will you tell him to come home right away, please?"

"I think perhaps you'd better come here. Perhaps you and Howard both."

"Why? Isn't Howie all right? Is he hurt?"

"He isn't hurt. He's upstairs sleeping. He came here in the middle of the night."

"Why didn't you call us then?"

"I'll explain that to you, and there are some other things we should talk about. I really think you should come here right away. I'd go to your house but I don't think I should leave."

There was another silence before Adele said, "Howard's already gone to the hospital. He's operating this morning. I'll come over as soon as I'm dressed."

A little more than half an hour later Ianthe, hurriedly finishing her own dressing, saw from her bedroom window Adele walking swiftly toward the house. In a moment more the knocker on the front door sounded and Ianthe tensed a little, half glancing in the direction of the room where Howie was sleeping. She went quickly downstairs to the door, opened it and said, "Come in, Adele."

"Is Howie really all right? Nothing's happened to him?"

"He's sleeping. He's not hurt or anything like that, but I wouldn't say he's all right. He's in a very upset state, and that's what I want to talk to you about. Let me take your coat."

"I think I'll keep it on. Thanks, Ianthe."

"Then let's go into the study. . . . I'll just shut the door, though I don't think there's any danger of Howie's hearing us."

Adele went to the fireplace and stood with her back to the mantel, leaning on it, her hands in her pockets. When Ianthe said, "Won't you sit down?" she shook her head.

"There isn't much time. I've got to get him home and washed and fed before school."

"I think he'd better be allowed to skip school today. You know what happened last night, I suppose?"

"The deer Howard hit when they were driving down from the cabin? Howard tried to make Howie kill it. He shouldn't have done that. But Howard's hitting the deer was an accident, of course. He couldn't have avoided it. Howie should be able to see that."

"I think perhaps he's been missing Spotty, his pet, more than any of us have realized."

"He hasn't talked about it at home, but I can understand that. But an animal he'd never seen before . . ."

"He's been worrying about Spotty; he's afraid Spotty can't look after himself alone. When this wild deer was hit, perhaps it made his anxieties about Spotty so real to him he couldn't stand it. Last night I woke up and heard him running up the drive. I found him on the kitchen porch, crying, and in such a state it was hard to find out what happened. He kept talking about Spotty and at first I thought it was Spotty that something had happened to, though I knew that wasn't possible with Spotty so far away."

"It's not normal to be that fond of an animal."

"Perhaps not, but he seems like such a lonely boy, Adele."

"I wish you'd phoned us last night. We weren't really worried about him—about his being safe, I mean. He knows how to take care of himself in the woods. I told Howard that if he hadn't come home by the time I was dressed I'd take the jeep and go and get him. But he shouldn't have this kind of breakdown. And he shouldn't have come to you."

Her eyes, resting on Ianthe, were bright and hostile, and Ianthe, turning away from the look, thought, At least she's jealous—she loves him enough to be jealous when another woman . . .

Adele straightened up and stood erect, her hands making fists in the pockets of her tweed coat. "If he's as worn out as you say, he can skip school, but there's no reason for him to stay here any longer. I think you'd better go and wake him and tell him I'm here."

"Adele—I'm afraid you'll think—I'm sure you will—that all this is none of my business. And it isn't really. I don't think an outsider should interfere between parents and their child except in very exceptional cases. But I've grown exceedingly fond of Howie. I've

289

seen a good deal of him since he's been coming here to see Spotty. Perhaps that doesn't give me a right to talk to his mother about him, but I have some things I want to say, so I'd like to do it all the same. Will you listen?"

Adele gazed at her in silence for a moment; then she said bitterly, "I suppose it's going to be all over town that Howard and I were so cruel to Howie that he ran to you for protection."

Ianthe flushed. "They won't hear it from me."

"I'm sorry. I didn't mean that. I didn't mean you'd talk. It's just that I've suffered so much from the gossip of this town. . . . I feel sometimes that we aren't allowed to have any private lives—that everyone's curious and no one's friendly. I was thinking of the town, not you. I don't think you'd gossip."

Ianthe was silent for a moment, then she said, "I think I can see why you feel that way. I should have realized it—we all should. I'm afraid we've treated you badly, and without reason—or perhaps for the bad reason that you're different from the rest of us—or we've made the mistake of thinking so. You come from a part of the country we don't know; you've been to schools that aren't like ours. You have a different point of view. . . . We're a close group, and perhaps we were a little afraid of what you'd think of us. What I'm trying to say is, I'm sorry."

Adele made a slight movement of her shoulders and stared at the floor in silence. Then she sat down abruptly in the chair facing Ianthe.

"What was it you wanted to say about Howie?"

"He's desperately unhappy, and that goes way beyond the tragic deer business. Adele, he can't go on being that unhappy. I'm afraid something will happen."

"What do you mean?"

"I don't know. I just feel he's in a dangerously emotional state, and that he was before this deer episode. You must have felt it yourself."

There was a pause. Adele looked thoughtful and very troubled, and Ianthe, watching her anxiously, thought she was making up her mind to talk without reserve and that she was finding this difficult. She gave Ianthe a clear, steady look, full of intelligence, that left Ianthe with the impression that her past judgment of

Adele had been superficial and inadequate. Then with a quick motion she put her hand in her coat pocket, pulled out a bandeau and slipped it over her hair. It held the curtain of hair away from her face as though she were voluntarily exposing herself, and Ianthe was startled to see in the sensitive, clear-cut features a resemblance to Howie.

Adele said, "I suppose he feels that Howard and I are against him. We did so want—Howard especially—to have Howie have the sort of career his father should have had. He's been a disappointment to us. We've thought he could be what we wanted if he'd only try. Perhaps we were wrong. Perhaps he really can't change from what he is."

"Then couldn't you both give him more freedom to be himself? Not try so hard to force him to be what you and Howard want? From what I've seen of him I would think he has it in him to develop into something very fine along his own lines. He's told me he wants to be a veterinarian. I should think that would be very much the right thing for him. Has he talked to you about it?"

"Not really. Howard is very much against it. He wouldn't discuss it."

"You wouldn't reconsider, I suppose?"

"Perhaps we should. This trouble about the deer has been a sort of crisis. We haven't had a chance to talk about it because it was so late when Howard got home last night. But I could see he was very troubled. Not angry with Howie any more, but very troubled. I'm sure he feels as I do that we can't go on as we have been."

"If Howard would agree to let Howie be a veterinarian I believe it would give him the feeling of security and hope he seems to me to need so badly."

"I'll talk to Howard about it." Then she said it more decisively. "I'll talk to him about it tonight." She rose. "You've been kind, Ianthe. I hope you know I really mean that. I must go now. If you think Howie should sleep it out, all right. But when he wakes up, tell him we won't scold him. Tell him we won't talk about the deer, if that is what he wants. And send him along home, will you please?"

"I'm not sure he'll go, Adele. You and I have talked things out, and I think we both feel better, but I'm afraid when Howie wakes up he'll be in the same emotional state he was in before. Last night he was feeling very resentful toward his father and saying that he'd never go home again."

Adele sat down on the edge of her chair, her hands on her knees. "But what . . ." She frowned and was silent.

Ianthe said gently, "He could stay here a while, Adele."

"And have all the old cats in town saying he ran away because we ill-treated him and you were so sorry for him you took him in? Thank you, no. No indeed."

"I think you and Howard need a little time to think all this out by yourselves and that it would be better for all concerned for Howie to stay here, for a few weeks anyway, or for as long as seems wise. If you want a reason to give people, you can say he's staying with me because, with Nat away, the house is very empty—God knows that's true enough—and he's staying with me to keep me company. I'd truly love to have him."

Adele jumped up again and for an instant Ianthe thought she was angry. She walked to the window, where she stood with her back to the room. She stood there a long time and Ianthe waited in silence.

When Adele came away from the window she moved slowly and Ianthe thought that perhaps she had been crying, for she seemed softened and, in some subtle way, younger. She did not go to her chair, but stood leaning back against the professor's desk, her hands curved around the edge.

"I suppose, since this town knows all about my affairs, everyone knows Howard and I haven't been getting on very well."

She said it with bitterness but without anger and Ianthe made no reply.

"I know well enough that Howie is the chief reason for that. We quarrel about him. We don't want to—either of us. I can see Howard hating it as much as I do, though in a different way. But we can't seem to help ourselves. We—" Her voice shook and she stopped. Ianthe saw her eyes glisten with tears and her fingers tighten around the edge of the desk. In a moment she said in a voice thick with emotion, "If Howard and I could just be alone for a little while . . . If we could just be alone together . . . I've been so upset about him—perhaps that's why I didn't see that Howie . . . But his disappointment in Howie has changed him so,

292

and lately he's been . . . lately I've been so worried about the effect it's having on him. If we could just be alone for a little while, I think he might be the sort of person he used to be and we could talk about things the way we used to, and then I think it would be all right about Howie . . ." She covered her face with her hands.

Ianthe rose and went to stand in front of her, and Adele took away her hands and the two women looked at each other. Then Ianthe said, "I'll take good care of Howie, Adele."

XXIV

THE MORNING OPERATING SCHEDULE was light, consisting only of an uncomplicated tonsillectomy that Dr. Perkins handled with style and rapidity. The administering of the anesthetic was simple, but when Dr. Moore came downstairs, Edna Judson thought he looked as tired as though this were the end and not the beginning of the day. There was something else about him that she had noticed just in the last few days, and noticed with concern. This was a just perceptible air of bewilderment, a suggestion, no more, of a loss of his customary sureness. To her anxious mind he seemed to have retreated inside himself and to be looking at all that was customary and familiar from a new point of view. There was much to cause him uneasiness; of this she was certain, for her own mind was no longer at ease. And whatever the outcome of the hospital's difficulties, and even if the hospital survived, there would be change. In small and unimportant ways it was already going on. It would not abate until it had altered all their lives, and Dr. Moore's, perhaps, beyond his adaptability.

She rose stiffly from her place behind her desk and crossed the hall, propelled by a vague need to have another look at him through the window as he crossed the parking lot to his jeep. She saw him at once, a massive, squared-off figure in his parka with the hood over his head. He was moving heavily, as though the reserve of his vitality had been eroded away, and she thought, We'll soon be old, both of us—both of us already dreading change.

From the wing one more hooded figure appeared, Perkins, walking slowly toward his car. For a moment the two cowled monks stood together talking; then they went their separate ways. Edna stood on at the window until she became aware of a thin stream of ice-cold air coming in around the old window sash. She held her hand against it. Time, and past time, for the storm windows to be in place. She had forgotten—another disturbing sign, it seemed to her, of the creeping up of old age. She stood a moment longer, wondering how it would seem to turn all these petty burdens over to a successor and be free. The thought was not pleasing. She glanced up at the sky and saw that the gray clouds had the over-burdened brooding look of coming snow, a mood of nature match-ing too well her own. She turned away from the window and left the office with her swift nurse's walk.

The dullness of the day had invaded the front hall, and when she sat down at her desk to work, she turned on the gooseneck lamp. The brilliance fell on her papers and on her blue-veined hands, making the surrounding shadows deeper. The hospital was quiet, and gradually her awareness of it narrowed down to the circle of light in which she worked. In the shadow the white of her uniform was of more moment, of more positive importance, than Edna Judson. Time passing made these relationships of light and shadow, of mind and substance, a settled state. She worked on and on while the activities of the hospital continued around her until quick steps on the stairs with a sound of urgency in them made her look up, and she saw Ianthe.

"Edna, Nat suddenly looks different. Something's happened. Can you come?"

The two women went together to the tower room where Na-thaniel Norton lay. He lay, as he had done for days, quietly, his body turned slightly on his side, his eyes shut. He was not sleeping, but held in a weird enchantment by the drugs, aware, perhaps, of being alive (though no one knows these things for a certainty) but unable to translate any awareness that might exist into physical motion. One hand, swollen and puffy from reaction to the injec-tion of fluids that were helping to prolong his state, lay on his own body. The other, bluish in color but normal in shape, lay on the bed beside him, and over this hand Ianthe put her own.

Edna stood beside Norton's bed and Ianthe watched her anx-iously. He lay straight and white and narrow, as he had lain now for many days. The only visible change was a slight translucence of the skin, a bluing of the lips. But there was something else, and it was this, first of all, that Edna saw, but with the eye of the mind, through the lenses of experience, for it left no outward trace. She saw that Nathaniel Norton's body had begun silently to relinquish its last hold on life and, resistance gone, to move toward death. This process, which was one of quiet dignity, was already far advanced.

Edna raised her eyes and met Ianthe's. For a moment their gaze held, and at the end Ianthe knew all that Edna knew. She said with no breath behind the words but with steadiness, "Is Ed here?"

"He's gone, Ianthe. He's gone to Warwick. He'll be outside of the radius his radio works in. I'll get Dr. Armstrong."

She went swiftly, and with a hope that was as near to a prayer as she ever came that Ianthe's trial would soon be over. She found Dr. Armstrong studying a chart in the nursing station.

"Doctor, Nathaniel Norton is going . . ."

He let the aluminum cover of the chart drop down, touched the pocket from which his stethoscope bulged to assure himself that it was there, and went down the hall with long strides. He pushed open the door of the tower room, glanced at Ianthe standing with her hand over her husband's, and stood looking down at Norton. He saw not what Edna had seen but only the physical signs that indicated the successive failings of the body's parts, a predictable sequence that could be estimated in Norton's case with accuracy. He watched for an attentive moment the slow, erratic breaths. He pulled his stethoscope out of his pocket, from habit warmed the diaphragm on the palm of his hand, parted the coverings, and applied it to Norton's wasted chest.

He did these things swiftly, with practiced economy of motion. The sureness that his fingers displayed his mind lacked. His acquaintance with Norton was of the slightest, having been confined to a few routine visits to the tower room when Moore was called away, and yet he felt about this imminent death a curiously personal inadequacy. The reason he knew to be that he had permitted the emotions surrounding it to come home to him. He had allowed himself to feel, and by doing so opened himself to a full knowledge of a doctor's inadequacy as well to those who live as to the dying. Not that he thought coherently about these things. He was as confused as an intern seeing death for the first time and not knowing from what angle death should be viewed, or how to preserve his own detachment. He took the instinctive refuge of those who find themselves in a similar predicament—he became stiff with aloof formality. He looked in Ianthe's direction without actually looking at her.

"Mrs. Norton, will you leave the room now, please, for a little while?"

She turned her clouded gaze on him and answered slowly, "No, Doctor, but if you don't mind I would like to have you leave the room."

He hesitated, staring down at nothing, and then very quickly, almost precipitately, he went out into the hall. He knew the wait would not be long. Opposite the closed door to the tower room he stood with his back to the stair rail, half sitting on it, and sought to evade a wave of self-awareness that threatened him.

In the room Ianthe made a small, soft sound. She leaned over the bed and slipped her arm under Nathaniel's shoulders, holding him close to her. Against her breast she felt the faint stir of his breaths that now came so lightly. She put her hand under his motionless fingers and let it stay there quietly. It was like this that her body felt his last breath. She knew when it came and that it was the last, and she held him as she had done before.

After a long time, without moving her arms from under his shoulders, still holding him against her, she groped for the push button that hung on a cord tied to the head of the bed.

David saw the red light above the door go on. He went in and stood by the bed, waiting while Ianthe drew her arm gently from under Nathaniel's shoulders. He bent over the bed, using his stethoscope once more. When he had finished, he drew the sheet up and smoothed it carefully. He knew Ianthe's eyes were on his face, but he avoided looking directly at her.

"His troubles are over, Mrs. Norton."

At first she did not speak or move. Then, a little unsteadily, she went to one of the windows in the tower and stood there with her back to the room. David watched her closely. When he was sure she was going to be all right, he said, "I'll ask Edna Judson to come. And I'll be in touch with Dr. Moore."

Before he had finished speaking he knew that his words were bringing back the normal world too soon. She turned toward him and he could see that she had not clearly understood and that she was trying to force herself to meet the normal world, and to be adequate and docile. He said, "I'm sorry, Mrs. Norton," without knowing clearly what he meant. He could feel the effort she was making to do what was expected of her. She said slowly, "Thank you, Doctor." After that she seemed to lose track a little, to grow a little vague. He stood a moment more, but he felt that she would be all right now, and that she would be able to make herself equal to the demands that would be made on her. He went out, leaving her standing there.

When Dr. Moore returned, afternoon office hours had begun. David heard his hurried steps in the hall, hastily excused himself from the patient he was seeing, and stopped Moore just outside the waiting room door. Moore stood with his hand on the doorknob, the hood of his parka thrown back, and David thought how worn he looked but how durable. In the language of the country, "seasoned timber." The strength he possessed had, to a degree, the quality of being communicable. David was aware of this only as a slight heightening of the atmosphere experienced in Moore's presence. He said, "I'm sorry to tell you that while you were gone—" And at once the experience of Norton's death assumed dimensions not felt at the time or comprehended now.

"Norton?"

"Yes, at eleven-fifteen."

"Is Ianthe all right?"

"Yes, I'm quite sure she is. I was considerably impressed by the way she stood up to it, as a matter of fact."

Moore made a sound that seemed to mean that no less was to be expected.

"I asked Miss Judson to look after her."

"Edna couldn't leave the hospital to go home with her. You should have taken her home." Moore spoke sharply. "I'd better see if she's all right. You'll have to handle those people in there." Moore jerked his head toward the waiting room. "I won't be long. Anything you're not sure about I'll handle when I get back." He started toward the front door. "Tell 'em I'm on an emergency. You should have taken her home, God damn it."

But when Moore reached the Norton house a little before three o'clock, there were cars in the drive and cars in front. Two women were going up the walk carrying packages. He knew the custom, old as this country, of bringing home-baked pies and cakes and doughnuts to a home where there has been a death, and so he could guess what these packages contained. News travels fast in a small town, and the procession of friends and neighbors that follows any death had already begun. He steered the jeep around the end of the village green and went back to the office.

At the end of the evening office hours he went to the Norton house again and he was relieved to see the cars had gone and the drive was empty. Faint light came from some of the downstairs windows, so he knew she had not gone to bed. He parked, and opened the kitchen door.

"Ianthe?"

Silence, except for the ticking of the clock on the shelf and a slow drip of a faucet. He came in and shut the door. Standing there, he listened with part of his mind while the other part was aware of having intruded on the strange, secret life of its own that a deserted kitchen seems to have. After a moment he called again.

"Ianthe?"

No reply, and his awareness of the silence grew to include the whole house. Worried now, he went quickly along the hall that led to the study, and there he found her. She was rising, dazed and uncertain, from a chair as though she had just realized there was someone in the house.

"Ianthe."

"Oh, Ed, it's you."

She came to him and he put his arm around her. She put her head down on the padded shoulder of his parka and wept. He held her there, arm around her, hand on the back of her head, deeply aware of her and of the softness of her hair under his fingers. He let her cry, making small, inarticulate sounds of comfort to her as to a child. In a short while her tears lessened. He felt under his parka for a handkerchief and she took it from him and wiped her eyes, still in the protection of his arm.

"I'm sorry I wasn't there, Ianthe."

"I'm sorry too, Ed."

"But there wasn't anything I could have done."

"I know."

"It's cold in here. Come into the kitchen and I'll make you coffee."

He half led her to the kitchen and put her into a chair by the table. She laid her arms on the red-and-white cloth as though their weight were too much for her.

"I'm so tired, Ed."

"That's natural enough." He was busying himself with the coffeepot, handling it with the economy of motion of a man accustomed to making coffee for himself. "I'm afraid you'll feel that way for some time. You must try and rest. Where's Howie?"

"I sent him up to bed. He didn't want to go and leave me. He's a dear boy, Ed—but I wanted to be alone. There've been so many people here today."

"I know . . ."

"Do you realize it's been five years, Ed, since Nat was first taken sick? I've forgotten what life was like before this happened to him."

Moore stood by the stove looking moodily down at the miniature fountain of coffee inside the glass knob on the percolator. Five years since the biopsy report from Warwick had lain on his desk and he had reached for the telephone. "Nat? Ed. Can you come into the office this morning so we'll have a chance to talk in quiet . . ." Picking up the report with the telephone at his ear, then nervously shoving it to the back of the desk. "All right, then, I should be through at the hospital at eleven o'clock." Nat in the patient's chair pulled around with his back to the light, so it was necessary to peer at him a little. Voice noticeably hoarser. "It's what you thought, isn't it, Ed? Cancer?"

"We'll operate . . . have it done at Warwick."

"And if we don't operate? If we just let it go? Perhaps that would be the best plan . . ."

"Of course we'll operate. Damn it, man, what do you think . . . Ianthe . . . Why, you may live for years, and in the end, die of something else, God knows what."

In his mind Moore could still see Nat's angular face in shadow, planes of dark and less dark, sunken eyes steady and sharp with intelligence. In a detached way that was oddly disturbing, Nat was curious about his cancer, and with his peculiar brand of courage he despised it, calling it instead "this stranger." Well, they had operated.

The coffee inside the glass knob was making small, passionate

300

explosions. He picked up the pot, carried it to the table and filled a cup for her, then one for himself. She stirred hers listlessly.

She put her hand to her forehead. "I feel as though I'm so near to some great and important understanding of life, but I can't quite capture it. But I think perhaps a person can only go through one experience of love with wholly pure emotions, and then only at first, only at the start of a relationship. After that—I know it now—any emotion one feels for another person will be qualified. Qualified by experience, because you've been through it before, qualified by thinking and comparing, and by the loss of some vitality that was in you. Wasn't it that way with you, Ed, after Matilda died? Could you ever love anyone the same way again, or feel the same about anyone dying?"

"I don't know, Ianthe. You're right, perhaps. But I know I could still feel very deeply about someone, if not just in the way I did when I was young. But I don't want you to close a door on life."

She stretched out her hand and laid it for an instant over his, then put both of hers around her coffee cup, as though the warmth of his hand had made her aware of the coldness of hers. They let the silence grow, and it took substance from their thoughts, changed subtly into shared peace, and then, its usefulness over, became again merely silence. Moore looked at his watch.

"It's late. You should be getting to bed, Ianthe."

He shoved his chair back and stood, and she stood too. For a moment neither made any further movement, both reluctant to end this interlude, both knowing it was finished and that each must turn toward the future.

═══ XXV

THE SNOW FELL STEADILY all night, and David, waking just before dawn, heard one of the giant snowplows going through the town. With daylight a wind rose and the snow came slanting in faster, blowing in strange patterns of whorls and swoops and upward flights. By midmorning the drifts were already high, the sounds of the town were muffled, and daylight had become a dim, whitish luminescence in which no object was clearly visible.

At the start of afternoon office hours Moore opened David's door, and walked in. "This is a real one, all right. Bet there won't be many patients in. Have to leave the jeep in the road tonight because I won't dare tackle that steep drive of mine even with the snow blade. . . . An emergency call just came in. There's a woman in a house most of the way up Mount Starvation with a pain in her belly. Her husband just phoned from the general store at Highland Three Corners. Know where that is?"

"In a general way."

"I'll have to ask you to go. Too bad, in this weather. They've just brought a girl into the hospital who's beginning labor. Edna says she'll keep, but I wouldn't want to go so far from town. The man will wait for you at the store and go back up the mountain with you. Name's Earl Hurdock."

"It really is an emergency, I take it?"

"Probably. Sounds like it. She's been having pain for about twenty-four hours and now it's bad."

David scribbled the name on a piece of paper and put it in his pocket. "Why didn't the husband bring her in?"

"All he's got to drive is one of those old high tractors, and by the time he got around to thinking he better borrow a car she was in too much pain to move, or so he says. Says the snow's drifted pretty bad. I asked him, could a jeep with a snow blade get through? He says he thinks so—most of the way, anyway—so you better take mine. Key's in the ignition. Sorry to wish this off on you."

In the falling snow the town seemed dreamlike. There were a few people on the street, muffled figures, each seeming alone. David walked past his car before he remembered the snowshoes in the trunk, and, feeling foolish, he turned back to get them. He put them in the back of the jeep on top of Moore's, that were dark with age and broader and longer than his own. Moore's would have served in a pinch, he thought. The old boy had faith in the honesty of the town, leaving them there, and leaving the ignition key always in the lock.

The road followed the frozen river out of town, and David drove cautiously, the windshield wipers rhythmically sweeping away the snow. Closed in by the curtains of the jeep, he felt snug and warm in a pleasant isolation.

After a time the road turned into the dim tunnel of a covered bridge over the Little Torrent River. He made the turn carefully, for it seemed to him that here and there the road was icy under the shifting snow. On the other side of the bridge the country was open, with few trees, and the snow seemed to be coming down faster. It was coming straight at him, and though the laboring windshield wipers kept half-moons of glass fairly clear, his range of vision ahead was cut down to a few yards.

Moments later the snow was driving so hard he could barely see the sides of the road, and, afraid of going into the ditch, he slowed down still more. He sat forward, leaning over the wheel, trying to see. The distance to Highland Three Corners he had forgotten, if he ever knew. Five miles, perhaps, or ten, or even twenty. Five miles would take him beyond the range of his radio telephone, and the thought of that made him uneasy. In front of the jeep the snow moved in intricate circlings, then seemed to divide and stream past the jeep on either side. He turned on his headlights, found he was facing a mass of oncoming snow as impenetrable to his sight as a wall, and turned them off again. His eyes ached from the endlessly repeated patterns of the blowing snow, his back ached with tension, and he felt alone in an uninhabited world.

Once the dark bulk of a truck loomed suddenly ahead of him,

and swerving, he felt the jeep bumping over the uneven margin of the ditch. Once, coming to the blurred outline of a crossroad he did not remember, and that seemed to him like no place in the real world, he climbed out to reconnoiter. He found a signpost, the crossarms high above his head, wearing a cap and mantle of snow that covered the lettering. He went back to the jeep and took the right-hand road for no better reason than that ruts half filled with snow seemed to indicate the truck had come from that direction.

With the world contained in the few feet of visibility between himself and the curtain of snow, time and distance and his objective lost their meaning. And so he did not know how long he had been driving when he came to a group of buildings, more sensed than seen, and guessed that he had reached the village of Highland Three Corners. He pulled the jeep alongside the porch of the village store, and saw a great hulk of a man just rising from a chair where he had been sitting as though this were a summer day.

"Doc Armstrong?"

"Yes. You're Mr. Hurdock?"

"Yup." Hurdock came down the steps with the light quickness of a man accustomed to use every muscle in his big body. "It's quite a storm we got. Don't know's the jeep kin git all the way up." He wedged himself into the narrow seat and slammed the door. "See you got snowshoes in the back. Good thing if you ain't used to breastin' drifts like I be, only this snow ain't right for 'em. This here's the turn."

They passed a house or two, then crossed a narrow bridge with no side rails, and began to climb. And David, wondering why on earth anyone chose to live in such a place, thought, as he had many times, about the strange juxtaposition of the primitive and the almost urban life along the highways. They were deep in the woods, and the road, hidden under snow, could have been at best little better than a track. The storm seemed lighter here, for the dense boughs of the hemlocks caught and held much of the snow as it fell.

Hurdock seemed rather to enjoy himself. They had come to a clearing where there was ice under the snow, and the jeep lost traction. "Real slippery, seems like. The sun melts the snow, then she freezes. Ain't much farther if you think you can make it."

David had no time to reply. The jeep slewed toward the edge of a steep drop at the side of the road and he stopped it with little room to spare. When he tried to start again, the wheels spun on the ice and he could make no headway.

"Let her back a bit and come up again real slow."

"I'm not used to this kind of driving."

"Just take her slow and don't stop."

David took her slow, letting the jeep roll backward, watching the road nervously through the snow-clouded rear window. Then he tried it again. "Real slow now," Hurdock said, leaning forward as though to help the jeep with the balance of his weight.

They came to the same spot, slewed sidewise and stopped. David said, "Maybe you'd better drive."

"You're doing all right. I'll git out and wait and when you git here I'll push."

That time they advanced perhaps three or four feet. "I didn't git a real good hold," Hurdock said. "My feet slipped. Try her agin."

This time Hurdock's feet went out from under him and he fell close to the spinning wheels. David turned off the motor.

"This is too dangerous. Can't we walk from here?"

"I guess we got to. Ain't far. Better put your snowshoes on."

For a short distance the going was easy, the motion a relief to muscles cramped and tense from the difficult driving. Then they came out on a knoll where there were no trees, and the snow, driven by the full force of the storm, enveloped them. David guessed the knoll was high and that the wind was coming across a long sweep of open valley. He pulled the hood of his parka closer around his face, but where the wind-driven snow touched his skin it stung like needle pricks. Under him the snow felt powdery and unstable, and beside him Hurdock floundered knee-deep and more.

For the first time since starting up the mountain road David had time to remember that he was on his way to see a patient and that he must deal with an emergency of unknown proportions. Then he realized that Hurdock was speaking to him.

"She drifts pretty deep along here. But 'tain't much further, Doc."

Then they were on a cleared path with the bulk of a house in front of them. And a moment later he was freeing himself of snowshoes, and saying, "Why in hell do you live in a place like this?"

"'Tain't nothin' less there's a storm. Like to live sort of away from things, but, good weather, this ain't remote. Come right in, Doc."

A blast of heat struck them as Hurdock opened the door, and with it a smell that was like the smell in old Alice Henderson's house. A woman's voice, high and weak, called out from another room, "You got the doctor, Earl?" And all at once David was tired to the point of exhaustion, tired to such an extent that his surroundings were blurred and his legs were trembling. Hurdock was walking quickly toward the bedroom and David followed, fumbling with the fastenings of his parka.

A woman with matted hair and pale, beseeching eyes lay on a sagging bed under a patchwork quilt. When David came in she smiled feebly and worked her mouth as though she thought she was saying something. He began his examination, aware that both the man and woman were watching his face all the time. He deliberately eliminated all vestige of expression. They had the look, familiar to all doctors, of expectancy and trust. They waited, their minds blank, putting themselves wholly in his hands. He wanted to shout at them, "*I'm not God*. This woman is very sick and the chances are I can't help her, so stop looking at me as though I were God."

Aloud he said in a strained voice that he tried to make uninformative, "How long have you had this pain?"

Hurdock answered for her. "It's maybe two, maybe three days since she was took, Doc. She's had like this before and got over it good, but this time it's worse than others."

And suddenly David was so angry he felt himself trembling with it, his face flushed and burning.

"Then why in heaven's name did you wait till now to call a doctor?"

Hurdock, stricken silent, stared at David with puzzled, pleading eyes. He put his hand on his wife's shoulder and she turned her head weakly to look up at him.

"We ain't doctorin' folks, Doc. Anyway we thought it was just somethin' she et."

To the woman David said, "I'm going to give you something to ease the pain," and when he had finished he said, "Come out in the other room a minute, Hurdock." David started in that direction, bethought himself, and returned to the bed. "Don't worry," he said, "you're going to be all right," and he turned quickly away from the expression in her eyes.

The other room seemed to be kitchen and living room combined. David led Hurdock to the far end of it where the sick woman could not hear, and as they neared the stove the intensity of the heat was stifling.

"Your wife's got an acute appendicitis and she's a very sick woman. She has to be taken to a hospital right away."

Hurdock made a sound that was like a groan, and the two men stared at each other in silence, every shade of feeling of the one toward the other momentarily forgotten in the problem confronting them both. Briefly, they were close. Then Hurdock said, "Ain't there somethin' you can give her to take, Doc? To fix her up, I mean. She ain't never been to a hospital and I don't guess she'd like it so much."

"No, there isn't. She's got to have an operation, and no time to spare. We can't take her down in the jeep. Have you got a long sled, or anything like that?"

Hurdock thought a minute and shook his head. "No, I guess not, Doc."

"I've got a two-way radio on my jeep. Are we within five miles of Haddon?"

"Just about, as a crow flies. Lot more by road."

"Then it should work. I'll go back to the jeep and call in and see what they can do at that end. I'll be able to follow our tracks all right. You stay here with her."

Going down, he faced the storm with more assurance, and when he crossed the open, windswept stretch he felt for the first time in his life a sense of mastery over the elements. The shelter of the trees, when he reached them, seemed friendly, the inside of the jeep a warm and desirable place. As he picked up the speaker of the radio, he listened to the vast silence of the hemlock woods. Then, miraculously, there was May speaking, and the emotion her clear, fresh voice stirred up in him made it necessary for him to steady his own.

"May."

"Oh, *David*."

"We're in a spot here. I've got to get Mrs. Hurdock to a hospital quick, and I'm stuck in the jeep partway up the road. An ambulance can't possibly get up here. Any idea what I can do?"

Silence.

"May?"

"Wait, I'm trying to think. . . . Listen, David, I'll send the ambulance to the Highland Three Corners general store. I heard the snowplow going through just now. . . . Highland has a volunteer fire department. I'll phone the store to call them out and send them up to get her with a sled, or a toboggan, if there is one. All right?"

"My God, yes. Sure it's all right, if it works. Tell them to hurry. Call Perkins and Moore. Tell them acute appendicitis and to stand by ready. Tell Edna to get the operating room ready. I'll follow the ambulance in. Thanks, May."

He sat in the jeep, tired out, but comforted. In a few minutes he heard in the valley down below him, muffled by distance and snow, the wail of the fire siren rise and fall. He sat in the jeep for a moment more, growing more aware of the silence of the woods and the cold penetrating his parka. Then he climbed out and fastened on his snowshoes. He struggled back to the house, conscious chiefly of the tingling of his legs. Once more in the kitchen, his mind stored away the trivial facts that Hurdock's head came close to the low ceiling and that the buttons of his plaid shirt strained across his big chest. Then he was sitting on a hard chair by Mrs. Hurdock's bed, inwardly fretting because of the delay, but touched that his presence so obviously reassured her.

After what seemed to him a long time there was a sudden commotion outside the house, voices and the sound of stamping boots on the kitchen porch. There were five men, big, husky young lads who said "Hi, Doc," one after another and who seemed to have things so well in hand that, gratefully, he let them take over.

They joked with Mrs. Hurdock and handled her with great tenderness while she smiled tremulously and blinked away weak tears. They laid her, bundled in blankets, on the toboggan. None of them wore snowshoes, and they pushed their way through drifts that to David would have been impossible. The procession, with David and Hurdock in the rear, arrived in very little time at the stranded jeep, and these astonishing young men paused long enough to push it around, sliding it on the ice that underlay the snow so that it faced downhill.

While this was being done, David went ahead to look at his patient, and from her nest of blankets she looked up at him with more gratitude than he had ever seen on any face before. She took her hand from under the blankets and he held it a moment, patted it, and tucked it back under the blankets again.

The drive down the mountain David found almost easy. He went ahead of Hurdock and the men with the toboggan, keeping to the ruts the jeep had made on the way up. He felt none of the tenseness and fear he had then, and he knew that in a like situation he never would again. He pulled up on the main road by the village store in what seemed to him a surprisingly short time. The ambulance, with a longer distance to go, had not yet arrived.

A woman with a coat thrown over her shoulders came out on the porch of the store and called to him. "Doc, come in and have a cup of coffee before you drive back."

He said, "Thanks, I will," and climbed out, feeling the driving snow pelting his face.

The atmosphere in the store was steamy and rich. A group of men in mackinaws and boots fell silent when he came in, but they all nodded to him. The woman set a cup of coffee on the lunch counter, and he threw back his parka hood and sat on a stool to drink it. All the men silently watched him.

They were not unfriendly, though he was only beginning to know these people well enough to understand that. After a few minutes one of them said with tentative boldness, "She took bad, Doc?"

He turned around on his stool with his cup in his hand to answer.

"We'll know more about it when we get her to the hospital."

After a pause another man said, "You takin' her to Doc Moore's hospital, or over to Warwick?"

"Dr. Moore's. It's closer, and there's no time to lose." He thought a minute, then looked from one to another of the interested, weatherbeaten faces. "Look here, will any of you people be going to Town Meeting at Haddon?"

"We ain't even in the same township."

309

He put his coffee cup down. Outside, he heard the whirr and swish of a snowplow and one of the men said, "There she goes." David took a sudden resolution.

"I want to tell you something I think you ought to know. I'm sorry you don't have a voice in the Haddon Town Meeting, because Dr. Moore is going to ask the meeting whether the town of Haddon does or doesn't want a hospital. Maybe you've heard about that?"

Several of the men nodded, and one of them said, "Seems like Warwick's kind of far away—for us here at the Three Corners, for example."

"That's the point exactly. I may as well tell you Mrs. Hurdock is in very serious condition. We're going to operate the minute we get her there. Everything will be ready and there'll be no delay at all. Even so, I'm not sure . . . But what I'm saying is, if we had to take her all the way to Warwick in this storm—it must be well over thirty miles . . ."

One of the men said, "Thirty-seven. Haddon's seven, near enough."

David took a deep breath. "I'm going to say something perhaps I shouldn't. I hope we can save Mrs. Hurdock at Haddon. If she had to go all the way to Warwick, I doubt very much if she could survive."

He said this with the utmost seriousness. Once he had said it, his thoughts turned inward, for he had just discovered that within the last hour and without having given it a single conscious thought, he had become a strong believer in the need for a hospital in Haddon.

There was silence; then someone said, "Listen!" and stood up. They all heard the wail of the ambulance siren coming toward them. They were all on their feet and going toward the door. Someone said, "There's Hurdock and the boys, too." David paused long enough to pull change out of his pocket to pay for the coffee. The woman refused to take it, and one of the men, going out the door, said over his shoulder, "Better accept it, Doc. That cup of coffee's like to be the only pay you'll ever git from this job." They all laughed.

Outside there was the ambulance and a state police car. The two troopers and the ambulance driver had already begun to transfer Mrs. Hurdock to a stretcher. As she was being lifted into the ambulance, she smiled weakly. "Good-bye, Doc."

He was enormously pleased. "I'll be seeing you at the hospital in a few minutes. You're going to be all right." He very much doubted that this was true.

The police car, with a growl of its siren, swung out into the road. David found himself surrounded by the husky young rescuers, shaking hands. They each in turn slapped the snow off their thick gloves and gave him grips that made him inwardly wince. He caught a glimpse of Hurdock sitting inside the ambulance, hunched up, his red mackinaw looking odd in the surroundings of white and chrome. He hurried to the jeep and started the motor. The ambulance moved into the highway after the police car and picked up speed in the track made by the snowplow. David waved his hand behind the curtain of the jeep to the group of men watching from the porch of the store, and followed.

XXVI

D<small>AVID—ASKING</small> <small>HIMSELF</small>, How does a hospital die?—decided the process was not greatly different from the onset of death in an aging human body. One part and then another begins to show wear, to threaten loss of function. The mechanism, without actually breaking down, ceases to coordinate efficiently. The end is foreshadowed.

Something resembling this process of disintegration, it seemed to him, was taking place in the little Haddon hospital. This or the other part of the mechanical equipment was continually needing to be tinkered with, and the repair was never wholly satisfactory. The ancient octopus of a furnace made the place either too hot or too cold. The turn of a faucet produced water that was red with rust, and the X-ray machine when called on too often failed to respond.

These things, though troublesome, were bearable; but the symptom that seemed to David far more significant was the weariness that recently had become apparent in the little staff. He imagined he detected this not only in Moore, which did not surprise him, but in such lesser things as the quality of the meals and even in the way Helen handled instruments in the operating room.

Edna, without having lowered her high standards in the smallest particular, had an air of grimly holding out until Town Meeting should have decided all their fates. That she was under considerable strain David guessed, for she had become more gaunt and rigid than ever. Since the out-of-season visit of the hospital examiners she had acquired the look of perpetually expecting disaster; it showed in the turn of her head and in the nervous start with which she reacted to any unexpected sound. Seeing her rise from her desk when any stranger opened the front door was enough to create in David's mind a picture of Edith Cavell rising to meet her executioners.

In a worn-out, dying human body David had sometimes seen an astonishingly tenacious hold on life. With similar tenacity Haddon Hospital reacted to the emergency of Mrs. Hurdock. David was amazed and impressed by the tight efficiency with which everyone concerned went into action, and he thought he had not, up to then, realized what a fine mechanism Moore had created.

Mrs. Hurdock, with drainage tubes sprouting from her body, lay now in the tower room at a cost that would come largely from Moore's own pocket. She was more dead than alive, but she was receiving the best nursing care that David was glad to admit he had ever seen, and there was a thin, bright strand of hope for her recovery.

David was thinking these things as he walked along the snowy street. The wind that blew on him was mild, and as he walked on, he undid two buttons of his parka and took deep, therapeutic breaths of freshness. All along the street icicles that were melting rapidly hung from the edges of the roofs. The falling drops made soft emphatic sounds that he liked, and he liked the feel of the slush under his boots. A man in a plaid jacket, carrying bunches of sap buckets in both hands, gave him a cheerful "Hi, Doc." Passing the hardware store, he saw that the display of skis that had been in the window all winter long had been replaced by an arrangement of paints and brushes, more in keeping with the season's change.

When he reached the corner, he saw across the street, where the green begins, the broad back of a woman whom he recognized as Ianthe Norton. She made a bulky figure in her thick gray coat and brown wool scarf tied over her hair. She was standing in front of a large cardboard thermometer with a red "mercury" on it and the words HADDON HEALTH CENTER lettered at the top. She seemed to be raising the level of the mercury to touch the eight-thousand mark, which, all things considered, struck him as astonishing. He knew the old house which would be converted to a health center had already been bought, or at least acquired on a mortgage almost equal to the purchase price, which showed, if nothing else, an optimistic attitude toward the future. This optimism, he thought, walking on, seemed hardly warranted, for what doctors would there be to practice in it? Not Ladd, who refused to leave the office he had built on the side of his house so long ago. And if the hospital went under, as seemed so likely, not Perkins either, or himself. Moore alone, perhaps, or perhaps Ted Barlow could be snared. . . .

David found May sitting up very straight against her pillows, the accounts she was keeping for the health center spread out around her. When she saw him, she gave him her radiant smile. "Oh, David," she said, smiling, "I'm so glad you've come," and began at once to gather up her papers. He watched her from across the room as he took off his parka and boots. He strode across the room and said gruffly, "Give me those damn papers!"

Grumbling at her, he collected them, disposed of them on a nearby chair, came back and sat on the couch beside her.

She drew away a little. "David, what's the matter?"

"I want to talk to you. All this has been going on long enough."

"What has? What are you talking about? You look so angry."

"Angry!" He reached for her hand and held it in both of his.

Her eyes, wide and serious, were on his face. Abruptly, she tried to take her hand away. She shook her head vigorously from side to side. "No, David, no."

"You don't know what I'm going to say. May, I'm not talking as a doctor. I think we've come to mean a lot to each other. Isn't that true?"

"Yes."

"Then, May, my darling . . . Do I have to say it straight out? I love you. I want to marry you."

"Don't think I haven't thought about us. . . . David, you mustn't feel this way about me."

"But *why?*"

"I don't want to talk about it. Please, David."

"But it doesn't make any sense. We love each other. All you have to do is one simple little thing. Let us get that leg fixed up, so you can lead a normal life. Is that so much to do to make us both happy?"

"David, don't. Please don't ask me. I'm so afraid of an operation. I couldn't—I just couldn't go through with it."

"But there's nothing to be afraid of. It's not an unusual opera-

314

tion any more. It's not even difficult for a man trained in vascular surgery . . . May, darling . . ."

He put his arms around her and held her close to him. She buried her face in his shoulder and he could feel the tenseness of her body.

"Darling, think about it. What kind of a married life could we have if you were an invalid? It wouldn't work, May. You haven't any choice in the matter. If you want to marry me, it's something you must do."

"Don't ask me, David. Please, please don't. I'm so afraid. I love you terribly, but I couldn't do it. I couldn't . . ."

Clinging to him, she burst into a storm of weeping. He let her cry, his arms around her. After a while the tears changed to anguished, exhausted sobs, and he stroked her hair gently. "May, May . . ."

"You're not going to make me, are you, David?"

He held her away from him. She lowered her tear-stained face and shut her eyes. She was not trembling now, but she felt weak and frail under his hands.

"You have to choose, May. I don't want an invalid wife. I love you very much, but I know that would spoil both our lives. You have to choose. Do you want to lie here on this couch all your life, or do you want to lead a normal, happy life with me? Remember, I'm not going to stay here in Haddon. When I go, that would be the end. Is that what you really want?"

She shook her head.

"Well, then . . ."

"Can't we talk about it later, David?"

"No. I want the answer now."

For a long time she said nothing. Her head was still bowed, her eyes shut. Then he felt a shudder run through her body, and she whispered something he could not hear.

"What, darling?"

She leaned toward him and he held her close to him again.

"I said—would you do it—would you do the operation yourself?"

"I wouldn't want to, May. I've been thinking we might take you to New York and have Fairchild do it. He's about the best there is."

"No, no. It would have to be you."

"It isn't customary for a surgeon to operate on someone close to him."

She sat up and pushed her hair back from her forehead. "It has to be you, or I won't do it. It has to be you, and Uncle Ed to be the anesthetist. And our hospital here."

"Dr. Moore wouldn't want to, and this hospital doesn't have the instruments—"

"I don't care. I won't do it any other way."

"I'll talk to Dr. Moore and see what he says. I doubt if he would want to do it. It would put too much strain on both of us."

"I can't help it. I won't do it any other way, I tell you. And another thing, David. Don't rush me. I've got to have a little time. I want to tell you myself when I'm ready."

He made no reply, and she put her hand in his. "You'll do that for me, won't you, David?"

After a moment he nodded. Then he put his arms around her and kissed her.

When David came down the stairs from May's apartment, he paused at the bottom to look at his watch. Dinner would have to be a sandwich and a cup of coffee in the office if he could find time even for that. He looked up to see Ianthe standing before him, and, without reason, he blushed. Equally without reason, it seemed to him, she laughed. It was a comfortable, understanding laugh, and it came to him suddenly that in a place where each knew so much about the others, his frequent visits to May could not have gone unnoticed. The thought startled him and as a result he failed to take in what she was saying.

"What was that? I beg your pardon."

"I said, are you coming to the auction tonight?"

"Auction?"

"You doctors! Ed didn't know about it either, but notices have been in most of the store windows for a week. An auction at the Town Hall of things that people have donated, to raise money for the Health Center. You and Ed could come together after office hours."

A few minutes later the two doctors met in the surgery between

316

their offices. Moore said, "We'll have to go, that's for sure. Be thankful it's not a grange supper."

"Why?"

"Scalloped potatoes in old-time milk pans. Too big to get more than warmed through—finest medium for germ culture there is. The ladies just won't learn. Last time I was up most of the night, and so was Ladd, treating half the town. Well, let's get to work. Looks like it might be light tonight . . ."

The Town Hall was a venerable building that had seen much of Vermont history. When the two doctors arrived, the place was nearly full, the air damp and steamy. The auctioneer, who was in full swing, with an ironstone pitcher in his hand, saw them, stopped and said, "Folks, we got doctors in the house. Doc Moore and Doc Armstrong just come in. You better bid spry now, you two. Whole town's got an eye on you." A ripple of pleasure went over the audience and there was a spattering of applause.

They found seats at the back. The auctioneer went on with his selling of the pitcher. David, turning to speak to Moore, was surprised to see that he had a look of glum depression and a worried frown creased his forehead. Then David remembered that in this same hall, not long from now, Town Meeting would be held, and it was that, it seemed to him, about which Moore was thinking. Then Moore raised his head and looked slowly all around the hall until he discovered Ianthe sitting near the front, and the sight of her, David thought, seemed to comfort him.

As the auction went on, some of Moore's amazing and rather touching capacity for enjoyment returned to him. Some bed sheets were put up for sale and Moore began to bid on them. He sat up straight, his hands on his knees, his blue eyes bright with interest, and made his bids in a loud voice, as though he wanted people to share the fun he was having. In a short time the sheets were his. Howie, in the capacity of auctioneer's helper, brought the stack of sheets to where they were sitting. Howie seemed to have lost a little of his shyness and David, wondering if that was Ianthe's doing, heard Moore say, "Got these sheets for Edna. She tells me the hospital supply is running low."

After a little David remembered that he too would be expected to buy something, and he gave his attention to the items going up

317

for sale. One of them was a knitted afghan in a rich dark red, and David shortly found himself its owner.

Then the auction ended and they were out in the street, walking by the long side of the green. The mild wind, heavy with dampness, was blowing, and the snow as they trod on it seemed to be largely water. Moore said, "Looks like a real thaw, all right. If it keeps up all night I better think about getting me up and have a look at the reservoir tomorrow."

"Why the reservoir?"

"When you get a fast thaw like this with the ground still frozen hard, water runs over the top and drains right into the reservoir from God knows where. Last year, this time, we had a lot of cases in town—not typhoid, but some of the look of it. I always thought the water might be to blame. This year I aim to find out, before the trouble starts, just whose barnyard and privy the surface water may be running by."

"Isn't that a job for the town health officer?"

"Yes, but he's a layman with no training for his job, the way it still is in a lot of Vermont towns. Shouldn't be, I guess. When we get this hospital question settled, maybe you and I better see about getting that reformed." Moore, with his arms full of sheets, moved a shoulder to indicate the afghan over David's arm. "What did you buy that thing for?"

"I thought May might like it."

"That red color with her dark hair—pretty. I haven't seen her lately. Been sort of leaving her to you. How is she?"

"She's consented to the operation."

In his astonishment Moore stopped walking, and the two hooded men with their odd burdens faced each other.

"Look here, you haven't been bringing pressure on her, have you? I don't want that."

"I've never understood why."

"Good God. I've tried to tell you. She's a strong-willed girl. She can force herself to do things that are hard for her. She drove herself right to the edge of a breakdown while she was in training. She's not over it yet, by any means, and you want to add to that the strain of an operation she's desperately afraid of. I won't be responsible for what happens if—"

"*I'll* be responsible."

"*You* will? Let me remind you she's my patient. I asked you for a consultation—nothing else. I didn't tell you to take her over as a patient, but that's what you've done—"

"Dr. Moore—"

"Taking over. That's what you've been doing with everything. Oh, I know you've been perfectly ethical. The perfect image of the doctor and the gentleman. But if my life work gets thrown on the scrap heap—if the town goes in for a lot of new medical experiments that nobody knows will work or not, it will be your influence doing it. . . . And now May. She's my own flesh and blood—all of it that's left to me. She's like my daughter. I love her. She's mine. . . . And now you tell me *you've* decided she's to have an operation —you, an outsider. It's too much. It's absolutely too much."

"Dr. Moore, I didn't want to tell you like this, but May and I are going to be married. That's why she's decided to have the operation."

There was silence. Moore held the pile of sheets against his chest as though to make a shield between himself and David. Twice his lips moved tremblingly, as though he were going to speak, and finally David said, "I'm sorry, sir. I know it's a blow to you."

"All right. All right. . . . Maybe I should have seen it coming."

"No time's been set for the operation. I'd rather see her have it soon, while she's keyed herself up to it, than have her have to wait. But there's something else you'd better know about. She's made it a condition of consenting to it that I operate and you give the anesthetic, and—it follows—here in this hospital."

A sound like a groan came from Dr. Moore.

"I agreed to it. What else could I do? We can borrow the instruments. And she would feel much easier, much safer if you gave her the anesthetic. If you are worried about her being afraid, that's a way you could help her and lessen her fear."

Dr. Moore breathed heavily, like a man who has forgotten how to sigh, and gave a hitch to his bundle of sheets.

"I don't want to talk about it any more now. It's a blow to me —yes. I don't want to talk about it. I guess I'd better say good night."

David watched him walk away. He moved slowly, his big shoulders stooping under the heavy burden he was carrying.

319

XXVII

ED MOORE SAID, "It's a remarkable thing you're doing, Ianthe. I can't say I like giving up the office where I've worked all these years, but it's a remarkable thing. And not the least of it is getting Tim Stoner to cooperate. I wish I knew how you did it."

Ianthe laughed, and he thought, it's like her old laugh, comfortable and pleasant; she hasn't laughed like that since Nat . . .

"I told Tim to put his glasses back on and listen to me. He saw town leadership getting away from him into the hands of a committee of women, and he humped himself to get out in front again. We couldn't have bought this place so soon without the bank loan."

They were standing on the walk that led to the front door of a fine old house, built in the early years of the nineteenth century when New Englanders had money to spend. The house, once pink brick, had been painted the color of Jersey cream, and this had mellowed through the years, fading almost white where its walls were exposed to the sun, retaining some of its original tint in the shadow cast by a giant elm. Boston ivy, now leafless, clung to the walls, forming an intricate branching tracery, like a giant nervous system. From inside the house came sounds of carpenters pounding, the blows of hammers synchronizing, breaking rhythm, synchronizing again.

"Still," Moore said, "it's remarkable that Tim lent the money to buy this place before the drive for funds was really started. That's not like him."

"He had a reason, and if I guess it right, it's typical of him. I'm sure he figures that if a health center is actually in progress and equipped as a clinic and a first-aid station, the town people won't see so much need for your hospital."

"All he wants is the added business for the bank that new plants at Silver Springs would bring. His attitude toward the hospital question is entirely formed by that."

"Ed, what do you think will happen at Town Meeting?"

"The people will be asked for an expression of opinion as to whether they want my hospital to keep open or to close. The moderator will put the question. I've talked to him and told him to keep it simple. He's been listening to that fellow Whitall, from the Public Health Service, and he thought an alternative should be proposed—a new hospital built partly by funds subscribed by the town and partly by a Federal grant. I told him the town wouldn't want that and couldn't possibly raise the money, and not to bring it up."

"And he won't?"

"I'm sure not."

"Then what?"

"There'll probably be a little discussion. Tim will have to have his say. Then those for and those against will stand, just as though it were a vote. It should all be over in a few minutes."

"They'll want your hospital to go on. If it's that or nothing—"

"I'm not so sure of it as I was."

"They will. But then won't there be the problem of money?"

"No, not after a vote of confidence from the town. Tim would have to lend me money. And Greer would come through—it's all he's waiting for, I'm sure. Let's go on in and see this place and get it over."

Just beyond the door Moore stopped as though the crossing of the threshold represented a new phase of his life that he was reluctant to begin. Aware of this, she waited for him, and he smiled at her ruefully.

"I suppose one of the signs of age is not liking change—in any form. The woman who comes in and cleans for me has started keeping the kitchen spoons in a new place. It's handier, but I hate it. I hate this." He gestured at the torn-apart interior of the old house. "The funny thing is, I hate them both with about the same amount of emotion. Another sign of age, I suppose. I don't want to start practicing group medicine even in this modified form. Young David's a fancy, modern surgeon, so specialized he doesn't know how to take out a pair of tonsils, though he's learned a lot from Howard. Restive because I'm not practicing medicine according to new standards I don't know anything about. I'm not able to, damn it. I wish the meeting were behind us, Ianthe. Show me what you've cooked up for me here in the way of an office. I'll tell you right now I won't like it, but let's see it."

A cubbyhole. The best of the four, but a cubbyhole. The longest wall was not long enough, he saw, for the old rolltop desk that had been his father's. He supposed he'd wind up with one of those flat things made out of linoleum and plumbing, with a bottom drawer too high to pull out and put his feet on. He looked at Ianthe, not knowing if she understood these things. "All right," he said. "All right. What next?"

"This big room is the reception room."

"I'll always see it as it used to be when I made house calls here."

"There'll be a desk in the hall for a receptionist or the nurse."

"I wish to God May could be behind that desk instead of getting married. I don't like any part of this business, though I'm getting used to the idea of her being in love with him. I suppose I should have seen it coming. You didn't seem surprised. I guess I didn't want to see. This operation troubles me too because I don't think she's ready for it. What's to be down these stairs? X-ray and so on, isn't it? It all looks so different than it did on the plans when Howard and I worked on them."

He followed her down the stairs and stood looking gloomily around while the hammers pounding overhead seemed to be striking inside his head.

"I've seen enough, Ianthe. You've done a wonderful job, but I've seen enough."

Whenever David was able, he brought a lunch of sandwiches and coffee from the dairy bar to May's apartment and they ate together. They both looked forward to this hour, and he came to rely on her light gaiety. But one day he found her sad and thoughtful.

"I've just been thinking how times flies, David, and now the Town Meeting isn't far away. I'm so worried about what will happen to Uncle Ed and the hospital. I feel as though everything is going to go to pieces. Can't you persuade him not to put the fate of the hospital up to the town?"

"I've tried. He's been so sure the town will want him to keep his hospital going for them, and that then he'll be able to get the money he needs. Lately, I've had a feeling he's not so certain, but we haven't talked about it since this coolness between us. He probably feels he's given his word and won't go back on it. Even if he weathers this crisis, he can't go on forever. He's sixty-five, isn't he? I've been thinking that perhaps this is the point at which he should retire."

"Oh *no!*"

"He's been too busy to keep up with modern medicine as well as he should. He feels at a disadvantage, I think."

"David, if this that's happening is the revolution in rural medicine that you and Ted and Mr. Whitall talk about . . ."

"It's only the beginning, May. All that's happened so far has come from *inside* the town. There are pressures building up that will dwarf anything a town like this could do for itself."

"I don't know that I like what's happening. We'll get better medicine, I suppose, but I'm not sure we're going to be happy about it. People in big cities aren't satisfied with the kind of medical care they get. Up to now, people in the country have been satisfied. I'm afraid that's going to change too." She patted the couch and he sat down beside her. "Your year in Haddon is nearly half gone, David. Have you thought about what you're going to do?"

"Only vaguely. I want to get back to vascular surgery; that's the only thing I feel sure about. But whatever I do, it must be in a place where you'll be happy."

"I'll be happy where you are, darling. But the idea of living in a strange place frightens me a little. In the new setup, wouldn't there be a place for a vascular surgeon?"

"Perhaps. It's hard to say at this point."

"Couldn't we just stay here?"

"I don't think that would be wise. But let's not talk about it now. There's something else we ought to discuss. The situation about the hospital is not clear. Dr. Moore is financed with bank loans until September, but if things go against him at Town Meeting, I should think he'd probably close up as soon as he could. If you still insist you won't have your operation in any other hospital, I think we should make plans."

323

"Oh, David—please . . ."

"It's that or another hospital, May. The first thing to do is to take you to Warwick for an arteriogram."

"I don't want to go back there ever, ever."

"May . . ."

There was a moment's silence; then she said in a small voice, "All right, David, if you'll stay with me."

"I will. I won't leave you a minute. Then I'll have to see about borrowing some special instruments. Warwick won't have what I want."

"I'm so frightened whenever I think of the operation."

"You must really try not to be. But I do wish you'd let me take you to New York and let Fairchild do the job."

"No, David. You promised."

"I know I did. All right—we'll get going with our plans. What's the matter, dear?"

"Oh, David, hold me tight. I'm so frightened. Promise me it will be all right and that you won't let anything happen to me. I love you so. I can't help being a baby, but I want to do what you want me to."

When David went back to his office he thought for a moment about what instruments he would need that the hospital did not have and where he might get them. Reluctantly, he put in a call for Adam Fairchild. Word came back that Dr. Fairchild was not available, but his nurse would be glad to take a message.

Dr. Fairchild's nurse was a friendly person whom he had known through all the years of his residency. She thought she could get the hospital to lend the instruments without troubling Dr. Fairchild. "In fact," she said, "I don't think I even need to mention this to him. If you will just tell me exactly what you want, Doctor . . ."

He told her and thanked her with the warmth of his relief.

A week later, on a February afternoon, when David had finished seeing a patient who had been in surgery that morning, Edna said to him, "Your instruments have come, Doctor. Helen is in the wing unpacking them. Did you see the editorial about the operation in the *Torrent Valley News*?"

"Good Lord, no. Why on earth did they think they had to write it up? I wish they hadn't."

"Oh, but we're all so proud of it. I never thought I'd see the day when this sort of surgery would be done in Haddon."

"It's pretty commonplace in cities."

"But not in small country towns. It's fine for us all to feel that country medicine is catching up. Then, since the answering service, everybody in town, almost, knows May. She always sounds so bright and cheerful when she takes a call. Everybody loves her."

David went down the corridor to the wing, where he found Helen in the big back room where, months before, he had met Ianthe among piles of vegetables. Helen, still wearing a cap and the smock she had worn under her gown in the operating room, was standing behind a table taking the instruments out of their cotton wrappings and laying them on a towel-covered tray. To David's surprise, Dr. Perkins was there, standing at the opposite side of the table, watching with interest. These days David never saw him without a tightening of the nerves, a hasty assembling of inner defenses, for Perkins's disposition was, to say the least, uncertain. Now one glance told him that Perkins was affable and blown up, as it were, to the full size of his personality. He had not been in a mood like this for a long time. Perkins waved a hand at the glittering objects on the tray.

"Pretty gadgets you've got here, Doc."

"I wouldn't want to undertake this job without some of these things here."

Perkins picked up an artery clamp, strong but delicate as a jeweler's tool. He opened and closed it several times and laid it back on the tray. "Makes ours seem clumsy."

Helen, who had been examining a reel of vascular silk, put it down and began to gather up wrappings. Perkins, hands in pockets, eyes smiling, rocked back on his heels and gave David a direct look that was both attention-compelling and amused, as though he knew a joke at David's expense.

"You'll need to modernize the OR equipment generally, Doctor, if the hospital survives. Perhaps it would help if we got together and made up a list of what you'll want, if you and May decide to stay on here."

Helen stopped gathering up wrappings and stared at him, and Perkins, hands in pockets, rocked back on his heels and grinned at her. He transferred the grin, which was bold and self-satisfied, to David, and left without another word. They both watched him until the door closed behind him. Then Helen said, "Does that mean he's got the Warwick job after all?"

"How did you know about the Warwick job? I thought it was supposed to be a secret."

"Nothing's ever a secret in a small hospital or a small town, Doctor."

"Shush, he's coming back."

The door opened and Perkins came up to the table. "I forgot to ask you, Dave. Who're you going to have assist?"

"I don't know. It's been bothering me. Someone from Warwick, I suppose, though I don't much like the idea of working with a stranger."

"Would I do?"

Startled, David stared at him. Perkins laughed, but it was not quite the heavy, coarse laugh with which David was familiar. David, feeling the hated flush creeping over his face, said hastily, "Of course. Sure. I didn't feel I could ask you, but I'd be honored."

For a moment the two men looked at each other with an almost total absence of expression, as if each were busy in his thoughts with a reappraisal of the other. Perkins was the first to be finished with this.

"I don't know a God-damned thing about vascular surgery. There almost wasn't such a thing when I trained. I'll find it interesting."

Helen was nervously laying the new instruments straight on the tray, doing this as meticulously as though she were preparing for the operation itself. Between the two doctors there was an easiness that had never before been in their relationship. Perkins said, "There're some questions I'd like to ask. Let's go see if those nurses have left us any coffee." Helen watched them go off together; then she put the back of her hand to her forehead as though this unusual atmosphere of amity had made her slightly giddy.

When David and Perkins were seated in the nurses' dining room with coffee and a handful of filched cookies that Perkins tossed on the table, David said, "There's nothing very complicated about this procedure, or there shouldn't be. Vascular surgery isn't diffi-

326

cult, it's just different. You won't have any trouble assisting—and it's very decent of you. I'll show you the arteriograms and exactly what I'm going to do. The thrombus is fibroid by this time, of course, and I'll cut it out and patch the artery. The only thing is, as of course you know, that you have to take care not to damage the intima of the artery in such a way that it would cause another clot to form in the future."

"What kind of anesthetic?"

"She's nervous, and I don't want to put any undue strain on her, so I want to use a general. I've talked it over with Dr. Moore and he agrees—feels even more strongly about it than I do."

"Ed's good at it. He has a special feel for the patient that a lot of better-trained anesthetists never get. A good many times I've seen him anticipate a reaction and be ready to handle it before any real indication shows up. It's a talent that wouldn't count for so much in one of the modern, highly scientific procedures that use respiratory cyclers and oscilloscopes. But where you have to sense a patient's condition with nothing much but blood pressure and observable signs to guide you, he's tops."

"I think he told me once he's had almost no training, but I agree with you, he's good."

Perkins laughed. "He's had so little formal training that you can almost say he's taught himself. Read it up, mostly. Then, a few years ago, he took a short course that Warwick put on to help out poor hick doctors like us." Perkins helped himself to the last cookie, and said with his mouth full, "He doesn't know anything but ether, nitrous oxide, spinals, and a little supportive use of pentothal, which he's damn careful about. Can't use cyclopropane in a building that's no more fireproof than this. Well, what say we get back to our jobs?"

They rose and, obedient to the discipline imposed by Edna Judson, they carried their empty coffee cups to the sink.

The night before Town Meeting there were few patients in the office, fewer than Moore could ever remember. Those that came seemed to him to be constrained, almost embarrassed, and no one made any reference to the next day's meeting. They behaved, he thought morosely, as though the old medical regime were already dead. When the last one had gone, Moore also left, quickly, without stopping as he customarily did for a few words with David. He went at once to Ianthe's house, and she, sitting by the fire in the study, knew by the sound of his voice when he called to her from the kitchen that he was in need of her. Rising, she summoned up her forces.

She had never seen him in such a mood as now. He was restless, close to irritability, showing strain, the humor and kindliness gone from his face. The change in him since morning shocked her. He went to the fireplace as though he needed to warm himself, jerked to a stop and said crossly, "Your fire's nearly out. And you're out of wood." He seized the handle of the wood basket and went with it to the shed. A moment later she heard him, through the doors he left open, angrily throwing down logs from the top of the pile. She waited, tense herself, and frowning because she did not know how to help him.

When the fire was mended, he drew a chair close to it and sat on the edge of it, leaning forward, elbows on knees, hands tightly clasped in front of him. She could not see his face, but she saw how the blue veins stood out on the backs of his hands and how rapidly he was drawing his breaths. Since he first came into the room he had not once looked directly at her.

They sat for a few minutes in a tight, uncomfortable silence; then she said, almost timidly, "Ed, won't you let me fix you a drink? I think you need one."

"Need one! Well, all right."

He made no move to help her, and when she came back from the kitchen she found that he had left his chair and was pacing up and down in front of the bookcases, still with the unfamiliar look of strain and anger. She put the drink on the table by his chair, knowing that he would ignore it for a while. When a few minutes had passed she ventured to say, "Ed, won't you come and sit down?"

He stopped his pacing by the desk, picked up an ornate paper knife, examined it as though he had never seen it before, and put it down hard. He turned to face her, but he still avoided looking at her directly, fixing his gaze on a corner of the fender.

"The town's already made up its mind. It doesn't want a hospital."

"Ed, we can't possibly know how people feel until Town Meeting tomorrow. I think you're wrong. You were so sure, a little while ago, that everything would be all right, that the town would support you."

"I've changed my mind."

"But why?"

"Tim Stoner's been at work, I'm sure of it. Telling people the real choice is between my hospital and a hospital at Silver Springs to attract more plants with workers spending money in Haddon. Money's his argument. And why should people want me and my hospital when the town could be richer without it? I was a fool ever to think they would."

"Ed, it's not like that. You're worried and you've distorted things. Won't you come and sit down?"

He looked at her then and she saw the suffering in his eyes.

"Ianthe, I'm going to retire."

"Oh, Ed, no."

"I've made up my mind. I'm not going to let them stage this farce at Meeting tomorrow. Soon as the meeting starts I'm going to get up and tell them I'm through. I'm going to retire. Let them do what they like. I'm going to tell them that."

"Ed, please. Let's talk about this calmly."

"I'm calm. I've never been calmer in my life, but I tell you I'm through. They can get on without me. And Howard will go to Warwick. They don't want him either. At the end of his year, or before, David will leave. Then the damn town will be without any licensed doctors but Ladd and they can see how they like that."

She rose and went to him and, taking him by the arm, led him back to his chair. He dropped into it and covered his face with his hands. She drew her own chair closer and sat down to wait. In a moment he dropped his hands, letting them hang dejectedly between his knees. The fire threw leaping, grotesque lights and shadows on his face, and she saw that the anger had gone, leaving him with a look of bewilderment and uncertainty and very great fatigue.

"I can't stand this happening to you," she said.

She knew her words did not reach him, for he said, "When you come down to it, Ianthe, he's the one to blame."

"Tim Stoner?"

"No, Armstrong. That was at the beginning of it all. He's given

329

the town a taste of something it's not used to. Everything was all right before he came."

She thought carefully how to reply to this, and it seemed to her that if it relieved Moore's feelings to make a scapegoat out of Dr. Armstrong, no real harm was done. She said gently, "You've forgotten your drink, Ed."

He drank a little and put the glass down, but not hard, and she was glad of this sign that some of the tension had left him. He gazed into the fire, silent, and she studied him, her forehead creased with worry, her eyes dark as pond water at night. Years of as selfless a life as a man can achieve . . . An old man now, or close to it, talking in bitterness about retirement, but without the money to make retirement possible. A few thousand, perhaps, from the sale of the hospital building and the vacant property beside it—both mortgaged, no doubt. His own house probably mortgaged too. Nothing more, and nothing to occupy a mind deprived of life's one dedication.

The ringing of the telephone in the hall startled them both. He got up at once, and she saw that it had recalled him to the habit of competence and prompt action. He said, "Chances are that's for me. I'll get it." He went out into the hall and Ianthe, listening, heard him say, "No, I can't, Edna. Give the call to Dr. Armstrong, will you?"

Ianthe, hearing him use Edna's name, remembered May had gone to the hospital that day in preparation for the operation on the day following Town Meeting. She thought she would ask him about her, and then she thought that it would not be wise to bring one worry more to the forefront of his thoughts.

He came back and sat down again, and for a long time he was silent. Then he said, "That's the first time since I came to Haddon that I've given a call to someone else when I was able to go myself."

He seemed shaken by the thought and Ianthe waited, saying nothing. A log on the fire broke with a shower of sparks, and he came out of his abstraction and looked at it as though he were surprised to find himself here by this hearth.

"Perhaps I'm unfair to him. I'm getting old, Ianthe, though I hate to admit it. Maybe things trouble me more than they should."

"I can certainly see why they would trouble you."

330

"No, I don't want to be unfair to David. Our medical standards here in Haddon are unacceptable to him. He's right. How—by what means—he and his medical generation are going to raise medical standards, give country towns better medicine, I don't know. Maybe the government will do it for them. That's their problem. I shouldn't balk it. I should even try to help." He raised his hand and scrubbed it over his face, then dropped it again and sat with it clasped loosely in the other hand. He smiled sadly at her. "I guess you better forget what I said earlier, Ianthe."

She felt tears come to her eyes. She rose and walked to the desk, and as she passed him she laid her hand lightly on his shoulder. She stood by the desk with her back to him and brushed a strand of hair off her forehead. Then, though it was gone, she brushed at it again. After a minute, she came back to stand by his chair. "Let me get you another drink, Ed."

He looked up at her, and his face looked calm and smoothed out, and she saw that he was very weary but nothing more. He took her hand and laid it against his cheek, making a little sound. Then he let it go and she went away to get the drink.

On the way back from the house call that Dr. Moore had given him, David stopped at the hospital in the hope that May might not be sleeping. He went slowly up the stairs and along the quiet corridor, past the empty nursing station, thinking that in less than twenty-four hours, at Town Meeting, the people would decide the fate of Dr. Moore's dream, his life work, his hospital. Quietly, he pushed the door of May's room open. The air in the room was fresh from the partly open window and scented by the late winter night. He heard a faint rustling sound and knew that she was not sleeping and that she had heard the opening of the door.

"May?"

"Oh, David!"

In the dim light he saw her holding up her arms to him and he went over to the bed and put his arms around her.

"I'm glad you've come, David, darling."

"You should be sleeping, my dearest."

She laughed softly. "They gave me something to make me sleep, but I've been trying to stay awake, hoping you'd come. I'm glad you came, David."

"You must try to sleep now, May."

"Does my voice sound funny, David? It's that stuff they gave me."

"Your words are a little thick."

"I hope things go all right for Uncle Ed at Town Meeting. I hope—"

"Don't think about it now, dear. Go to sleep."

She felt warm and soft in his arms. He held her close. He knew he shouldn't rouse her, but he couldn't help himself. He kissed her. After that, he held her close again and she made a sound like a sleepy bird. He stroked her hair and then her cheek, and when he did that he found that her cheeks were wet with tears.

"Don't cry, darling. Why are you crying?"

"Because I love you so, David."

"Don't cry. Don't cry, dearest. There's just this one thing to get through, and then we'll be happy."

"I'm happy now, David. I'm frightened, but I'm happy."

"Don't be frightened. Everything is going to be all right. Can't you sleep now, May?"

"Yes, I think so, if you stay here. I'm not frightened when you're here. I'm only frightened when I'm all alone."

"I'll stay here for a little while. I'll stay till you're asleep. Try to go to sleep now, May."

He straightened the covers over her. He brought a chair and put it beside the bed. She felt for his hand and held it between both of hers. Close to her like this, he could still feel the warmth of her body, and it seemed like herself, reaching out to enclose him.

"Are you all right now?"

"Yes, darling, I'm all right now."

XXVIII

PEOPLE WERE CONVERGING on the lighted doorway of the Town Hall, dark rivulets of them coming from all directions. Dr. Moore, who had left his jeep in front of the office, avoided them by taking the almost deserted path through the green. He plodded heavily along, thinking that he had never been so aware of the town's identity as he was each year at Town Meeting. He knew there to be wide differences of opinion among these people but there was also, and more fundamentally, a unity. In the drawing together that was now taking place, the individually weak were becoming the collectively strong, the separately ineffectual the unitedly potent. In the end the decisions they made were, for the most part, wise and good. He was content to defer to them.

As he came up the steps toward the broad doors, those near him greeted him, and if there was constraint in the greeting it was so slight that he was not sure it was there. Inside the door he stood still and looked around him. The hall was already well filled. Howie, his leather jacket open, leaned against the wall by the door. Dr. Moore said, "Hullo, Howie."

"Hi, Dr. Moore, I've got a message for you from Dad. The hospital has been trying to reach you to tell you that he's got an emergency in the operating room and he and Dr. Armstrong will be late. He'll come soon as he can but he may not be able to make it."

Alarm seized Dr. Moore. "Do they need me? What about the anesthetic?"

"He says no, to tell you he can manage. He's using a spinal and he's got Miss Judson on duty. I guess you sort of miss May Turner, don't you? She could have gotten the message to you in your jeep."

333

"We miss her more than 'sort of,' but it won't be for long. Is Mrs. Norton here?"

"Yes, she's down front."

But Dr. Moore had seen her and was already making his way down the sloping aisle. She was sitting in the center of the hall toward the front with a vacant seat beside her that he assumed, with gratitude, was intended for him. He edged sidewise through the row toward her. When he was beside her she said, "Ed . . ." and he made an inarticulate sound that conveyed more than words. Up on the platform the three selectmen were already seated at one side of a long table, and the old town clerk sat at the end. He sat sidewise, facing the hall, one thin, old hand on the top of his cane, gazing into space as though brooding on the unimaginable woes of old age. Jim, the pharmacist, seeming unnatural in his role of moderator, leaned on the lectern and waited for the hall to fill.

Moore bundled up his parka and put it under his seat, and after that he sat lost in thought. There was comfort in having Ianthe beside him and in knowing that there was no need to talk to her. He wished that Howard were here, and in the same instant was glad that he was not, for his temper was too unreliable. Vaguely, Moore realized that the meeting had begun. Ianthe touched his arm and smiled at him, and he acknowledged this with a silent movement of his lips and a sigh of which he was not aware. From time to time some words penetrated his consciousness, fragments about such things as street lighting, the water system, taxes, zoning, the need to relocate the dump. Speeches were made; there were replies and counter replies, some heated, some delivered with the dry humor that is the special gift of this land and that on a more ordinary occasion would have delighted him. All was well ordered, and the moderator's gavel sounded only occasionally. Then Ianthe touched his arm in an urgent way and he came out of his thoughts and sat straight, his head raised and his eyes on the moderator.

There was a pause, and in it the hall grew still with expectancy. The moderator grasped the sides of the lectern and leaned forward.

"The subject that will now be presented to this meeting cannot be decided by a vote. You will be asked for an expression of opinion. It will be put to you in the form of a question. Speeches for

334

and against will be permitted, subject to the usual controls. You will then be asked to express your opinion, for or against, as though this were a vote. We on the platform are aware that this is an unusual, though not an unknown procedure. The expression of your views will be an important service to the town." He paused and looked down at Dr. Moore, and said more slowly, "Before the question is put, I think you should hear from Dr. Moore."

The hall was very quiet. Moore rose slowly, and as he turned to face the people, Ianthe folded back his seat to give him room. For a moment he stood there in silence while in his mind the unity that was the town dissolved and became people he had long known. Smiling, he looked from one to another all around the hall. He wanted to speak to them. Then, as he was about to begin, a stir at the back by the door caught his attention, and he saw that Howard and David had just come in. Suddenly he felt glad and full of life. He waved to them; then strongly and with confidence he began to speak.

"A while back my hospital and myself were attacked publicly. It was a pretty vigorous attack. I was told that my hospital had seen its day. It was said that Haddon doesn't need a hospital any more, now that we've got good roads and Warwick is only thirty miles away. It's been pointed out to me that Warwick Clinic is many times bigger and better-equipped than my hospital.

"As you all know, my hospital is my own, except for a share in it that Dr. Perkins has. Now, I might say that as it is mine, I can do what I like with it. I can sell it, or I can close it up or I can go right on running it, provided I can afford to."

A faint stir that was not quite a laugh went through the hall. Dr. Moore put his hands behind him and lifted his voice a little. "What I do about it is my own business. Technically. Only I've never run the hospital that way. I started it originally because I thought I could practice better medicine with a hospital than without one. I've tried to run it with the good of the town the first consideration. Now, certain people want it closed. Certain people. I'm not sure they represent the real view of the town. When this attack started, I said publicly that I would come to you, the people who live in Haddon, and ask you what you want. If you don't want my hospital any more, whatever your reasons may be,

335

I'll close it. If you do want the hospital, I'll find some way to keep it going, to improve it and bring it up as near to good modern standards as I can. I want you to discuss it now as much as you need to. I want your thoughtful, honest opinion that I may be guided by it. That's all I have to say." He looked once more around the hall, turned, nodded to the moderator, and sat down.

There was an outbreak of excited talk. Someone shouted, "We want Doc Moore's hospital." Someone else called out, "No we don't. Shut up." Then there was so much shouting that the pros and cons could not be distinguished and the gavel was pounding. Moore turned in his seat, hooking his arm over the back, and slowly surveyed the hall. He saw Perkins still standing by the door, also surveying the hall but with a look of belligerence that Moore found disquieting. Near him was Moriseau with some men from other plants known to Moore only by sight. He wondered absently what they were doing here and then he saw Stoner on his feet, arm raised, waiting to be recognized by the moderator, and not far away Greer was sitting. There was still a good deal of noise but now he realized that people were shouting to the moderator, "Look behind you. Look behind you." Moore jerked around in his seat to see the moderator, looking bewildered, slowly turn his head.

The old town clerk was struggling painfully to his feet, and Moore thought, Poor old boy. Now, what . . . Slowly the old man, his eyes fixed unswervingly on his objective, approached the lectern. Moore watched, hypnotized by the suspense of that precarious advance. A tremulous hand clutched at the lectern, the moderator stepped aside to make room, and Moore let out the breath he had been holding. He glanced over his shoulder and saw Stoner reluctantly sitting down.

The hall had grown quiet, and the quavering voice, high-pitched and sharp, said what Moore, unbelieving, thought was "Cart before the horse." He said it again, as though with relish and this time Moore knew he had heard correctly.

"Cart before the horse."

A sort of convulsion, an inner tumult, shook the ancient frame. Moore, alarmed, prepared to rise, realized that the upheaval was, however improbably, laughter, and sank back to listen.

"That's the way you get issues confused. Take it a step at a time—that's the way to do it. Look here, now. First step isn't 'Do we want Moore's hospital?' First step is 'Does Haddon want a hospital of any sort?' Answer that, then you don't confuse the issue with feelings about Moore. Answer that first, then if you want a hospital in the town, then ask do we want Moore's or some other kind of hospital." He turned with short, carefully planted steps and fixed the moderator with a stern, admonitory eye. "You do it like that."

People were clapping, and Moore was not sure whether the applause was for the substance of the old man's words or relief that he had got safely through them and was on the journey back. Moore turned to Ianthe and found her watching him. Someone behind them said, "By God, the old boy's right, at that." The moderator, looking distracted, took hold of the lectern by its sides as though he needed to regain steadiness. Moore realized that Stoner was on his feet again, and he and Ianthe both turned in their seats to watch him.

The moderator said, "Just a moment, Tim. The question's not been put yet. The form of the question is now: Is it the intention of this meeting that there should be a hospital in Haddon? We aren't talking about Dr. Moore's hospital now. Just would the men and women of Haddon like a hospital here? All right, Tim, you can have the floor."

"Mr. Chairman. Ladies and gentlemen."

Moore thought, Here it is. We're right at the heart of it now. And he set himself to listen, eyes narrowed, watching, sitting motionless.

"The question just put to this meeting is without meaning." Someone called out "Why?" and Stoner raised a hand for silence. "It is without meaning because there is no way that Haddon can have a hospital even if its citizens want one here. Let me explain. There are only two kinds of hospitals that need be discussed. The first is Dr. Moore's hospital, which is privately owned. The second is a new hospital built partly by funds granted by the government, partly by money voluntarily contributed by all of you here. Let me talk about Dr. Moore's hospital first.

"Dr. Moore, and Dr. Perkins who owns a share of the hospital, are fine men and outstanding physicians."

There was an outbreak of applause, and Stoner waited, smiling remotely, while it swelled and died. Moore drew a long sigh and resumed his watching.

"They have served the town well. Dr. Moore has maintained his hospital in the best interest of the town, but with increasing difficulty. The bank has helped, but year by year his deficit has grown. In my opinion, he has come to the end of the road. This is through no fault of his own, but is the inevitable result of rising costs. He not alone lacks funds for running expenses, but the building and equipment are antiquated. A great deal of money would be required to modernize them. I am not going to guess at how much, but be assured the sum would be a large one.

"Where is he going to get it? Not, I regret to say, from the bank, for the bank has regretfully concluded that it can make no more funds available."

Ianthe touched Moore's sleeve. "Ed, where is Harlan Greer?"

"Over there on Stoner's left." For a moment he let his eyes rest on Greer, who was sitting still, as though posed for a portrait, watching Stoner but with no shade of expression on his face. Moore stared at him intently for a moment and then, with perceptible loss of vitality, with grim discouragement, returned his gaze to Stoner.

"I don't think I need to say anything further about Dr. Moore's hospital except to repeat that it has served the town well and is deserving of all our gratitude. The other choice is the so-called voluntary hospital. With the help of Mr. Whitall of the Public Health Service, I have looked into the cost of such a hospital. To build and equip one of adequate size, designed for future expansion, would cost in the neighborhood of six hundred thousand dollars. Of this the Federal government might be expected to pay half. That leaves three hundred thousand to be raised by the people of Haddon. Do I need to say that this sum is too large?"

Stoner paused and looked around the hall. There were shouts of "No!" and the moderator pounded the lectern with his gavel. When quiet was restored, Stoner went on.

"But there is an alternative to a hospital in Haddon which you may not have thought of but which I think you would find thoroughly acceptable. That is to have a hospital at Silver Springs. The plants there need—in fact, must have—hospital facilities nearer than Warwick, and a hospital there would, I feel sure, draw more industry. Silver Springs is only eight miles from us here, and, moreover, we will shortly have good first-aid equipment at the Health Center. The conclusion is absolutely clear. Haddon does not need a hospital, but Silver Springs does."

Stoner sat down. Moore pressed thumb and finger to his eyes, then shook his head as though to clear it. After that he moved his feet, first one and then the other, as though he felt they needed to be planted more firmly. There was restless movement in the hall, and the moderator was silent, seeming to grope for lost bearings. The man behind Moore said, "Who's that just stood up in the back?" and Moore turned around to look just as the moderator said, "You want to address the meeting, Mr. Moriseau?" Moore, turned almost completely around in his seat, caught Perkins's eye. Perkins lifted his shoulders and gestured with one hand, though what Perkins intended to convey he did not know. He wished Perkins were down here in the row beside him, and then he wondered if, all these years, he had not put more reliance on Perkins's strength than he knew.

These thoughts had lost him a little of what Moriseau was saying, but as it seemed to be only an introduction of himself to the meeting, that did not matter.

". . . and also I am chairman of the Silver Springs Council on Industrial Health. It is in that capacity that I wish to speak. Mr. Stoner has said that the Silver Springs plants need a hospital nearer than Warwick, and that is absolutely correct. In the past the plants have used Dr. Moore's hospital and, with the exception of a tragic incident last September, that arrangement has been wholly satisfactory. I must add, however, that the Council feels the hospital needs more beds, much new equipment, and better diagnostic equipment to maintain its usefulness. It is our understanding that there is no sure way that Dr. Moore can achieve these ends. It is against our policy to give financial aid to a private institution, however worthy. However, if there is not to be a hospital in Haddon, there must be one at Silver Springs. In some important ways this would not suit us as well. Silver Springs is, as you know, almost wholly an industrial community, and so the responsibility for running such a hospital would inevitably belong to

339

the Council. We are reluctant to undertake this, and I doubt that a hospital dominated by the companies would adequately meet Haddon's needs.

"A little while ago the Council decided that if a voluntary hospital in Haddon became a possibility, the plants would contribute toward it the sum of one hundred thousand dollars."

Talk, loud and excited, broke out all over the hall. Ianthe leaned toward Moore. "Ed, what will this mean?"

He said, "I don't know," and found he was tired almost beyond endurance. His hands were shaking, and he held one over the other and shut his eyes. He felt Ianthe's hand resting on his arm and he leaned a little toward her. Then he opened his eyes and drew in a long breath, and with fortitude forced his attention back to what was taking place. There was still noise in the hall and the gavel was pounding. Then the moderator said loudly, to quell the last of the noise, "The Chair recognizes Dr. Harlan Greer," and Moore moved heavily around in his seat.

Greer was standing, smiling thinly, with two long fingers resting on the back of the seat in front of him. To Moore it seemed that Greer was careful to avoid looking in his direction. A hot wave of resentment went through Moore and he listened to the precise enunciation with a frown.

"Before Dr. Moore came to Haddon, my father practiced medicine here. He was a real country doctor of his day. I don't know what he'd think of things as they are now. Some of it I don't think he'd like very much, but that's beside the point. What I rose to say is, as a memorial to him I want to give a fund bearing his name to the proposed new voluntary hospital. The sum I have in mind is seventy-five thousand dollars." He raised a hand to quiet the beginning of applause. "I also want to add my word of tribute to the fine hospital that Dr. Moore has maintained in spite of so many difficulties for all these years."

Moore covered his face with his hands and, remembering that people were looking at him, took them down again. There was tumult in the hall. The moderator had left the lectern and was standing with his back to the people, leaning on the table, conferring with the clerk and the three selectmen. In the hard, overhead light they seemed to Moore's tired brain to have taken on a sharpness of outline, an intensification of detail, beyond reality. A voice in his ear said, "Pretty near time they sugared this meeting off, ain't it, Doc?" and he had a moment's difficulty in bringing the words into focus.

The moderator returned to the lectern and stood there, leaning on it with one arm, holding the gavel hanging at his side, letting the tumult lessen by itself. When there was quiet again, he spoke in an easy conversational tone.

"Some of this isn't exactly parliamentary, but since it's not to be a regular vote, we up here on the platform don't think that matters so much. Now it's getting late, it's almost midnight, and I'm not going to recognize any more speakers. But for form's sake, let me put the original question again. Do you think it desirable for the town of Haddon to have a hospital? . . . All those in favor signify by saying aye."

There was a roar of sound. Ianthe leaned close, said, "Ed . . ." and left her sentence unfinished.

"Contrary-minded?"

Moore turned to look sharply behind him but he could identify none of those who shouted "No."

"The ayes have it. Are you ready for the next question? Let me state it first. Do you want Dr. Moore's hospital, if he can find a way to keep it going, or—"

Moore raised his head and shouted, "I'll find a way," and there was a burst of applause, cut short by blows of the gavel. Ianthe said, "Oh, Ed—this is it," and leaned close and put her hand under his. He clamped his fingers over hers. His head was raised and he was breathing hard as though this were the end of a round in a fight.

"—or . . . let me finish . . . do you want a new hospital, to which the people of the town would be expected to contribute a hundred and twenty-five thousand dollars? Now, since this isn't an official vote, I am going to curtail further discussion from the floor. Ready? Those in favor of having Dr. Moore continue to run his hospital best he can, signify by saying—"

There was a roar of sound. In the midst of the noise Ianthe was saying, "Ed, that must be it . . . Ed, that must be it . . ." He squeezed her hand, not knowing that he hurt her. Tears came to her eyes and she shut them.

"All those in favor of a voluntary hospital—"

Again the sound was very loud, but he couldn't tell, he didn't know . . .

"Ed, which was it? Which was it, Ed?"

He shook his head and looked at the moderator, his expression anxious and uncertain. Apparently the moderator was uncertain also, for he turned to the table where the three selectmen, standing now, were gazing at the people, trying to estimate the volume of sound. The one named Jake Miller said loudly, "Ask for a standing vote, Jim." Moore growled something inaudible and Ianthe said, "What, Ed?" but, alert and attentive to what was going on, he did not answer. There was absolute stillness, but the moderator brought down his gavel and the sharp crack echoed in the spaces overhead.

"The result was not clear. We will have to have a standing vote. Those for Dr. Moore's hospital . . ."

Ianthe was standing. Moore had swung around to see what was happening. Those who had stood were beginning to sit down, settling into their seats.

"All those in favor of a voluntary hospital . . ."

Moore looked at the standing people and shook his head. Then he straightened around in his seat and shook his head again. Without knowing it, he had Ianthe's hand once more.

"The voluntary hospital has it."

Moore turned to Ianthe and saw on her face, turned to him, a look of so much pity and unhappiness that he felt his lips begin to shake. He rubbed his hand over them and tried to smile at her. Then he knotted his hands together and twisted them and stared in misery at the floor.

The gavel came down again. "Well, folks, I guess that about winds things up. If someone will move—"

"No, it doesn't wind things up." Perkins's voice was loud, and harsh with controlled anger. "No one has asked if this town has a *right* to ask Ed Moore to go on ruining himself for the people in it. It seems to me the town owes him something for all the labor and expense . . ."

Moore said, "Oh Lord . . ." and, miserably, turned to try to put a stop to this and realized his helplessness.

"I don't mean he should be paid. All the money this town has couldn't pay for what he's done for the people in it. I mean, give him an honor he deserves. Make him administrator of the hospital you are going to build."

There was a storm of shouts and clapping and foot stamping. The moderator had put down his gavel and was clapping, and Moore lowered his head and heard above the thud of Ianthe's hands, "Yes, Ed. Yes." Then, still clapping, the selectmen got to their feet, and then all the people in the hall rose.

Perkins had not finished, and when the noise died down he said, "How about it, Moriseau—would the Council care to make that a condition of the gift?"

Moriseau replied without standing. "Federal approval of an administrator would be necessary, but of that there can be no question. Yes, we would like to make it a condition. We certainly would."

"Good. Greer, how about you?"

Greer nodded meagerly and said, "Yes, of course."

"Ed, maybe I should have consulted you first, but . . . how does the idea sit with you?"

Moore half rose and said, "I'd have to think about it." Then he straightened up and looked around him a little dazedly. "Thank you." Suddenly he smiled, said "Thank you" again with more emphasis, and sat down.

"And now"—the moderator laid his gavel down and looked at his watch—"it's after midnight. If someone will move that the meeting . . ."

A little while later Ianthe and Dr. Moore stood in the light of a streetlamp by one of the white posts with the carved pineapples on their tops. People were still going past, homeward bound in cars and on foot along the snowy street. Moore said, "When you lose a part of your life, it takes you a little while to realize it. I can't believe it's happened and that I've lost the hospital. I can't imagine my life without it. I feel like an old man, Ianthe. My bones ache."

"Come in and have a drink, Ed. It's late, but you need it."

Moore hesitated, looked at his watch and said, "No, I'd better not. It's too late. May's operation is tomorrow and I have to be in the hospital by six-thirty. I've got to try to get some sleep, if I can."

"I forgot about May. Well . . ." She stood for a moment in silence. "Well, good night, Ed."

"Good night, my dear."

XXIX

THE OPERATING ROOM WAS READY, and the quiet there was thick and paralyzing to the nerves. It slowed movements, giving them the weight and substance of a dream. It italicized sounds, robbing them of their proper context in reality. The faint click of instruments being laid out, the brief hiss of oxygen, the creak of a rolling stand.

On the operating table May lay in suspensive lethargy, her muscles held captive by sedatives, her eyes like dark openings into a troubled soul. To Dr. Moore, looking down on her from the end of the table behind her head, she seemed to have lapsed into the docility of despair. Her loveliness had a lost, little-girl look that made him long to take her in his arms and comfort her. He leaned over and spoke to her softly.

"Are you all right, my dear?"

She tilted her head back to look at him, and he saw light come into her empty eyes.

"Is that you, Uncle Ed?" Her words were thickened and slurred by the sedative, but she managed, as though with difficulty, a faint, tremulous smile. "You look . . . so funny . . . in those clothes."

Amused, he mentally surveyed himself—the white smock tied untidily around his middle, the white cap covering his thick hair down to the horizontal lines on his forehead, the gauze mask hanging under his chin—and he returned her smile.

"Are you going to be a good girl now?"

She nodded and he saw that his words had made her ordeal seem so imminent that she could not bring herself to speak.

"There's nothing to it, May, nothing at all."

At the other end of the room, Edna, in her ordinary uniform, but also with a mask hanging ready under her chin, was moving around, busying herself with the mechanics of preparation. Helen, in green gown, gloves, and white cap pulled over hair and ears, mask covering nose and mouth, stood on her platform at the foot of the operating table. She was laying out instruments in rows, gazing at her work with thoughtful introspection.

Moore drew a white stool close to the head of the operating table, thinking, as he almost never failed to do, that sometime he would get a new stool with a circumference better suited to his posterior proportions. Seated, he was in an enclosure, on one side a rolling stand covered with paraphernalia, on the other the anesthetic apparatus with its pendant green and blue cylinders of oxygen and nitrous oxide, and in front of him the operating table and the top of May's head. He felt at home in this restricted but efficient space where he was able to function in semiprivacy. He picked up the black face mask that was attached by tubing to the anesthetic apparatus and straightened May's head.

"All right now?"

She nodded, moving her lips and wetting them with her tongue. Her eyes had grown wide and dark again.

"There's nothing to this, May. All you have to do is breathe the way you always do."

She nodded again. He turned a knob, and the mask began to make a faint, sibilant sound as he lowered it to her face. Edna came to stand at May's side, and Moore, holding the mask steady with one hand, exchanged with her a long look. There was a tear on May's lashes, crystal-bright and quivering. It ran down and dropped on his wrist. Feeling a twinge of guilt for having withdrawn from her to solace himself with Edna's sympathy, he bent his head down close to speak to her.

"I'm right here, May. It's all right."

The words of her reply were blurred and indistinct, but he thought she was saying, "Where is David?"

"He'll be here soon. We'll all be right here with you. Quiet, now."

She drew a long, tremulous sigh.

The operating room grew quiet again. From time to time Moore glanced at the dials on the anesthetic apparatus, then up at the clock on the opposite wall. The dials indicated a mixture of eighty percent nitrogen and twenty percent oxygen. The clock read seven-forty. He squeezed the black rebreathing bag against the side of his leg and took from the rolling stand the clipboard that held the anesthetic record sheet. In the space reserved for the name of the operation he wrote "Patch and," hesitated in doubt of spelling, and slowly wrote, "angioplasty."

Not by fanfare, but through small things like this unfamiliar name, was one made aware that the new era had arrived. In this it was like one's own aging, the change unnoticed until one awoke to find age a reality. And between these awakenings there seemed no grasp of intervening time, so that one appeared to grow older, not gradually, but by a series of shocks to the incredulous mind. The intervals between the sudden awareness of age seemed to grow briefer; at each recurrence the ego cried in amazed disbelief: This can't be happening to *me*.

Under Moore's right hand, which still held the mask, May turned her head sharply. She drew her hand from under the sheet, groping desperately, the half-anesthetized mind causing the motion to be formless and undirected. Moore held the mask close, and Edna took the hand and held it between hers. Moore glanced at the clock and saw that the time was seven forty-five.

"All right, May, it's all right."

One hand on the mask, the other on the rebreathing bag, Moore watched Edna cautiously putting May's hand back under the sheet. Then she put in place a low screen across her chest that would divide him from the operation. Watching her, he thought how quick and efficient she still was, and wondered vaguely what her age might be. May's arm lay on the arm board now, almost at right angles to her body, half-opened hand palm up. Edna wrapped the gray blood-pressure cuff around the arm, and put the rubber bulb within Moore's reach.

May's body, subdued now, was not in her control, but the mind was still seeking to escape. She made a guttural sound, startling in the quiet, then noises of urgent distress, words jumbled and run together. The sounds rose to a high, frantic babble. Moore, his hand shaking a little, pressed the mask closer. The babble subsided into moaning that changed to whimpering and died away.

He shut his eyes a moment, feeling the crisis and its passing in his own nerves. Then he roused himself, made an adjustment in the mechanism of the anesthesia apparatus, and a faint odor of ether rose around him. He increased the flow until the dials showed an equal mixture of ether and nitrous oxide. He glanced at the black rebreathing bag, saw that it pulsed rhythmically with May's breathing, and looked up at the clock. The time was three minutes after eight. He squeezed the bulb of the blood-pressure cuff, nodded to himself in recognition of the healthy blood pressure registered there, and made an entry on the chart. And he was thinking, I'm just as skillful at this as I ever was. Then why am I uncertain? No, not uncertain—that's too strong a word. Not even unsure, but I don't feel sure, I question myself. Is that because I don't believe May is ready for this operation, or is that only an excuse I am making for myself? Is it really something else? Age? Am I losing something that I'll never have again? No—no, that can't be true. This minute I can feel myself doing these things as well as I ever could.

He leaned over May's head and carefully pulled her eyelids back, first one and then the other. (No tremor in the hand . . . none at all.) The lids resisted him slightly; the pupils were dilated, and the eyes, controlled now by some mechanism deeper than thought, moved slightly. The pupils would shrink, and when that happened she would have gone beyond the sense of pain; she would be, in the language of the operating room, "ready."

The sides of the rebreathing bag were rising and falling with the soft rhythm of sleep. The room was once more quiet, and Edna had left in temporary pursuit of her many duties outside. Helen, her preparations complete, stood with crossed arms behind her instrument table. Her smoothly rounded face outlined by the coiflike cap, the enveloping green gown, the solemn eyes staring at nothing with fixed intensity, gave her the aspect of a sculptured medieval saint.

Beyond the closed door in the scrub room there were sudden sounds of activity. Then Armstrong pushed open the door and looked in. Not yet gowned, he wore a white smock and cap, and it seemed to Moore that even in this unprepossessing garb he carried with him an air of competent responsibility.

"How are we coming?" Brisk, normal, his manner checked the mind's vague wanderings.

"Fine, she's fine."

"About ready, are you?"

348

"I haven't got the tube in yet."

A nod of understanding. Then he came to the side of the table and looked down at May over the screen. He was satisfying himself, as a doctor, of her condition, but without any change of expression the impersonal scrutiny began to soften and it was evident that he had forgotten Moore's presence. Moore, looking up from his seat on the low stool, seeing the change come over David, felt something like jealousy of the young man on the threshold of a new medical era, with his life and his love before him.

Then David turned away and Moore felt a light current of air from the closing door. He could hear sounds of the running water and of a brush being vigorously applied as Armstrong began the meticulous scrubbing of hands and arms. Then he heard Perkins's voice, loud and casual, and conveying as it always did an impression of forcefulness.

"How are they getting on in there?"

Then Armstrong's reply, inaudible above the sound of running water.

Though nothing of moment had happened, the tempo had quickened. Moore watched the motion of the rebreathing bag, and Edna, coming back just then, stood near him.

They both saw it—the outward swell of the bag and its collapse, then no more movement. The bag hung limp, its sides caved in. They watched it, waiting. The seconds passed beyond and way beyond the point at which she should have breathed, and still the bag hung motionless. Edna, tense with watching, shifted her position restlessly, and Moore said, "It's her subconscious fighting us. She'll have to breathe in a minute." He put his hand on May's cheek and stroked it as though she could feel his encouragement. The black bag continued to hang limp. "I guess we'll have to help her . . ."

He squeezed the bag. Then he took his hand away and watched. The bag showed no motion. He put out his hand to squeeze it again, and before his fingers touched it, the sides swelled out, collapsed, and swelled again. "Good girl, good girl, May." Edna smiled and moved away. Moore glanced at the clock.

The passage of time was so strange a thing. One noted it exactly, noted it on the chart, yet the sense of time's passing was sometimes swifter, sometimes slower, than the measured, carefully

349

noted minutes. Almost as though there were two times, the one belonging to the clock with its sweep hand going round and round without pausing, the other your personal, secret time, the time you knew to be true. . . .

"I'll tube her now."

Edna came back now to watch, though she had seen this a hundred times.

Moore took up the intratracheal tube, held May's mouth open with his fingers, and started to slip the tube into her throat. At the first touch her throat contracted and her chest heaved. He withdrew the tube and Edna said, "It's queer how they sometimes resist, even when they can't feel anything."

"That's her subconscious again. She's not quite far enough under and she's afraid of this operation and so she's fighting me."

Facing this ordeal, not with confidence but only with courage. And now, with consciousness and courage both vanquished by the fumes of the ether, her youth seeming so vulnerable, so lovely . . .

He bent over her, feeling that they were as close in spirit as though she were his own child and that now, this moment, they shared an understanding.

He sighed, and reached again for the intratracheal tube. This time the tube slipped in, and he fastened it with strips of adhesive across her face. Then suddenly Perkins and Armstrong were in the room, and the strange loveliness of his secret communication with May was destroyed. Confident and dominating, they prepared to take May for themselves.

One watched with apprehension seeing the whole scene at once. Seeing Helen, no longer in her trance, but with the same fixed look, helping the two surgeons into their gowns. Watching them, but with a mounting, senseless resentment as, gloved hands clasped like priests, they approached the table.

This is the moment. . . . Now preparation ceases and doing begins. Now, as they move to opposite sides of the table, the prerogatives of this intricate small world shift to them . . . then the slight feeling of wrongness in seeing Perkins not in his customary place but at the assistant's side of the table . . . taking his place there and smiling that insensitive, that near brutal, smile at this joke on himself. . . .

350

"By God, it's the first time in fifteen years I've stood here. I'm not sure I'll know my anatomy from this point of view."

The loud voice, the loud laugh that, because it was May on the table, literally flailed one's nerves. . . . Edna regarding Perkins with no expression at all, Helen turning on him her long, thoughtful stare. Armstrong moving away, hands still clasped, to study the lighted X-ray films on the wall, studying them as though he were not already thoroughly familiar with them. Then turning back to look down at May with intense, expressionless face, and the sense that Perkins's laugh was still vibrating in the air. Looking down at May strapped to the table and covered with a sheet, both arms outflung and fastened to arm boards in the pitiful facsimile of surrender. . . .

Moore, still nursing his unreasonable resentment, watched Armstrong push the sheet back to expose the injured leg. Edna set beside him a basin of disinfectant and a forceps with a gauze swab clamped in its jaws. David reached for the forceps and Perkins spoke again.

"Here, I'm forgetting. That's my job today, David."

Saying it, Moore thought, without the taint of buffoonery, without the loud, coarse laugh, so that suddenly you felt yourself to be in a working relationship with him once more. David had yielded place to him, and Perkins was using the swab to scrub the area where the incision would be made.

"This makes me feel like an intern again."

And now it was possible to smile because it was said with simple enjoyment. Moore saw that even David felt this, for his mask moved with the smile it concealed.

The feeling of not being truly a part of these proceedings, of being cut off by more than the screen from what was going on, became so real to Moore that it was startling to be spoken to by David.

"Is she taking it all right?"

"Yes, fine. She's fine and steady now."

Impossible to keep a slight coldness out of the voice, but was there not coldness in David's voice also?

The forceps that held the swab clattered back into the basin. Moore, suddenly remembering, pulled his mask up. Then he spent a disturbed moment thinking he might easily have forgotten, that perhaps he had reached the time when he must guard himself against forgetfulness. He who for a lifetime had watched calmly while others were beset by old age . . .

He forced himself to abandon these gloomy thoughts and concentrate on what was being done. Perkins was saying to David, "All right, you paint while I do a quick second scrub." Edna had taken away the basin of antiseptic and brought a pan of brilliant red Merthiolate. . . . Perhaps one could tell even from the way David held the forceps with the gauze in its teeth while he painted on Merthiolate what kind of surgeon he was. Slow and steady. None of Perkins's flashing brilliance, but everything he did backed up by solid knowledge . . . Bending forward now with the intent look of a surgeon who has no thought beyond what he is doing.

At this stage of an operation, when one had nothing to do but squeeze the rebreathing bag and keep on squeezing it, one had too much time to think. To make one's self—in that phrase Ianthe borrowed from some Greek philosopher—"a stranger to the familiar." And so see what, through seeing frequently, one never really saw at all. David's face—not now the face he had brought to Haddon. That had been smooth and its expression slightly pompous. This face was older, as though he had just lately arrived at the far margin of youth. The smoothness gone, and at the corners of his eyes new lines of tension. Hollows where no hollows had been, skin stretched thinly over bone, eyes tired.

Moore, feeling himself yielding to a sympathy he was not willing to harbor, busied himself. He squeezed the bulb of the blood-pressure cuff and found that her pressure had fallen, though not enough to cause concern. He tried her pulse and found that too within normal limits, but he frowned.

Then David was speaking in the new way he had, as though he could read one's thoughts, saying, "How do we stand?"

"All right. Pulse one hundred, blood pressure one hundred over eighty."

Perkins, you saw, was watching David with a frown, as though he thought David far too meticulous about these preparations, but watching with interest because what was being done was something he had never seen before.

Moore also rose to watch. David, with a spray can in his hand, was spraying the area he had just finished painting red with Merthiolate.

"What's that you're using?"

Perkins answering, as though to keep hold of a part in this, "Bacteriostatic adhesive."

Helen taking the can now and holding out a sheet of sterilized plastic. David, with Perkins's help, spreading it smoothly onto the adhesive. The plastic forming a tight, outer layer of skin.

Then David's sharp "Are we ready?" jolting the nerves, because now . . .

"Ready."

The flash of the scalpel as Helen pressed it on David's palm, and his brief scrutiny of the blade.

Sitting down again, Moore was thankful for the stool, and for the screen cutting off his view, because, even after all the years, that first sweep of the scalpel . . . A faint sound—a sound never heard in this operating room before—the cutting through of the plastic and the first layer of skin beneath as though they were one . . . bringing a wave of nausea that for an instant made him again the frightened, sickened intern of long ago.

David, in that official voice, saying, "Time?"

Edna answering, "Five after nine, Doctor."

A faint click, meaning that David had laid aside the scalpel that would not be used again for fear that bacteria, still undestroyed, might be carried deeper into the wound.

The mind saw this as clearly as though the eyes watched, the screen concealing the reality. But the eyes, looking up, could see Helen high on her platform, with a new scalpel in a gloved hand . . . not *Helen's* hand, but a hand belonging to this ritual . . . The bright flash of moving steel, and Helen, individuality submerged, becoming motionless and watchful.

And again the eyes of the mind unwillingly watching what could not be seen—the scalpel cutting deep, not as though it were a thing being held and guided, but as though it were a living extension of David's arm.

Closing the eyes meant seeing it more vividly. Even pressing thumb and finger hard against the lids would not blot out the

353

springing apart of the flesh as the knife passed, or the yellow nodules of fat rising to stand upright . . . Hating this as he had the first time he had seen it happen.

He tried to forget what was going on and confine his thoughts within the restricted space he occupied. He tried to make himself feel that he and she—that part of her that was in his keeping—shared its privacy. He put his head down close to hers and in his mind he said, "It's all right, May, it's all right. It's not for long, May."

Knowing no one would be watching, he stroked her hair, the feel of the soft curls overwhelming him with tenderness. But a part of his mind still insistently followed the operation.

The wound held open by retractors, Armstrong and Perkins bending over it. The rasp of a hemostat biting closed a bleeder. The swift motions of David's hands with the black suture, tying down these bleeders, and the walls of the wound speckled with these black suture knots . . .

Moore pulled his mind away with a jerk. Becoming brisk, over-brisk, he checked pulse, respiration, blood pressure. Then he checked again, because—

"Dave, her pulse is weak, blood pressure eighty."

David making no sign but a slight, spasmodic tightening of his shoulders. A swift glance from Perkins. "Watch her. Bring her pressure up if you can." Edna, long forceps in her hand, hanging bloody sponges on a rack to be counted, putting the forceps down on the towel stretched over the high pail and coming quickly to the rolling stand to be there if needed. The hypodermic needle exactly where the hand went down to grasp it . . .

The surgeons not changing their pace or their concentration, but aware now of urgencies beyond their field. Then again the rubber bulb and the snort of air in the blood-pressure cuff, the upward swing of the needle to 100, and the long sigh of air escaping from the cuff.

"It's coming up. She's all right, Dave."

David tipping back his head. Edna seeing and moving swiftly with a piece of gauze to wipe his forehead. Perkins pausing with his hands resting on their heels to say, "We're almost down to the artery."

Moore, aware of all this to the last detail, was at the same time

354

thinking, Keep a close watch on her now. Don't let the mind . . . And the mind responding to this command so strongly that the body suddenly feels young.

Busy now with a need to use up an excess of strength. Making entries on the chart with a firm hand, picking up the used hypodermic with the bit of cotton under the needle and laying them to one side. Lifting things merely to put them down again. The left hand never ceasing to squeeze the rebreathing bag. And the monitor in the brain so sensitized that it notes a difference in sound when an instrument strikes another or strikes the metal of a tray. Howard's breathing is audible and David's not. There has taken place under May's skin the subtle change that appears when, for some time, the body has been sustained by something other than air.

The operating room had again entered on one of those phases of quiet efficiency that always seemed to Moore to become all of life without foreseeable end. Keeping close watch on May, he still knew that David and Perkins were working well in partnership. Keeping constant track of time, he was nevertheless startled when David spoke.

"There it is. There's the artery."

He was pointing with the tip of an instrument down into the wound. Edna was at Moore's back with a riser in her hand. "Do you want to stand on this, Dr. Moore, and have a look?"

Not wanting to, but standing on it and relinquishing the rebreathing bag to her, he looked into the wound. There was the femoral artery in the channel it shares with the great femoral vein that returns used blood to the heart. The tip of David's pointer was resting on a slight bulge, a slight misshaping of the artery.

"There's the trouble, right in there. When we open it we'll find the clot that has hardened into fibrous tissue. We'll cut away all we can and put a patch, a plastic patch, on the artery."

Speaking, Moore thought, as though this were a classroom, with that direct, pure, scientific interest that seemed characteristic of these younger men. Did he, just at this moment, remember this was May? . . . The artery rising and falling as the heart forced into it waves of blood. Pulsing strongly above the obstruction, more feebly below. As David put his fingertip first above and then

355

below, and doing it again and again, feeling the flow of her blood, did he remember this was May's lifeblood he felt?

Moore got off the riser and put his own fingers on the carotid artery in May's neck, feeling the pulse—wonderfully the same pulse David was feeling—the pulse too thin and rapid as though the anesthesia had not been able to conquer her fright.

David was lecturing again, saying, "We will dissect the artery free in this whole section, put tapes under it, above and below, to tie it off."

Who is he talking to? Only Perkins listening, and he has heard it all before.

"All right, let's go. Metzenbaum scissors, please."

Moore, watching the scissors move from Helen's hand to David's and feeling the rigors of his hard stool, saw that Perkins was not following the work the scissors had begun to do along the side of the artery, but that he was staring at Armstrong with thoughtful fixity. When Howard looked like that, he was estimating, and bringing into play all that was incisive and calculating in his nature. Estimating David, not as a person, not as one surgeon estimates another. Seeing in him the new generation with new skills. Getting him into perspective because it is important to do so—and important to see himself also in that perspective. Then— his thoughts so clear in his unguarded eyes—coming to a decision, not about David but about himself. Seeing himself in contrast to the new environment that had been forming so swiftly around them all. Satisfied, somehow, and so concluding this brief, swift introspection . . . Bending now with attention returned to the operation he had never before seen. But not at all as though he had never seen it before. Contributing some quality of his own. Not experience, since what he was seeing was outside his experience. But bringing to this the end product of other, different experiences—confidence. And adding to this a special quality rooted in his own nature—boldness.

Moore sighed, returning from this brief gathering of philosophic wool, and concentrated his attention on his own fingertips resting against the artery in May's slim neck. He felt nothing. Startled, he pressed harder and felt a faint throb, and could not tell whether he was feeling the movement of her blood or the pulse in his own fingertips. He seized the stethoscope and pressed the disc hard against May's neck.

He heard the beat, faint even with the magnification of the stethoscope, but it was there, and continuing. He felt himself let out, in a long sigh, the breath he did not know he had been holding, and felt a prickling in his finger ends.

"Pulse very weak."

Not hearing his own words because of the intensity of the listening. The pulse far off, faint . . . *thump* . . . *thump* . . . so faint it might be only a projection of the will to hear . . . *thump* . . . Silence.

Silence spreading out and growing large. One second more of desperate listening, and a voice, loud and not like his own, saying, *"I'm not getting any pulse."*

The clatter of a dropped instrument. He turned the oxygen to five, then to ten liters a minute and shut off the ether almost before the thought that he must do so reached his consciousness. There was an instant of feeling the rush of oxygen against his wrists before he pressed it hard against her face. Holding it there, he used the stethoscope again, listening.

Silence and intense listening, and then he realized Perkins was speaking to him urgently. "Ed!"

Without moving the stethoscope, Moore looked up.

"Ed, is it fibrillation or cardiac arrest?"

"Arrest."

"Then you're not getting anything at all?"

"No."

Listening so intently for a heartbeat made David's words more a motion of the lips than sound. "Heart . . ." The rest of it lost, but the meaning clear. The heart must be started—and at once—by a shock, a blow.

Perkins's wide gesture seemed to sweep David aside. "I'll handle this."

The mind must be divided in order to listen for the faintest heartbeat and at the same time keep track of what they . . .

The silence filling the ears, becoming established . . . Listening to it was making soundless Howard's violent jerking off of the sheet that covered her to drop it on the floor, and Edna's swift

357

move to pull it away from his feet. Soundless too his call for epinephrine, but the glass cylinder with the long needle was going from Helen's hand to his. The driving of the needle between her ribs into the heart—a sight to shrink from, but even with eyes turned away, the slight jerk of the body as the needle went in.

It should be now . . . now the heart should beat . . . Moore bent over, forcing all the senses to listen for the beat, however faint it might be, but impossible not to feel those others waiting and watching, so that only a headshake would tell them. . . .

Silence, then a sense of Perkins moving swiftly . . . Perkins's hands, one on the back of the other to give him the strength of both arms, bringing them down together on the sternum bone to put pressure on the heart—bringing them down hard and at once lifting them again . . . the shock of the impact felt through the stethoscope like a blow . . . Impossible not to watch and to note each happening . . . Perkins looked swiftly at the clock. And his doing that a reminder that there are only a few minutes in which a stopped heart may safely be started again without causing permanent damage to the brain. How many minutes? Three? Three and a half? Four? Certainly not more. . . .

Blows, and between them the possessive silence. Then Perkins calling out loudly, as though everyone had gone deaf, "Riser." Edna moving swiftly to bring a riser, and pushing it hard against Perkins's heels so he would know it was there without having to look. And Perkins, standing on it, better able . . . David, standing back, his hands clasped in front of him, still instinctively guarding them from contamination.

"Ed?"

"No beat yet, Howard."

And Howard drawing a deep breath so that the next blow . . . More strength than David could have . . . The blow, and with it, under it, a sharp crack, the sternum breaking. . . . Then David making a sound like a groan and the next blow falling higher to avoid the break, but the ends of the broken bone moving the skin . . .

"Ed, was that a beat?"

"No."

The lifeless jerking of May's body under the blows becoming suddenly sickening, making it necessary to sit down on the stool

358

to concentrate on listening. Then the two women saying together, "Three minutes." So they too knew about the time limit.

A blow, another and another.

Then no more blows, and Perkins breathing hard and leaning
his whole weight on the table edge.

"That's it. That's all I can do. I'm sorry, Dave."

But still listening long after there was no longer any use.

Slowly, Moore took the stethoscope out of his ears and laid it
aside. Then he moved his hand over his face again and again as
though he could scrub away what had happened. He buried his
face in his hands, and thought, I'm too old . . . I shouldn't have
things like this to contend with. I'm too tired. . . . I don't know
what I could have done that I didn't do . . . I don't know. . . . I
shouldn't have let David . . . but he was so sure . . . Perhaps I
could have saved her, but I don't know how . . . I don't know . . .
I'm tired . . . May . . .

He felt a touch on his shoulder and he lowered his hands to see
Edna's wrinkled face above him, faded eyes looking down at him.
He felt a tremor in his body like palsy and a weight of hopeless-
ness too great to struggle against.

"Edna, we're too old."

"Not yet, Dr. Moore."

He shook his head and turned away, sitting hunched over,
fighting the palsy. He was dimly conscious of Edna's leaving the
room, but he made no effort to be aware of anything beyond the
confined space in which he sat. After a while he remembered the
flow of oxygen and reached to turn it off and found that Edna had
already done so. He moved to take the mask off May's face and
had to wait for the sudden blurring of his sight to clear.

The gauze mesh over his mouth and nose was suddenly stifling
and he pulled it down. Then he pushed his cap back off his head,
letting it drop behind him on the floor. Shakily, he picked up the
chart and held it on his knee to complete the record, but though
he looked at the clock intently, and repeated the time to himself
again and again, it was a little while before he grasped it clearly
enough to make the final entry.

The effort to concentrate cleared his head a little, and he
looked up to see Perkins bent over the table. He was working without urgency, and though his hands were hidden by the screen that

359

was still in place across May's chest, Moore knew that he was closing the incision as carefully as though May were alive.

David was standing very still and looking as though he were beyond thought and almost beyond feeling. Moore watched him as he might a stranger and saw him slowly turn away and walk unsteadily toward the scrub room door. With his hand on the door he leaned against the frame, his forehead pressed against the wood as though he felt the room reeling around him. Then with an effort he straightened up and stumbled through the door.

Moore was vaguely aware that Perkins had raised his head to watch David for an instant, and that afterward he worked faster as though he intended to finish quickly what he was doing in order to follow David into the scrub room. Helen was still up on her platform, holding a long suture thread and needle ready to hand to Perkins, and watching him as intently as though the operation were still in progress. Then Moore realized that Edna was beside him again, saying, "I brought you some coffee, Dr. Moore."

He drank most of the coffee and his trembling stopped. She had stayed near him, and now she said, "I could finish, Dr. Moore."

"No, Edna, I'll do it."

She left him then and he bent over May. Slowly and carefully he peeled the adhesive off her cheeks and slipped out the tube. He found some alcohol and a piece of cotton on the instrument table and gently cleaned the marks of the adhesive off her face, and when he found a spot where the edge of the tube had marked her lip, he made a small, wordless sound of pity.

Then there was nothing more for him to do, and Edna was pulling back the rolling stand. The way she did it made it clear that she wanted him to go because there were still duties that she and Helen must perform. He started to get up from his stool and sat down again and put his hand gently on the side of May's face, stroking it as he had done hours ago to comfort her.

When he stood up, he saw that Perkins had gone and the brilliant lights in the center of the dome had been turned off. The two women were busy at the side of the room and he felt that Edna was watching him anxiously, but he did not look in her direction. He was still standing there uncertainly, not able to focus his mind on what he should do, when Perkins came back from the scrub room. He crossed the room to Moore and took him by the arm.

"You'd better go to David, Ed. This should end whatever's the matter between you. And keep him in the scrub room until . . ." Perkins glanced toward the table. "All right now, Ed? I'll see you downstairs later."

Moore walked slowly toward the scrub room, his eyes averted from the table where May, unsheeted for her final bath, lay white and still and lovely. He found David sitting on a bench by the wall. He no longer wore his gloves and long green gown, and his cap and mask lay on the bench beside him. He was sitting hunched over, his face hidden by his hands, and he did not look up when Moore moved the cap and mask and sat down beside him.

They sat there for some time, until Edna came and stood in the doorway. Moore looked up, and she nodded and went away again. Moore laid his hand on David's shoulder, and said gently, "Come on now, David, we must go." His voice was husky and not like his own. They went out together through the empty operating room.

═══ XXX

Late that night David was sitting on the front steps of Dr. Moore's darkened house. He had been sitting there a long time, waiting for Dr. Moore's return. He was thinking of May with a slow, unprogressive movement of the mind. He had no real feeling of her at all. He knew that at some future time it would come again, but now she seemed to have left him so completely that he could not evoke one single, living image of her. At length he abandoned the effort and gave himself, with weary lassitude, to listening to the varied sounds of the night. The air was chill with the damp of a February thaw, and he thought he heard running water all around him, like the voices of a hundred rills. His numb mind recorded a sound like infinitely distant gunfire as a car rattled over the loose planks of a covered bridge a mile away. Near him a sleepy bird twittered once and was still.

At last he heard a car laboring up the hill, and the wide arc of Moore's headlights swept over him. Then the familiar jeep came bounding toward him over the ruts and potholes of the drive. David was standing on the steps when Moore came from the drive and stopped, peering up at him.

"David, is that you?"

"Yes, sir. I wondered if I could talk to you a few minutes."

Moore made no reply, but he came up the steps and opened the front door, leaving David to follow him inside. Moore dropped his bag on a table and went to a closet under the stairs to leave his coat. David hesitated, then took off his own coat and laid it on a chair. Returning, Moore led the way to the living room and turned on an overhead light. The light gave dreary emphasis to the shabby, ill-considered furnishings. Unread journals of the American Medical Association were stacked on a center table. The hearth, gray with scattered ashes, gave the impression of not having harbored a fire for a long time. Two chairs stood by the bleak hearth, one of dark and prickly plush with an antimacassar askew on its back, the other of cracked black leather, hollowed into certain positive contours by years of sustaining the same heavy weight.

Moore led the way to these chairs, stood defensively in front of the leather one and, waving toward the other, said, "Sit down." Moore himself sat as though every tired bone in him were seeking its special resting place. He put his hands on his knees, his fingers spread, and said, "Well, David?"

David gathered himself for effort. "Dr. Moore, why did May die? What was the cause of her death?"

"That's not an easy question, David."

"Nevertheless, I can't live with myself until I've answered it. I have to know whether or not I was in any way to blame." Moore gave him a swift, hooded look, and David said, "Surely, when we examined her we didn't overlook anything. The ECG didn't show any heart condition that made her a poor operative risk. Then why did she die?"

"We'll have to answer that question as soon as we can, David. Tonight we can't do more than guess. Operating table deaths that can't ultimately be explained are rare—you know that. It isn't always one cause you can put your finger on and say, 'This is it.' Sometimes it may be caused by an aggregation of seemingly trivial things, not any of them, singly, of any importance."

"Do you think that may have been what happened in May's case?"

"I just don't know and I somehow think we never will. She was very afraid of the operation. Though fright isn't a recognized cause of death, perhaps someday science will find a reason why it's at least an important factor. I believe it is, and I think Perkins does. He told me once about a case . . . Well, never mind. Tonight, I'm willing to think that if she hadn't been so afraid she might not have died."

"Then, if that's true, I shouldn't have pressed her and—oh God, you were right, I shouldn't have pressed her."

"We don't know that's true, David."

After that Moore was silent for so long a time that the strain of this long day, the despair and the feeling of personal guilt overwhelmed David and he once more hid his face in his hands. Then he dragged his fingers downward as though he could rake away all subterfuge and untruth. Moore saw emerge a haggard, white face and eyes deep with earnestness and despair, and he was moved to relinquish a little of the harshness with which he had been protecting himself against his own sense of guilt. Speaking as though to questionings in his own mind, he said, "I saw her state of mind more clearly, I think, than you did. I let myself be pressured into your point of view. Originally, May was my patient. Fundamentally, the responsibility was mine."

"I knew she was afraid. I wanted her to be well. I didn't understand . . . I didn't see . . . I forced her . . ." David twisted his fingers together in agony. His voice caught in a sob. "I forced her . . . I knew this weakness in myself—that I'm not good with people, that I don't understand how people feel . . . I knew that about myself, and yet I forced her . . ." He buried his face in his hands again. The rest was incoherent.

Moore once more rose and paced the floor, his own face lined and sad. Once he stopped and looked toward David's hunched figure and seemed about to speak, but he resumed his pacing without having said what was in his mind. Gradually, as his inner conflict subsided, his expression softened. He returned to the fireplace, and before going to his chair he laid his hand lightly on David's shoulder.

"Tomorrow you and Howard and I must sit down together and review both surgical and anesthetic procedures to try to find out what factors may have been involved."

David nodded in agreement and they were silent, but presently he sighed as though he felt the burden of the many thoughts that had not been put into words.

"There's something else on my mind. May and I never had time to make any definite decisions about our future—where we were going to settle . . ." He stopped speaking for a long moment until he was able to regain a measure of control. "She wanted me to stay here in Haddon but I didn't think that would be wise. I wish I had told her I would stay. Now I think I would like to as a sort of memorial to her. That is . . . I know we haven't been getting on as well as we should lately—but perhaps things will be better now.

What I'm trying to say is, I'll stay if that meets with your approval."

"My approval!" In a sudden blaze of anger, Moore slapped the arm of his chair. "What's that got to do with it? I'm on the shelf. I'm an old man, David. I feel like an old man. I'm not to be a doctor any more. Administrator—what's that? It's not being a doctor. I don't know anything about the kind of medicine that's practiced today; I don't know anything, I tell you. I don't know anything at all. I'm finished. Everyone knows it, so they are going to make me an administrator. I tell you I'm finished."

With this outburst Moore plummeted to depths he had never in his life reached before. He came to the surface bewildered, shaken, irresolute, but he saw the world he had briefly left in a new light. He rubbed a trembling hand over his eyes and forehead and said in an unsteady voice, "I shouldn't have burst out like that. This has been a terrible day for both of us."

"Dr. Moore, experience like yours—my God, if I had only listened to you about May. . . . Your experience and knowledge of the town and its people is something that none of us can ever hope to have. You'll use it to enrich your new position in a way no outsider possibly could. Haddon is lucky to have you here, and the people know it."

"That's what Ianthe says."

"And she's right."

"It's damp in here. Let's have a fire."

"Let me build it."

"I've just remembered something."

Moore got up with sudden energy and went off toward the kitchen. David took wood and newspaper out of a bushel basket, and for a few moments of concentration he gave himself to the masculine, possessive satisfaction of laying sticks of firewood after his own fancy. He was holding a match to his creation when Moore returned, carrying a bottle and two glasses. These he set on the mantel shelf.

"I got this stuff when you first came to town, Dave, as a sort of welcome, but somehow we never got around to drinking it. Maybe now's a good time." He poured liberally into the glasses. "Sit down. Sit down."

He gave a glass to David, but before picking up his own he went around the room turning on lamps. Then he switched off the overhead light. Bleakness vanished, shabbiness became an atmosphere of well-worn comfort, and as he came back to his chair the leaping flames lit up a half smile.

A moment of silence passed, but it was one of those silences that sometimes achieve more than words. In it, both men adjusted themselves to a new relationship, and finding it in every way acceptable, let themselves inwardly expand. Moore said, "Your staying here in Haddon would be a fine thing for the town, David, but I don't think you should decide under these circumstances. Wait a while. Take your time. We'll talk about it some more. I'd like to have you; that goes without saying."

"I lack the experience you have."

"What's experience without knowledge? About half of the diagnostic techniques now employed weren't heard of when I left school. Ninety percent of the prescription drugs didn't exist twenty years ago. That goes for almost all the antibiotics, antihistamines, tranquilizers, and steroids, and more of them being put out every day. Advances are coming so fast, and so many of them, that the day a doctor leaves school he starts to slip behind. . . . And how am I to keep up? How is any busy doctor going to keep up? We can't afford to go back to school every few years as we should. What's the answer? I know there are closed-circuit television courses for practicing doctors, and lectures, and floods of mail, all aimed at continuing a doctor's education, but it's all of it just a drop in the bucket compared to his needs, and anyway, how's he going to find the time?

"I tell you, David, once the only problem of medical education concerned the youngsters in school. Now the problem of how to keep doctors educated after they leave school is just as important. And nobody has the answer. Well, here's to you and all young doctors. I didn't mean to deliver a lecture."

Moore drained his glass and rose to pour fresh drinks. "But just let me say this. The problems a country doctor has to face are different from a city man's. He needs some special preparation for a country practice, and almost nothing, so far as I know, is being done about it."

David looked thoughtfully into the bottom of his glass. "I can

366

speak for his need for special training from my own experience. A residency in country medicine in the new hospital, perhaps? Or maybe you should call it small-town or exurban medicine since there's darn little real country any more. Maybe that's something the new hospital might consider doing."

Moore regarded him, shrewd eyes squinted as David had so often seen him look when he was studying a patient. After a moment of thought Moore said slowly, "Maybe it's something to think about—for whoever comes after me to think about. I'm doubtful if it will work, because I think that one of the things that's keeping young doctors from coming to the country is that they're scared of the variety of knowledge a rural doctor has to have. But yes, maybe it's something to think about. Always assuming any of us has time to think." For an instant there appeared in Moore a gleam of the old, endearing humor, before his face returned to the tired sadness that had become its settled expression.

═══ XXXI

SPRING CAME RELUCTANTLY.

The month of May slipped by and June expanded into glory. On a day of drifting clouds and little breezes Moore became briefly aware of time's passing. Beside a cornfield he climbed out of the jeep and stood on the gravelly roadside, blinking like an old dog in the sun, and letting the warmth of summer work inward to his bones.

After that he took no more notice of things like these. Of July, warm and concerned with growing, he was scarcely aware. August with its misty mornings filled with sunshine dust he was far too busy to enjoy. But one day toward its end, in a moment of clarity, he realized that the changes that had been churning up his life had stabilized and become the established order. They were not in process but in being. He did not like any of it. He no longer felt easy or sure in the pursuit of duties that had no resemblance to the medical practice of thirty years, but he had in honesty to admit to himself that not all of it was wholly bad.

It had been decided that his old hospital was to be allowed to function until one wing of the new one was ready to open. Another of the alleviations was that he had been permitted to keep his old office. By the end of August the new Health Center was in operation, but the cell that he was to have occupied there was thought to be too small for the needs of the new hospital's administrator, though the hospital was still in the blueprint stage. David occupied the cell that was to have been Moore's. Ted Barlow—already shorn of the illusion that private practice would provide more leisure than his residency—occupied a smaller cell. In the smallest was a young surgeon who had been lured there by guaranteed earnings of more than he was worth. The three serious young doctors in their white coats gave the Health Center the authentic atmosphere of a clinic, and if the patients who came here felt timid and uneasy, and missed Moore's shabby waiting room, they were correspondingly impressed.

Dr. Moore's waiting room was no longer shabby. A women's committee, called the Haddon Hospital Auxiliary, had banished the old wicker settee, the worn-out rug, the old-fashioned lamps, and all the other furnishings. The walls had become light tan; the dark varnished woodwork was painted cherry-red. A desk, that seemed to Moore an undesirable mating of rubber and bathroom chrome, stood catercorner, facing toward the door. Behind the desk sat a self-confident product of a Burlington business school named Doreen—a name that produced in Moore a slight queasiness whenever he was forced to use it.

For the use of visitors, there were three tan chairs made of molded plastic, their shape suggesting some obscure and perhaps obscene medical purpose. The only picture in the room was a large pencil-and-wash drawing, somewhat misleading in the vastness of the perspective, of the new Haddon Hospital, which would soon be built on the vacant land next to his old hospital. The single-storied, flat-roofed building, some walls of which were green, some tan, looked to Moore like something one might find on Mars. When, in his goings and comings, he was forced to pass this picture, he kept his eyes averted.

All these changes in the office that he had occupied for so many years made him feel as a shipwrecked mariner might who, standing on the deck of the glistening new ship that has rescued him, watches his own sorry but beloved craft sinking under the waves.

About his own office he stood firm, refusing to have it altered in any way. The familiar clutter had the same power to soothe him as the sound of the river below his windows. And when Ianthe said, "You really should spruce this place up a little, Ed," he was indignant.

"I'll do nothing of the sort. My whole life, everything about it, has been changed. I'm going to have one place that's the same."

On one occasion, while Moore was out, Doreen attempted to bring some sort of order into the chaos of his desk by sorting and filing papers as she had been taught. When he discovered what she had done, his fury reduced her to tears. David, who was an unwilling witness of this, was shocked by the violence of Moore's rage until he perceived that it was not the handling of the papers that had angered him, but the invasion of the last stronghold of his former way of life. His was the anger of a man beset, the trembling anger of futility and age, and David was deeply affected by this scene. Afterward Moore was contrite and bought Doreen a box of chocolates, which she ate in an orgy of self-pity.

In theory, Moore had ceased to practice medicine, and a good deal of Doreen's time was taken up explaining this to former patients, all of whom thought an exception should be made for them. Many of them, denied access to Moore in his office, went to his house. They would rap on his door at mealtimes, or wait for him to come home from his office, or telephone him late at night. Some of them he prescribed for, but they were those with the simpler ailments, such as any intern could have handled. The others he told—brusquely, to conceal his bitterness—that, like it or not, they must go to the young men at the Health Center.

About other things than the rejuvenation of his office he became immovably stubborn. He would not, for example, part with the old red jeep, though he would be making no more house calls in the back country. And he still refused to put on a white coat, though he was now the only doctor at the hospital who did not do so. His attachment to his old tweed jacket seemed firmer than ever, and he continued to wear it until the day came when he was forced to move out of his hospital office in order that it might be converted into a doctors' common room. Then he carried the jacket to his Maple Street office and hung it on the coatrack, but he never put it on again.

When Edna saw him leaving the hospital with the jacket thrown over his arm, she said, "I'm sorry to see you taking that away, Doctor. It seems like the end of old times."

"They've gone already, Edna."

"I've been thinking, Dr. Moore . . . Sometime before the bulldozers come to pull this place down, I think I'll go to California to live with my sister."

"I never knew you had a sister."

"And a niece too. She's head nurse on the OR floor of a big hospital out there."

370

"I'll be sorry to see you leave, Edna, though I think I know how you feel. You're the one person I consider indispensable. But so long as you're happy . . ."

He stood for a moment by the front door looking unutterably miserable, and the afternoon sun, coming through the panel of stained glass, flecked them both all over with spots of colored light.

Of the numerous unpleasant things that happened to Dr. Moore during that incessant summer, the one he considered the worst, though it was essentially trivial, was that he was forced to sit for his portrait. Brooding about how to distribute the blame for this, he thought that Ianthe had been largely at fault, along with that superannuated gadfly, Harlan Greer. Even Edna had been disloyally pleased with the idea.

The occasion for all this was the visit of Greer's portrait-painting niece. By what Moore considered great mischance, she had come to Haddon to recover from an illness, and Greer, who had paid the bills, conceived the idea of getting some return for his money by having her paint a portrait to hang in the new Haddon Hospital.

Persuading Moore to sit for the portrait took all Ianthe's skill. He went through with the ordeal of two sittings, fidgeting and mumbling about the waste of time. After that he flatly refused to sit again, and the picture had to be finished from some snapshots that Ianthe found.

The finished picture troubled Ianthe, however, for it forced her to see Moore as he was and not as the image she held of him in her mind. The Moore she had known for years had lived deeply, intensely, in the present. When she thought of him, it was as she had seen him hundreds of times, hurrying along the street, bag in hand, head lowered, and frowning in concentration on the problem before him.

The Moore in the portrait looked like a well-dressed man of achievement. But he seemed to have come to a troubled, uncertain halt, to be looking around him as though he were no longer sure where he was going, and as though he had just discovered that there was no urgency and no goal toward which he must hurry. The painted expression was one of reverie rather than thought.

Because of these things, Ianthe's first sight of the portrait was a shock to her. She involuntarily cried out, "Oh, no!" and she pressed the back of her hand against her mouth as though to stop herself from saying more. Greer and his niece were looking at her expectantly and she struggled to retrieve herself.

"I mean, he looks like that, I know. But you see, I see him in a different way. You've made him look important, and he is that, though he doesn't know it himself, and he isn't important in the usual sense. I don't know how to say what I'm trying to . . . You've made him look like a famous doctor, but he isn't that. He isn't even known three counties away . . . You've made him look like a great man, and he is, he really is, but not in this way. The wonderful quality he has is just for all of us here—for the town, the hospital, the people. You've taken him out of context, and you can't do that without losing the whole meaning of his life. . . . And you've made him look as though his work is finished. . . . It hurts so to see him look like that."

Suddenly her eyes were full of tears. Greer and his niece stared at her in aloof astonishment, and after a moment, when she could master her voice she said, "I'm sorry. I'm really sorry. I've said unforgivable things. It's just that the painting has made me see what I didn't want to see—that his real work is finished."

Everyone else who was given a preview of the portrait, except Edna, thought it very fine indeed, and to these the famous-doctor look gave him new prestige. Edna simply thought it a bad likeness, since it was not the Dr. Moore she knew, and after the first glance she avoided looking at it. Ianthe was unable to stop thinking about it, or to free herself of the emotional burden that the portrait had imposed. This burden took the form of a depression that was always with her, and that made her seem to those who knew her, including Dr. Moore, quite unlike her usual self. Moore, worried by it, concluded that she must still be suffering from Nat's death, but she would not talk about it to him, and he felt shut out and lonely.

Characteristically, she tried to master this heavy state of mind by activity. She set herself many household tasks, and when she found these did not help her, she only worked the harder. She took herself sternly to task, asking herself why a mere portrait, however unlike the original, should occupy so much of her mind. She thought at length about the disparity between the image and the man. And then quite suddenly one day, while she was in the study dusting the old professor's books, it came to her that the cause of her distress was not the portrait but the man himself.

She stood motionless beside the bookcase, a worn copy of Homer in one hand, a duster in the other, while her mind hurried along this avenue of thought as though he waited for her at its end. Moving swiftly, her thoughts lost their sharp coherence and became images, and, as in a dream, she saw him waiting with a look about him she knew well. It was the look of pleased astonishment with which he met the few and always unexpected pleasures of his life. And then she saw that her perception was superficial, and that what she was really seeing in him was something deep that was true and steadfast. She knew he had always been these things, but now, in her daydream, she saw that they related to her. Alone in the room though she was, he was closer to her than he had ever been and she more aware of him. The dream slowly faded. With the back of the hand that held the duster she brushed her hair off her forehead. She looked all around the room, surprised at its new aspect and that the mote-filled beam of sunlight coming through the window had a quality she had not perceived before. Smiling a little, she put the book she was holding back on the shelf.

After this she found that she could think about the portrait with no more than healthy dislike. When the women of the Hospital Aid Committee, of which she was a member, proposed to make a ceremony of its unveiling, she did not oppose it. The unveiling was to be combined with a ceremonial breaking of ground for the new hospital, and the whole town was to be invited. The ground breaking was a little premature, but good weather in Vermont is not to be wasted, and the town was in a party mood. Ianthe said to Edna, in private, "He'll simply hate it."

When Moore heard about the project he came storming to Ianthe in protest. To him she said with decision, "I know, Ed, I know. But I'm afraid it's something you'll have to do with as good grace as you can." They were sitting in wicker chairs behind a screen of morning-glory vines on Ianthe's back porch, with cups of coffee in their hands and the percolator on a low table within reach. He put his cup down hard and answered her in a tone of the utmost exasperation.

"Good Lord, Ianthe, haven't I suffered enough?"

"The town wants to honor you."

"Damn the town. I'm tired, Ianthe. I tell you I'm tired all the way through to the bone. I'm trying to do this new job they've given me, and I wish they would leave me alone. I'm tired."

She poured him another cup of coffee, which he drank fiercely, but after a while his angry muttering died away like a retreating thunderstorm.

On the afternoon of the ceremony, all the flags in the town were out, as though this were the Fourth of July. The sun shone brightly, the air was cool and incredibly clear, the footsteps of passersby rang out with brisk decision, and the flags flapped and streamed in the wind. After lunch, Edna phoned Moore at his Maple Street office to ask if Doreen could come to the hospital and help with the flowers.

"Flowers?" Moore said. "What flowers?"

"Everybody's sending them, Doctor. Every store in town, and lots from people's gardens."

"Flowers! What do people think this is—my funeral? I'm not dead yet—not quite. Yes, you can have Doreen, and mighty welcome to her."

With Doreen's departure and the cessation of her eternal typing, a great quiet descended on Moore's office, and he told himself that now perhaps he could get some work done. But the voice of the river grew loud and complaining, he felt the emptiness of David's former office and the abandoned surgery, and the old waiting room seemed populous with vanished patients. He did no more than sit and stare at the papers on his desk while his sense of solitude grew. After a while he gave up all thought of work, locked up the office and drove the jeep to the refuge of Ianthe's house. He found her putting trays of little cakes, destined for the party, into her car.

"You're not leaving yet, are you?" he asked her in alarm.

"Not for a while. I just thought I'd get this done."

He held the screen door open for her, and when the last tray had been carried out she said, "It's such a nice day. Shan't we sit out here on the porch?"

"I want to hide."

He locked the screen door behind them—a thing he had never done before. He did not wait for her to precede him, but led the

374

way, tramping heavily down the hall. But at the study door he stopped; then, to her surprise, he turned away and entered the seldom used room on the opposite side of the house where, to her memory, he and she had never sat before.

This room was lovely and uncomfortable, furnished with gracefully insubstantial chairs and tables that had been new long ago when the house was built. He sat down, a little belligerently, at the end of a hard sofa beside an exquisite marble mantel and glowered as though he had set himself to wait for this day to do its worst to him. She settled herself, not very comfortably, beside him.

"Dear Ed—is all this really so difficult for you?"

"What do you think it's like to have your town behave as though you were dead? They're expecting me to go to my own funeral."

"Aren't you being a little extravagant? You know they don't think of it that way."

He made no reply, and, looking with troubled eyes at his bent shoulders and gloomy profile, she waited, hoping he would open his heart to her about those things she knew really troubled him. Not this ceremony, for that she knew to be at most only an exasperating embarrassment about which he was making this undue fuss to relieve feelings tortured by quite other matters. He sat leaning forward, his hands hanging limply between his knees, an attitude of hopelessness that wrung her heart. She thought he had forgotten she was there beside him, unless perhaps he felt in her presence a background of sympathy. It seemed to her that she did not so much ease his pain as create an atmosphere in which he could freely give this pain expression. This role did not trouble her as it might a woman who needed positive and continued recognition of her personality. She would gladly be of help to him in any way she could, and if no better means presented itself she was content merely to let him groan aloud.

Smartly, he hit the palm of his hand with his fist. "I tell you, it's a mockery. Everything I do these days is a mockery. Things would get along just as well, in some ways better, if I weren't here at all. I'd almost better be on the shelf. Those new doctors in their damn white coats and their formal manners—do you know that not one of the four of them has asked my advice about anything?"

"Nevertheless, you can keep them from making mistakes, and—"

"I didn't keep David from making a mistake. I went right along with him."

She drew a secret sigh because she felt they were slipping into one of those discussions—characterized less by sense than by the recalling of bitter incidents—that in the end achieve no good purpose.

"You know about people, Ed. They don't," she said, and felt that she had not remedied this fault to any great extent.

"They think they do. They think they know more about people than I do because they heard some lectures on psychiatry in medical school. In my opinion all they learned were some fancy names for things about men and women that good doctors and good priests have always known."

"Ed, think back—when you were young and first started to practice, didn't you, perhaps, pretend to be self-confident and assured to hide feelings that were really just the reverse? I seem to remember a big young man with a very new bag and a most important frown. . . . Did that young man go to Dr. Ladd for advice, though Ladd was older and knew the town?"

Moore laughed, but without mirth; then he looked interested and thoughtful, and when she saw this, her heart warmed to the fairness, the open honesty, of his mind.

"You know, Ianthe, you may have put your finger on one of the reasons why Ladd and I never got on very well, why he drew off and kept his practice to himself. I never thought about it that way before. Well . . . But there wasn't the distance, medically speaking, between Ladd and myself that there is between me and these youngsters at the Health Center. The other day young Barlow used some words—I had to ask him what they meant. . . . It isn't only that they know more about the science of medicine than I do —they base it on a different set of premises, a different point of view. I suppose you might say that the older men, who don't know much about the science of medicine, tend to overestimate the value of the art. Young men fresh from learning the science and lacking experience in the art tend to underestimate the value of the art. That's true enough as a generalization, I guess. And I suppose you might say there isn't really very much the older generation can do about guiding the younger. Or even should do.

376

We'd be working at cross purposes. No, I think the best thing we older doctors can do is to get out of the way of these young men. Leave them free to work out their own destinies. That's about what I've come to think, anyway, though it doesn't make giving up any easier. No, Ianthe, the fact is I shouldn't even be in this administrator's job. The fact is I've outlived my usefulness."

"Oh no, Ed, that's not true. I'm willing to grant that there's a great deal in what you've been saying, but not that there isn't a place for you in the medical life of Haddon. That's simply not true."

As though these emotions had exhausted him, Moore sat listlessly contemplating bitter thoughts. Ianthe, wrapped in thoughts of her own, leaned back in her corner of the sofa, hands folded in her lap. From time to time she glanced with soft, warm eyes at Moore, as though she were waiting for a propitious moment to draw him out of his reverie. Sounds of the village street came muted into the room. A gilt clock, ornate symbol of a generation long dead, ticked rapidly. The sound, barely audible, seemed a breathlessly hurried, self-preoccupied effort to keep abreast of time's swift passing. Ianthe, listening, was filled with a panic sense of being, herself and Ed, rushed onward, hurtled helplessly into the unknown.

Moore drew a long, unsteady breath, and without taking his eyes off the point in space on which they were fixed, he laid his hand, palm up, on the sofa between them. She put hers into it. And as though he had not really expected this, as though it brought back to him a sense of living and of enjoyment, he turned to face her and found that she was smiling. He made a sound deep in his throat, wrung out of him, inarticulate because the flood of feeling that swept into him had swept away words. She leaned a little toward him, her fingers tightening on his.

"Ed, I've been wondering . . ."

"What, my dear?"

Her lips moved as though she would speak, but she seemed unable to form words. In her mind Ianthe had rehearsed what she wanted to say, but now she found she had no use for the elaborate sentences that had then seemed to her effective. He was leaning toward her, gripping her fingers tightly, a look of sympathy mingled with strained anxiety on his face, as though he knew that what she was trying to say would be of great moment to them both and was uncertain whether its purport would be good or ill.

"What is it, my dear? What is it you've been wondering, Ianthe?"

He spoke with wonderful gentleness and laid his other hand on hers, so that he held hers between both his own. He felt a tremor go through her, and as she bent her head he saw the blood come rushing into her face.

"Tell me, Ianthe."

"Ed, I've been wondering . . ."

Her fingers tightened on his hand and she gave a sort of gasp of resolution. ". . . wondering when you're going to get around to asking me to marry you."

He sat perfectly still and stared at her. She raised her eyes to him, her cheeks still bright with color, and there were sparks of laughter in her eyes. A great smile spread over his face, and she was laughing aloud. He laughed too, a roar of laughter, and hitched himself along the sofa closer to her. Then neither one of them was laughing and they were gazing into each other's eyes, intently searching. And each was conscious only of this searching and of the slow, rich beginnings. He made a sound that was at once anguished and final. Then he drew her slowly into his arms and bending over her, he put his head down on her breast. She held him close.

After a time she felt rather than heard a long, deep sigh of peace. He raised his head, and in a manner that was almost convulsive in its sudden strength he drew her close and kissed her.

When the long kiss was over, they did not move apart, but rested each in the other's embrace, while old and bitter wounds began wonderfully to heal. In the silence the little gilt clock ticked industriously, as though the silence belonged only to itself. It seemed to gather its forces, and there took place an inner and creative convulsion of mechanisms that produced a whirring sound. There followed a pause on a high level of expectancy, and then the realization, the giving out of four clear, perfect notes.

Ianthe disengaged herself gently, and Moore at once attempted to possess himself of her again, saying, "This is incredible, Ianthe —wonderful and incredible."

378

She answered with a smile of woman's wisdom, and seeking to repair the damage to her hair, she said, "It's four o'clock. I have to go and help get the party ready."

She did not move at once. She seemed lost in thought, but about what, Moore could not tell. He moved back to his corner of the sofa and sat, one arm along the back, knees crossed, watching her possessively. After a moment the full force of his astonishment struck him and he said as though his whole soul were in it, "I'll be damned." This brought her out of her reverie and they laughed, then laughed again because of their delight in laughter. She rose and he, like a docile, great dog, pleased with himself and his world, followed her to the kitchen, where he went straight to the screen door and unfastened the hook.

She had a coat in her hands, the same drab, comfortable coat she had worn for years, and he helped her into it.

"Before you go you'd better tell me what time I have to show up at the party."

"Five, I should think, dear. Not much after."

Her use of the small endearment of familiarity pleased him inordinately. He smiled at her in a way that, in a man less chastened by the buffetings of fate, could certainly have been called masterful.

"I'll stay right here until then."

He started to hold the door open for her, let it shut again, and with determination took her in his arms once more.

Though he began to miss her the moment she was gone, he was not really lonely. The house was too full of her. He went from room to room, looking around him with as much interest as though he had never been here before, but actually seeing nothing at all. His mind was churning with ideas that jostled each other out of completion, and remembered impressions of what had just happened, bright as meteors, flashed through his thoughts. He sat for a while in the study and tried to put this mental chaos in order, but his blood was flowing with too wild a swiftness. He got up and went back to the kitchen as being the room most suggestive of activity. He discovered the percolator on the stove, shook it and, receiving a reassuring sound, turned on the flame. There were a few used dishes in the sink and these he washed and set with care in the draining basket. The domed cover of a cake dish caught his eye, and lifting it, he found one piece of chocolate cake inside. He ate it. Suddenly he realized that he felt a quite strong desire for a drink and said aloud, "And why the hell not?" The coffee was now making sullen noises and there was a dark fountain inside the glass knob. He turned the burner off with a quick, decisive motion.

He drank his Scotch at the kitchen table, and as the drink took effect, emotions rose in him in a way not unlike the coffee percolating. Some of them made him feel strong and assured and confident of the future. But some of them—those that came from thoughts of his desire to cherish Ianthe and to fill her life with happiness—made him feel timid and as inadequate as a snail that has lost its shell.

Finally he remembered that time was passing, and he looked at his watch to discover that it was already after five. He sighed and rose, but even then he found small reasons for delay, so that it was nearly five-thirty when he let the screen door bang behind him. The sunshine had the remotely golden quality peculiar to September afternoons, and the streets were deserted. He guessed ruefully that most of the town had already gone to the party. Examining his feelings with clinical interest as he drove along, he found that though he did not feel anything resembling pleasure at the prospect of what he would shortly have to endure, he did not feel quite so intractably rebellious as he formerly had. Making this discovery, he sought for the reason, and found it to his satisfaction in Ianthe. Now he had something to sustain him—something that would sustain him, he felt sure, in far greater trials than this. He swung the jeep into the parking lot with a great exuberant swoop— and discovered that there was a car in the narrow slot that was, by hallowed tradition his. He judged by the caduceus emblem it bore that it belonged to one of the new young men. In a spirit very like mischief he parked the jeep in such a way that the culprit would not be able to move by so much as an inch.

As he crossed the parking lot, looking up at the hideous pile of his beloved hospital that would be so soon replaced by a modern blight, his mood sobered. It grew close to somber as his gaze shifted to the large tent in the weedy plot next door where the party was already most audibly in progress. The massed chatter had, he thought, the noise quality of a birdhouse in a zoo. Shortly he would have to go there, receive a beribboned spade and lead a procession to the strains of the high-school band. They would march solemnly out of the tent, and he would "break ground" for the new hospital by digging up six inches of weedy, symbolic sod.

Moore grunted and mounted the steps to the open front door. Edna was not at her desk. He stood for a moment irresolute, missing her acutely. Then, partly with a vague intention of further procrastination, partly in pursuance of a habit track worn deep in his mind, he turned his steps toward his former office.

The decorating committee had been busy here also, and it was an office no longer, but had become a common room for the use of the staff doctors. Comfortable chairs and smoking stands replaced his possessions, and there was a couch where once his desk had stood. The lone piece of his furnishings to survive was the glass-doored bookcase on the top of which had stood the photograph of his dead wife and his dusty student microscope. The shelves no longer held his antiquated medical books. In their place were piles of white coats neatly stacked and folded.

Moore stood in the middle of the room and let the change have its way with his feelings, as though exposure could at last bring immunization. The long past lay in shadows behind him, but on the horizon of the future the sky was bright. He had gone through a time of torment when it seemed to him that his usefulness was over, but he had come through that more or less unscathed. Looking back on those distressful days, he had the beginnings of a perception that what had happened need not be thought of as personal failure, but rather the change of circumstance and condition that comes after a lifetime to all men. And it came to him that old age is like a birth into a world where the conditions of life are different but not necessarily distasteful. The passage through the birth canal he had found exceedingly painful, but all that now lay behind him. Figuratively looking about him at this new landscape, he perceived that there was work to be done here, and if his usefulness was not to be of the same order as in the past, it was usefulness nevertheless. There was progress here, and if he did not meet it with blind resistance, he might hope in a small way to influence its course. And above all, like the sun in the sky illumining this new land, there was affection, an end to loneliness, love.

Standing there in this changed, familiar place, he faced the future without resistance and without resentment, but nevertheless he paid the past the tribute of a sigh. Time pressed and he could not linger here. He took off his topcoat, and finding with pleasure that the antlers Perkins had given him still hung on the wall, he hooked the coat on one of the branches. He hesitated, the old-time twinkle of amusement came into his eyes, and he took off his jacket and hung that too on a branch of the antlers. With a quick, firm step he went to the bookcase, and taking what seemed to him the largest of the white coats, he shrugged his big shoulders into it. The starch in the sleeves resisted him and he forced his arms through them.

The long fitted coat was definitely too small for him. He buttoned it all the way down and the buttons strained across his chest, but when he stood up straight he found he could breathe without too much feeling the restriction. There was a mirror on the wall, but it did not occur to him to examine himself in it.

When he went out into the hall, he found that Edna was once more at her desk, the absurd cap tipped forward as she bent over her work. No party for Edna. Since someone must stay by the patients, she would, as a matter of course, assume it should be herself. When she saw Dr. Moore, she rose and stood there as always, tall, Gothic, thin, a sentinel of time. She saw the white coat. As Moore, pleased with himself, advanced toward her, it seemed to him that without any flicker of change in her expression she glowed with understanding. He thought the cap made the very slightest nod as of approval. For a moment the air between them was filled with wave on wave of regard and memory as their eyes held each other's gaze. Then with a breadth of gesture, with humor, finality, and with style, he put his hands behind his back and walked out of his hospital.

About the Author

MRS. YOUNG'S ADMIRABLE ABILITY to project the life of a New England town stems partly from the facts that, though born in Ohio, she considers herself a New Englander by inheritance, and that she spends several months of every year near Woodstock, Vermont. Her understanding of the medical aspects of her story comes from practical experience as a nurse in hospitals, from the research for two books on the history of surgery, and from taking part in the lives of several Vermont hospitals.

At various times of her life, Mrs. Young has served on the faculties of both Yale and Western Reserve University and, during World War II, as a consultant to the Secretary of War and the War Manpower Commission. She has also been a dancer and a stage and costume designer. Several of her apparently widely divergent fields of expertise have been the subject of her fiction and nonfiction books. A list of these appears in the front of the book.